WHAT
REMAINS
TRUE

OTHER TITLES BY JANIS THOMAS

Something New
Sweet Nothings
Say Never
Murder in A-Minor

WHAT
REMAINS
TRUE

A NOVEL

JANIS
THOMAS

LAKE UNION
PUBLISHING

Text copyright © 2017 by Janis Thomas
All rights reserved.

Published by Lake Union Publishing, Seattle

www.apub.com

Amazon, the Amazon logo, and Lake Union Publishing are trademarks of Amazon.com, Inc., or its affiliates.

ISBN-13: 9781542048248
ISBN-10: 1542048249

Cover design by Rex Bonomelli

Printed in the United States of America

For Auntie Hilary
Despite the losses, we find the laughter . . .
Love you so.

PART ONE: A DAY IN THE AFTERMATH

ONE

Jonah

Sometimes I hear Mommy crying in the middle of the night. She's in the bathroom, her head pressed hard into a bunched-up towel so she won't wake anybody. If I had arms or hands or fingers, I'd touch her on the shoulder. Just so she'd know I'm here.

Sometimes, when no one else is around, she screams like someone's stabbing her or something. But mostly it's crying.

Sometimes all three of them cry at the same time, Mommy, Daddy, and Eden. All together. It sounds like a song Mommy used to play in the car when we were driving somewhere, but it wasn't crying in that song, it was laughing. Lots of different people with different voices laughing together. I liked that better than the crying. If I still had ears, the crying song would hurt my head. But I don't have a head anymore, or a body, or anything. So the crying just whispers through me and reminds me what it's like to be sad, even though I can't feel it.

I'm not sure what's happened to me. I know I died. Kind of like my goldfish, Fred, only I'm not floating on top of the water waiting for Mommy to flush me down the toilet. But I feel like I'm floating somewhere.

Daddy told me once that when we die, we go to heaven, but I know I'm not there. I haven't seen God yet, or any angels.

I see places I've never seen before, like the crawl space above my room and the gardening shed, which I was never allowed inside 'cause of all the sharp tools, and the closet that has the water heater in it. I can slip through the cracks in the door and slide around the metal tank, then slip out the other side.

But I haven't left the house or the yard since the "very bad day," which is what Mr. Escalante calls it whenever he talks to Luisa about the day I died. Luisa works for Mrs. Martin next door, and sometimes she brings lemonade out to Mr. Escalante or coffee or something else to drink, 'cause Mr. Escalante does both the Martins' yard and ours at the same time. Now when Luisa brings it, Mr. Escalante shuts off the lawn mower and limps over to her, and they talk quietly so Mommy won't hear them. They both shake their heads and look at the ground, and Mr. Escalante always sees something on the ground, like a weed or something, and bends over to pull it out. I think he does it on purpose so that he won't see the tears in Luisa's eyes. And by the time he stands up straight again, she's already wiped them away.

I don't think I'm a ghost. Mrs. Hartnett, my teacher, read us a story on Halloween about ghosts, and they all were mean and tried to scare people. I'm not mean. I know that because Mommy always told me the same thing. "You're such a good boy, Jonah. You're such a nice boy, Jonah. You're such a lovely, sweet boy, Jonah." I don't think ghosts are nice and lovely and sweet and good. So I must not be a ghost.

I think I'm supposed to do something. But I can't figure out what. 'Cause I don't have a body anymore. So I'm mostly just waiting. And listening. To the crying. Hoping it will stop.

TWO

Eden

I told them I didn't want to come today, but they didn't listen. They don't listen to me anymore.

They used to, before. We'd all sit around the table at dinner, and Mom and Dad would make us talk about our days. Jonah never said much. Mostly finger painting and jungle gym stuff, kindergarten stuff. Mostly. Sometimes he'd talk about the stupid jerky kid Jesse, who was always getting into trouble for doing stupid jerky things. Sometimes he'd talk about books. He was learning to read, and he liked this one book a lot—*The Little Rose*—and he could read it good, too, even though it was a first-grade book. But mostly he'd talk about coloring and drawing pictures. He loved to draw pictures.

Mom and Dad would ask me to tell them about my day, and Mom would put down her fork and knife and look at me full-on, her blue eyes totally focused on me like I was the only one in the room, and I'd tell her about school, from start to finish. Dad would listen, too, but he'd still be eating, even though he'd nod and ask questions, sometimes with his mouth full, and Mom would give him a smack on the arm and tell him he was being a "bad influence on us" for talking with food in his mouth.

Mom and Dad don't ask me about my day anymore. They don't ask me anything anymore. Mom doesn't even really look at me. Her eyes have changed, like they can't really focus on anything. They're shiny, and not just from tears. I heard Aunt Ruth say something to Luisa about medication. I don't know what that means. I had to take medication when I got an ear infection last year, but I'm pretty sure it didn't make my eyes shiny, so Mom must be taking a different kind of medication. A kind of medication that makes her not listen to me anymore.

I don't think Dad is taking medication, but he doesn't listen to me, either. His eyes aren't shiny, but he has this really deep crease between his eyes always, like he's thinking hard about something, trying to figure something out. The kind of look he used to get when we did puzzles at the dining room table or played Wii bowling in the living room or when he helped me with fractions. Now, he has that crease all the time, but he just wanders through the rooms of the house like he's looking for something, but never finds it. And when I talk to him, he turns his head and looks at me, but like he's looking through me, like whatever he's trying to find is right behind me, and he never answers my questions quite right. Like, yesterday, I asked him if he knew where my softball helmet was, and he told me he didn't think it was going to rain today.

They said it was time for me to go back to school. It was Aunt Ruth, actually. She did all the talking while Mom sat on the couch with her shiny eyes staring down at her hands in her lap. Dad was standing by the window, looking out at the front lawn, with that crease in his forehead that looked like it hurt. And Aunt Ruth kept talking, saying things had to get back to normal at some point.

I wanted to argue with her that things would never get back to normal. Normal was walking my little brother to the kindergarten gate, not because I wanted to, but because my mom and dad made me, but I kind of liked the feel of his chubby little fingers holding tight to my hand like I was his champion or something and would protect him from anything that could hurt him or scare him. Normal was going into Mrs. Hartnett's class every Tuesday and Thursday for kinder-readers—they put me with my brother 'cause that's the way they do it with brothers and sisters—and listening to him read and helping him with the big words that he couldn't understand, but a fifth grader, his reading buddy, could tell him what they meant. Normal was walking home from school with my friends, pretending Jonah wasn't there, but always checking, every few minutes, to make sure he was only four or five steps behind me, rolling my eyes when he called my name.

Nothing would ever be normal again without Jonah.

But I kept my mouth shut because I knew Aunt Ruth wouldn't change her mind, and with Mom and her shiny eyes and Dad and his creased forehead, she's kind of in charge of things right now.

So here I am, and Mr. Libey is writing something on the smart board, and Betsy Morgan is staring at me and whispering to Ava Landou, and Matt Boyles and Josh Hannapel and even Ryan Anderson are trying not to sneak glances at me but failing epically, and all I want to do is disappear. Melt into my desk chair and slide into a pool of nothingness on the floor of my homeroom.

Mr. Libey writes out a long-division equation on the smart board and looks around the room. "Who can tell me the answer, my friends?"

I know the answer; it sits smartly on the end of my tongue. But all I can think is, *Who cares, who cares, WHO CARES?*

THREE

SAMUEL

The sheet of paper stares up at me, mocking me with its blankness. The pencil in my hand mocks me with its impotence. I've been sitting at my desk for the better part of an hour, trying to make sense of my own sketches. My vision for this house was so clear when I began. But that was before. Now, I can't remember why I put the walls where they are.

I need to focus. It's never been a problem. I could always rely on my ability to tune out the rest of the world and get down to work. My sketches and blueprints and schematics and 3-D virtual tours were an escape for me. I could shelve my personal problems, slough off any issue that was plaguing me, allow the stress to seep from my pores as my work enveloped me and carried me away.

But this is not a problem I can shelve, nor an issue I can slough off. This is not stress. This is grief. Overwhelming and insidious grief that refuses to be ignored or denied or temporarily tucked away.

Ruth thinks we need to see a counselor or find a group. I know she's trying to be helpful, and I don't disagree that counseling might be a good idea, especially for Eden. But I'm not sure I can handle it right now, and I sure as hell don't think Rachel can. Rachel isn't able to handle anything. Rachel can barely make it to the bathroom on her own.

I wipe away the beads of perspiration that have erupted on my upper lip, can feel the dampness in the armpits of my polo shirt, the film of sweat pooling at the base of my spine. My office is cool, but my innards churn and burn, as though I'm running a marathon. A constant coil of tension twists within my gut. A jackhammer headache throbs just above my eyes.

Survival is the worst physical challenge there is.

A quiet tap on my door. The door opens a second later, and Greta peers in. She holds a cup of steaming coffee in one hand. I nod to her. She enters and crosses to my desk, sets the mug down slowly, carefully, as though she's afraid she'll spill the coffee. She gazes down at me, her eyes searching mine. I look away.

"How's it going?" she asks, her voice soft.

"I'm having a tough time concentrating," I admit.

She places a gentle hand on my shoulder, and I have to force myself not to recoil.

"Maybe it's too soon for you to be back," she suggests.

I want to snap at her, *Someone has to work—someone has to pay the bills.* But I know she is trying to comfort me. Greta cares about me. She hates what's happened, just like everyone else. And, like everyone else, she has no idea what to say to me.

She rotates her hand in small circles on my shoulder. I want to shrink away from her, but I don't want to hurt her feelings. How can I tell her that the touch of her hand feels like molten steel burning into my flesh?

"I'm just so sorry, Samuel." No one calls me Samuel. When Greta first started working here, she called me Mr. Davenport. I told her "Mr. Davenport" made me feel like I was a hundred years older than her, and she'd laughed her twentysomething laugh that wasn't flirtatious on purpose. She decided to call me Samuel, because she thought it sounded more respectful than greeting me with the übercasual Sam. For a while, I was reminded of the sisters in my Catholic grade school, but after a while, I grew to like the way it sounded from her lips. "I wish there was something I could do to make it better."

I have heard this exact phrase more times than I can count over the last four weeks. Each word that makes up this detestable sentence is like a shard of glass pressed against my eardrums.

"I know," I tell her, then push her hand from my shoulder. She tries not to look hurt, fails, bites her lower lip, and takes a step away from me.

She knew Jonah. I brought him to work with me on a handful of occasions, and she dutifully took him for ice cream or sandwiches; she made a little play area on the far side of my office where she provided him with pencils and crayons and reams of plain white paper. She oohed and aahed over his childish drawings, complimenting his skills and telling him he was a chip off the old block, and he'd smile even though he had no idea what that meant. Greta loved Jonah, but then, everyone loved Jonah. You couldn't meet my son without instantly falling in love with him.

And now he's gone.

The sob rises from my chest and I force it down, then cough violently from the effort. Greta eyes me worriedly, and I wave her away. "I'm okay." I pick up the mug and take a sip of coffee, set the mug down again.

"What can I do?" she asks.

Nothing. There's nothing anyone can do.

I clear my throat. "Call Laydecker and see if he can move our three o'clock to tomorrow. Please. I'd like to be home when Eden gets there."

She stares at me for a long moment, then nods. Wordlessly, she crosses to the door. As soon as she closes it behind her, I bend over and retch into the waste bin.

FOUR

RACHEL

My eyelids are too heavy to open. My tongue is thick and lazy in my mouth. I taste bile. Did I throw up? I did, I know I did. My nostrils are filled with the scent of vomit, but I can't remember when. I'm shaking. I'm curled up on my side beneath my covers, my knees tucked into my chest. Like a fetus in a womb. This is how a fetus feels. Fetus. *Fetus.* What a funny word.

No, it's not funny. Nothing is funny. Nothing will ever be funny again. But why? I can't remember. Something happened. Something awful. I burrow more deeply under the comforter and farther away from the memory of the awful something. It's there, just outside my grasp, but I don't reach for it, because then I won't ever want to leave this bed, this oasis, this escape.

I'm suffocating my baby. I feel his arms around my neck, his soft body beneath me. I'm crushing him. No. Not my baby. Too small. Too soft. A stuffed animal. Yarn. Monkey. The monkey . . . No. I don't want to think about it.

I have to get up. I have to. The kids will be home soon. They'll need a snack. And then dinner. Maybe there's something in the freezer. *Freezer. Fetus. Frisbee. Femur. Fleeting. Foible.* So many *F* words. *Fuck.* I never say *fuck.* I should say it more. I would say it now if I could only make my mouth work.

How can I get up if I can't even make my mouth work or open my eyes? Why are my lids so heavy?

I remember. Pills. Lovely pills that make me not happy but also not like every inch of my skin is on fire. Why was my skin on fire? It's not, not now, but it was. Was that yesterday or last week or last month when I was screaming, both inside my head and outside my head and my skin was burning and I felt like I was being disemboweled? Now there's a word. *Disemboweled.* Fuck.

I shrink away from these thoughts, these disemboweled, skin-burning, head-screaming thoughts, because I know they will take me to the something-awful place, and I cannot go there. I have to get up and make a snack. I think about the snack, even as my stomach twists (disemboweled) and my head pounds (screaming) and my skin itches until I want to claw it off (burning).

Snack. *Rachel, focus. Snack.* Peanut butter and crackers for Eden and apples with almond butter for Jonah, not because he has a peanut allergy but because he likes the almond butter. The woman at Trader Joe's thought that was interesting. That's what she said. *That's interesting.* Almond butter. I think I'm out of almond butter. I haven't been to Trader Joe's in a while. But I don't need almond butter, or do I? I do, for Jonah. Peanut butter for Eden and almond butter for . . .

Jonah.

I sit up suddenly and force my eyes to open. The daylight sears my retinas. Through the spots of white obscuring my vision, I see him, perched on the end of the bed, smiling at me.

Hi, Mommy.

Jonah.

My vision clears. And I remember.

Jonah.

Oh my god oh my god oh my god. JONAH.

I'm screaming again.

FIVE

RUTH

I hear the scream, and the keys slide from my grasp. I curse softly, then drop my carry sacks on the porch and scramble for the keys. The screaming continues. My fingers are shaking. I can't unlatch the bolt. I stop and take a deep breath, then turn the key and push through the front door, leaving the groceries outside.

The dog is standing at alert at the bottom of the stairs, its long nose pointing to the second floor. It sees me and immediately lowers itself to the floor and bows its head submissively.

I hurry up the stairs two at a time and rush to the master bedroom. The smell of vomit assaults my nose, but I don't linger on the question. Rachel is on the bed, clutching that damn stuffed monkey to her chest, rocking back and forth and screaming. Tears stream down her cheeks.

"Rachel," I say, but she doesn't hear me. I move quickly to the side of the bed and reach for her. As soon as she feels my fingertips brush her arm, she lashes out blindly, smacking my wrist hard enough to make me wince.

"Rachel! It's me Ruth. Rachel!"

I grab for her again, clutching her arms and pressing them tightly against her sides so that she can't swing them. A deep moan bubbles up from her chest and ends with a blistering wail.

"Jonah!"

She goes limp then, and I wrap my arms around her and hold her to me. Her moans turn to wrenching, full-body sobs, with intermittent cries of her son's name. We sit that way for what seems like a long while. I don't allow myself to move or shift, but the stench of the room—the vomit from the trash bin next to the bed, the unwashed, sweat-soaked bedding, the rank odor of grief emanating from my sister—begins to make me nauseous.

"Jonah," she mewls.

"I know, honey. I know." When I'm certain she is calm, I ease her back down onto the bed. She stares at the ceiling, then throws her forearm over her eyes. The stuffed animal lies limp at her side. Her lips are cracked and crusted at the corners; her normally rosy, freckled skin is pale, with half-moon bruises under her eyes. Her strawberry-blonde hair is greasy and slick at the scalp and matted at the ends.

"I saw him," she says. "He was here."

The pills are talking. I slowly rise from the bed and walk around to the nightstand to inspect the bottle. I can't tell how many she's taken today. Guilt gnaws at me. I shouldn't have left her in charge of her own medication. I shouldn't have left her alone. But then, someone has to take care of the household. They were out of almost everything. I had to go to the store. The casseroles and premade meals from friends and neighbors are long gone. What was I supposed to do? Let them starve?

I remember the groceries on the porch. "Rachel, I'll be right back."

"Don't go." Her voice is like a child's. I know I should feel sorry for her, and I do, but suddenly I'm angry. This is not my sister.

"Rachel," I say sternly. She flinches, but I continue. "I'm going to bring in the groceries and put them away. Then I'm coming back up here, and you're going to bathe."

She shakes her head back and forth.

"I'm not taking no for an answer. I'll carry you if I have to."

"No, no, no."

14

"You stink, Rachel." I know it's harsh, but I can't help myself. If my sister were on the outside of this grief, looking in on someone else, she would do the same thing. "You stink and your room stinks and you can't live like this."

She doesn't say anything. I grab the bottle of pills and tuck it into my pocket, then cross to the window and pull the curtains wide. I slide the window open all the way. Rachel scoots up against the headboard, scans the nightstand, then squints at me.

"Where are my pills, Ruth? I need one."

I cross my arms over my chest and shake my head.

"I need one. You don't understand, Ruth. You don't know what it's like. I can't take it, I can't, I can't . . . " She is starting to work herself up again. I go to her and lay a hand on her cheek.

"You have to get through this, honey."

"I want a pill."

"After. Your. Bath."

She glares at me, then gives a slight nod. She grabs the monkey and burrows under the covers, turns away from me onto her side. I release a sigh, then stand and walk to the bedroom door. Just as I step into the hall, I hear her muffled words.

"He was here."

SIX

Shadow

Dark Female is back. I hear her car before she comes in the house. It creaks and shudders when she turns it off. Not like my master's car that hums soothingly or my mistress's car that whispers, and I'm not sure it's her until she slams the car door. Her car-door slam sounds hollow.

Dark Female is outside when my mistress starts to howl. I jump from my bed and run to the bottom of the stairs. I'm not allowed up there, but my mistress is in distress. I should go to her. But the front door opens, and Dark Female rushes in. She looks at me like she always looks at me, with angry eyes like I've been a Bad Boy, but not angry eyes like my master when I stole the bacon from the counter—his eyes were angry but also laughing a little at the edges. Dark Female looks at me like she wants to hurt me, but I don't know what I did to make her want to hurt me.

Maybe I did a big Bad Boy thing. I must have. But I am good and faithful to my humans. I sometimes do small Bad Boy things like chew pillows and chair legs and Little Female's stuffed animals and Little Male's softballs, and sometimes I try to run out the front door when the cat across the street hisses at me. But I'm a Good Boy. "Good boy." That's what my humans always say to me. They did before. They don't talk to me much now, but that's okay because I know they are sad.

They are sad because Little Male got hurt. They think he is gone. He's not gone, not completely. I still see him sometimes. He looks different, and I can't smell him at all. But he's here.

My mistress is still howling, but Dark Female gives me another angry look, and I lie down on my haunches and lower my head. Dark Female runs past me and up the stairs.

She smells like food and fear.

SEVEN

JONAH

I'm pretty sure Mommy saw me today.

She was talking about snacks. Or thinking about snacks. It's kind of funny because I can hear the words in her head as if she was saying them out loud. But it made me happy that she was thinking about making me a snack, even though I can't eat it. I wanted to make her smile and know that I was happy she was thinking a good thought about me.

I don't like peanut butter. It sticks to the top of my mouth and makes me talk funny and Eden makes fun of me 'cause I sound like a baby. Almond butter is yummy and doesn't stick to my mouth and make me talk like a baby. It goes down my throat better. Or it did before, when I had a throat.

So I went into Mommy's room. I don't know where I was before I heard her words. Sometimes I just am, but I'm not anywhere. It's kind of like floating in a swimming pool when your eyes are closed and you don't feel anything or think anything or do anything, but you just are. But then I heard Mommy talking about my snack and I thought of being where she was and then I was just there, kind of sitting on her bed, but not like I used to. I couldn't feel the bed under me. And Mommy sat up and looked at me, right at me, not through me like when I sat next to Dad on the couch and his eyes saw the clock on the mantel instead of my chest, which was right in front of him.

She said my name and then her eyes got really big and she started to scream, and I didn't like that sound so I just thought about my room and I went there. I could still hear Mommy screaming even though I was down the hall, and it was loud, not like she was in my room with me, but like her screams were inside me, and I didn't like that at all, so I thought of floating and the pool and then I was nowhere, but somewhere away from the screaming.

And then, I don't know how I could tell, but I knew everything was quiet again, so I thought about Mommy and I was back in her room. But not on the bed. I didn't want her to see me and start screaming again, so I kind of slid into the corner of the shadows by the wall. I'm here now and I know she can't see me 'cause she's in the bathroom, sitting in the bathtub with water and lots of bubbles all around her.

I can't smell now, but I remember Mommy's baths always smelled really good. She said it was lavender, a kind of flower, and she had me repeat the word until I got it right, until I could say *lavender*. And I told my teacher that I could say *lavender* and that I knew what it was and she was really proud of me.

Auntie Ruth is in Mommy's bedroom. She pulls the comforter off the bed and throws it on the floor, then pulls the blankets and sheets off, too. Her lips are white with frowning, and her nose scrunches up as she bundles up the sheets and tosses them outside the bedroom door. Every few seconds, she goes to the bathroom and looks in.

"You okay, Rach?" she asks.

Mommy sometimes doesn't answer and sometimes she says, "Go away" or "Leave me alone" or "Can I have a pill?" Auntie Ruth's frown gets bigger, but she keeps working, putting new sheets on the bed and tucking them under the mattress.

I always loved that, when I got into bed after Mommy made it fresh, with the sheets and blankets tucked in under the sides and pressing down on me. It felt nice and safe and cozy. Maybe Mommy will feel nice and safe and cozy when she gets back into bed. I liked the way the sheets smelled, too. That word Mommy taught me was easier. *Tide*, she said. I didn't tell my teacher that one because even a baby can say *Tide*.

Auntie Ruth runs the vacuum and then she goes into the bathroom and washes Mommy's hair. Mommy makes angry sounds when Auntie Ruth tries to brush through her hair, kind of like Eden does when Mommy brushes through her hair. Mommy and Eden have the same hair—that's what Mommy always says. When Eden cries out, Mommy says, "I know, honey. You got your hair from me."

Auntie Ruth has different hair from Mommy even though they're sisters, just like Eden and me have different hair. Mine is dark brown like Daddy's. Or it was. Auntie Ruth's is darker than Mommy's, at least on the bottom it is, but not on top 'cause the top of Auntie Ruth's head looks kind of gray, like my nanny's was. The bottom of Auntie Ruth's hair is kind of like the color of the stuff Mommy drinks with dinner, or sometimes before dinner, too, or after dinner, the stuff in the tall green bottle. Sometimes Auntie Ruth drinks the stuff from the green bottle with Mommy, but I don't think that's why the bottom of her hair is that color, 'cause if it was, Mommy's would be, too.

Auntie Ruth helps Mommy out of the bathtub and wraps a towel around her. Mommy just stands there while Auntie Ruth dries her off, then leaves her to come back into the bedroom to get some clothes. Mommy is naked. A *nudist*, I think. One time when I got out of the bath and the towel dropped to the floor, Mommy laughed and said, "Nudist!" And I asked what was a nudist and Eden said it's someone who doesn't wear clothes, dummy, like she was so much smarter than me, which she is, but only 'cause she's bigger, and Mommy got cross with her and told her not to call names. Mommy made Eden 'pologize and Eden said she was sorry, but I think she only meant it a little bit, not all the way.

Mommy looks really skinny, not like she did before when I would see her get out of the bath looking all pink and smelling of lavender. Her bones are kind of sticky-outy. Her boobies used to be round, but now they kind of flop down flat. And her belly that used to poof out just a little bit, which felt nice when I laid my head in her lap, kind of like a little warm pillow, is all sunken in and doesn't look comfy at all.

Auntie Ruth comes back into the bathroom holding a pile of clothes. A pair of sweatpants that Mommy used to wear when she cleaned the house or sat on the couch with Eden and me eating popcorn and watching Dora and Diego, which Eden said was for babies but watched anyway. And the yellow sweater with the unicorn on the front, my favorite thing Mommy ever wore because the unicorn looked like it was about to fly off her sweater and into the room. Mommy said that it could happen and Eden rolled her eyes like that was never going to happen, but Mommy said it could if you believed hard enough, anything could happen.

I look up at Mommy's face and her cheeks are wet, but not from the bath. Her eyes are crying again.

"That was Jonah's favorite sweater," Mommy says, but her voice is kind of choky. Auntie Ruth takes in a breath and throws her arms around Mommy, even though she's still naked, and then Auntie Ruth's crying, too.

I don't want to hear the crying. I think of being nowhere and then I go.

EIGHT

Eden

This has been the worst day in my entire life. I know I'm supposed to say that the Jonah Day was the worst, but it wasn't. Not for me. Everything was crazy that day, not just after it happened, but before, too. And after it happened, there was a lot of yelling and sirens, and people rushing out of their houses and Aunt Ruth sent me up to my room so that I couldn't see anything, even though I already saw it.

But today was way worse, because on the Jonah Day, nobody knew anything and today, everybody knows everything.

I'm so mad at Mom and Dad, but even more mad at Aunt Ruth, because she made me come to school, and I don't think I'm ever going to forgive her for that. Mom and Dad wouldn't have cared if I stayed home for another week or another month or even another year. They don't care what I do or don't do right now. Maybe someday they will again, but they don't now. So why did Aunt Ruth have to think she was all parenty and knew what was good for me? She's not my mom or my dad. She doesn't even have kids. Like she knows what's best for a kid. She's not even married anymore.

I'm mad at my teacher, Mr. Libey, for looking at me all day with those eyes of his. Which were sad but also kind of afraid, like maybe he was thinking about his own kids and how bad things can happen no matter what and there's nothing you can do about it. I heard one of my mom's friends talking about that on the day of the funeral. "You just can't keep them safe," she said, dabbing at her bright-pink lips with her handkerchief that now had big bright-pink rings all over it. "No matter what you do, you can't keep them safe."

And Mr. Libey kept looking at me and then looking at his cell phone, which I know for a fact has a picture of his kids as his screen saver. I asked him about them once, when I was at his desk turning in my math worksheet and I happened to see the picture of the two curly-haired girls with matching dresses and matching missing teeth in the front of their mouths. He said they were Hailey and Shaley, and I thought Hailey was a cool name, but Shaley was stupid and that he'd named her Shaley just so her name would rhyme with her sister's.

And he didn't stop the other kids in my class from whispering about me and passing notes, even the ones I thought were my friends. He made some stupid speech about being kind and considerate of "your school companions," which was code for "the girl whose brother is dead."

But he didn't seem to notice that everyone was still pointing and smirking and frowning at me. Well, everyone except Aimee Joyce and Corwin Kwe. They're nice and don't say anything mean about anyone, not even the kids who tease them.

And I'm mad at Mrs. Hartnett *and* Mr. Libey for totally poning me in kinder-readers. Because they didn't think about the fact that, like, I had no one to read with because my kinder-reader partner was my *brother* and my brother was gone. Duh? And Mrs. Hartnett got really round owl eyes and then started sniffling and everyone turned and looked at me, everyone in my class, and also the kindergartners, too. And because the teachers didn't know what else to do with me, they sent me up to see this lady in the front office called Mrs. P, who isn't married, according to Kylie Barnard—"at least not to a man." I've never talked to Mrs. P before, but I know from listening to teachers talk when they think I'm concentrating on my work, that Mrs. P gets the kids who have "issues" or "problems" or are on something called an IEP, which I think means they're dumb or something.

Mrs. P smiles like she isn't really happy at all, and that kind of creeps me out. She asked me how I'm doing and how it is to be back at school and if I need anything. I told her fine and fine and no. She told me I could come talk to her anytime, that she'd be here, and that I could talk to her about anything, and then she smiled that creepy smile and I knew right then and there that I was never going to talk to her about anything ever.

And then at lunch, I had to buy because my mom didn't pack me a lunch because she's taking medication that makes her not do any of the mom things she's supposed to do. So I had to buy lunch but there wasn't any money in my lunch account because my dad forgot to refill it, not because he's taking medication, but probably because the crease in his forehead is causing brain damage or something. So the lunch lady kind of pats my hand and pushes a tray over to me and says I can pay the school back tomorrow. And I take my lunch over to the table where the whispering stops suddenly and everyone looks at me.

I used to sit with Carlee Rhodes and Ava Landou, but they turn their backs to me and start being all jokey with Ryan Anderson and Matt Boyles, like they don't even know me, like they didn't come to my tenth birthday sleepover and eat pizza till midnight, like we didn't do a whole singing dancing routine to "Single Ladies (Put a Ring on It)" for the talent show last year where we all dressed up like Beyoncé. I feel my cheeks get hot and I know they're probably all pink because they always get pink when I'm embarrassed. Even Ryan, who I thought was different, even *he's* being all jokey, and that really hurts my feelings.

Aimee Joyce smiles up at me, then scooches over to give me space. I almost want to hug her for being so nice to me. But then I look down at my lunch tray and there's a shiny red apple on it and I think of Jonah and I get this weird kind of choking feeling in my throat and I know I'm going to start crying, and I can't let that happen in front of all my classmates, 'cause even though I have a good reason to be crying, I'll still be the crybaby until I get to middle school, and maybe even after that.

So I turn around and throw my tray in the trash, and I hear the lunch lady behind me calling to me about wasting food, and I just run and run, out of the lunch area and into the building and down the hall to the activity room. No one's allowed in at lunch 'cause there's no teacher or anyone to watch you, and it was dark, but I went in anyway and I just sort of sat in the corner on the carpet and hugged my knees into my chest and just sat there for a while, crying and hiccuping and trying not to think about the very bad day and the thing I did, because when I think about it my stomach hurts.

I thought about going to the nurse and telling her I didn't feel well and having her call home for someone to pick me up. But I didn't think being home would be much better than being here. And I knew that after lunch there was only PE, and I figured that being outside and playing kickball would make me feel better, but then Ross Llewelyn, this total weenie, said that I couldn't play because I was grieving and that would make me suck. And the PE teacher, Miss Wells, didn't even tell him not to say bad words like *suck*. She just nodded with a sad face and said I could sit this one out.

So now school's finally over and I'm standing out in front of the school, waiting. No one told me they'd pick me up from school today, but I guess I thought maybe Aunt Ruth would come. I watch all the cars come and go until there's nobody left to pick up except me. Mrs. P steps out from the front office and turns and looks at me. She takes a step toward me, that creepy smile coming back to her lips, and I hustle down to the sidewalk away from her.

"Eden, are your parents picking you up?" she calls to me.

I don't answer, don't slow down, just head down the street toward the next block.

My friends, the ones I usually walk with, are nowhere in sight.

I can't help myself. I keep looking behind me, expecting to see Jonah.

Worst day of my life.

I start to run.

NINE

SAMUEL

When I pull up to the house, I see Ruth's Nissan at the curb. My relief is tempered by an irrational feeling of resentment. I'm glad Rachel is not alone, that her sister is taking care of her. But when Ruth is around, which is all the time now, I have to be on guard. I'm not allowed to be the grieving father. I'm not allowed to express what I'm going through, because it might upset Rachel further. I don't want to upset my wife. I've done that enough. But a part of me rails against the injustice. Rachel gets to fall apart, but Sam has to hold it together. Sometimes I don't want to hold it together. Sometimes I can't.

I went to the park on my lunch hour today. Not a wise move. Greta offered to get sandwiches and come with me. I politely declined. I told her I needed to be alone. I refrained from telling her that keeping on my game face was exhausting. That accepting other people's ministrations of sympathy was akin to being burned at the stake. I needed to be away from the solemn stares and the downturned glances and the shaking heads of regret.

Greta nodded and told me she understood, but she doesn't. How can she? She's young, single. Her parents and grandparents are still alive, for Christ's sake. She doesn't have children to love and care for and make dreams for and grieve over. I'm glad she doesn't understand. I wouldn't wish that kind of understanding on anyone.

The park was empty when I first arrived. I found a bench not far from the playground, and as I sat, I watched, with mounting dismay, the onrush of toddlers and tykes and their mothers or nannies, with their strollers and diaper bags and coolers full of snacks.

I thought I could handle it. I thought I could sit there and watch the children play and laugh and climb and slide. But then I saw him, a little boy, four or five, with dark ringlets framing his face and skin like porcelain and a wide grin, and I thought, *Jonah*.

I pictured myself rising from the bench and crossing the rubber floor tiles and grabbing that child and running, holding him under my arm like a football while I fumbled with my cell phone, calling Rachel and telling her to go to the school and get Eden, that I'd found Jonah, that he wasn't dead, and we could all be together as a family, but we'd have to run far, far away to be that family—the four of us, Sam, Rachel, Eden, and Jonah, who was not Jonah but could be if we made him so.

And then I realized that I was thinking the thoughts of a fucking madman, and with the nannies and mothers and children looking on, I buried my head in my hands and sobbed.

I can't sob, here in my home. I can't bury my face or slouch or falter. I have to pretend that everything is okay. Not good, not great, but okay, moving forward, moving on. What bullshit.

As I alight from my car, I see the neighbor woman, Beatrice Martin, dump a sack of trash into her bin. She eyes me nervously then tries on a smile. It looks like a grimace.

"Sam," she says, and I nod to her and try a smile of my own, but I can't quite get my mouth to obey.

"Hello, Bea."

"How's it going?" Her words are measured and sincere. I've heard them countless times in the past month from countless people—Carson Gregson, my business partner; Greta; Sal at the dry cleaner's; Phil at the diner; Hugo Escalante in his thick Ecuadorean accent—just to name a few.

"It's going," I tell her.

"You want I should bring over another chicken casserole?" she asks. "I'm happy to do it."

Her casserole is good. She made it for us when we first moved in. We scraped the pan clean and raved over the cream sauce, Rachel and I, congratulating ourselves for our good fortune to live next door to a bona fide casserole goddess.

The last casserole she made, the day after the accident, went from the oven to the trash.

"That's okay," I tell her. "Don't go to any trouble."

"You know me," she says. "I like to be of service."

You like to tell Escalante how to trim the hedges and cut the rosebushes, I think, then chide myself for the ungenerous thought. Beatrice has been a good neighbor. She cares about my family. She has cared for my children when Rachel and I needed her. She is a busybody and a know-it-all when it comes to gardening, but she is not a bad person. Her casserole is her way of coping. I only wish I had as simplistic a way of coping.

"That would be very nice," I tell her. Then I turn away from her and trudge to my front porch. I don't know what awaits me on the other side of the door. But I will face it, whatever it is. I have no choice.

When I walk into the living room, I'm surprised to see that the curtains have been pulled back and the windows are open. The smell of cleaning solutions fills the air, and every surface—the hardwood floors, the tabletops, the mantel—is freshly wiped. The house is cleaner than it's been since the day of the funeral.

Even more surprising is that Rachel is seated on the couch, her legs crossed beneath her, a shawl wrapped around her shoulders. Her hair is curly, spilling down her back, and she wears clean clothes, sweats and the yellow sweater with the unicorn on the front. She holds a cup and saucer in her hands, and she gazes into the cup as though trying to read tea leaves on the bottom.

I set down my briefcase and walk toward her, slowly so as not to startle her. She doesn't look up, but I see her body tense slightly. Beneath the shawl, I see the stuffed monkey, its arms spanning Rachel's waist. My own shoulders tighten.

"Hello, Sam." Ruth's voice comes from behind me. I turn to see my sister-in-law walk through the dining room. She wears her usual expression—the slightly-disappointed-that-I'm-not-someone-else look, which she quickly covers with a smile. Her smile is like my neighbor's—pained.

"Hi, Ruth." I turn back to Rachel. "Hi, Rach. How are you feeling?" She still doesn't look up at me. "Hi, Sam," she says softly.

"She's feeling much better, aren't you, Rachel?" Ruth takes the seat next to Rachel and pats her knee. "Much better. She's had a bath, and she even managed a piece of toast with honey."

"That's terrific," I say with a little too much enthusiasm. Rachel shrinks into the couch. I lower my volume. "I'm glad."

I stand awkwardly for a moment. It would be nice to sit next to my wife, but there isn't room for me with Ruth there. There isn't room for me in my bedroom, either. Rachel's grief has taken my place. I glance at the bedding folded neatly and stacked on the easy chair. Ruth has laundered it—the sheets have that crisp, clean look about them. Ruth has been sleeping in the guest room at the back of the house. It's only right that she has her own bed, that's what I keep telling myself, even though the couch is horrible for sleeping and I hardly manage to get an hour or two at a stretch and I wake each morning to searing back pain that only a handful of Advil can touch.

"I've made tea, if you'd like some," Ruth says. What I'd like is two fingers of bourbon, neat. That will have to wait.

"I'll get it."

"I'll come with you," Ruth says, and I feel my jaw clench.

She doesn't say anything until we are safely in the kitchen, out of Rachel's earshot. Shadow lies on his bed in the corner. His tail thumps enthusiastically when he sees me. He starts to get up to greet me but freezes when Ruth enters. He lies down and tucks his head into his chest.

I cross to the far counter where the teapot sits, lean against the counter, and wait for Ruth to speak.

"She had another bad day, Sam. I went to the market—I wasn't gone for more than forty-five minutes. When I came back, she was screaming. She'd been sick. I think she took too many pills at once on an empty stomach."

I remember retching into my trash bin at work. No pills necessary.

I tell Ruth the same thing I tell her every day, because she needs to hear it, to feel validated. "Thank you for being here, Ruth. I don't know what we'd do without you."

She nods as if she agrees. And she does. My sister-in-law is grieving. She loved Jonah. But I think she secretly likes the fact that my family would be completely fucked without her help. Our need gives her power. She has none in any other area of her life.

"She looks . . . better. Better than she has in weeks," I say, pouring some tea into a waiting mug.

"She's clean, Sam. That's all. And medicated. Which I'm worried about. We can't leave the pills with her anymore. We have to start doling them out. She can't be trusted to stick to the dosage."

"I know Rachel is in bad shape, but I think you're being a little dramatic."

This wouldn't be the first time my sister-in-law has created a non-existent issue. It's happened frequently over the course of my marriage.

Ruth withdraws the bottle of meds from her pocket and hands them to me. "I have to go home and get some things, Sam. You keep these for now."

Worry blanches her features. I try to reassure her.

"Ruth, Rachel would never go overboard. You know that. She's grieving, she's devastated. But she's not going to do anything stupid." As I say the words, I realize that I'm not completely sure if they're true. I don't know the woman sitting on the couch in the next room, the woman who won't look at me and barely speaks to me and banished me from my bedroom. What is that expression? The one about how dealing with challenges and tragedies reveals the character of the person? If that's true, then I'm screwed. And so is Rachel. And God help Eden, because her mother is totally gone.

Ruth sniffs, then gives me a pointed look. An I-told-you-so look even before she tells me. "She thinks she saw Jonah."

"What?" I stare at her. "She dreamed about him?"

"No, she says she saw him. Sitting on the end of her bed. Uh, *your* bed. Floating on the end of your bed. And then he disappeared."

"The meds, right? She was hallucinating." Even as I say the words, some deeper part of me wonders—hopes, prays—if it's possible that Jonah could still be here. Ridiculous, I know. Absurd. Again with the fucking madman business. I focus on Ruth.

"Of course she was hallucinating, Sam. But that's not the point. If she continues to hallucinate and see Jonah, and she thinks he's a visiting spirit, and then she thinks the only way she'll get to him is by becoming a spirit herself, well . . . I called her GP, and she's worried, too. She suggests we start cutting back, start the weaning process."

A fist of tension forms in my gut. "Right now, Rachel needs those pills."

"She needs counseling, Sam. For crying out loud, it would be good for all of you. The three of you need to talk to someone, or get into a group."

"We've been through this before, Ruth. Now isn't the time. We're not ready."

"Now is exactly the time. How long are you going to wait? Until my sister goes completely insane or winds up an addict?"

The fist tightens. I don't want to see a counselor. Things might come up. Things I'm not prepared to explain. Things I need to discuss with my wife first. I can't say this to Ruth. So I placate her instead.

"I'll think about it. I really will."

"You should do more than think about it, Sam. This is serious."

Indignation swells inside me. "You think I don't know that? My son is dead. It doesn't get any more serious than that."

She looks stricken, but I don't apologize. I'm too angry. Not just at Ruth for her presumptuousness, for thinking she has the right to tell me what I need, what *my* family needs. But angry at the world, at Rachel, at God, at Jonah for leaving us, at myself for my part in his death. I want to lash out more, to rail against her, to tell her to get the hell out of my house. But I can't. Of course, I can't. I take a deep breath instead and gaze at my mug, at the amber liquid that has long since cooled. I set the mug down, then glance at my watch. Ruth stares out the kitchen window, and I can only assume she is trying to think of something to say to me, some biting retaliation for my outburst. Uncharacteristically, she remains silent.

I keep my tone even. "Can you please try to get that fucking thing away from her?"

She turns to me. "The monkey?" She shakes her head with disdain. "I think you should focus on more important issues, Sam. And I'll ask you not to use that kind of language with me."

I bite down on a scathing comeback, close my eyes, open them when I stop seeing red. "I'm going to go pick Eden up from school."

Ruth takes a breath and sighs. "Doesn't she usually walk?"

"Yes," I reply. "With Jonah."

"You're too late," she says. "She'll be walking through the door any minute." She doesn't meet my eye, just swipes my mug from beneath my fingers and dumps the contents into the sink. "You didn't want that, right, Sam? Too cold." She turns on her heels and stomps out of the kitchen.

After a moment, when I hear her murmur to Rachel, and I can tell she has taken her seat next to her sister, I cross to the refrigerator and reach for the cupboard door above it. I pull out the Maker's Mark, then grab a highball glass from the adjacent cupboard.

For a while I stare at the bottle, thinking of the curly-haired boy on the playground.

I pour out three fingers and down them in one gulp.

TEN

RACHEL

The ticking of the clock on the mantel echoes through my brain. The sound is unpleasant. I'd like to smash the clock into pieces, but I don't have the energy to get up from the couch. I can't smash it anyway. I don't have a hammer. And it's my mother's clock. *Was* my mother's clock. She bequeathed it to me. *Bequeathed.* I want to say the word *bequeathed* aloud, just to see how my mouth feels when I say it, but I don't want to sound crazy. Ruth is right next to me, pretending not to watch me.

I'm not crazy. Just so tired. So very, very tired. My thoughts shift back and forth, in and out and around. I try to hold one for a moment. It disappears, just like Jonah.

I reach beneath the shawl for the monkey, just to make sure it's still there.

I want to go back to bed, but Ruth won't let me. She has become my mom. My mom. What was I thinking about?

The clock. Bequeathed. Mom *bequeathed* the clock to me. That's right. We found the Post-it note with my name written in broad strokes on the back of it. And that really pissed Ruth off, finding that Post-it, but I was there, too, so she couldn't pretend it wasn't there. Ruth really wanted that damn clock. I should have let her have it. It's ugly and loud and any minute that dumb little cuckoo bird is going to pop out and make that annoying cuckoo sound. *Cuckoo, cuckoo.*

Jonah loved the clock. *Don't think about Jonah.* When he was three, he used to sit on the floor in the middle of the room for hours at a time and just watch for the bird. *No no no.* And when it popped out, he would giggle and giggle and giggle.

Stop. Don't think about Jonah. I can't think about him. My boy, my precious baby.

My cheeks are wet again. They're wet all the time, but my mouth is always parched, like I'm emptying out all of the water in my body through my tear ducts.

The sofa cushions feel like gelatin. I could sink into them, let them envelop me, suffocate me. Death by faux-suede couch cushions.

I want a pill. Ruth only gave me one, wouldn't give me another. She always did like to torture me, ever since we were kids. I need another one. Or two. One isn't enough. One only takes the hard edges away from the world, blurs the lines a little bit. But two is better. Fuzzy-thought making. Three is when I threw up, but then I saw Jonah, so I need to take three so I can see him again. He was there.

He was there.

He wasn't there. Jonah is dead.

Ruth puts her hand on my shoulder, and I flinch. She removes her hand.

"Where's Sam?" I ask. He was here a minute ago, wasn't he? I want to tell him about Jonah.

No. I don't want to tell Sam. I can't talk to him, because then I'd have to look at him and I can't look at him, not right now. I don't know why. Jonah is in his face, or his face is in Jonah's, the same nose, only bigger, the same jawline, only without the baby fat. I don't think that's the reason, but when I look at Sam, I start to feel like my insides are being run through a meat grinder.

"He's in the kitchen."

Good. Stay in the kitchen, Sam.

"Daddy was a butcher."

"No, honey. Dad sold insurance."

"Daddy was a butcher who used the meat grinder every Sunday night, making sausages for the week ahead."

"What is that from?" my sister asks. My sister. I should have given her the stupid clock.

"A story." A story I used to read to Jonah.

How can I still be crying? I'll turn into a salt statue and the wind will blow through the windows Ruth opened and I'll disintegrate. She'll have to vacuum again.

"I want another pill, Ruth. Please."

"Why don't we wait until Eden gets home, honey. You can ask her about her day. Talk to her for a few minutes." *With unfuzzy thoughts.* She doesn't say it, but I know she's thinking it. "Her first day back might have been hard."

"Back where?" I can't remember where my daughter is. I have a daughter and a son. No, just a daughter now. Where is she? School. Yes, school. She's in fourth grade. No, fifth. My daughter. Jonah was in kindergarten.

Was *was was was.*

"I want a fucking pill."

"Rachel."

I've shocked my sister. I said the f-word. Out loud. If I still knew how to laugh, I would. Instead I start to moan. It starts in my belly, and I feel it rise upward through my chest, into my throat. I open my mouth and let it out as a howl.

"Jesus Christ, give her a goddamn pill!" Sam. I lower my head, clamping my mouth shut, and stare at the tea. I hate tea. *I hate tea, Ruth. You know I do.*

I hear him, my husband, the man I promised to spend my life with. *Till death do us part,* we'd said. But until whose death? He's still my champion, even now, telling meanie Ruth to give me a pill. *Thank you, Sam. I can't bear to look at you, but thank you.*

I see his shadow cross the room, hear the rattle of the pills as he hands the bottle to Ruth. His shadow moves beyond my sight line, toward the front door. I want to ask him where he's going. I don't care, though, so I don't.

Goodbye, Sam. I saw Jonah on our bed this morning.

ELEVEN

RUTH

"Where are you going?" I ask my brother-in-law. I see the splotches of red on his neck and know he's had some liquor.

"I'm going to get Eden," he snaps.

"Do you really think you should be driving?" He stops at the front door and glares at me, and I know I've gone too far. But I can't help myself. "Be careful." I try for sincerity, but my words sound like a warning.

"You too, Ruth."

He turns and walks out, slamming the door behind him. I close my eyes and breathe deeply.

I know why my sister married Sam, with his movie-star good looks and easy charm. High school quarterback and homecoming king and wunderkind architect. He wasn't like the other boys she dated, the losers and dropouts and potheads that mooched money off her and pushed themselves between her legs because she let them. Samuel Davenport was solid and successful and kind and attentive and so damned reliable. He always showed up. But I don't trust him. He is still a man, and men are incapable of maintaining any of their good qualities for very long. I should know.

There's something going on with him, something I can't define. Yes, he's grieving. We all are, for goodness' sake, but there's something holding his attention that might be attached to his grief or parallel to it. I don't know.

What I do know is that he's being completely unreasonable about the counseling issue. How could he not want to explore every possibility of healing his family? The desire to keep everything private is so typically male. It makes me furious that he is unwilling to do everything in his power to help Rachel. I've seen how he looks at her, the mixture of compassion and disgust. I can't blame him for that, though. I must look at her the same way. Her grief has swallowed her and spit out someone who looks like my sister but who is unrecognizable in every other way.

"Is he gone?" she asks, her voice a whisper.

"Yes."

She raises her head. Beneath the fragrance of the shampoo and the soap I used to scrub her, I can still smell the faint odor of vomit and despair. She looks directly at me, but there is no warmth in her gaze.

"You heard my husband, Ruth. Give me a pill." Her countless tears have forged tracks down her cheeks. Her expression is haunted; the blue of her eyes has paled. I can't bear to look at her, this woman who used to be beautiful and vibrant and alive. I keep my gaze steady so that she won't know how hard it is for me to look at her.

"Don't you want to be here for Eden?" I ask as calmly as I can manage.

"I was here for Jonah," she says, then she mumbles something I can't make out, even though I'm only inches from her.

"Eden needs you, Rachel. You can't ignore that."

"Silly Ruth. Silly, stern, serious Ruth. Socially inept Ruth. Celibate Ruth. No, *celibate* starts with a *C*, doesn't it?"

Her words are like a punch to my gut. Because they are true. Not silly, no. I have never been silly. But stern and serious and socially inept. Those are true. And celibate, yes. I haven't been sexually active since my husband left me eighteen months ago.

"Sad Ruth. Sad, single, submissive, superior, schoolmarm Ruth."

She is taking sick delight in her alliteration. I feel nauseated. "You're being unkind, Rachel."

"I'm sorry," she says, but she doesn't sound sorry. She sounds like a teenager, the teenager she was a hundred years ago. *Sorry, Ruth, I didn't mean to ruin your sweater. Sorry, Ruth, I didn't mean to steal your boyfriend. Sorry, Ruth, but not* really *sorry.*

She stands up suddenly and hurls the teacup across the room. It smacks against the wall and shatters, the remaining tea and scant tea leaves raining down on the carpet I vacuumed moments ago.

I jump to my feet and tension courses through my system, causing all of my muscles to contract. I suck in a breath and blow it out between my clenched teeth, willing myself to relax. Tension triggers my fibromyalgia. And, of course, I'm out of my medication. The effects of last night's dosage are starting to wear off—I can already feel the tenderness in my joints and the pull of fatigue and the way the muscles of my shoulder blades are starting to ache. Those muscles are always the first. I don't know why. But soon the pain will spread in both directions, up to the base of my skull and all the way down to my toes, and I won't be able to function, let alone take care of anyone else. I should have gone home for my refill when I went out for groceries, but I would have been gone twice as long. God knows what kind of shape Rachel might have been in if I hadn't come when I did.

When Sam gets back with Eden, I'm going to have to excuse myself and go home. But right now, I've got another mess to clean up.

"Well done, Rachel." I reach into my pocket and pull out the bottle of pills, twist off the cap, and shake one out onto my palm. "Here."

She snatches the pill from my hand and puts it into her mouth, swallows it dry.

"You need to drink some water," I tell her, but she is already moving away from me toward the stairs. "Drink some water before you lie down."

"I will," she says, then turns to face me. Her expression is bleak. "I'm sorry," she says, and this time the apology sounds sincere. "I'm going to be better, okay, Ruth? Just not today. I just can't today. I just need some time."

A month has passed since the funeral. Thirty-six days since the accident. I wonder how much time my sister needs to get better. I wonder if she will ever get better.

"I know you do," I tell her and watch as she slowly climbs the stairs, one hand clutching the railing to steady herself, the other cradling the monkey.

I cross to the far side of the living room and kneel down on the carpet, my knees in full protest. As I carefully pick up the pieces of the teacup, I think of how a split-second impact can shatter everything.

TWELVE

SHADOW

Little Male is sitting next to me on my bed. I have three beds. One is here in the food-smelling room, the room I like best because every now and then one of my humans drops something on the floor that tastes better than my food. Which is good, because sometimes my humans forget to feed me for a whole day, and if I didn't get the dropped things I wouldn't eat.

One bed is outside on the hard ground next to the house. It's old and smells like dirt and another dog, the before-me dog, and I can tell by his smell that I would have liked him even though his smell is old and tired.

One bed is in the room with the couch that I didn't chew because it tasted funny after my mistress sprayed something on it. Dark Female is in that room now, so I wouldn't go in there, even if Little Male were not sitting with me.

I sniff, but I still can't smell him. His touch is different, too—his fingers are not fingers, but more like a gentle breeze ruffling through the fur on my neck. It feels good but different than it did before. Still, it is a kind of touch, and I don't get much touching anymore.

My master doesn't look at me with angry eyes, but he doesn't get on the floor and rub my body and scratch my backside and thump thump thump me with his hand and say, "Good boy." He doesn't pull on my rope with me pulling it the other way, me pretending to let him win and give over the rope, because a human could never get a rope from me if I didn't want him to. But at least he doesn't look at me with angry eyes.

My mistress doesn't play with me, either. She doesn't see me anymore. I don't think she really sees anyone.

Little Female sometimes pats my head, but then water starts to leak from her eyes and she shoves me away like I did something bad, even though I don't know what I did.

But Little Male still loves me and thinks I'm a Good Boy. He's telling me that now, and his voice is not a voice, but like the sound of the train whistle from so far away that none of the humans can hear it, but I can. Little Male giggles and says, "I love you, Shadow."

I hear my mistress climbing the stairs. If I was allowed up there I would go, too, just to lie beside her bed, even though I don't have a bed in her room. I would lie down next to her just so she would know I'm there, even though I don't think she would. But I'm not allowed to climb the stairs, and Dark Female is out there in the couch room and I don't want to see her and her angry eyes. So I stay here in the food-smelling room, with Little Male and his whisper giggles and breeze touch, and hope my humans don't forget to feed me, because I know Little Male can't feed me even if he wanted to because his fingers are made of wind.

THIRTEEN

JONAH

Shadow is sad, just like everybody, only he doesn't cry with his eyes. But I can tell. He's happy when I sit next to him. He knows I'm there, but he doesn't start screaming like Mommy, or barking, or anything. He kind of tries to lick me, but I can't feel his tongue like I used to, that big pink tongue that isn't wet or drooly but kind of feels rough and tickly at the same time. But I know it means that he likes me there petting him, even if he can't exactly feel my fingers.

I wish I had real fingers so I could draw pictures. Maybe in heaven, if I ever go there, God will give me a great big pad of paper and some big fat markers. Mommy only let me use crayons, 'cause the one time she gave me markers I accidentally drew a big sun on the wall of my room that Eden said looked like someone barfed up yellow on the wall. Mommy told Eden not to say that, but then she was all mad 'cause the sun wouldn't come off and she told me I could only use crayons from now on 'cause crayons you could wash off the wall.

But I bet God would let me use markers, 'cause I bet you could wash heaven markers off the wall.

I can hear Auntie Ruth in the living room. She's talking to herself, but not like Mommy talks to herself. She sounds cross. She's trying to be quiet, but I can hear her 'cause I can hear everything when I want to and nothing when I want to and that's like a superpower, I guess.

Then she stops talking to herself and comes into the kitchen holding broken pieces of a cup in her hands, but all careful, like she's afraid they're gonna cut her. She dumps them in the trash, then smacks her hands together, not like clapping, but like trying to get the itsy-teensy pieces of cup off them. Shadow lifts his head, 'cause sometimes people clap when they want a dog to come, but Auntie Ruth gives Shadow a really mad look and he puts his head down.

"Stupid damn dog," Auntie Ruth says. "They should have put you down."

I don't know what she means. *Put you down.* But I know the d-word is a curse, 'cause Daddy said it one time and Mommy made him put a dollar in the curse jar. And I know that if Auntie Ruth used a curse, then the rest of what she said is probably very bad, because Auntie Ruth never, ever uses curse words—at least that's what Mommy always said. Whatever it means, I know Shadow is upset. He's shaking just a little bit, so I try to cover my whole body on top of his and give him a hug. I know he can't exactly feel it the way he could before, but I think he kind of feels something 'cause his body stops trembling.

I hear Mommy upstairs in her bed, but I wait till Auntie Ruth leaves the room before I go to her so that Shadow won't be alone with Auntie Ruth saying bad things to him. As soon as Auntie Ruth goes back to the living room, I wish myself upstairs. I kind of fold myself into the wall so I don't surprise her like I did before, but she's asleep. I can tell she's sleeping because her mouth is open and she's snoring a little bit, so I move closer because I know she won't see me if she's asleep. She's holding Marco, and that makes me happy, but also sad 'cause I can't hold him myself.

When I'm right next to Mommy, I put my hand on her forehead, like she used to do with me when I had a cough or a tummy ache or a sore throat, or when I was just saying I had one 'cause I wanted to stay in bed. I can't feel her skin under my fingers, but for just a tiny bit, I can hear her sleeping thoughts.

She's in a tunnel, a really long one, with water covering her feet, and there's really bright light coming from both sides of the tunnel and she doesn't know which way to go and she's really, really upset, but then I think maybe she feels me because her sleeping thoughts whisper and they sound like they're talking to me. *Which way should I go?* And I don't know which way she should go, but I kind of know that it doesn't matter which way, it only matters that she goes, so I kind of try to put myself in the tunnel with her, but I can't, and she's still asking the question, so I think of my favorite color, green, and with all my might I think of making the light on one side of the tunnel green. And then it is green, so bright, like the Emerald City from *The Wizard of Oz* or something, and Mommy sees the green light and starts walking that way and I can tell she feels not happy, not really, but better than when she was just standing there.

And then I feel like maybe she's going to wake up and I don't want to make her scream, so I take my hand that isn't really a hand away from her forehead. She makes a funny sound, like a kitty cat or something, and she moves her head, then rolls over, but then she starts snoring again, so I know she's still sleeping.

I don't know how I got into Mommy's dream. I have to think about that. I have to think about why I'm still here and not in heaven. What I'm supposed to do before I can go.

I watch her for a few more minutes, but I don't touch her forehead again.

FOURTEEN

EDEN

I swallow huge gulps of air. My heart is racing, and my lungs feel like they're going to explode. I started running at Chestnut Street, two whole blocks back, and I haven't stopped once. I'm not looking behind me anymore, either, because I know that Jonah isn't there. But it's like I have to *make* myself not look back, because it's the knowing he's not there that's the awful part. And the shame of remembering that when he was there I wanted him not to be. But when I'm running, I can't look back, so I keep going even though my side is on fire and my backpack weighs a ton and I'm probably going to have a heart attack and die right here on the sidewalk.

I see my dad's car coming toward me down the street and I stop and bend over, clutching my stomach and forcing myself not to throw up, which I really think I need to do. Dad slows down, then does a U-turn and pulls up to the curb next to me. A part of me is happy to see him, but another part of me, a bigger part, wants to be mad at him and yell at him and ask him why he didn't pick me up from school, why he made me walk down the street by myself, checking for Jonah until I had to start running.

Maybe if I do actually have a heart attack and die right here in front of him, he'll feel really bad. But I know he already feels really bad. When he leans over and opens the door for me, I see that the crease is still there between his eyes, and his eyes are kind of swollen, and his face is kind of red like he's been scratching it.

"Hi, piece of pumpkin pie," he says. But he doesn't say it the way he used to, when his face would be all happy and goofy smiling and he looked and sounded like a cartoon character. His words are flat and the car engine muffles them. And when I get in the car, I don't think he even notices that I'm about to keel over, that I'm sweating and wheezing and all red in the face, which I know I am. He just turns his creased-forehead, itchy face toward the windshield and pulls from the curb without saying anything about me or to me, or anything at all. I hug my backpack to my chest and stare out the windshield, too.

I want him to ask me how my day was so I can tell him it was the worst day of my life and maybe he'll feel sorry for me and not make me go back to school tomorrow. But then again, maybe he'll get all mad and the crease in his forehead'll get even bigger and he'll tell me that the worst day of my life should be the day Jonah died and how could I pick any other day than that one because it was the worst day of his and my mom's life so it should be mine, too. And then I'll have to start thinking about that day and the things I did that I don't want to think about, so I try to keep my mouth clamped shut, but I can't get enough breath through my nose, so I open my mouth, but I try to not make open-mouth-breathing noises, like Darth Vader.

We're home in two minutes. Dad pulls into the driveway. He just sits there, not moving at all, just staring at the garage door, like something's written on it and he's trying to read it. But obviously there's nothing written on the garage door. I reach for the car door handle.

"Eden." My dad's voice sounds funny, thick like ketchup, like he's got something in his throat but can't get it out. I let my hand sit in midair for a few seconds, waiting to see if Dad's gonna say anything else.

He looks at me but looks away really fast, like maybe it hurts his heart to look at me. And I almost want to tell him to look at me because I'm his kid and I'm here even if Jonah isn't and that I wish Jonah would come back, too, but he's not coming back and so he and my mom are going to have to start looking at the kid they have left, because if they don't I'm afraid I'm gonna just disappear.

"I . . . Eden . . . I don't . . . ," he starts to say in that ketchup voice, and I can tell he wants to say something, but it's making him hurt and that makes me feel like I'm going to start crying and if I start crying, I know that will make him feel worse. And then I get mad because my own dad can't say anything to me, my dad who's supposed to be strong and brave and like Iron Man, not just because he kind of looks like Robert Downey Jr. but also because he's a dad and is supposed to be a little bit of a superhero.

"I have to go pee," I say, even though I know he doesn't like it when I say *pee*. He likes me to say, "I have to go to the bathroom," but I kind of don't care what Dad likes right now, because even though he came and picked me up, which means he must care about me, he doesn't care enough to talk to me anymore. I grab the door handle and shove the door open, then drag my backpack out of the car and run up to the house. I hurry, but not just because I want my dad to think I really do have to go to the bathroom but because I want to get away from him and his crease and his ketchup voice as fast as I can.

I drop my backpack just inside the door. I know Aunt Ruth will holler at me, but I don't care. I run up the stairs two at a time, trip halfway up and bite the tip of my tongue, which really hurts. I feel my lip start to tremble and that choking feeling in my throat, and I pick myself up and keep going. I hear Aunt Ruth calling me from downstairs, but I ignore her and run straight into my bedroom and slam the door. I walk across my room and go into the bathroom, 'cause even though I don't really have to pee, I need to pretend. So I stand in front of the toilet and count to twenty, then flush.

The tears start to come. I grab some toilet paper and press them against my eyes, pushing really hard, like maybe that'll make the tears stop. There's a knock at my bedroom door. It's Aunt Ruth or my dad.

It won't be my mom. Her bedroom door is closed, which means she's sleeping.

"Eden? Honey?" Aunt Ruth. "It's me." Like, duh. Who else would it be? "Can I come in?"

There's no way to stop her, even if I wanted to, because we don't have locks on our doors. I wish we did, not just so I could keep her out, but because if we did, maybe Jonah would still be alive.

I will not think about that, I will not think about that, I will not think about that!

Aunt Ruth opens the door and pokes her pointy nose into my room. Her hair is pulled back in a bun, like I used to have to wear for ballet, only mine had to be really neat and Aunt Ruth's is all messy with strands of hair falling out of it. Her hair is mostly reddish brown but has lots of streaks of gray in it. My mom used to whisper to my dad, when she didn't think I could hear, that it was no wonder Aunt Ruth couldn't find someone when she didn't care enough to color her hair anymore. Which is kind of funny that my mom said that, I guess, because now Mom doesn't care about anything.

Aunt Ruth holds my backpack out to me, and I think she's going to say something cross, like "Don't leave this downstairs," but she doesn't. Maybe it's because she sees I'm crying or maybe it's because she's not feeling well. Her face, now that I look at her, is really kind of white, like more white than usual, and there are circles under her eyes. Not as big or dark as my mom's. My mom's look like someone punched her, like on the Popeye cartoons. But Aunt Ruth's are still dark.

"I thought you might need this for homework," she says.

I nod and take the backpack from her. I don't tell her thank you like I should, but I'm afraid to talk, afraid I'll have a ketchup voice like my dad.

And plus, I'm still mad at her for making me go to school.

"How was it at school today?" she asks.

And now I don't care if I have ketchup voice or not, because she needs to know what she did to me. "It was terrible and awful and horrible and the worst—" I stop myself before I say the rest. "It was the worst."

"I'm sorry," she says, and she looks like she actually means it. She shakes her head sadly. "I'm sure it will get easier."

"No, it won't. I hate it there. Why did you make me go? It's not fair."

"Eden. You have to go to school. It's the law. You were out for three weeks. The school district sent a letter to us and to the state."

"I don't care."

"I know."

"Dori Wilson and her sister are homeschooled," I tell her. I only know that means they don't have to leave their house if they don't want to. And that sounds just okeydoke with me. "Why can't I be homeschooled?"

She smiles, but it's not really a smile, I can tell. "Because your mother or father or I would have to homeschool you, and none of us are in a position to do that right now. Maybe when your mom gets better, you can talk to her about that."

Is she ever going to get better? I want to ask the question, but I'm kind of afraid of the answer, so I hold it on my tongue.

"I have to go home for a little while," she says, and my heart pounds really hard in my chest, like when I was running. Aunt Ruth can be strict, and she sent me back to school, which was really mean, but she's the only one around here who talks to me. Mostly about chores and how much TV I can watch and that kind of thing, but it's better than nothing.

"Don't worry," she says, reaching out and touching my cheek, like she can tell what I'm thinking. "I won't be gone long." She pulls her fingers away from my face, and I watch as she starts to rub her right wrist with her left hand, and her face scrunches up the way Jonah's used to when Mom put alcohol on his scraped knee. "There's a very nice sandwich in the fridge for you in case you get hungry. You can have a bag of chips and some milk with it, okay?"

I nod, feeling the choky feeling in my throat again.

I don't want to be alone in this house, with my mom and her shiny eyes and my dad and his creased forehead. Every minute that goes by feels like hours. Aunt Ruth says she won't be gone long. But it might as well be forever.

FIFTEEN

SAMUEL

After Ruth leaves, I pour myself another Maker's Mark, two fingers this time. The first belt hit me hard, especially since I hadn't eaten lunch, and I probably shouldn't have driven to pick Eden up. But it was only two blocks, thank God.

When Eden got into the car, I knew she was upset. Her face was red and she was huffing and puffing, and her eyes had that haunted look that all of us have. I didn't ask her if she was okay. I should have. But I just couldn't. She would have needed me to make things better for her, and I can't right now. So I pretended not to notice her distress. Then when we got home, when I pulled into the driveway, I tried to talk to her. And again, I couldn't. My throat closed up and I was afraid I'd start blubbering, like I did at the park today. I couldn't let that happen, not in front of my ten-year-old daughter.

I am a terrible father now. I used to be a good father. Not the best, certainly not Father of the Year, but good. I always prided myself on that fact. I never worked weekends so that we could have family time, and I was available most evenings to help with homework and read stories and play with Matchbox cars and Barbies, even though it was difficult for me to satisfactorily make the Barbie voice for Eden. I was always there for my children.

Now, I have only one child. My insides twist at this realization. I've had it many times over the last month—*I have only one child*—and it always takes me by surprise. The wound is torn open, and the pain is fresh and immense.

I wonder if I will ever be a good father again, the father Eden deserves.

Maybe soon. Maybe, if I can just pull myself out from under the weight of grief. Fucking treacherous grief that colors everything a bright shade of rage. Rage that my son was taken from me. It's difficult to see the light at the end of the tunnel, to imagine that there will ever be a time I'm not consumed with grief and rage.

Time heals everything, Tuesday, Thursday . . .

Rachel sang that song on our second date. We were at a Japanese restaurant that had a karaoke lounge in the back. Rachel's confidence was bolstered by sake and Sapporo, as was her voice, and although the notes didn't come out perfectly—she is no Céline Dion—she was wonderful, emotional, committed, and won the first prize, a free shot of Jägermeister, which I used to my full advantage later that night when I carried her to her bedroom.

Time heals everything, this day, next day. If I'm patient the hurt will end and one fine morning, my heart will mend.

One fine morning. I pray for that one fine morning.

Eden is in her room doing her homework, according to Ruth. I haven't checked in on her, but I tell myself I don't need to. Eden is very responsible when it comes to school. She likes to do well. She likes to get good grades and impress her teachers. I wonder how Jonah would have done in school. Maybe he wouldn't have gotten the best grades, but he probably would have been the most popular kid; he would have had countless friends, would have been good at sports, and his teachers would have loved him even if he didn't quite excel academically because he was so damn charming and had dimples so deep you could almost see the back of his head through them.

Fuck. Fuck fuck fuck.

I grab the glass of bourbon and step outside into the backyard. Shadow follows me and immediately goes to his bed, does a quick circle, and lies down. I pat his head and briefly scratch under his chin, and he looks up at me adoringly with his brown eyes, as though I've just bestowed upon him the greatest gift in the canine kingdom.

I drop my hand to my side, then reach into my pants pocket and absently trace the shape of Rachel's pill bottle. Ruth had passed the pills to me, unceremoniously and without a word, before she left. Now, they sit heavily in my pocket. I move along the wall of the house to the stacked brick barbecue. I kneel down and open the metal door to the storage cupboard and feel my way past the sodas and waters and beer. My hand closes around the pack of cigarettes, and I pull it out. I take one of the cigarettes out, light it with the lighter hidden in the pack, then tuck it away, back behind all of the drinks. I move to the very corner of the property, where the trash and recycling bins sit, and smoke the cigarette in between sips of bourbon.

I quit smoking for Rachel. It was my one really bad habit, and she disapproved mightily, telling me flat out that she could never spend her life with a smoker. So I gave it up. For her. Because I wanted her that badly, loved her enough to commit my life and my lungs to her. But now she is unwilling to do anything for me, unwilling to be present, which in some ways I'm glad for, but in other ways not so much. So I stand here and smoke, enjoying every draw.

When I'm down to the filter, I stub it out on the corner of the concrete, then toss it in the trash bin. Rachel won't find it. Rachel doesn't take out the trash anymore or do anything anymore. And if Ruth finds it, well, fuck her.

I go back into the kitchen, Shadow at my heels. I look at the dog. He seems thin, and I wonder when he ate last.

"I'm sorry, boy," I tell him, and his ears perk up and he pads over to my side and leans his full body weight against my leg. I pat him on his back three times—thump thump thump—then cross to his dish and fill it with food. He rushes to the bowl as if he hasn't eaten for a decade and noisily inhales the kibble.

I polish off the bourbon, consider pouring myself another two fingers, then think better of it. I wash the glass and dry it with the dish towel and put it back in the cupboard, erasing the evidence of my sin even though I shouldn't have to in my own house. I run my fingers past my nose, return to the sink and wash the cigarette stink off my hands, then wash my face for good measure, using the dish soap, which is probably terrible for facial skin, but who gives a fuck, really? Then I bury my head in the dish towel and try to keep myself from crying.

When the emotion, strong and pungent, passes, I leave Shadow to his emphatic feasting. I climb the stairs to the second floor and wander down the hall to Eden's room, carefully averting my gaze from the door on the right, which is closed and has been for weeks.

I knock softly on the door, then push it open. Eden is seated at her desk, her back to me, hunched over a notebook.

"Do you need any help?" I ask and am relieved that my voice sounds normal and that I manage to get the entire sentence out without choking on a word. She snaps her head in my direction, and her look of surprise is like a slap to my face, as though she can't believe I'm actually talking to her. I force myself to look at her, not turn away or drop my eyes, even though it takes all of my willpower to do so.

I watch as her lips turn up slightly at the edges.

"It's just Language Arts," she says. "I got it."

I nod and try to smile at her, my lovely daughter who deserves a father who can speak to her more freely than I can.

"Good. Let me know if you need me."

"Okay, Daddy. Thanks."

My heart squeezes in my chest. Eden hasn't called me Daddy for two, maybe three years. I can't bear it. I pull the door closed and wander down the hall to my bedroom.

The curtains are closed, but I can make out the outline of my wife's body in the bed. She lies on her side facing the window, away from me, and I'm not sure if she is sleeping or awake. I move around the bed and see that her mouth is open. I hear the familiar sound of her sleep breathing, which is like a snore, but not rough-edged or annoying like I know mine must be. I sit on the edge of the bed, perched and ready to escape should she start to stir.

In sleep, in the darkened room, Rachel looks like the woman I married, if a bit thinner. The curve and hollow of her cheekbones, the strong chin and perfectly arched brows, the slender neck, the sea of strawberry-blonde hair that my fingers used to grasp like a lifeline when we made love. When she is awake, she is a gross caricature of the woman she used to be, with the bruised circles under her eyes and the vacant stare and the slouched posture as though her grief is a constant pressure on her shoulders, pushing her down and down and down. But now, as she sleeps, I see the woman I fell in love with, and I have the urge to reach out and stroke the skin of her arm, to curl up beside her and spoon her and pull down her sweatpants and push myself inside her and lose myself to her sweetness.

"You smell like cigarettes." I jerk with surprise at the sound of her voice.

I don't know how to respond, so I say nothing. She rolls over onto her stomach, pulling the stuffed monkey with her, kicks out her leg, and falls asleep again. I consider taking the stuffed animal from her grasp—it's time she let go of that goddamned thing—but I don't want to wake her again. I watch her for another moment, then quietly leave the room.

SIXTEEN

RACHEL

I was having a dream. Jonah was there. I couldn't see him, but I felt him, like he was hovering somewhere nearby. I was in a long tunnel, and I didn't know which way to go. I was stuck, my feet in water that wasn't really water—it was like soup, thick and heavy and pulling at my shoes. And then I saw the green glow of light from one end of the tunnel and the soup became water and I could move, and I did, toward the green light.

Green was Jonah's favorite color.

I'm awake now. I wish I was still asleep. Not that it's better there. Sometimes the nightmares come. The chasing-Jonah nightmares where he's just out of my grasp and I'm running after him and I can almost feel the fabric of his shirt on my fingertips, but he always pulls away at the very last second, and the dream always ends with an echoing thump, and I wake myself out of it before I see what the thump means, even though I already know what it means. But at least in the nightmare, Jonah is alive, smiling and pumping his legs and giggling until the very last second.

I was awake when Sam came in, but I pretended not to be. I could feel his eyes on me, and then I could feel the weight of him on the end of the bed, and I knew he was just sitting there, watching me. My thoughts were still fuzzy from the pill. They aren't as much now, just a little fuzzy, but when Sam was here they were all jumbled together, still wrapped up in the tunnel dream. I said something to Sam—I can't remember what it was, something about cigarettes? But that doesn't make sense, because Sam doesn't smoke anymore.

The glowing red digits from the clock on the nightstand tell me it's just after 6:00 p.m. I'm in bed at six o'clock on a Monday evening. Or is it Tuesday? I'm not really sure, but then, it doesn't really matter what day it is. Every day is the same. Every day is the same. Misery and pills and tears and screaming, and feeling like I'm missing a limb or a vital organ, some part of me that makes me whole, but it's not a limb or an organ, it's my son.

I know that I should push back the covers and get out of bed, do something useful, like make dinner for my family, something I used to do. But I'm not sure if I can remember how to use the oven or a frying pan or a knife.

The pill has worn off enough for me to understand my thoughts— at least most of them. And I'm aware, now, at this moment, that even as I choose to escape these every-day-is-the-same days, that I am also allowing myself to slip farther and farther away from my own life. I am being selfish. I have stopped being a mother to my daughter, when she likely needs me most. I've stopped being a wife to my husband, although I'm not sure he wants me to be his wife anymore. He wants another one.

No, wait, that's Ruth. That's what my ex-brother-in-law, Charlie, told Ruth. Not me. *Charlie* wanted another one.

The only thing I haven't stopped being is the little sister in need. Ruth likes it. I think she missed taking care of me or thinking she needed to take care of me, all these years I've been with Sam. When we were kids, she acted like a second mother, always telling me what to do, how to behave, criticizing my outfits, my friends, my aspirations or lack thereof. She was there for me when I needed her. Yes, she was. But I think she secretly took great satisfaction in my screwups, which were plenty, like they made her feel better about herself. And then, after all, I ended up with the perfect life, the perfect husband and two perfect children. Maybe she started hating me a little bit for that.

Now, she can pity me. She can feel better about her own life by seeing the hell mine has become. And she can torture me by holding back my pills.

But she's right, Rachel. You need to cut back.

A sharp phantom pain slices through me at the idea of being completely lucid and sober all the time. Always, every moment of every day, I'll be totally cognizant of the fact that Jonah died, is dead, is never coming back, will never grow to be an adolescent or a man, never fall in love, have children, win the Nobel Peace Prize or a Pulitzer. He will always be a memory, ever fading. I just can't bear it. Cannot bear it. But the alternative is for me to fade away until one day there will be no reason not to take the entire contents of the bottle and disappear.

But then you'd be with Jonah.

And my daughter will be motherless. And my life will have meant nothing.

I will myself into a seated position, swing my legs to the side of the bed. I grab the monkey and wrap his arms around my neck, then push myself to my feet. My knees buckle, and I sit down, hard. My head is spinning. I take a deep breath and wait until my vision clears. Then I try again. This time I manage to stand without falling back down. I still feel dizzy, but I ignore the sensation. My feet slide along the carpet—I can't seem to lift them—but after a moment of hard labor and heavy breathing, I'm standing in front of my dresser and gazing at my reflection.

What I see is a horror.

I avert my eyes and my gaze lands on the closet door, which is open about six inches, revealing one of Sam's sport coats, which is encased in the plastic wrapping from the dry cleaner. And as I gaze at that plastic wrapping, something stirs in my memory, a thought loosens, an idea or fact or scenario I should recall. Words collect themselves in my head—angry words, my husband's voice, my own. And I'm just on the very border of knowing when I suddenly push the thoughts away because I know, with cold certainty, that I do not want to remember.

I call for Ruth, over and over again, drowning out the angry voices and colliding thoughts, grasping at the edge of the dresser to keep myself from falling over, wondering if I can make it back to the bed or whether I need to throw up, and if so, whether I can make it to the bathroom.

Ruth doesn't come and doesn't come. Why should she? I was awful to her. I said horrible things to her so she'd give me a goddamn pill.

Ruth. I'm really sorry. I didn't mean any of it.

The door opens, and blessed relief fills me until I see my daughter's face peering in at me.

I let go of the dresser and fall to the floor.

SEVENTEEN

RUTH

I have to admit it, I'm glad to be home, even if home isn't much, just a cramped one-bedroom apartment that I'm allowed to live in thanks to the guilt and shame of my ex-husband. My alimony includes the rent and a small monthly stipend, which is barely enough to cover my bills and groceries, and I try not to think about the sprawling estate on the outskirts of town in which he lives with the woman who was able to give him children. Three at last count, darling twin girls who were growing in his wife's womb even before he left me, and an infant son who will hopefully have my ex-husband's receding hairline, although I know it's unkind to wish that on an innocent babe.

I put my purse down on the table by the door and glance at the pile of mail stacked there. I take three steps into the miniscule kitchen, with its outdated Formica counters, peeling laminate cupboards, and decades-old appliances, the tired peach curtains in the window, the ones I brought from my old house and promised myself I'd replace but still haven't. After spending so much time at my sister's house, I am struck by the stark contrast between this sad excuse for a kitchen and Rachel's kitchen. I think of her gleaming blush-rose granite counters and dark cherrywood cupboards and Viking oven and Sub-Zero refrigerator. It would be perverse to envy my sister with what she's going through, but I feel a tinge of jealousy nonetheless.

In the corner of the room sits a small round table with a single chair shoved beneath. I rarely eat at the table. Its diminutive size and the lone chair remind me of my solitary existence. Mostly I take my meals on the couch with my constant companion, the television.

My meds are in the cupboard next to the refrigerator. I keep them there because the fridge reminds me to eat something when I take a pill. I don't have time for a meal. I need to get the drug into my bloodstream and soon. Every muscle in my body aches, the kind of ache that throbs in time with your heartbeat, expands with every passing moment until it crosses over to bright, excruciating pain. Right now, I'm at the precipice between throbbing ache and excruciating pain. I need to get off the ledge.

I reach for the new vial of pills on the second shelf of the cupboard and spend a few precious seconds trying to twist off the childproof cap. My fingers will not cooperate. *Press down and twist, Ruth. That's all. Press down and twist.* Finally, I manage to pop the lid, and I shake out two of the tablets, one for the dose I missed this morning and one for this evening's dose, which I usually don't take until after dinner. But I need it now.

I yank open the fridge and grab the carton of milk, and then I do something I have never done in my entire life. I put the pills on my tongue, then open the milk and drink from the cardboard lip of the carton. This act is so foreign to me that I end up spraying milk onto the Formica counter, but not before I swallow down the pills.

The relief is instantaneous. I know that my reaction is completely psychological—there is no way the drug can possibly go to work that quickly. But knowing that the medicine is traveling toward my stomach is enough. My brain sends the signal to my body that help is on the way, and slowly I feel all of my muscles uncoil.

I stand still for a few minutes, then put the milk carton back in the fridge and use a dish towel to wipe the errant milk from the counter. I grab a loaf of wheat bread and pull out a slice, then eat it greedily. I'm anxious to get the calories into my system, hoping the bread will stave off the nausea that sometimes comes when I don't eat.

Walking with measured steps into the living room, I feel the push of the medication that might or might not have an actual, *tangible* effect on the pain. The drug is an antidepressant, which is ironic because I never thought of myself as depressed, not back then. The fact that my fibromyalgia reared its ugly, monstrous head the same month I found out I couldn't conceive was something I compartmentalized and stripped of its importance. My doctor pointed the correlation out to me, and I remember shrugging my shoulders and telling her, in no uncertain terms, that regardless of the timing, my pain was very real, and was there something, *anything*, that might help?

I detest the woman I've become, the woman crippled by her physical challenges, who lives a solitary existence in a tiny apartment with no pets and no plants, whose sole joy is watching *Dancing with the Stars* every Monday night.

I was a teacher, a hundred years ago. My life had real purpose. I taught eighth grade and took pride in steering those awkward, self-loathing middle schoolers toward high school, giving them confidence to take their next steps toward adulthood. And then being a wife gave me purpose. And then I lost it. Right up until Jonah's accident.

My stomach churns with the realization that I've felt more alive in this past month, when I've been holding my sister's family together, than I have since Charlie left. My sister's tragedy, the death of my beloved nephew, has actually made me more vibrant, more productive, more present. How awful I am. How sad and pathetic and awful I am.

I grab the stack of mail next to my purse and head for the couch. Before I sit down, there is a knock at my door. The sound is so unfamiliar to me I almost don't recognize it. I set the mail on the coffee table, then cross to the door. I peer through the peephole and feel my chest tighten. On the other side of the door is my downstairs neighbor, Judd.

I open the door and stare at him.

"Hi, Ruth." His eyes are kind, his closed-lipped smile genuine.

"Hi."

"I don't want to bother you. I just wanted to give you this." He hands me a small, folded piece of paper. "It's my cell number. Just in case you ever need anything. Or you want to talk. Or . . . anything. I'm here." No mention of a certain bottle of wine. He probably drank it already. I shouldn't care. I *don't* care.

"Thank you," I say. Nothing more. I close the door slowly and stand unmoving until I hear his footsteps retreat to the elevator. I press my forehead against the door. The wood is cool against my skin.

After a moment, I push myself away from the door. I shuffle to my purse and tuck the piece of paper into a side pocket, then return to the couch. I take a deep breath and pick up the mail and begin to riffle through the envelopes. Bills mostly, and advertisements. But at the bottom of the stack is a smallish envelope, cream, with my ex-husband's company address. First Judd, and now this.

My hands shake, not with pain this time, but with anticipation. My heart beats rapidly; I can feel my pulse pat pat pat in my temples. I know there will be no declaration of love or regret for what he's done or entreaties for me to take him back. My curiosity is equal to my trepidation. Perhaps he wants to renegotiate the settlement; perhaps he thinks he's being too generous, or his *newish* wife thinks he's being too generous and has demanded that he cut back on my monthly payments.

Before I allow my thoughts to run away with themselves, I carefully open the envelope and pull out the handwritten note, unfold it, and gaze down at Charlie's familiar writing. I smile to myself, remembering the first time I got a note from him, back when he was courting me. In this technological age, I was surprised that he had taken the time to write to me longhand instead of just sending me an e-mail or composing the note in a word-processing program and printing it up. He'd grinned and told me he was old-fashioned, that printouts and e-mails seemed so impersonal. Handwritten notes were the only way he communicated with people he cared about. I remember how my face grew warm at his words as I realized that he was talking about me. He *cared* about *me*.

During the divorce, I received only e-mails and texts, as though he was making a point. *I don't care about you anymore, Ruth.*

But now this, this note card. He still cares?

Oh, for heaven's sake, just read it.

He begins with *Dear Ruthie*, and I swallow hard at his addressing me with the nickname he, and no one else, used. I keep reading.

> I know this letter is long overdue. I just wanted to let you know that I have been thinking about you these last several weeks and that you are in my prayers, for whatever that's worth. I'm not sure that God hears me anymore, based on my behavior, but he might when the prayers are for you. I was saddened to learn about Jonah, and I regret that I was unable to attend the services, although I'm not sure how you would have felt about me being there.

At the time, when it first happened, I was furious with Charlie, that he hadn't called or sent me a card or sent flowers to the family. It was as though he was trying to erase his past, to extract himself from my life completely. But the days became longer and Rachel spiraled out of control, and when he didn't make an appearance at the funeral, I was forced to accept the reality of divorce. Divorce is not just about the separation of two individuals. It's the separation of families. A drawing of lines, never to be crossed. My family is now solely mine. Your family is yours. *His family is his.*

The family we were going to create together is gone forever. No, Ruth, it never was. It was a mirage. I keep reading.

I'm not trying to defend my absence, he continues.

But my father became gravely ill, and I was called to his side, as the doctors believed he might soon pass. You remember how William is—refuses to go along with anything the doctors say, and of course, he is still with us and probably will be for a long while. But those few weeks were chaotic.

I regret not being there for you. I regret that I was so consumed with my own challenges that I didn't even think to send flowers or condolences. I hope you will accept my sincere apology and that you will not think worse of me (or worse than you already do, with good reason . . .).

I know how much Jonah meant to you, how much both your sister's children mean to you, and I am so very sorry for your loss. Please let me know if there is anything I can do to be of service to you.

With affection, Charlie.

I reread the note, being mindful to not let my tears fall onto the cardstock and mar the ink of his words. Even now, after eighteen months, after he has created a new family that doesn't include me, Charlie is the person who knows me best in the world. I hate him for that. I hate him because he was my soul mate, but since I couldn't give him children, I was no longer his. I hate him for being a man, for having that need to procreate—to have his own biological offspring—in order to validate his existence in the universe. I hate him for not loving me enough to look past my graying roots and my useless uterus and ignore the shiny penny in front of him, she who practically gave him a gynecological report touting her fertility in order to steal him. I hate him for allowing himself to be stolen.

I hate him because I never trusted men, never opened myself up to them, always assumed the worst about them. Until Charlie. He came along and changed my mind, and I was happy, happier than I ever thought I could be, until he changed my mind back, irrevocably. And there will never be another Charlie, and possibly there will never be another man. I hate him because he doesn't need me anymore.

I fold the note and slip it back into the envelope, then glance at my watch. I should get back to Rachel's. *They need me,* I think. But I am suddenly so weary, I could fall asleep. I lean back against the cushions and close my eyes.

Immediately, an image of Jonah comes to mind, a memory from— God, less than two months ago. (Is that possible?) We were on the front porch together, sitting side by side on the steps, which my joints disapproved of, but which delighted my nephew. Rachel's children have always meant the world to me, not just because I love them, but also because they are the closest thing to me actually having kids of my own. I treasure our times together, even if I might not be the most fun or enjoyable company they have. I know they always prefer Taylor to babysit for them, the girl down the street who plays Twister and lets them eat whatever they want. But I would do anything in the world for those children and they know it, which was why Jonah forced me to sit down "Right on your bottom!" and I did. Of course I did.

He was gazing reverently at a bug on the concrete path, a caterpillar slowly making its way toward the side of the house. Jonah was pointing out the legs and the bristles on its back and the stripes of brown and white and explaining to me that this creature was trying to find a safe place to attach in order to make its chrysalis, which he pronounced "krisliss."

"It's gonna turn into a big beautiful butterfly, Auntie Ruth, with bright orange-and-black wings, and it's gonna pol'nate Mommy's flowers in the backyard."

I'd chuckled sardonically and said, "Only if it doesn't get eaten by some hungry bird."

Now, in my head, I see his reaction anew. His expression grew troubled, as though he'd never considered that such a tragedy could occur, but now that I'd suggested the possibility, it was almost a certainty that the caterpillar was doomed. Tears squeezed out of the corners of his eyes. And instead of reassuring him, I'd said, "Honey, that's just life. For little creatures like that guy, the odds aren't good."

What the hell was I thinking? How could I have been so thoughtless? Jonah was five years old, for goodness' sake. Instead of allowing him to enjoy the wonders of nature, I'd managed to rob him of his awe. It isn't the worst thing I've done, I know. But thinking of it now fills me with shame.

I open my eyes and stare at the drab beige wall of my living room. I would give anything to go back to that moment, to change what I said to him.

You bet it is, Jonah. It's going to be the most beautiful butterfly in the world.

EIGHTEEN

Shadow

Dark Female is gone. I don't know how long she's been gone. I can still smell her scent, the sweet-pungent odor of her clothes, but it's fading. She will come back, and I will hide from her angry eyes, but she's not here now, so I can lie on my couch-room bed until I hear the shudder of her car outside.

My master is on the couch, sitting on the edge of the cushions, his hands on his knees, like at any minute he's going to stand up. But he doesn't stand up, just sits there. The big black screen on the wall is alive right now. There are people on the screen talking to my master, but I don't think he hears them. He is staring at the coffee table, the one with the scratchy leg where I chewed a long time ago. I don't remember chewing it, but I remember that if I do now, I'll get angry eyes and angry voices, not just from Dark Female, but from my master and my mistress, too. So I won't chew it.

My master's eyes are so sad. I don't want them to be. If his eyes are sad, that means he is sad, and I don't like that. I know why he is sad, and why Little Female is sad and why my mistress is sad. I wish I could tell them that Little Male is here. He isn't here with me now on my couch-room bed, but I know he is nearby, somewhere in the house. I think knowing he's somewhere in this house, that he hasn't gone to another place yet, would make my humans happy. But I don't know how to tell them.

I stand and pad over to the couch. I sit next to my master and nudge his hands with my head. His hands feel cold. Maybe because they were holding the glass on the chewed-leg coffee table. Now the glass is empty and on the table, but his hands are still cold. They don't move. I feel them, limp on my head. I nudge them again. And then I feel my master pat me. He pats me with one hand. It doesn't feel bad, but it's not as good as when he strokes my fur or scratches under my chin. And then I feel his fingers scratch my ears, and I can't help it, can't control my tail, which thwack thwacks against the carpet.

"Good boy, Shadow," my master says. His voice is quiet and low and not a happy voice, but not a mad voice, and Good Boy is what he always calls me when I'm doing something right, so my tail thwack thwacks again.

And then I hear a slight thump from upstairs and Little Female cries out, and even as my ears rise, my master is up on his feet and running to the stairs. I trot behind him and stop at the first step. I'm not allowed up, I know I'm not. I'm a Good Boy, and a Good Boy doesn't do Bad Boy things on purpose. But I want to be up there with my humans and make sure they're okay.

I lift my paw and lower it on the first step. I feel my body start to shake with the knowing that I'm doing something that is a "no" thing. Then I hear another cry from upstairs, from Little Female, and the loud words from my master, not angry but upset, and the crying-sobbing sound of my mistress, and I keep going, up up up the stairs until I'm at the top.

Little Male is sitting on the top step. He isn't smiling.

NINETEEN

JONAH

I like my house. And I love my family—Mommy and Daddy and even Eden, who lots of times said kind of mean things to me, but then she'd do nice things, too, like find my blue crayon when I couldn't and give me her last french fry from her plate and make up funny songs to make me laugh when I was sad or had a cold or something.

But now my house is full of sad. Mommy doesn't look like Mommy anymore and Daddy looks like Daddy, but like he's not all the way here, like he's a picture instead of a person and someone left the picture out in the sun all day and it's kind of fadey. Only Eden looks like Eden, but her thoughts are all kind of jumbled together and mad and sad and crazy, all at the same time. She thinks about how Mommy and Daddy don't listen to her anymore, that no one listens to her anymore, and I want to tell her that I'm listening, but I don't know how.

There might be a way to tell her, kind of like showing Mommy the green light in her dream. I have to think about it some more.

I still remember everything from before the bad day, but it's getting a little bit smaller in my brain. But I like remembering before, because nobody was sad.

Mommy used to read me books before bed. Sometimes she'd pick 'em and sometimes I would, and she'd climb into my bed with me and I'd scooch up next to her and put my head on her chest and she'd wrap her arm around me. I could feel her heartbeat and also I could kind of feel the air going in and out of her, and she felt warm and cozy and most times I'd kind of fall asleep while she was reading, but that was okay because I always knew the end of the story anyway.

She'd make me macaroni and cheese out of the blue box because that's the one I liked, even though she said it wasn't as healthy as the kind in the orange-and-white box. And she let me put ketchup on it, too, which always made Eden make an ucky face. I remember how Mommy would sing songs when she was sweeping, not songs I knew, like "The Wheels on the Bus Go Round and Round," but songs with funny words like "Lay down, Sally" like she was talking to a dog or something, and sometimes Daddy would come in and start singing with her and he'd take the broom and set it against the wall and they'd dance together until she'd start to giggle and swat him away and tell him she needed to finish the floor.

Daddy would take me to T-ball and he always wore the same color cap as our team shirts, which he called something else that starts with a *J*, but I can't think of it now. And he'd cheer for me real loud and clap real hard and tell me I was doing great even if I didn't make it to first base, or if a ball went right through my feet. And some days, when he wasn't working, Daddy would take me in the backyard and practice throwing and catching with me, and after a while, after I caught lots of his throws and threw back to him as hard as I could, he'd get this big smile on his face and say, "That's my boy," which was funny 'cause of course I'm his boy, but the way he said it made me think it was kind of more special.

One time we went to the beach, the whole family, even Shadow, where the waves were so big, and I was scared, but Mommy and Daddy held both of my hands, one of them on one side of me and the other one on the other side of me, and they'd kind of lift me in the air when the wave was high. Eden was bigger and she wasn't afraid, and she got to play by herself in the water as long as she didn't go too far out. But sometimes she'd come over to us and take Mommy or Daddy's hand, and then it would be all four of us holding hands in a row, and we'd laugh and giggle as the water sprayed us in our faces. And Shadow would romp around us, and he'd make happy barks and bite at the foam. And I liked that, being all of us together. And when we got tired and hungry Mommy always had sammiches for us, baloney for me and Eden and turkey and something that looked like grass for her and Daddy, and dog bones for Shadow. And we'd sit on the big blanket with the stars and the moon on it and eat, not talking but just being happy.

And I remember when I was playing on the jungle gym at school at recess and Joey P. started grabbing my foot, not being mean, just playing, and I fell down and my forehead hit the ground and split open and there was blood everywhere. Daddy was at a contention or something and Mommy was somewhere else, I'm not sure where, and Auntie Ruth had to come to the hospital. And she sat with me the whole time, holding my hand and talking to me all nice and calm and telling me I was a brave boy and she loved me and everything was going to be just fine, and this doctor had to stitch up my forehead and Auntie Ruth didn't go away and didn't let go of my hand, not one time.

I remember all of those things, and everything else, too. Maybe 'cause I'm still here. Maybe when I go away forever, I won't remember anything anymore, and I'm not sure how I feel about that. Maybe it will be better 'cause you can't miss something you can't remember, and if you don't miss it, you won't be sad.

I don't know how long I'm going to be here, but I'm starting to not like being here. At first it was nice 'cause I got to see everyone even though they couldn't see me, and that made me feel all good and safe, 'cause I can still remember all the good stuff from before. But now, with the sad all big around me, I just kind of want to go. But I can't. I thought about being way up in the sky, just like when I think about being nowhere and when I think about being with Mommy or with Shadow or whoever, and then I'm there. I wished for the sky, but I didn't go to the sky. I didn't even go to the ceiling. I just stayed where I was, but now I can't remember exactly where I was when I wished it.

I'm at the top of the stairs right now. I heard Mommy fall down and Eden call out something, but I didn't make myself go there because I kind of didn't want to see what was happening 'cause I know it's all about the big sad thing. So I came here instead.

Shadow is coming up the stairs even though he knows he's not 'llowed. He stops and makes his head go sideways, and I know he sees me. I don't put on a happy face like I usually do when I see him, because I'm not happy. I'm scared that I'm going to be stuck here with all the crying and sad people. I want Mommy and Daddy and Eden to be happy again. Even Auntie Ruth, too, but I'm not sure she was happy even before the bad thing happened to me. But she still smiled at me and patted my knee and played Candy Land, but not on the floor, at the kitchen table 'cause she said her knees told her she couldn't play on the floor. I didn't know knees could talk. Mine never did. But it was still fun to play with her, even if it wasn't on the floor.

I clap my hands for Shadow to come to me, but he doesn't hear the sound of the clap because I can't make a sound anymore. I hear the clap inside my brain, but not outside my brain. I wish there was some way I could make a sound that I could hear outside my brain, 'cause maybe then I could make Mommy and Daddy and Eden and Auntie Ruth hear me, and I could tell them not to be sad anymore.

TWENTY

Eden

My mom's eyes are all round, not as shiny as they have been, but open really wide, and I think that might be worse than the shininess. She cries out and falls to the floor, and then I cry out, too, because I don't want her to hurt herself.

I run over to her to make sure she's okay, but she bats my arm away, hard enough that it smarts. She shakes her head back and forth and starts to laugh, but not a happy laugh. It's, like, a really mad, scary laugh that makes my stomach feel sick. I want to put my hands over my ears to block it out, but I don't want to make her feel bad.

"Mom, Mommy, are you okay?" I ask her, making sure not to touch her so she won't bat at me again. She's still laughing, but all quiet now, her shoulders hunching over.

"The dry cleaners," she says with a gravelly voice that doesn't sound like my mom at all. I don't know what the dry cleaners have to do with her falling down and her crazy laughing. I'm about to ask her when Dad comes running into the room. He sees me and Mom on the floor, and the crease in his forehead gets even bigger.

"What the hell?"

A part of me wants to tell him he has to put a dollar in the curse jar, but I'm smart enough to know that now is not the time for that.

"She fell down," I tell him. "And she hit my arm," I add, which isn't exactly true, but I just want to see if he's listening to me. He doesn't answer, so I guess not. I'm not surprised, but I kind of hoped he'd say something, you know, like a normal person would say when their kid told them her mom just hit her. Like, he'd say, "I'm so sorry, Eden. I'm sure she didn't mean it." And I'd real fast say, "Oh, no, Dad, she didn't mean it at all, it was an accident, like it wasn't even really hitting, she just batted my arm away," and he'd be all relieved. But nope. He doesn't say anything, just rushes over to us and puts his arm around my mom and scoops her up and over to the bed, totally ignoring me.

"Rachel, Rachel," he says. "What is it? Are you okay?"

"You took it to the dry cleaners. You had it fucking cleaned, you bastard."

I am definitely not going to tell her she has to put money in the curse jar, even though the f-word is worth like five dollars, and she never says the f-word—I only heard her say it one time when she burned her hand really bad on the stove. But I'm not going to say anything to her when her eyes are like that, and I know, *for sure*, I like them better when they're shiny.

"Rachel, calm down," my dad says, and he's gripping her wrist really tight and his voice isn't mean but totally intense. But Mom just kind of snarls at him, like the cat across the street does to Shadow when he's out front.

"Let go of me, Sam! What did you think, that I wouldn't remember? That you could just have it cleaned and I'd fucking forget?"

"Rachel!" My dad's voice booms through the room, and I sit down hard on my butt and I feel that choking thing in my throat. Dad looks at me, kind of not *at* me but in my direction, and when he speaks to me, his voice is all calm, but like he's working really hard to keep it calm. "Eden, please go to your room and shut the door, and I'll be in to see you in a minute."

I gulp and nod and jump to my feet and race out the door toward my room. Shadow is at the top of the stairs, his nose pointed at my mom and dad's room, like he's going to go in there to make sure everyone's okay. And I can't let him do that, because my mom and dad are already mad enough and he's not allowed upstairs and I don't want them to yell at Shadow, because he's a good boy.

I grab his collar and yank him down the hall and into my room. He weighs a ton, but he comes easily, like he's really glad to see me and glad I'm bringing him with me. My dad might be mad when he finds Shadow in my room, but I'm just going to tell him I was scared and having Shadow with me made me feel better. I think that might make Dad feel kind of guilty, so he won't yell at me or Shadow. But you know what? I don't even care if he gets mad at me. In fact, I *hope* he gets mad at me, because then he'll have to talk to me.

I shut the door behind me and pull Shadow over into the corner of the room where my beanbag chair sits. I fall heavily upon it, and Shadow nuzzles into me and licks my face. I wrap my arms around him and hold him tight and pretend I can't hear the muffled, angry words of my parents from down the hall.

Shadow trembles, and I rub the fur on his back and tell him what a good boy he is. I think about what Aunt Ruth said, right after the accident, about how Mom and Dad should "just put that mutt down." Thinking about her saying that makes me shudder, because I know what it means. Mary Pickle's parents had to put down their dog because it bit a little kid. Aunt Ruth said that to my parents because she thinks what happened to Jonah is Shadow's fault. But I know better.

Feeling guilty, I press myself against Shadow. He's making whiny noises in his throat, and he keeps pointing his nose toward the wall. At first I think he's looking in the direction of Mom and Dad's room, you know, because he's worried about them, but then I realize that he's looking at my bed. And the way he's frozen, with the hair on his neck kind of standing up, makes me feel goose bumps on my arm. But I don't feel scared, just, like, weird.

"Jonah?" I say, and I have no idea why I say it. Jonah is dead. He can't hear me. He's in heaven. But I say it again anyway. "Jonah?" And then I feel really stupid for calling my brother's name out loud, and I'm really glad no one else is here to hear me say it. Well, no one except Shadow, and he won't tell on me.

My eyes start to sting, and I realize I'm crying. Again. Shadow stops looking at my bed and starts licking my cheeks, mopping up my tears. I try to make them stop. I'm so tired of crying all the time. But the thing is, I miss Jonah a lot.

When he was here, he kind of bugged me, you know, like little brothers do. He couldn't help it. He didn't mean to. He would try to get me to play with him, and he'd get all pouty when I wouldn't, and he'd always want to show me things, like the totally disgusting bugs he'd find, and his drawings, which were silly stick people and stuff, but only because he was little, and how high he could jump and how fast he could run and the LEGO towers he built, which were kind of crooked and ugly-looking. And I would, like, be totally bored and sometimes I'd say mean things and his mouth would start quivering, but he didn't give up. There was always something he wanted to show me, because I was his big sister and he wanted to impress me. And sometimes I'd say nice things, not just to get him off my back, but because he was just a little guy, so the things he did were actually kind of good. But I didn't really do that very often.

Jonah had this way of giggling with his whole face and these really big dimples in his cheeks and he was really cute, which also kind of bugged me, 'cause everyone was always saying how cute he was and they never said that about me anymore.

When Mom and Dad brought him home from the hospital, he was just this tiny little thing wrapped in a fuzzy blue blanket and he was, like, totally bald and cried all the time. My mom told me I was a big sister now, and that a big sister was a very important job and I had to take it very seriously and she knew I would be great at it. And I felt kind of proud, you know, that she thought I'd be great at it. And Jonah, when he could talk, he would say things like, "Eden, you're the best big sister ever."

I feel really bad and awful, because I was not the best big sister ever. Not even the second or third best sister ever. I was a totally sucky big sister, and I know I'm not supposed to say *suck* or *sucky* or anything like that, but it's true.

There were some times when I was nice and I meant it, too. Because he really was sweet and always trying to make me smile, and when he fell down or got sick, or the time he got stitches in his forehead, I would make up silly songs to get him to laugh. His favorite was the one about farting, and he asked me to sing it to him all the time, even when he wasn't sick or hurt or anything. And I'd always do it, too, just because I liked the sound of Jonah's laugh, until Mom would make me stop because she said, "*Fart* is not an appropriate word." And Jonah and I would laugh even harder, sometimes till we started farting ourselves, and Mom would throw up her hands and make a kind of mad face, but she was laughing, too.

Sometimes, when there was a storm, Jonah would sneak into my room, and I thought that was funny, you know, that he didn't sneak into Mom and Dad's room like I used to do. I asked him why he came in my room, and I probably sounded annoyed or something, but he just kind of shrugged and said my room was closer and when he went into Mom and Dad's room they were making a tent and there wasn't any room for him. I didn't know what he meant by "making a tent"—not then, anyway. I do now 'cause Janey Markowski told us about sex and what happens and then she showed us a scene from some grown-up TV show called *The Affair* on her iPhone.

But anyways, Jonah's eyes were always kind of scared from the storm, and I let him come into my bed and lie beside me in the dark, and we'd watch for lightning and then count the seconds until the thunder. And his breathing would get all loud and deep and he'd fall asleep, and I'd say, "Oh, great!" But deep down inside, I didn't mind him being there. I liked it. I liked making him feel safe, and that made me feel safe, too. I remember he always smelled like Johnson's baby shampoo.

Shadow lifts his head suddenly and turns it toward my bed.

Maybe it's 'cause I was just thinking about it, but I swear I can smell Johnson's baby shampoo in my room.

TWENTY-ONE

SAMUEL

I don't know what to do. I've always been completely in control, the kind of man who knew what to do in any given situation, but in this moment, with my wife lashing out at me in a way that is completely foreign to me, swinging her arms, kicking me, throwing accusations at me, I'm at a loss, stranded on a stormy sea in a rowboat with no oars.

When I raise my voice, she gets louder. When I try to pin her arms to her sides, she shoves me off her with the strength and agility of an Olympic wrestler. For the first time in weeks, I wish my sister-in-law were here. Ruth would know what to do.

She sits on the end of the bed, that fucking monkey around her neck like a noose, staring daggers at me, breathing deeply and offering a moment of quiet. I reach into my pocket and feel the outline of the bottle of her pills.

"Why did you do it?" she asks.

I don't have an answer that will satisfy her, or me, for that matter. I know what I've done and what I haven't done, and I've tried to focus on the latter, congratulating myself for the things I chose not to do. But my truth is different from my wife's. "We shouldn't talk about this right now, Rachel. You're out of your mind with grief over Jonah."

"Don't you say his name to me! Don't you dare bring him into this. He's gone because of *this*, Sam. You know it and I know it."

I shake my head no. I've thought the same thing over the past month, castigated myself for my role in the death of my son. *The death of my son.* How is it possible that those words are a reality in my life? I bear my guilt with stoic solemnity and Maker's Mark, while Rachel bears hers with escapism and pills. I blame her as much as she blames me, but in this game, her hand trumps mine.

"Bad things happen, Rachel. It's no one's fault. We can't blame ourselves." *Even though we do,* I think.

She throws her head back so far I have the crazy idea that it will topple off her shoulders and roll across the bed. She lets out a strangled cry.

"He's gone because of this," she says again. Suddenly, she stands up and walks over to me, and I force myself not to flinch.

"I need a pill," she tells me with icy calm. "You're right. We shouldn't talk about this right now. I need to rest. The doctor said so. I need to sleep. Give me my pills."

I stare down at her, trying not to look too hard at her sunken cheeks and hollowed-out eyes and the translucence of her skin.

"I'll give you *one*, Rachel," I say.

She starts to seethe with anger but has the decency to keep her voice down. "Give me my prescription, Sam. It's my name on the bottle, not yours, not Ruth's. I'm an adult, and I have complete control of my faculties, even if you don't think I do." She jerks her hand out, palm up, a demand. "Give me my fucking pills."

Rachel never says *fuck*. She's said it twice in the last five minutes. I hold her gaze, and her expression softens, and suddenly she looks like the woman I've loved for more than fourteen years. "I won't do anything stupid," she says quietly. "I just want to sleep."

"Just one?"

"Yes, damn it. Just one. Just one, I promise, okay? Give them to me. I'm not a child."

I withdraw the bottle from my pocket and show it to her. She reaches for it, and I pull it away. "Give me the fucking monkey, Rachel."

Her whole body spasms, and she glares at me. Slowly, and with what looks like great effort, she pulls the monkey's paws apart. The squawk of Velcro echoes through the bedroom. She holds the stuffed animal out to me. It hangs limply from her grasp. Tears stream down her face. I almost change my mind, but I don't let myself. I take the monkey and hand her the bottle of pills.

I glance at the bed, at the side where I used to sleep. I wonder if I will ever make my way back to this bed, if I will ever be invited back to this bed.

"Rachel, I . . ."

But she is already backing away from me, retreating into her grief. Her head drops to her chest, and I hear the sob. I want to go to her, to wrap my arms around her and press myself against her and push away the torment she feels. But I know she will resist. Her body will stiffen, and she'll lash out again and say something that will break us more than we are already broken. So I stay where I am, arms at my sides, wishing we were the kind of couple who endured tragedy together, soldiered on united, held each other up, held each other close. We are not.

"You need to check on Eden," she says, her voice a hoarse whisper. "Make sure she's okay."

"Come with me, Rachel. Let's check on her together."

Her head jerks from side to side. "I can't. I can't. I know it's terrible, *I'm* terrible, but I can't right now."

"You're not terrible, Rachel," I tell her. It's a lie. She is terrible. Our son is gone, but our daughter is here, alive, suffering, and Rachel cannot even pretend to be a mother to her. I'm no better, except that I am able to pretend.

"I love you, Rachel." The words tumble out of my mouth without my permission, without thought. They are true, but unwelcome. Rachel says nothing. Her shoulders rise and fall with silent sobs. She doesn't look at me.

Defeated, I turn and walk out of the room, closing the door behind me. I wander down the hall toward Eden's room, wondering what I can say to my daughter to explain what just happened. The Maker's Mark sloshes around in my stomach, not pleasantly, and I know I should eat something to absorb the alcohol, but all I want is another two fingers of bourbon. What a fucking pair my wife and I make. Rachel has her pills, and I have my bourbon. *What does Eden have?* I ask myself. *How does she cope?*

I stop at Jonah's room, turn the knob, and push open the door. I can't bring myself to step inside. I toss the monkey to the bed. It lands on the pillow, upright. Staring at me. I quickly shut the door and continue to Eden's room. I knock softly on her door, wait a moment, then open it and peer in. Eden sits on the far side of the room on her beanbag chair. Shadow lies with his front legs across her lap. Eden's arms encircle his chest, and her head rests against his head, her eyes closed. Shadow, alerted to my presence, eyes me dubiously but doesn't move.

My instant reaction is anger. Shadow isn't allowed upstairs. The carpeted floors cling to his discarded fur and dander. But then I remember what Eden just witnessed, and I realize I have no right to the anger I feel. Her mother doesn't make her feel safe, nor do I. At least Shadow can give her some reassurance.

"Eden?"

She raises her head slightly but doesn't open her eyes. Her voice is muffled by Shadow's thick coat. "Is Mom okay?"

How like my daughter, to ask after her mother before anything else. Her question fills me with shame that I haven't put her well-being ahead of everything, as I should. I take a tentative step into the room. It smells of dog, and I feel my nasal passages react.

"Your mom's really sad. Just like you are. Just like I am and Aunt Ruth is."

"She didn't seem sad," Eden says. "She seemed really angry and, like . . . like, crazy."

"I know she did." Two more steps and I'm at the edge of the bed. I sit and gaze down at the top of my daughter's head, at the crown of strawberry-blonde hair, the same shade as her mother's. "I know it's hard for you to understand." I take a breath and sigh. "It's hard for me to understand, too," I admit, and Eden looks up at me as though I've just made an important revelation. Her eyes are puffy and swollen and red, and it hurts to look at her, to see my ten-year-old's pain, but I force myself to not look away. "Everybody is different, right? Everyone is different and unique, isn't that so?"

She nods, almost imperceptibly. "And everyone is sad in different ways, too," I tell her, but my explanation sounds feeble.

"Why is Mom so mad at you?" she asks, and the question is so innocent, so unknowing, bereft of an agenda and made from simple curiosity. I don't know how to answer, what I can say that will make sense to her.

"Mom's mad at everything right now. That's the way she's being sad."

"Is she mad at me?"

"Oh, no, honey. Not at you." Another lie. Because I know, on some horrible level, Rachel is mad at Eden for being alive and needing her when she can't bear to be needed. "Never at you."

"Are you mad at me?" she asks, her eyes glistening in the near dark. "For Shadow being in my room?"

I let out a chuckle and see Eden visibly relax. "No, piece of pumpkin pie. I'm not mad." I reach out to her, stroke her hair, then put my hand on hers. She looks surprised, and I can't pretend I don't know why. I haven't reached out to her, haven't held her hand or stroked her hair or even really looked at her since Jonah died. I feel the urge for another shot of bourbon and quickly tamp it down.

"Come on. Aunt Ruth left some sandwiches in the fridge. I think we both could use a sandwich, don't you?"

She lets me pull her to her feet. Shadow groans, then stands and shakes himself, as though he's soaking wet. Eden squares her shoulders and looks at me.

"Dad. There's something I want to talk to you about." She sounds like she's thirty-five years old. "About the day . . . " She swallows. "You know, the day Jonah . . . the accident."

My stomach clenches with the memory of that day. What did Eden hear? How much does she know about what happened between her mother and me?

"But I don't want to make you upset."

"That was a very bad day," I say, and she nods solemnly. "And I definitely think we should talk about it at some point." She nods again. "But maybe we should wait until we can talk with Mommy, too." I am a coward. A bastard and a coward.

Eden nods. "When do you think we can all talk about it?"

I wish I knew. "Soon, honey. Really soon. I promise. Now, how about that sandwich?"

She nods and lets me lead her out of the room. Shadow follows at our heels. When we reach the top of the stairs, she glances at the closed door of the master bedroom.

"Mom said the f-word," she whispers, her mouth turned up in a ten-year-old grin. "Twice."

I allow myself to grin back at her. "I know, right?"

"She owes the curse jar, like, ten dollars." I nod in agreement, then watch as her grin morphs into a frown. "I'm not gonna make her pay, Dad."

I nod. "I think that's probably for the best, at least right now."

Eden starts down the stairs, her mood suddenly lifted, her hand still in mine. "Can we have a show dinner?" she asks. I can think of twenty reasons why we shouldn't. But I don't give voice to a single one.

An hour later, after enduring an episode of *Dancing with the Stars*, which Eden claims is Aunt Ruth's favorite show, my daughter gets up from the couch and kisses me on the forehead.

"The crease is better," she says. "Not much, but a little. I'm gonna go up and read for a while, okay, Dad?"

"Okay, my girl. I'll come up and check on you soon."

She nods and goes to the stairs. Once she's out of sight, I reach up and touch the skin between my eyebrows. I feel the deep furrow Eden referred to and massage it for a moment. Then I get up and carry our paper plates into the kitchen and dump them in the trash bin. I move to the cupboard above the fridge and pull out the Maker's Mark and pour myself a shot. I drink it in one swallow, then return to the couch. It's after nine o'clock and I'm surprised that Ruth hasn't come back yet, but a part of me is glad. I channel surf for a few minutes and land on an old Humphrey Bogart movie. My finger stills on the remote as I remember the night Rachel and I saw this film at a theater in downtown New York.

I don't want to think about Rachel then. So vibrant and impulsive and spontaneous and *alive*. That Rachel has gone away. And I don't know if I will ever see her again. I think about the way she used to skip, *skip*, down the streets of Manhattan and sing Beatles songs at the top of her lungs and make alphabet pancakes and spell out words of adoration to her kids with them and carve the most elaborate Halloween pumpkins on the block—hell, in the whole neighborhood. I wonder if I will ever see that Rachel again, the one I fell in love with, the one who never failed to surprise me, who made me laugh at myself, who danced with me in the living room, who gave me head in the bathroom of my office and straddled me in the driver's seat of my Highlander while the kids were napping in the backseat, who picketed the school district when they threatened to raise the class size, and charmed the socks off my potential clients and championed me when I lost an account.

The woman upstairs is a woman I don't know, and despite the fact that I had something to do with her transformation, I can't help but grieve the loss of the amazing person she was before. God, I hope she comes back. Not just for me, but for her.

I lower the volume on the TV and stare at the screen. Shadow turns around and around on his bed and finally settles.

God, I miss my wife. Almost as much as I miss my son.

TWENTY-TWO

RACHEL

It's no one's fault. What a load of crap.

I sit perched on the edge of the bed, *my* side of the bed. I could be on the other side, if I wanted. Sam's not here. He sleeps downstairs on the couch. Because Ruth told him it was for the best. Because I told her I couldn't sleep with him beside me. And Sam being Sam, he didn't fight or argue or insist that he sleep in his own bed, beside his wife.

I don't want him here, don't want to have to look at him or endure his duplicitous touch or feel his studied, long-suffering gaze. But I wonder, just for a moment, how I would feel about him if he claimed his place in this bed, in this room, if he'd argued against leaving both. Would I feel differently about him? Or would I resent him more?

It doesn't matter.

Where is the monkey? I miss him. I shouldn't have given him to Sam. Again, it doesn't matter. Jonah is gone.

And yet I can smell him, my son, suddenly, as though he just walked by. The baby powder, macaroni and cheese, and dirt-from-playing-in-the-garden scent. I draw in a long breath through my nose and I can definitely smell him, and I wonder, not for the first time in this last month, if I have gone completely, certifiably insane.

I can't smell Jonah because Jonah is not here because Jonah is dead.

But you saw him, Rachel.

No. I saw what the pills made me see.

No. He was here.

How many pills have I taken today?

Who cares?

I can't get that smell out of my nose.

I hear the whispered voices of Sam and Eden at the top of the stairs just outside my room. I can't make out the words. I feel a brief, intense flash of guilt over my behavior in front of Eden. She must think her mother is a monster. But the scent of Jonah overpowers my remorse. I can't even recall how I acted, what I said, Eden's reaction. I know I could access the memory if I tried, but the smell of Jonah is too strong, blocking out everything else.

I turn my head, just slightly, because I am afraid, and there he is, sitting at the head of my bed, resting against the headboard, smiling a close-lipped smile.

"Jonah," I say. But in a whisper, because I don't know if Sam and Eden are still outside at the top of the stairs, and I don't want them to hear me, because if they do, if Sam does, he'll come in here and make me think I'm crazy, which I know I am, and he'll tell me I'm not really seeing Jonah, which I know I'm not, but if no one stops me from thinking he's here, I can pretend that he is.

His mouth is working, but I can't hear what he says, can't make out the words. I don't know if they mean anything, truly, or if they are just the musings of a five-year-old boy. I stretch my hand out to him, and he reaches for me, too, with his right hand, and at the point where our fingers should meet, should touch, I feel only air. And that makes me want to scream, but I don't want to frighten him, my baby boy, my angel. Because this afternoon, when I saw him at the foot of my bed and started screaming, he vanished. So I hold the scream in.

I ease myself closer to him, but the closer I get, the less I see him. As though he is an optical illusion, smoke and mirrors, only the smoke is my pills and the mirrors are my desperation.

"Don't go," I tell him. His expression shifts from the happy smile to a look of concern, a look that is not typical for a five-year-old, a look that Jonah never made when he was alive.

When he was alive, his expressions ranged from content to joyful to puzzled to curious to intently focused, like when he found an interesting bug in the yard or discovered animal shapes in the clouds. He was a bright, precocious, happy child, engaged with the world around him.

But this Jonah, this phantom who might or might not really be sitting at the head of my bed, looks worried. I want to tell him not to, *don't worry, everything's okay*, because a five-year-old shouldn't ever wear that expression. But I can't, because everything is not okay, everything is awful, terrible, horrible, unbearable without him.

The image of my son begins to shift, to quiver, to fade even more, and I cry out, "Jonah!" He touches his nose and grins, and my tears are sudden and fierce.

When he was four and contracted strep throat and couldn't speak without immeasurable pain, he and I came up with signals, a kind of sign language. If he needed something, he would pantomime it, but if he was fine, in need of nothing, he would touch the tip of his index finger to the end of his nose. It became a thing for us, a secret communication between us to let the other know we were *just fine*.

I want to be able to touch my nose for him, but again, I can't. I'm seeing my dead son. That in and of itself is a pretty big indication that I'm not *just fine*.

An instant later, Jonah is gone. I squeeze my eyes shut, then open them, but all I see is the wooden headboard and the disheveled pillow on which I sleep.

A memory blooms in my mind from two years ago. My mother had just passed, the cancer quickly and efficiently taking her. My grief was tempered by all of the bureaucracy and business dying creates, the endless forms and phone calls and arrangements that needed to be taken care of. I was sitting at the kitchen table, a completed life insurance form and my cell phone in front of me. Jonah, three at the time, wandered into the kitchen and climbed into my lap.

"Are you sad, Mommy?" he asked, and I nodded my head. I was sad and tired and overwhelmed. "Are you sad about Nanny?"

"Yes, honey. I am."

Jonah didn't know what death meant. No child does.

"Nanny went away," he said solemnly.

"Yes, she did."

"But where did she go?"

I took a deep breath. "She went to heaven, baby."

"Where's heaven?" he asked. "Is it far away? Can we go see her there?"

"It's very far away. And we can't see her again except in our dreams." I had just had a very vivid dream the night before in which my mom had hugged me and told me she was "feeling all better now."

"But heaven is a wonderful place, Jonah. Beautiful, with angels all around. Nanny's happy there, so even though we can't see her, we know she's safe and happy and looking down on us with love."

"Does everybody go to heaven?" He shifted in my lap so that he could see me.

"I don't know," I said, opting for honesty.

"Will I go to heaven?" he asked, still searching my face.

"Yes, honey. You will definitely go to heaven. But not for a very, very long time."

He turned to face the table and leaned back against me. His dark curls were getting long, and I absently thought he was due for a haircut and wondered if we could fit one in before my mother's funeral.

"I can't wait to see Nanny again," he said softly, and I slipped my arms around his middle and held him close, rocking him back and forth until both of us were nearly asleep.

I glance at the bottle of pills on the nightstand and wonder why I'm seeing my son since I only took one pill. And then it hits me.

Why is he here? Why isn't he in heaven? My brain can't make sense of these questions. Jonah was the sweetest, most wonderful boy in the world. Why haven't God or the angels snatched him up and taken him to his kingdom, where my mom could lavish him with her bounteous love?

Maybe he's stuck here. My heart starts to race at the thought. Maybe he can't find his way. Maybe the angels are urging him on, but he can't hear them. I have to help him. I have to help him find his way to heaven. It's my responsibility as his mother. He deserves heaven, and I have to get him there.

I reach for the bottle of pills.

TWENTY-THREE

Ruth

I awake with a start, disoriented, not knowing where I am. Darkness has fallen, and the room is full of shadows. The living room. *My* living room. The digital clock on the cable box reads half past six. I've been asleep for more than two hours.

I jump up from the couch, relieved that my muscles are obeying the commands from my brain without much protest, but my relief is tempered by my guilt. Guilt that I have left my sister's family alone for so long. Rachel is a mess, Sam is incapable of dealing with her, and Eden, God bless her, needs the stability of my presence, whether she knows it or not.

As I half jog to the kitchen and grab my pills, a seed of worry sprouts in my gut. I don't know the root of this sudden apprehension. I am not superstitious, nor do I believe in telepathy, and even if I did, I'm far too common a woman to possess such a power. But this feeling, this sudden fear, compels me to hurry, to quicken my pace, despite the fact that my legs are not equipped to handle such velocity.

I grab a carry sack from the cupboard and bring it with me to the bedroom. I pull fresh underthings from the drawers and clean clothes from the closet and stuff them into the bag. I go into the cramped bathroom and relieve my bladder, and when I wash my hands, I am careful not to look in the mirror, because I am afraid of the image I will see.

Five minutes later, after making sure all of my appliances are off, even though I didn't use them during my brief visit, my Nissan shudders to life. I try to be grateful for what I have rather than bemoan what I don't have, but sometimes I resent the fact that Charlie got the Porsche. Especially since he bought his new wife a Land Rover. But the Nissan works, and how ridiculous would it be for a middle-aged woman with gray hair and sagging breasts and plump, useless breeder's hips to drive a sports car?

Worry gnaws at me, but I drive at the speed limit and stop appropriately for questionable yellow lights.

It won't help my sister if I get into an accident.

As I ease onto the freeway, I think about Rachel, the Rachel before Eden and Jonah, the Rachel before Sam. The girl I helped to raise.

Our mom was a good mother. But after Dad died, she had to support us on her own, and when she went back to work, I had to pick up the slack of caretaking. Rachel was impetuous; she was the baby and got away with anything because she could charm my mother out of her anger. In truth, she could charm me as well, but I took the role of stand-in parent seriously and used any opportunity that came up to teach my sister important lessons about life. She looked up to me and resented me at the same time. She made fun of me because I chose to study instead of going out with boys and because I eschewed drinking even when Mom was gone for the night and would never catch me. Rachel would sneak the Kahlúa out of the cabinet, pouring water in the bottle to make up for what she drank. I would threaten to tell Mom, but I never did. Instead, I would watch her closely and make her drink water and give her aspirin and, finally, drape a blanket across her when she passed out on the couch.

She never thanked me, never made any noises of appreciation. Not until later, not until after that boy.

His name was Casey Holdaway. He was a beautiful bum. He looked like Brad Pitt, and he was affable and funny and as ambitious as a sloth. I might have had a slight crush on him even though he was two years younger than me and totally focused on getting into my sister's Calvin Kleins. I don't think he even knew my name, but he recognized me as a possible ally and so he joked with me and maybe even flirted with me in order to get closer to her. And although I admit to the occasional fantasy about him, I recognized him for what he was. I warned Rachel off him, but she mistook my ministrations for jealousy and careened headlong into his arms.

She came to me, one night, when Mom was on the late shift, crying, her mascara halfway down her face. She'd been at a party, and Casey had been on the arm of another girl, a slut called Amber, and they'd been making out in front of everyone. I told her not to worry, that she was better off without him, that she would be fine, but she'd sobbed and sobbed and then she threw up, right there on my bed, and I knew, before she even told me, she was pregnant.

I took care of her. There was no other choice. I could have betrayed her to my mom, but that would have led to misery for everyone. And she was so brokenhearted, so small and afraid and alone, and she needed a champion. I had always been that for her, even if she didn't recognize that fact. So I lied to our mother, and I took her to the clinic, and I cared for her afterward, and I went to Casey Holdaway's house a week after the abortion and I shattered his windshield with my father's sledgehammer that had been lying dormant in our garage since his death.

And Rachel, still recovering and pleading the flu to our mother, took my hand and pulled me to her side and thanked me, tearfully, her emotions uncontained. She told me I was the best sister ever and she would always be grateful to me, indebted to me, and that she loved me.

I've held that memory since she was fifteen. It has kept me from hating her in her moments of complete self-absorption. It has kept me at the ready to validate her praise.

I reach the turnoff for Rachel's neighborhood. The seed of worry has blossomed into absolute terror. Something is wrong, I know. I have no hands-free device, but I reach for my cell phone anyway. I call Rachel's cell, knowing she won't answer because it lies unused in its charger downstairs. I hang up and call Sam's cell phone. He doesn't answer, either. I call the house phone, but the call goes immediately to voice mail, which is no surprise since I helped them change the setting when they were overwhelmed by all of the phone calls from friends and relatives.

I put my foot on the accelerator, exceeding the speed limit, then have to brake suddenly at a crosswalk that lights up seemingly by magic. I idle, looking at both sides of the street, trying to find the pedestrian responsible for this unwanted delay. There is no one. I curse softly, then press down on the accelerator.

Three minutes, I think. I try to counsel myself. I tell myself that my worry is unfounded. All is well. If it weren't, surely I would have heard from Sam. *All is well. All is well.* As well as it can be, considering the fact that Jonah is dead.

I reach the familiar tract of houses and make the turn onto Rachel's street. When I pull to the curb in front of my sister's house, I take a deep breath and let it out on a sigh. I don't know what I expected to find, but there is nothing out of the ordinary. Lights blaze from inside, and I can see the flickering light from the television in the living room. There are no fire engines or paramedics, no curious neighbors—all is as it should be. I grab my bag from the passenger seat and get out of the car.

I approach the front door. I think back to when I arrived earlier this afternoon, when Rachel was screaming. She is not screaming now. All is quiet. Slowly my pulse returns to normal.

Shadow starts to bark.

TWENTY-FOUR

SHADOW

Something is wrong. I can smell it from where I lie. I raise my head and sniff the air. The smell is coming from upstairs, from my mistress. I raise my ears to listen for sounds from my mistress, but the screen on the wall is alive and very loud.

My master and Little Female are sitting on the couch, their faces turned toward the screen, watching flat humans behave strangely. Sometimes, my master and Little Female laugh at the flat humans, and the sound pleases me, because I haven't heard them laugh in a very long time. There are plates on the chewed-leg table with food that Dark Female made. I know because I smell her on the bread.

I have been sitting on my couch-room bed, not lying down, but sitting up watching my master and Little Female eat, waiting for one of them to drop something on the floor or give me a taste. I'm not hungry because my master remembered to feed me, but I can always eat, especially if it's human food.

But now, the smell from upstairs draws my attention, pulling me away from my master and Little Female and their food. I creep away from the couch and move to the stairs. My master doesn't notice and neither does Little Female.

Most smells make me happy, even the ones that make my humans hold their noses and frown and cry out while waving their hands back and forth in front of their faces. But this is not a happy-making kind of smell. This smell makes me afraid, makes my ears flat and my tail curl down between my back legs.

I know I'm not supposed to go up there, even though I went up before and my master didn't give me angry eyes. I'm still not supposed to go. I don't know what to do, so I lie down on the cool floor right by the bottom step and listen for my mistress's call.

Little Female rises from the couch and walks toward me. She pats my head and says, "Good Shadow." She speaks a few words and then tells me stay. I know that word. Right now, with the afraid smell, I don't like the word *stay*. I make a small whining noise in my throat, but Little Female is already up the stairs and down the hall. She didn't stop at my mistress's door, but then Little Female has a human nose, not a dog nose. I hear the door to Little Female's room creak closed.

The afraid smell is worse. I can't stay, even if Little Female told me to. I have go.

I stand up, then put my paw on the first stair. I take a step up, then another, feeling a little bit like a Bad Boy but not being able to stop myself because I sense that my mistress is in distress. The smell gets stronger with each step I take until there is only the smell, nothing else, not my master or Little Female or there-and-not-there Little Male. The fur on my neck rises all by itself, and I am afraid, but I am a Good Boy *and* a Brave Boy, so I keep going even if I don't want to.

Up I go until I'm at the very top of the stairs. I move to the door on the right side. My mistress is on the other side of this door. Her smell seeps under the crack. I make the whining noise again and scratch at the door, and it opens just a little bit, but I don't see my mistress or hear her, either.

The smell is burning the inside of my nose and my head and I don't want to get any closer to that smell because it hurts, but I have to because I am a Good Boy and I know my mistress needs me, even if she isn't calling me like she usually does when she wants me to come.

I let out a single bark, but my mistress doesn't answer. My master and Little Female don't hear me. I lift my forepaw and press it against the door, and the door opens enough for me to walk in.

It's dark inside this room, but I don't need light to get to my mistress. Her scent, underneath that smell, leads me to her. I pad around the side of the bed and see her. She lies on her side with one arm flung out, the hand at the end of it touching the table beside her, where a plastic bottle sits open. I know what open and closed is, because open means I can reach my head into the container of food and grab some, and closed means I can't. Her eyes are open, but I can tell that she is not seeing anything. Her breathing isn't right—she makes gurgling sounds and her chest rises and falls rapidly, in short bursts like it hurts to breathe, and the afraid smell is coming out of her mouth.

I make the whining sound and push my head under her hand. Her hand flops off me. I chuff at her, but she doesn't move. Her breathing changes again—she's wheezing and choking and I can tell that the smell is death.

I start to bark. And bark. And bark. And I don't stop.

I hear Dark Female rush into the house downstairs and make shouting noises at my master. My master and Dark Female come into this room, and my master grabs my mistress and shakes her, shouts at her, rocks her, while Dark Female talks into her metal toy. Little Female stands at the open door, her eyes very big and round, until Dark Female grabs her arm and drags her to her room. I hear the sirens in my ears. Then the squeal-whine of tires. I'm still barking as the heavy tread of footsteps sounds on the stairs, as strangers push on my mistress's chest and put something in her mouth and pierce her arm with the sharp end of a long tube.

Dark Female shushes me and scolds me with her angry eyes and angry face, but I stay in the room, barking, until the strangers lift my mistress onto a long table with no chewed legs and carry her from the house.

I follow my master to Little Female's room and see him put his arms around her and hold her, then take her hand and lead her to the hallway. Her eyes are crying, but she pats my head, and I feel better that she knows I'm there.

I follow my master and Little Female downstairs, where they meet Dark Female. Her face is angry, but her body is angry all over, too. I feel it coming out of her. Big sad plus big angry. She looks at Little Female but not at my master. The humans go to the front door and outside and I want to go with them, I want to not be alone here, but I know they won't let me come.

The smell is smaller now, but still here. I go to the food-smelling room and walk to the farthest corner, as far away from the smell as I can. I lie down and put my head on my front paws. I look at my bed. It would be nice if my bed were over where I am. But I'm not going to go to my bed until the smell is even smaller.

And then I see Little Male. He comes into my sight, and my tail starts to wag. But when he is all the way there and I see his face, my tail stops wagging. Because he is not smiling. His face is not wet, but I can tell he is crying.

And then he is gone.

PART TWO:
A DAY OF
COUNSELING

Therapist Journal: 5/15/17

Patient: Rachel Glass-Davenport, age 36
Referral: Archibald Deever, MD, PhD

My initial meeting with Rachel Glass-Davenport (from here on to be referred to as RGD) took place at Mercy Hospital on May 15, 2017, at three thirty in the afternoon. Her husband, Samuel Davenport, and her sister, Ruth Glass, were present for introductions and provided background information. Her physician, Elizabeth Hamill, MD, as well as the attending psych resident, James Lahey, MD, discussed her case and went over her chart with me.

RGD was brought in to the emergency room on May 14, 2017, at 7:43 p.m. after ingesting as many as one dozen fluoxetine. Gastric lavage was performed in the emergency room, and patient was stabilized by 8:32 p.m. and admitted to Mercy.

When asked the reason for the attempted overdose, RGD said she was trying to help her son (deceased, April 15, 2017) find his way to heaven.

Samuel Davenport and Ruth Glass reported that RGD has been suffering from severe depression following the death of her son (Jonah Davenport, age 5). RGD has been unable to function, refuses to get out of bed, refuses to perform normal tasks, no longer plays a parental role to her daughter (Eden Davenport, age 10), avoids personal grooming, including bathing, and eats only when forced or coerced.

Ruth Glass reported to Dr. Lahey that RGD claims to have seen her son on the day of the overdose.

RGD was extremely thin, her skin had a grayish pallor to it, her eyes were

sunken in their sockets. She was slow to react to my presence, had difficul-
ty focusing her vision and stabilizing her gaze, appeared not to understand
many of my words, refused to answer most of my questions, although not
with hostility, only with ambivalence.

I informed RGD that she was getting better and that she would be released
from the hospital in a day or two. RGD became visibly upset. I informed her
that I would be helping her and her family get through this difficult time.

RGD was unable to calm herself and reported that Jonah (son, deceased)
had found her at Mercy and she couldn't leave because she didn't know if
Jonah knew the way back to their home.

RGD became increasingly agitated, started to thrash her arms, nearly pull-
ing out her IV. I depressed the call button for the nurse, who entered within
twenty seconds and immediately administered 4 mg lorazepam through IV.
Follow-up Scheduled: ___X____Yes____No if so, when: _Monday, _May
22, 2017__9:30 a.m.___

TWENTY-FIVE

MADDIE

Grief is my business.

Sometimes I feel ashamed that I profit from the tragedies of others. But most of the time, my guilt is tempered by the knowledge that I am helping people to heal.

I treat young and old, in various stages of grief and at various levels of grief. I once treated an elderly woman who lost her husband and her parakeet in the same month. She was fine with the loss of her husband—"He was a jackass"—but her parakeet's death left her inconsolable. I treat children who've lost their parents and parents who've lost their children, spouses who've lost the loves of their lives and husbands and wives who don't know why they're grieving because they couldn't stand their partners, siblings with survivors' guilt, best friends unable to go on without their touchstones, people who've lost limbs or jobs or the ability to do the things they were able to do before.

There are those who don't understand why I do what I do, who can't comprehend why I would make the choice to surround myself with so much loss. But I remind them that every person on the planet is surrounded by loss. Life itself is a series of losses, is it not? In this world, happiness and fulfillment are products of successfully dealing with our losses.

Aside from the various race- and gender-related challenges I've faced over the course of my life, I have also suffered numerous tragedies, and those compelled me to do what I do today. When I started the psych program at university, my goal was to be a high school guidance counselor. I wanted to work with inner-city kids at that dubious stage when they can either embark on the path to success or careen toward mediocrity or failure.

Just before I got my degree, my parents were killed in an auto accident, and suddenly I was an orphan with no brothers or sisters and no family to speak of. At the time, I suppressed my grief, compartmentalized it, buried it where I thought it could do me no harm. I threw myself into my schooling, graduated with honors, and found comfort in the fact that my parents would have been proud.

Two years later, when I was midway through my doctoral program, my fiancé was one of the many victims of a shooting spree in a local restaurant that involved a disgruntled employee. My professors allowed me to take a sabbatical, and for six months I couldn't leave my apartment, could barely get out of bed.

It was through the kindness and compassion and determination of one of my fellow doctoral candidates, my friend Jessa, that I was able to work through my grief and become a functioning human being again. She counseled me every day, in between forcing me to do my laundry and make my bed and eat my meals. She offered me tools to help me step outside into the sunshine and accompanied me when I finally dared to go to the restaurant where Paul had been killed, holding my hand tightly and monitoring my heart rate and reminding me to breathe when I forgot. She told me that happiness was not some elusive force that only showered down upon the deserving, but a choice we all make despite the fact that life is hard.

A year later, Jessa died from an undiagnosed brain tumor. Her death, but more importantly, what she did for me in life—giving me back mine—inspired me to do what I do. Helping others through their grief not only fulfills me and helps me deal with my own loss, it is a way for me to honor Jessa's legacy.

I have been married for seven years and have a good, if somewhat unorthodox, marriage, not only because I'm black and my husband is French-English. My husband works three hours away and keeps an apartment near his firm where he sleeps Monday through Thursday. On Friday, he works a half day then takes the train home, and we spend the weekend together. Our friends often question this arrangement. Secretly I think they're jealous. But it works well for us I don't know that our marriage would survive if we were to live together full-time. My days are long and emotionally charged, and because I must remain stoic for my patients, I require a lengthy decompression period at night, and it is impossible to decompress with an audience. Peter, my husband, FaceTimes me every night, but only after I text him that the coast is clear. Sometimes I talk to him about my day, after the intensity has faded, either through a hot bath or yoga or a run. And he is always an active and compassionate listener, asking questions when appropriate and occasionally offering insight. But most nights, I steer our conversations to lighter arenas and enjoy the sound of his voice as he tells me anecdotes from work.

Madelaine Meyers Grief Support and Counseling Services is thriving. I have a good reputation in my field, and I work hard to earn it. My practice occupies the ground floor of a brownstone, and I am proud of the comfortable, welcoming, and nonclinical space I have created. My sessions are longer than most therapists', because I don't believe that fifty-five minutes is enough time to get to the root of an issue, introduce a new tool, or analyze a particular memory or dream. These things take as long as they take, and I would never want to cut short a patient on the brink of a breakthrough. I don't charge exorbitant fees—I am midlevel at best—and I take insurance. My patient roster is full, every day, every week, month, and year. Tragedy happens daily, and grief is ever present.

When Archie, one of my old professors from university who now works in family practice, called me with a referral, I told him I couldn't take any more patients, especially not a family. We talked for a long while, and he related to me the story of the Davenports—the death of five-year-old Jonah and the failed overdose of his mother—and by the end of the conversation, I was going through my calendar to see if there was some way I could work them into my schedule.

"Ruth, the mother's sister, is an old dear friend of mine," Archie said. "She's been through some difficult times, and now this. I care very deeply for her, Maddie. These are good people. If there's any way . . ."

And because Archie helped me establish myself when I was first starting out, and because he'd never asked me for anything in return, I made a way.

TWENTY-SIX

SESSION ONE

The Davenport family is waiting in the reception area when I arrive at my practice on Monday morning. They are early. Rachel Glass-Davenport is seated on a chair, her sister beside her, her head lowered and her shoulders hunched over. Samuel Davenport stands with his hands in his pockets, gazing at a print on the wall, not really seeing it, I suspect. The little girl—Eden, I recall—sits apart from her aunt and her mother, her nose in a book, her knee bouncing up and down rapidly.

My assistant, Nadine, stands and smiles at me from behind her desk.

"Dr. Meyers, the Davenports are here for their appointment," she says in her calm, melodic voice. Aside from her impeccable credentials and sterling character references, I hired Nadine Walters for her voice. In a room that is often filled with heightened anxiety and emotion, a voice with certain characteristics—a nasally pitch or a high squeak—will only make things worse. A helicopter could crash through the front door of the practice, and Nadine would inform me with the same intensity she might use when telling me I have something in my teeth.

"Thank you, Nadine." I look from face to face, hoping to meet eyes with each family member, but the only person looking at me is Ruth Glass. She wears an expectant, almost desperate expression.

"Good morning," I say. "Nadine, why don't you show the Davenports to the family room. I'll be there in a few minutes."

Nadine nods and moves around the desk. She is full figured but moves with lightness and grace. Her long black hair is shiny without a trace of gray, despite the fact that she is well into her forties. "Please come this way," she murmurs, then makes a slight sweeping gesture toward the back of the brownstone.

I watch Ruth get to her feet, then turn and lean toward her sister to help her up. Samuel moves to help, but Ruth waves him off. He turns to his daughter and puts his hand out to her, then lifts her out of her seat. She keeps her hand in his. They follow Nadine to the second door on the left.

I go to my office, stow my purse, and boot up my computer. Check my schedule for the day and charge my phone. Three minutes later, I walk into the family room.

As per its name, this space might be found in any home—comfortable couches with plump pillows, a couple of easy chairs, a coffee table stacked with magazines and children's books, a toy chest in the corner, and a television on the wall. In the far corner is a kitchenette with a small refrigerator full of various nonalcoholic beverages, a countertop with a sink, a coffee machine, an electric kettle, and a basket with an assortment of herbal teas.

Rachel is seated on one of the couches, eyes cast down. Samuel is pacing, and Ruth is investigating the tea bags. Eden sits on the floor by the toy chest, carefully perusing its contents. All eyes, save for Rachel's, turn to me when I enter.

"Again, good morning," I say. I cross to one of the easy chairs and sit. I carry nothing with me, no notepad or clipboard, no recording device. When I perform a group intake, I like to be unfettered and rely solely on my senses and intuition. If I'm busy taking notes or checking to make sure the session is being recorded, I miss too much. I have found that this method allows my patients to relax and open themselves up more.

"I'm Dr. Madelaine Meyers. You can call me whatever makes you most comfortable, including Maddie. It would be nice if we could all sit down together." I stop speaking and wait. After a moment, Ruth crosses to her sister and sits beside her. Samuel looks at the two women for a moment, and I can't decide whether his expression is one of longing or resentment. Possibly both. Finally, he sits on the other couch. Eden gets to her feet and wanders over, gives me a doubtful look, then slowly lowers herself into an easy chair next to me. She sits on the very edge, as though she wants to be ready to spring up at any moment, and clutches her book to her chest. I can't make out the title, but the cover picture is dark, with clouds and lightning on it.

"First, I want to say how sorry I am for your loss. I didn't know Jonah, and I'm not going to pretend that I know exactly how you all are feeling. I have experienced the loss of a loved one. Several loved ones. I'm telling you this so that you'll know I can empathize." I turn to Eden. "Do you know what *empathize* means?"

She nods solemnly. "It's like when you can understand something because it's happened to you, too."

"That's very good. If I ever use a word that you don't know, please feel free to ask, or if I ever say anything that doesn't make sense, let me know, and I'll try to do a better job of explaining. Okay?"

She nods again and I smile at her. "Good." I look around the room. "That goes for everyone. Okay?"

Ruth nods. Samuel clears his throat. Rachel doesn't move.

"I'd like to talk for a few minutes about why you've come to see me and what your expectations for our time together are. After that, I'd like to meet with each of you individually . . ."

"How long is that going to take?" Samuel asks. He isn't angry, just impatient.

"I think about twenty minutes per person."

"I have to go to work."

"How about I meet with you first? Does your family have a way home?"

"I have my own car," Ruth says defiantly. "I brought Rachel."

I nod. "Good. Is that acceptable to you, Mr. Davenport?"

"I suppose."

"Do you mind if I call you Samuel?" I ask, and he flinches at my question.

"I would prefer Sam."

"Fine. Thank you, Sam. So, let's begin. Why don't we talk about the reason you've come to see me."

No one speaks. Sam turns his head away from me. Ruth sits forward and pats her sister's hand. "Well, we—"

"You're going to help us feel better," Eden chimes in. "Because we're all so sad, and it's kind of like we're trapped in the sadness, like it's quicksand or really thick mud and our feet are stuck and we can't get out, and you're going to give us a really strong rope and pull us out."

"That's a very good explanation, Eden. Is it okay if I call you Eden?"

"That's my name, so I guess it's okay."

"Would anyone else like to add to Eden's explanation?"

"I'm worried about my sister," Ruth says. "As well as the rest of the family. But I think Rachel needs the most help. I mean, obviously, considering what just happened. And yes, you can call me Ruth."

"Thank you, Ruth. What about you, Sam?"

"What about me?" He looks at me, then pointedly checks his watch.

"What are your reasons for being here?"

"I'm sorry, Dr. Meyers, but that feels like a useless question."

"Please don't be sorry about expressing yourself."

"My son died. My wife is in trouble. We're all grieving. That's why we're here."

"Would you agree with Eden that you feel stuck in your grief?"

I watch him ponder the question. He glances at Rachel. "Yes."

"Okay. Rachel? Would you like to tell me why you're here?"

She doesn't look at me. When she finally speaks, her voice is a monotone. "Because we're stuck."

"Thank you, Rachel. Thank you all. Each of us are individuals, and we all deal with our grief separately. But a family is also a unit. And it's important for all of you to be on the same page as to why you're here as a family. What about your expectations for our sessions? Would anyone like to comment?"

Sam chuffs, much like a dog. Ruth shoots him a glare. Eden kicks her feet out, and Rachel just sits there, motionless.

"Sam, I understand that my questions might seem rhetorical or, perhaps, irrelevant. But I ask them for a reason. What are your expectations for our sessions?"

"I don't have any," he says. "I don't believe in therapy. I believe in moving forward."

"And are you?" I counter. "Moving forward?"

He throws up his hands. "I'm trying."

"That's good," I tell him. "That's very good."

I glance at Eden, who is concentrating on her feet, and Ruth, who is shaking her head, and Rachel, whose head is down, and I decide not to push them further. I have seen this kind of resistance countless times. Pushing is counterintuitive and can lead to a total shutdown. Patience and persistence are far more effective.

"Why don't we begin the individual sessions? Ruth, Rachel, Eden, help yourself to anything. If you're hungry, there are snack bars and crackers in the cupboard. And the remote control for the television is in the drawer of the coffee table. Sam, if you'll follow me?"

I walk to the door of the family room. Sam looks at Rachel for a long moment, then smiles at Eden. "See you later, piece of pumpkin pie."

The girl jumps from her seat and throws her arms around Sam's waist. He gives her a brief hug, then pats her back.

"'Bye, Dad," she says. "Have a good day at work."

"I will, honey. You take care of your mom and Aunt Ruth, okay?"

Eden gives her father a dubious look, and he chucks her under the chin. She reaches up and pulls at his tie, forcing him to bend over, then she whispers in his ear. I can just make out her words.

"Do you think Dr. Meyers can help us?"

I force myself to look at the floor. Sam glances at me—I feel his gaze upon me—but I pretend I didn't hear his daughter's words.

"I hope so, honey," he says to her. "I really do."

TWENTY-SEVEN

SAMUEL DAVENPORT

"Am I supposed to lie down?" he asks, jerking a thumb in the direction of the couch. We are in the room I use for my private sessions, a small space with good light from a south-facing window. On one wall is a couch, and catty-corner to the couch is an easy chair. A straight-backed chair faces both, and a desk sits in the corner, out of the way.

"You're welcome to lie down if you'd like," I tell him, and he snickers. "You can lie down or sit or remain standing. Whatever makes you most comfortable."

He paces the length of the room in three seconds, turns and gazes at the Kertész print hanging over the couch.

"Melancholic Tulip," he says.

"You like Kertész?" I ask.

He shrugs. "Not particularly. I mean, he's good. But I prefer Ansel Adams. I guess that makes me a cliché."

"Ansel Adams is a wonderful photographer," I say. I walk to the desk and fetch a clipboard from the top drawer. My notes are sparse, usually a single word, but they help me to recall my sessions. I go to the straight-backed chair and sit. "I have an Ansel Adams in my house."

"Original?"

"Clearing Winter Storm," I say, and he whistles.

"Nice."

I wait a moment. Then, "Would you like to sit, or do you prefer to stand?"

"Look, I'm sorry about what I said in there." He gestures toward the door. "About not believing in therapy."

"This is a safe place, Sam. You're free to say whatever you want to say. As long as you're not verbally abusive." I give him a grin. "I'm not easily offended. The fact that you're here tells me you have, at least, some modicum of belief in therapy."

"My parents went into therapy," he says. "A month later, they filed for divorce, so, as you can imagine, I'm not a big fan."

"Then why are you here?" I ask.

"I'm here because of Rachel." He stares at me, a challenge.

I meet his stare. Samuel Davenport is a very handsome man, with dark-brown hair and brown eyes and a strong jaw. In the past twenty minutes, I have determined that this is a man who is used to being in control, who despises chaos, who has, for his entire life, had the world on a string because of his looks and charm. But the huge crevasse between his eyes betrays him. He never expected the horrible hand life dealt him, and he no longer knows how the world, how *his* world, is supposed to work.

"Your wife is in crisis."

"I didn't need to come here and spend whatever it is you're charging me to know that!" He takes a breath. "I'm sorry."

"I told you, Sam. I have a thick skin. I don't want you to edit yourself. But in order for me to help you, and Rachel, I need you to . . . I need you to open yourself up to the possibility that this is a good thing. If you come into this guarded or doubtful or suspicious or without any faith at all, I won't be able to help you. You've made a commitment to come here. For your wife, for your family, and whether you think so or not, that means you're also here for yourself."

His head drops to his chest. I watch as he takes a few deep breaths, in and out. His shoulders relax for the first time since he's been here.

He raises his head and looks around, as if seeing the space for the first time. Then he wanders to the easy chair closest to me and sits.

"Ruth thinks it's my fault. I know she does. She's probably right. I shouldn't have given Rachel the bottle of pills. I just, I never thought she'd . . . I mean, she seemed coherent, and she seemed like she wanted to be in control. I thought that was a good sign."

Samuel Davenport is omitting an important piece of information. I don't know what it is, but I can tell by the expression on his face. He changes the subject, and I allow it.

"I love my family," he says. "I loved Jonah." He shakes his head. "I *love* Jonah." I nod, but he's not looking at me. He's looking at his lap. "He's my son, you know? He'll always be my son. He was supposed to . . . he was . . . he was going to carry on my name. That sounds so stupid, doesn't it?"

"No, Sam. That doesn't sound stupid at all. A son to a father is a remarkable and unique relationship."

"I love Eden just as much."

"Of course you do. But a father's relationship with his son is different than with his daughter. Just as a mother's relationship with her daughter is different than with her son."

He continues to stare at his lap. I look at the blank page in front of me; my pen is poised but remains motionless.

"Sam?" He raises his head, but his eyes don't meet mine. He stares at a spot just past my head. "Tell me about Jonah."

He smiles, a genuine smile. "Jonah was a great kid. Funny, you know? I mean, he was only five, but he had a great sense of humor for a five-year-old. He would come up with the canniest observations about things. Way beyond his years." The crease in Sam's forehead deepens. "I'm trying to think of an example—there were so many. But I can't think of one. How can I not think of a single one?" He shakes his head. "He'd say this, whatever it was, and Rachel and I would look at each other, like, what the fuck? Excuse me, I'm sorry."

"The f-word is permissible, Sam. No worries."

"I can't believe that I can't give you a single example."

"Tell me something else about him," I say.

He thinks for a moment, then holds up his right hand. "He had really big hands, long fingers. Much bigger than other kids his age." He drops his hand to his lap. "Rachel wanted him to take piano lessons. I thought sports, like football. I mean, I supported him taking piano lessons, but I really thought he'd be a great football player. Rachel hated the idea. She'd always remind me about football injuries and head trauma and that kind of thing." He lowers his head again. "Now he's never going to do either."

"What else, Sam?"

Sam takes a deep breath, clears his throat, manages another smile. "He was curious about the world around him. He loved bugs. He didn't have any fear of bugs, no matter what kind they were. He used to find them outside, or sometimes inside, and he'd go to his insect encyclopedia and look them up, and then he'd tell us all about them. He wouldn't let Rachel kill a spider. He'd get a cup and trap it, then take it outside and release it. It used to drive her nuts."

He is quiet for a moment, remembering. I let the silence stretch out until he gives me a questioning look.

"You said something earlier about wanting to move forward. What does that look like to you?"

"I don't know. Forward. I want to move forward. I want to wake up in the morning and not have this be the first thing I think about. I want to get to the point where this whole terrible, horrible thing that happened isn't the thing that defines me, to myself and to everyone around me."

"That's very well said, Sam."

"But then I feel fucking guilty for even thinking that. Because it was my son, and I should think about it every waking minute of every day and it should define me because it's my fau—" He stops himself, stands up suddenly, and crosses to the window.

I consider his words, and what he stopped himself from saying. That Jonah's death was his fault. It's common for parents to shoulder the burden of their child's death, but I suspect there's more to it. I want to dig deeper, but his posture tells me to tread carefully. I make a note to circle back another time.

"Were you home on the day of the accident, Sam?" He nods without turning around. "So you were there and saw Jonah, you watched as they took him in the ambulance. You were there at the hospital when they pronounced him."

"Yes," he says, almost angrily. "We were all there that day. Even Ruth. Why are you asking me this?"

"I know the memories of that day stand out for you right now. It's important for you to allow yourself to think about Jonah as he was before, when he was alive and full of life. You need to keep those memories close; you need to celebrate the child who saved spiders and made keen observations and had a great sense of humor."

"It hurts to remember him that way, knowing he's gone."

"But those things you cherish about him are the things that will pull you through your grief. Eventually. Have you and Rachel been able to talk about him, about the way he was before?"

He turns to face me. "Rachel and I haven't been able to talk about anything." Spots of color appear on his cheeks. "She's been . . . she's been in bad shape."

"Do you feel that Rachel's situation is keeping your family from moving forward?"

He lets out a sigh. "Yes."

"Are you angry with her?" He doesn't answer. "Remember, Sam. Safe place. You can say anything. There's no judgment."

"Bullshit. I'm sorry, Doctor, but there's always judgment. You can pretend to be unbiased, but if I say that I'm angry with my wife for having a nervous breakdown after her son got killed, then you're going to think I'm a bastard."

"It doesn't matter what I think, Sam—it only matters what you think. And by the way, I don't think you're a bastard. I think you have every right to be angry."

He looks at me with an almost hopeful expression, then shakes his head ruefully. "I guess I just never expected this from her. I never expected her to fall apart. Rachel was the coolest girl I'd ever met. So enthusiastic about life. That's where Jonah got it from. She was amazing. And now she won't even get out of bed. And Eden, my God, poor Eden. It's like Rachel's forgotten she has another child. And then she goes and does what she did. I just . . . It's just . . . I know things like this break up marriages. And she and I have things we need to work out. But we can't do that unless she decides she wants to start living again." He rubs his forehead with his hand. "Please help her. Please help all of us."

He looks down at his feet and chuckles with little humor. "Listen to me. You'd think I really believed in this shit."

"Maybe someday soon, you will," I tell him.

"Maybe," he says without enthusiasm. "Maybe I will."

TWENTY-EIGHT

RUTH GLASS

"I've already been in therapy," she says right off the bat. She sits on the couch, perched on the edge, her back straight, her hands folded in her lap. "I know how this works."

I smile. "That's good."

She offers the answer before I ask the question. "I had a difficult time after my husband left me."

"Thank you for telling me."

"He left me for another woman," she says. "Actually, he left me because I couldn't give him children. He has three now. Children."

"That must have been very difficult for you."

She shrugs. "Not much I could do about it. Therapy helped. Helped me to realize it wasn't my fault. That I'm not defective."

"Of course you're not," I assure her, although I think she still bears the blame. She tells herself it's not her fault, repeats what her therapist tells her—that she's not defective—but she doesn't really believe it.

"I haven't seen Dr. Moore since Jonah, well, you know . . . I'll probably go back to him at some point. But I felt it was important to be a part of this." She gestures to me, to the room around her. "I'm the one who got them to come." I smile noncommittally. She continues. "Anyway, I'm not here to talk about myself. I'm extremely worried about my sister." She glances at the door. "Do you think they're okay in there?"

"I asked my assistant to do some paperwork in the family room. She'll keep an eye out."

Ruth nods. "Thank you. I'm sure she's fine. Eden was watching *Cupcake Wars*. She loves that show. We watch it together sometimes. Or *Dancing with the Stars*. That's my favorite. During the commercials, Eden will get up and start dancing around the room." She sniffs. "Well, she used to, anyway."

"You love your niece very much," I say, and Ruth smiles.

"I love them both. Eden and Jonah. I'm like their second mother. I mean, not that I'm even comparable to how Rachel is as a mom. Or how she was, before."

"She was good with the children?"

"Oh, yes, she was wonderful. Very involved. She loved to play with them. Really play, not just make the motions. I'm not good at that kind of thing." She sighs. "Which is probably why God didn't want me to be a mother. I mean, I play with them, but it doesn't come as naturally to me. I'm talking about myself again. I'm sorry."

"You have nothing to apologize for, Ruth."

"Rachel was a wonderful mother. I pray she will be again, for Eden's sake. Eden needs her, now more than ever. I'm just not capable of filling Rachel's shoes. I mean, I'm doing everything I can for all of them. I'm basically running the household, doing the laundry and the cooking and the cleaning. Don't get me wrong, I'm happy to do it."

"The Davenports are very lucky to have you."

"Oh, no, I'm not looking for praise. Anyone would do what I'm doing. Especially after what happened. Especially after what I . . ." She stops talking, and I watch her closely as she pulls a tissue from her purse and dabs at her eyes and nose. I wait for her to speak again. When she does, her voice is soft.

"Rachel wasn't trying to kill herself. It's important that you understand that."

"Okay."

"My sister would never do that."

Except that she knowingly took a handful of prescription drugs. In my experience, that means she was definitely trying to end her life.

"And it's my fault. I should never have left the pills with Sam. I shouldn't have left at all, except that I had to go home. I needed my medication. You see, I suffer from fibromyalgia. But I left very strict instructions that Sam was not to give the bottle to her."

"Because you were worried that she would take too many?"

"No. I don't know. Maybe. But not on purpose. I just knew she wasn't thinking clearly. Earlier that day, Rachel thought she . . ."

"Go on, Ruth."

"My sister isn't crazy, Dr. Meyers."

"No one is saying Rachel is crazy."

Ruth stares at me for a long moment. "She told me she saw Jonah, earlier that day. She said he was sitting on her bed. Obviously, she was hallucinating, but she swears it was real."

I recall Dr. Lahey mentioning as much. I make a note on my clipboard, and Ruth gives me a nervous look.

"What are you writing? Am I allowed to ask?"

"Something I want to discuss with your sister. About seeing Jonah."

Ruth is suddenly distressed. "She'll be angry with me. That I told you."

"She might be, yes," I say. "But her well-being is more important than her anger toward you, wouldn't you agree?"

She looks at her hands. "Of course. I just . . . I'm the only one she trusts right now."

"She doesn't trust Sam?"

She gives a bark of laughter, not a pleasant sound. "She can't stand to be near him. Barely speaks to him, doesn't look at him, won't let him touch her. He sleeps on the couch downstairs, for goodness' sake."

Sam didn't mention this to me. I make another note, but this time Ruth doesn't question me about it, only nods with apparent satisfaction.

"I think she blames him for Jonah's death," she says then quickly adds, "not that it was his fault. It wasn't anyone's fault." When she says this last, her eyes shimmer, and she dabs at them, soaking up the tears before they fall.

"Bad things happen. They just do." She says it like a mantra, as though she is trying to convince herself.

"Yes, Ruth, they do."

She doesn't look at me, just gazes at the tissue she clutches. "They just do."

TWENTY-NINE

EDEN DAVENPORT

"I wish Shadow was here."

"Who's Shadow?" I ask.

"My dog. He makes me feel safe."

"You don't feel safe here, Eden?"

She avoids the question. "Do you have a dog?"

I shake my head and smile. "I have a cat."

She frowns. "You don't like dogs?"

"No, I love dogs," I tell her. "But I'm gone so much it wouldn't be fair to have a dog. Cats are easier. They don't require much attention. They pretty much do what they want."

"What's your cat's name?"

"Cleopatra."

"Queen of the Nile."

"That's right. She's definitely the queen of the house."

Eden is sitting on the couch with her knees tucked into her chest, a protective position.

"If you would like to bring Shadow with you next time that's okay with me."

Her eyes light up. "Really?"

"Is he potty trained?"

"Oh, yeah, for sure. He only pees and poops outside on the grass."

"That's good. Then he's welcome." I lean forward and rest my elbows on my knees. "So, what color is your room at home?"

She scrunches up her nose in thought. "Well, two of the walls are yellow, and one of the walls has pink wallpaper with yellow and light-purple flowers on it, and the fourth wall isn't really a wall, it's my closet, and the doors are white."

"That sounds like a lovely room."

"It used to be, like, all white, but then when I turned nine, my mom said I could decorate it however I wanted. I got to pick the paint colors and the wallpaper. And my mom painted it and put up the wall-paper all by herself."

"All by herself?"

"Well, I helped a little, but mostly she did it herself. She did Jonah's room, too. He was only three, so he couldn't pick out his own colors or anything, but Mom got blue paint and used some of the yellow paint from my room and put up this really cool border that has LEGO *Star Wars* pictures on it."

"Wow. She sounds like a really cool mom, huh?"

The corners of her mouth turn down. "She was."

"She *was*?" I repeat. Eden purses her lips but says nothing. "She's not cool anymore?"

The girl remains silent. Such a pretty thing, with freckles on her cheeks and nose and bright-blue eyes and strawberry-blonde hair just like her mother's.

"Eden?"

She lets out a breath. "If you can't say something nice, you shouldn't say anything at all."

"You know, that's true. But in here, it's a little different. In here, we get to say whatever we want to say, even if it doesn't sound nice. And the things you say won't hurt anyone, because you're only saying them to me, and maybe what you tell me can help me help your family to get better. Does that make sense?"

She nods. "I want my family to get better. I want my mom to get better. I want her to be like she was before. But I know she never will be."

"Why is that?"

"Because!" She kicks her feet out angrily. I'm glad for it. Up until this moment, Eden has been too calm and composed. She needs to unlock her emotions if she is to work through her grief. "Nothing will ever be the same without Jonah! Duh!"

"You're right. It won't be the same. But do you think it's possible that it could be good again? Different, but good?"

She considers my question. "Not unless my mom gets better. But it's like, she doesn't even want to. She just wants to lie in bed and be sad and think about Jonah. And that makes me feel sad and mad at her, too, and mad at myself because of what happened."

"Eden, why are you mad at yourself for what happened? It's no one's fault. You know that, right?"

She doesn't answer, just gives me a stony look as she tucks her knees back against her chest.

I repeat her aunt's words to her. "Bad things happen. They just do."

When her silence continues, I make a note and change directions.

"What's the biggest thing you would change about your mom right now, the one thing that would let you know she's getting better?"

She chews at her bottom lip. I consider how to rephrase the question, but before I do, she answers.

"I would want her to know I'm there," she says. She puts her hand to her throat and coughs a little, then sucks in a breath. "It's like, she doesn't see me anymore. She doesn't see anyone."

Except Jonah, I think. The one person who isn't there.

THIRTY

Rachel Davenport

"I don't want to be here," she says. She sits on the couch, her posture as it was in the family room, shoulders hunched, head on her chest. "I just want to go home and go to bed. I'm so tired. So, so tired." I know she is still being medicated, although strictly monitored with a lower dosage. The effects of going off an antidepressant cold turkey can be devastating. Rachel is lucid, although markedly sluggish.

"I understand," I tell her. She shakes her head, almost imperceptibly.

"No, you don't. You say you do, but you don't."

"As I mentioned earlier, I have experienced loss, Rachel."

She raises her head and stares at me. "Was it your child? Your baby boy?"

"No."

"Then it's not the same." She drops her head.

"May I ask you a question, Rachel?"

"Stop saying my name as if you know me." Her words are slow and measured and devoid of aggression or force. "You don't know me."

"You're right. But I'd like to get to know you if you'll let me."

She turns to look out the window, her eyes faraway. "You don't want to get to know me. If you knew what kind of person I am, you wouldn't."

"What kind of person are you?"

She faces me, then closes her eyes. "It doesn't matter anymore."

"Why doesn't it matter what kind of person you are?"

"Because it's too late to change anything."

"What would you change if you could?"

"Everything. I don't like talking. It takes too much energy. I'm so tired." She stretches out across the couch, resting her head on the arm. She stares at the ceiling. "This is more comfortable than I thought it would be."

"From what I hear from the people who know you, you're a terrific person," I tell her. For a moment, I think she didn't hear me. Then she shifts on the couch and turns her head to face me.

"Maybe they don't really know who I am."

"Why don't you tell me who you are."

She returns her attention to the ceiling. "Can I go home now? I really don't want to be here. I don't like being outside the house right now. Maybe someday I will again. Maybe I'll like going out and doing the things I used to do."

"What kinds of things did you used to do?"

"I don't know. I can't remember."

"Did you like going to the movies?"

"I guess."

"How about shopping?"

"Not really. Sometimes, maybe. If there was a good sale."

"What about hobbies?"

"Writing. I have a blog. *Had* a blog."

"That sounds interesting. What else?"

Rachel continues to stare at the ceiling. She is quiet, but I can't tell whether she's pondering my question or if she has checked out of the conversation. A moment passes.

"Do you believe in ghosts?"

Her question takes me by surprise. "Do you believe in ghosts, Rachel?"

She laughs quietly. "I asked you first."

I smile, even though she isn't looking at me. "In all honesty, I don't know if I believe in ghosts. I believe there are a lot of things in the world that we can't explain." I pause. "On the day you took the pills, you thought you saw Jonah."

"Ruth told you?"

I don't confirm or deny. No use throwing Ruth under the bus. "It was in your chart from the ER. Dr. Lahey made a note."

Rachel purses her lips. "I did see Jonah. I didn't *think* I saw him. I did."

"Okay."

"You say 'okay' like you don't believe me. But he was there."

"I say 'okay' because I believe that you believe it."

"But you don't."

"Rachel, I wasn't there. I only know what you're telling me. Did Jonah talk to you? Did he say anything?"

"No. I think he wanted to, but he didn't, or couldn't. I don't know."

"Had you taken any of your medication when you saw him?"

"It wasn't the pills. And I'm not crazy." She pushes herself up to a seated position and looks directly at me. "I wasn't trying to kill myself. I just wanted to help Jonah. I was worried that maybe he's stuck, like he can't move on, and I wanted to help him get to heaven. Jonah belongs in heaven. He was a perfect, sweet, wonderful boy who shouldn't be stuck in this awful place where perfect, sweet, wonderful boys can be taken away in an instant because their mothers were too caught up in bullshit and neglected them!"

"Rachel, I need you to take a couple of deep breaths, okay?"

She presses her fist against her mouth and stifles a moan. Then she follows my directions and takes two deep breaths, letting them out on a sigh. I circle back to what she just said.

"Rachel, you didn't neglect Jonah."

Tears stream down her cheeks. I stand and carry the box of tissues to her. She looks at the box as though she has no idea what it is. I set it on the couch next to her.

"You don't know what I did or didn't do," she tells me, her voice soft and terse at the same time. "You weren't there." Using my own words against me.

"Would you like to tell me what you did that you feel was neglectful to Jonah?"

She shakes her head and wipes her nose on the sleeve of her sweater.

"Would you like to talk about something else?"

"I just want to go home. I'm so tired."

"I know you are, Rachel. But you're here already. Might as well use our time. I really want to help you and your family. And in order to do that, I'm going to need you to talk to me . . . just a little bit, so I know how best to help you."

She doesn't respond, just stares at me expectantly. The tears have stopped, but her eyes are swollen and her nose is red and wet.

"Can you talk a little bit about you and Sam?"

Her shoulders tense at the mention of her husband's name.

"Sam," she says, as if testing out the word. "Sam is Sam, green eggs and ham."

"How long have the two of you been married?"

"Thirteen years."

"How did you meet?"

A moment passes. "Blind date."

"I met my husband on a blind date, too. Where did you go? What did you do?"

She gives me an ambivalent look. "We met at a club." I nod and wait for her to continue. "It was near the campus, walking distance." Her expression shifts slightly as she connects to the memory. "It was one of those places with the drums and the neon paints."

"I've never been to one, but I've heard they're fun."

"I suggested it, you know, when we talked on the phone. I wanted to see . . ." Her voice trails off.

"What, Rachel? What did you want to see?"

"I don't know. I guess I wanted to see if he was . . ." She shrugs. "Adventurous. I used to be. Adventurous. Now I don't even want to leave my house. My bed."

I urge her back on track. "So you suggested the club and he agreed?"

She nods. "He told me he'd be wearing an Eddie Munster T-shirt. You know, from that old TV show? And there was this guy at the bar when I got there, and he was wearing an Eddie Munster T-shirt." She looks at her lap. "He wasn't really . . . I mean, he was so . . . He wasn't at all what I expected. He didn't look anything like my friend Leah described. And I thought maybe I could just sneak out without him seeing me. I didn't want to be mean, but he . . ." She shakes her head. "I figured I could call him later and tell him I got food poisoning or something." A quiet chuckle escapes her. "So I kind of backtrack to the entrance, and just as I'm walking out the door, in comes this other guy wearing an Eddie Munster T-shirt. What are the odds? And it was Sam. Looking just like my friend said he would. And he got this big smile on his face and took my hand, and that was it."

"That's a great story. Thank you for sharing that with me. How long did the two of you date before you got married?"

She stands suddenly. "I don't want to talk about Sam anymore." She moves toward the door, wringing her hands together, her anxiety rising with each passing second. I can tell that she is done.

"I want my sister," she says. "I want Ruth. I want to go home. I'm sorry, Doctor. I'm really sorry. I'll do better next time. I promise. I just need to go. I just need to go *now*."

I follow her to the door and put my hand on her arm. "It's okay, Rachel. I understand. And you've done very well today. You should feel really good about taking this first step."

"Feel really good," she repeats, her voice hollow. "I'm afraid that I won't ever feel really good about anything ever again."

"I know. That's why you're here." I squeeze her arm and watch as her eyes fill with tears. "Come on. I'll take you to Ruth."

THIRTY-ONE

MADDIE

I let myself into the house and head straight to the kitchen, where I pour myself a tall glass of water. I drink it slowly, staring out the window to the darkened yard, and thinking about the Davenports.

I catch movement in my peripheral vision and turn to see Cleopatra slink toward me. She rubs herself against my ankles and starts to mewl. Her coat is silver gray, shiny and sleek, and her eyes are peridot green. I kneel down and stroke her, and her purr is instantaneous. She allows me to pet her for thirty straight seconds, then turns and trots across the tile floor to her bowls. I dutifully follow her and grab the bag of cat food from the cupboard and measure out a quarter cup. I freshen up the water and leave her to it.

A half an hour later, I'm on the couch, wearing my yoga pants and a loose-fitting T-shirt, rolling a joint. On particularly difficult days, this is how I decompress. With marijuana. I tried drinking wine, which I enjoy, but the nightly calories wreaked havoc on my waistline. A psychiatrist friend of mine offered me a prescription for medical marijuana, which he said helped him unwind. The particular kind of weed I smoke is mild. It relaxes me without making me crazy, helps me to distance myself from my patients' grief, and occasionally it opens my mind to possible treatment solutions for particularly difficult situations. I only take one or two hits, never more.

Peter texted me earlier to let me know he had a dinner with the partners of his firm and didn't know how late he would be. I sent a reply, telling him not to worry, to enjoy the inevitable cigars and cognac that accompany such a meal, and if we couldn't FaceTime tonight, we'd make up for it tomorrow.

Cleopatra has graced me with her presence. She lies on the other side of the couch, summarily ignoring me, but the fact that she is within reaching distance speaks volumes. I know that if I scooted closer and started to pet her she would jump down and move to another room, so I pretend to ignore her and am content with her aloof company.

I light the joint and take one long draw, hold it in for a beat, then exhale slowly. I set the joint in the ashtray on the coffee table and recline against the back of the couch.

The Davenport file sits next to the ashtray. This morning's sessions are still fresh in my mind. I thought of the family throughout my day, between patients, at lunch, on the drive home. Something is going on with each of them.

When faced with a devastating loss of a family member, most healthy, well-adjusted individuals will experience survivor's guilt. It's natural. But with this case, each person exhibits feelings of guilt that run far deeper than I would expect. During their sessions, each one apologized, even when an apology wasn't necessary. Each confessed or, at least, almost confessed to having done something wrong, something that caused Jonah Davenport's death.

Jonah was hit by a car. He was not neglected or abused or battered by his parents. He was not pushed down the stairs by his older sister. He didn't find his aunt's fibromyalgia meds and take half a dozen of them. What happened was an accident. A terrible, horrible, tragic accident.

I reach over and pick up the file, open it, and gaze down at the smiling face of a five-year-old with enormous dimples, curly brown hair, and intelligent, amused brown eyes. I stare at Jonah's image for a while and try to imagine him as he was in life.

I think of how Sam described him, the precocious child with the enormous hands and affection for bugs.

"I don't kill spiders, either, Jonah," I tell him. "I get my husband to do it."

Peter and I discussed having children and opted not to. I was thirty when we met, and he was thirty-seven. Neither of us was too old to have them, especially in this day and age. But Peter had never felt the need and I was ambivalent, for good reason. I'd already endured the loss of my parents and my fiancé, all of whom had the supreme misfortune of being in the wrong place at the wrong time. I thought about my parents' car accident and the shooting, and I wondered, how on earth can you keep a child safe? And the answer that came to me was, *you can't.*

So I buried my biological clock and agreed with Peter that we didn't need to have children, that I would be fine without them. And I have been. My life is fulfilling. I work with many children, and helping them gives me a kind of maternal satisfaction. My relationship has never suffered sleepless nights or the waning sexual desire of the sudden shift of focus that couples experience and men tend to resent. In my life, I try not to waste time with regret or wondering *what if.* But there have been rare moments over the last ten years when I've pondered the other path I could have taken.

Now, as I look upon Jonah Davenport, I know, with all my heart, that I made the right decision.

"They love you, Jonah," I tell the photograph. "They love you and they miss you and they don't want to let you go. They're holding on to you. But they're holding on to something else, too. Each of them. What is it? What are these things they cling to?"

The photograph can't tell me what I need to know. But my intuition tells me that if I can get the Davenports and Ruth Glass to open up, they will find the map that will safely guide them through their grief.

My cell phone chirps from the coffee table, and I set the file down and pick up the phone. A text from Peter. Going to be an early one. No cognac or cigars. Thank goodness. I'm exhausted from you keeping me up all night last night. I'm about to fall asleep in my mashed potatoes. FaceTime in 30? You can sing me a lullaby.

I smile and text him back. I'll see you then.

I set the phone down, get up, and head into the kitchen, suddenly hungry. I pull a premade kale salad from the fridge and eat it standing up at my kitchen counter, watching the clock on the microwave, waiting for my husband's call.

PART THREE: THE DAY BEFORE

THIRTY-TWO

JONAH

I'm up, I'm up, I'm up! Mommy hasn't even come in to get me awake, but I'm already up 'cause I can't sleep 'cause I'm too excited to sleep. Today is the big Easter egg hunt. They call it a spring egg hunt at school, which I don't think sounds as good, and everybody knows it's an Easter egg hunt, but Daddy says they call it a spring hunt because they don't want to make anybody upset. I don't know why anyone would be upset about saying Easter, 'cause Easter's a really fun holiday and on Easter morning I get a big basket with chocolate bunnies and jelly beans and Peeps. But Auntie Ruth says the Jews get mad about Easter. I don't know what Jews are, but I don't argue with Auntie Ruth, and anyway, I don't want anybody to get mad, so if they want to call it spring egg hunt, that's okay by me.

I'm not as excited as I am on Christmas morning, but almost. Christmas morning is better 'cause Santa brings lots of presents. Eden says Santa is a figent of my imagination. I don't know what that means. I don't think I have a figent, at least not last time I checked, but I do know that Santa always gives me what I want, like the LEGO *Star Wars* Millennium Falcon that I put together in only one day and Mommy said I was a genius for doing it so fast. Anyways, it's not like Christmas morning, but it's pretty darn good, too. In some ways, hunting for eggs is better than hunting for bugs, 'cause you can't eat the bugs—'cept

Daddy says that some people *do* eat bugs, but not me, no way. I'd have to kill 'em first, and I'd never kill my insect friends.

Anyways, today I get to hunt for yummy eggs, and tomorrow I get to hunt for bugs, which is the best of both worlds.

I climb out of bed and go to my dresser. Mommy usually pulls my clothes out for me, but I'm going to do it myself this morning. I pull out my pants and a shirt and a clean pair of unders. Mommy and Daddy have a rule about clean unders every day, so I take off my jammies and put them on top of my dresser for later, then take off my unders and put them in the hamper, then put on the fresh ones. Then I pull on my pants and put on my shirt and I run for the door. Then I remember that I forgot to get socks, so I run back to the dresser and grab some socks from the top drawer and stuff them into my pocket for putting on downstairs.

Eden's door is still mostly closed, like it is every morning. She's not up yet. Mommy always says she has to drag Eden out of bed, but she doesn't really do it, 'cause that might hurt Eden. This one time, I heard Mommy yelling that she was going to pour a glass of cold water over Eden's head if she didn't get up right that minute. But her yelling wasn't mad yelling, it was kind of laughing yelling, and I knew she wouldn't do it 'cause Mommy's too nice to pour water over anybody's head.

Mommy and Daddy's door is still mostly closed, too, but I know Daddy is already up and at 'em 'cause I can smell that coffee smell from the kitchen. I go to Mommy and Daddy's bedroom and I look inside and see that Mommy is still in bed, her head on the pillows and her arm kind of slung over her eyes, but I can tell she's almost awake 'cause she's not making that snoring noise, and when I push open the door, she takes her arm off her eyes and looks over at me and smiles real big.

"Good morning, my angel boy," she says. "You're up early."

"I am," I say back. "It's the spring egg hunt day at school."

"Is it really?" she says in that kind of surprised kidding voice she sometimes has. "I didn't know that."

"You did, you did!" I holler at her. I climb up onto the bed, and she scoots over and gives me a big hug. I really love Mommy's hugs because her arms are strong and she does it like she means it, not like Auntie Ruth, who kind of pats you on the back and then pushes you away, like it's a chore or something. Don't get me wrong, I love my auntie. I just don't like her hugs too much. But Mommy's are the best, probably 'cause she's my mom and I'm her best guy.

"I guess maybe I remember something about an egg hunt at school," she says. "Look at you, already dressed. Wow, you're getting to be such a big boy. You won't need me for too much longer, will you?"

"I'll need you forever," I tell her, because she's my mom, and even when I'm all big and grown-up, she'll still be my mom.

She hugs me again, and my nose smooshes against her neck and her hair tickles me and I smell flowers.

"Why don't you go downstairs and ask your dad to put some bread in the toaster for you? I'll get dressed and wake up Eden, and I'll be down lickety-split."

I nod at her, then remember how naughty Eden can be about getting up. "We can't be late for school, Mommy. Not today. Any other day, but not today."

She makes a serious face. "We won't be late."

"Promise?" I ask, just to make sure.

Mommy crosses her heart. "We will not be late. That's the truth, the whole truth, and nothing but the truth, so help me."

"Okay, then," I say, and Mommy smiles.

"Love you, my guy."

"Love you, too, Mommy."

I jump off the bed and run to the door, then go down the stairs. Shadow is standing at the bottom of the stairs, kind of like he's been waiting for me. I pet him on his back, then scratch at his ears 'cause that's what he likes, and he licks the side of my face with his big pink tongue.

My feet are cold, so I sit on the very bottomest step and put my socks on. Then I put on my shoes and tie the ties like Eden showed me. I get it wrong the first time, but then I get it right the second time.

I go to the kitchen. Daddy's sitting on a stool at the counter, and he has his big mug that says "World's Best Dad" on it that Eden and me gave him for Christmas, even though it was really Mommy who bought it and wrapped it and then had Eden and me write our names in the card. Eden said my writing was too sloppy, but Daddy read it just fine and he was so happy to get our present, he got up from the floor where he opened it and went into the kitchen to put some coffee into it. He uses it every morning unless it's dirty from yesterday. Then he uses the Minion mug instead. I like the Minion mug better 'cause I love the Minions—they're so funny—but I know he likes his "World's Best Dad" mug, so I don't say anything about it. I'm just glad he likes the present from Eden and me.

"Hey, Buster Brown," he says when he sees me. He gets off the stool and bends his knees so that I can look right at his face. "Are you ready for some coffee?"

I can't stop the giggle. "I don't drink coffee, Daddy. I'm too young."

He makes a funny oops face. "Of course you don't. What was I thinking?"

"Eden says coffee stunts your growth." I don't know what *stunts* means, but the way she said it, I know it's not a good thing.

"Well, lucky for me, I don't need to grow any more," Daddy says. He stands up tall and walks to the fridge. "So, what's your poison? OJ? Milk? *Almond* milk?"

I'm big enough to know that he's only joking about poison. It's a funny thing to say about something I'm going to drink, but grown-ups sometimes say funny things and don't even know they're funny.

"OJ?" I ask, and he nods.

"Coming right up."

"Mommy says can you put some toast in the toaster?" I ask him.

"Your wish is my command."

I know what that means, 'cause I saw *Aladdin*.

"Thanks, Daddy," I say, and he smiles at me, then reaches down and picks me up and gives me a squeeze.

"You're very welcome, Jonah bologna."

He sets me down and goes back to the fridge and pulls out the OJ and the loaf of bread.

"So, what's on your agenda today?" he asks.

I don't 'zactly know what a 'genda is, but I think it's like what I'm going to do. It's silly that he asks, 'cause he knows what I'm going to do. But it's fun, too.

"It's the spring egg hunt at school today," I say and feel myself get all excited all over again.

"That sounds like fun. I wish I could have a spring egg hunt at work."

"You could, Daddy," I tell him. "You could hide eggs all over your office and let your friends find 'em."

"You know what?" he says. "That's a great idea. It's too late to do it this year, but next year . . . Will you help me hide them?"

I smile at my daddy, happy that he needs my help. He's like a superhero guy—he fixes everything when it breaks and he can lift really heavy stuff and he can draw anything and he knows everything about sports. Him needing my help makes me feel glad. I already can't wait till *next* year.

THIRTY-THREE

EDEN

I can hear Mom coming down the hall, and I put my pillow over my head. I hate getting up in the morning. I know I'm not supposed to hate anything because *hate* is a bad word and Dad says that hating can make you sick. But I've always hated getting up, and I've never felt sick because of it. I don't know why school can't start later. I mean, like, why can't we go at ten or eleven instead of eight fifteen? It's stupid. I'm not supposed to say *stupid*, either, but it just is.

"Good morning," Mom says from outside my door in her happy voice.

"I'm awake," I tell her from under the pillow.

"Wonderful," I hear her say. "Why don't you get out of bed and get dressed without me having to yell? We have to get to school on time this morning. You know what day it is, right?"

I let out a groan, and I know she hears me because I can feel her in my room next to my bed. All of a sudden, the pillow is yanked off, and my mom's big face is staring down at me. I roll over away from her and pull my covers over my head.

"It's spring egg hunt day," she says, like I didn't know that already. They've been talking about it at school all week, like it's some big deal. It's not, not for me, because fifth graders don't get to look for eggs—we just get to watch the little kids look for eggs and make sure they find them and don't wander off too far from the school. Like that's a big deal. I'm sure.

"I don't get eggs," I say from under my blankets.

"You know your brother will share," she says. And I know she's right. Jonah will give me anything I want, even the cookies-and-cream eggs that are his favorite. He'll give them to me to make me love him because he's not sure I do. Of course I do, he's my brother, but I let him think maybe I don't just to get the cookies-and-cream eggs.

"You know what else today is?" my mom asks, yanking at my covers. "The last day of school before spring break."

She's right. I hadn't thought of that. Just one more day, then we're off for a whole week. Some of my friends are going skiing. I don't know what Mom and Dad have planned, but I know it's not skiing. Still, it'll be fun just to not have to go to school.

I throw off the covers and sit up in my bed. My mom is smiling at me and now that I'm, like, totally awake, I can't help but smile back.

"I like spring break," I tell her.

"A whole week of sleeping in," she says, then she winks at me.

"I can handle that," I say, and we both start to laugh. She leans over and gives me a kiss on my cheek and I reach up to hug her, which I kind of don't do very much anymore, now that I'm getting older. She looks kind of surprised but then puts her arms around me and squeezes.

"See you downstairs in a few, okay?"

I nod and she leaves and I climb out of bed and head to my closet. I put on my favorite pink-and-yellow dress and grab my white espadrilles. My pink sandals would go better with my dress, but the school doesn't allow shoes with no toes, so I can't wear them. I pull a scarf down from the rack, a scarf that belonged to Nanny, and tie it around my neck, then I go into the bathroom and try to brush through my hair. Mom said I have to start taking responsibility for my hair, but it's hard to get through the tangles. I'll have to ask her for help and she'll give me that face, but she'll help because Mom always helps when you ask her.

I give up on my hair and go downstairs with it all tangled and hanging down my back. Shadow is standing at the door to the kitchen, and he licks my hand when I walk by him. I stop and pat him on the head and tell him he's a good boy, and he makes a snorting kind of sound and follows me into the kitchen.

Jonah's already sitting at the table with a plate of toast and a glass of OJ in front of him. He looks up at me and smiles.

"Hi, Eden!" he says, and I feel my lips wanting to smile, but it's totally not cool to be so excited to see your annoying little brother, so I kind of wave at him as I go to the fridge.

"Hey, piece of pumpkin pie," my dad says. He grabs my arm and swings me into him so he can give me a kiss.

"Morning, Dad," I say.

"Dad," he says, kind of like an echo of me saying it. "I sure miss you calling me Daddy. It happens, I know. You're growing up. But I miss it." He makes a really dopey sad face, kind of like a clown would make, only without the makeup.

"You're silly, Dad. And anyways, Jonah still calls you Daddy."

"Anyway," my dad says. "Not anyways."

"Okay, Dad. Whatever."

My mom walks in, and Dad turns to her and says, "Whatever."

She looks at him then makes a *W* with her thumbs and index fingers and holds it up in front of her face. "Whatever," she says. After a few seconds, they both start laughing, and I don't know why it's so funny, but in a minute I'm laughing, too, and then so is Jonah and then the four of us all are laughing, and even though it's like, totally lame, it kind of feels good.

I pull some milk out of the fridge, then turn to Mom. "I need help with my hair."

She raises her eyebrows at me. "I can see that."

Dad has already put the box of cereal on the kitchen table, so I take a bowl from the cupboard. For just a really small second, I think about how I couldn't reach the bowl cupboard when school started last year, but now I can. Mom and Dad said I had a growth spurt, which sounds kind of icky if you ask me, but it just means that I got a little bit taller. And my tummy kind of stretched up, where before it was a little bit sticky-outy. I like being a little bit taller, and not just because I can reach the bowl cupboard. But because I'm going to middle school next year and I want to look like a sixth grader.

I go to the kitchen table and take the seat next to Jonah, then grab the box of cereal and pour some into my bowl. Shadow is sitting next to the table pretending not to watch us eat, like he always does.

"I'm so excited!" Jonah says to me. "You know what today is, right, Eden?"

I roll my eyes even though Aunt Ruth says it's not polite.

"It's spring egg hunt day!" he hollers, like it's the best thing that ever happened to him.

"I know already," I say. "Big deal."

"Yeah, it is," he says, like he thinks I was seriously saying it was a big deal. "I'm gonna find lots of eggs, Eden. And I'm going to give you all the cookies-and-cream ones."

I'm about to say something mean, like how the egg hunt is totally lame, but then I think about what he said, really think about it, and I get this kind of weird tight feeling in my chest. My brother is just a little kid and he bugs the crud out of me, but even though he's only five, he's always thinking about me and wants to make me happy. And I feel kind of ashamed that sometimes I'm not very nice to him.

"You don't have to give me all of the cookies-and-cream ones, Jonah. You should keep them for yourself. They're your favorite."

"But I want you to have them 'cause you like 'em, too," he says. And he smiles at me like I'm the best sister in the world, even though I know I'm not.

"How about we share them. Fifty-fifty," I say, and he scrunches up his nose like he has no idea what I mean. "Fifty-fifty," I repeat. "Half for you and half for me."

He nods happily. "Fifty-fifty."

I hold up my hand for a high five, and he slaps at it, misses the first time, then hits it the second time.

"Hurry up, guys," Mom calls from the other side of the kitchen. I look over and see that she's next to the fridge, holding a mug of coffee in her hands, and Dad is standing next to her and looking at her funny. She looks at him, but like really quick, and then looks away really quick, too. "We can't be late for school today."

"I've, like, heard that a million times already," I say, but still I eat really fast. When I finish my cereal, Mom does my hair, and it hurts so bad when she brushes through my tangles. I try not to cry, but sometimes I can't help it.

I grab my backpack and Jonah's, too, just to be helpful, and Jonah and I follow Mom to the minivan. Jonah is giggly and excited, and I kind of want to roll my eyes again, but I make my eyes stare straight ahead while he sings about Peter Cottontail coming down the bunny trail.

Mom pulls up to the outside of my school, and a kid in my class, Dane Terry, opens the door for us. It's called valet service, and I did it last month and I'm gonna do it again at the end of the year. Jonah gets out first, I get out second, and Mom gives us a wave, then drives off so the cars behind us can pull forward.

"Kindergartner?" Dane asks, because the valet kids have to walk the kindergartners to the kindergarten gate.

"I'll take him," I say, like I say every morning. I look down at Jonah as he reaches for my hand. This time, I can't stop my eyes from rolling.

"We don't have to hold hands, you know," I tell him.

"Mommy says," he tells me back. And she does, and I'll get in trouble if he tells her I wouldn't hold his hand. So I grab his chubby little fingers and we walk to the kindergarten gate and I'm kind of annoyed about it, but then when he lets go of my fingers at the gate, I kind of miss how his hand feels in mine, all warm and stuff.

"'Bye, Eden!" he says really loud. "See you at the egg hunt."

I nod, embarrassed, then duck my head and walk to my class.

THIRTY-FOUR

SAMUEL

The coffee finally finishes its second brew cycle. Eden takes a seat at the kitchen table next to Jonah as Rachel crosses to me. We stand side by side, my wife and I, listening to the final chuff and wheeze of the machine.

"I think that might be the best sound in the whole world," she says.

"Better than the laughter of your children?" I ask, and she gives me a sideways grin.

"It's a tie."

I grab Rachel a mug from the cupboard and set it on the counter next to mine, then pull the carafe from the machine and pour. Rachel tops both mugs with half-and-half, then turns and leans back against the counter. She takes a few sips of coffee and gazes at the center island.

"Why didn't we ever get bar stools for the island?" she asks.

"We still can," I say. "Any reason in particular?"

"So I could bring a stool over here and just sit next to the coffee machine until the pot's empty and I'm fully caffeinated."

"If you want, I can design a built-in pullout chair for you right here." I tap the cupboard behind her.

"What a guy. Always thinking." She looks at me, and her expression turns serious. "Hey. Are you okay?" she asks.

I focus on my coffee.

"Sure, why?"

"You tossed and turned all night." She scoots in closer to me and uses her sexy voice. "Maybe if you'd taken me up on my offer, you would have slept better."

I force a chuckle. It sounds false. She steps away and grabs the dish towel from the oven handle. She wipes a drop of coffee off the counter and glances over at me.

"What's going on, Sam?"

"Work's a little crazy, the usual. Don't worry about it."

"It doesn't feel like the usual," she says. I turn and look at her, expecting her scrutiny, but her attention is on the kids.

"Hurry up, guys," she tells them. She glances at me, her expression unreadable, then she turns back to them. "We can't be late for school today."

"I've, like, heard that a million times already," Eden snipes. Honestly, I don't understand kids' obsession with the word *like*.

And *dude*. *Dude*, it seems, is a cross-generational word. We used it when I was growing up, and kids use it today. Thankfully, Eden hasn't embraced it, but I know, sooner or later, it will become a major part of Jonah's vocabulary.

"I'll be back in twenty minutes," Rachel says. "Will you still be here?"

I glance at my watch, even though I already know the answer. "I have to leave in ten."

She looks disappointed. "You sure you're okay? Do you want to meet for lunch to talk?"

I shake my head. "I've got a lunch meeting." Even as the words come out of my mouth, my stomach turns over. I kiss the top of her head. "I'm okay, honey. Really." Not really.

"Mom. Hair."

She gives me a last speculative glance, then turns to Eden. "You could say please."

153

"You're the one who doesn't want to be late," Eden reminds her.

Rachel gives Eden a wide-eyed look. "And it's your hair not mine, missy. I don't expect you to grovel, but *please* would be appropriate."

"What's grovel?" Eden and Jonah say at the same time, then they both laugh.

"It's what your dad does when he wants a special kiss."

"Funny," I say. "It's what your mom does when she wants a new piece of furniture."

Rachel throws the dish towel at me, and we both laugh.

"I still don't know what that means," Jonah says.

"It's when you get down on your knees and beg because you want something so much," Rachel tells him.

"I'm not doing that," Eden says.

"I'm not asking you to," Rachel says. She crosses her arms over her chest. "I'm waiting."

Eden sighs. "Will you *please* do my hair, Mom? Pretty please with a cherry on top."

"And whipped cream!" Jonah chimes in. "And almonds and chocolate sauce."

"Yes, my lady, your wish is my command."

This is the Davenport dynamic at work, jokes and questions and laughter. I love the interplay of my family. I know I would miss it if I didn't have it.

Rachel follows Eden out of the kitchen. I finish my coffee and rinse the mug in the sink as Jonah gets up from the table. I watch him take the crust from his toast and hold it out to Shadow. Very gently, Shadow takes the crust, then trots to his bed, where he proceeds to devour it. Jonah brings his plate over, sets it on the counter, and looks up at me.

"I'll find some eggs for you, too, Daddy. And for Mommy and Auntie Ruth. I'll find so many, we can all have them."

His brown eyes are twinkling, and his wide grin makes his dimples look huge. My heart gives a tug. I reach down and ruffle his hair.

"Thank you, little man."

"I'm not a man," he says, then giggles.

I pretend to be very serious. "Not yet, you're right. But you will be very soon."

He throws his arms around my waist and squeezes my middle. "Love you, Daddy."

I bend over and hug him back. "Love you, too, Buster Brown."

He pulls away. "I gotta go, Daddy."

"I know. You can't be late."

He races toward the living room, then stops and turns to me. "What's your favorite kind of egg?"

I think for a moment. "Peanut butter."

He smiles. "That's good. You can have 'em all."

"How very generous of you."

"What's generous?" he asks.

"It's when you give a lot of what you have to someone else."

He contemplates this then gives me a doubtful look. For a five-year-old, he's got the doubtful look down. "I don't think it's me being ge-ner-ous, Daddy. 'Cause I don't like the peanut butter eggs."

I smile at him. "But you like the cookies-and-cream eggs." He nods vehemently. "And you're going to share them with your sister." He nods again. "I would say, my guy, that you are extremely generous. The proof's in the pudding."

He nods back at me. "Okay. Good. I'm glad we got that settled." He races out of the room before he can hear my laughter.

When they're gone, the house is quiet. I take my mug from the dish drain and pour half a cup, leaving the rest of the pot for Rachel. I carry the mug to the table and sit down. For a moment, I'm lost in my thoughts. I love my family. I do. So much it hurts sometimes. But. *But.* No, there is no *but.* Except, there are temptations. And possibilities.

Shadow watches me from his bed. As if sensing my conflicting thoughts, he rises and pads over to me and lays his head on my thigh.

His soulful eyes dart up at me, then dart away, then dart back to me. Ordinarily, I would shove him off my work slacks, worrying that his hair will leave a trail. But his warmth and sensitivity soothes me, so I stroke the fur of his head and neck instead.

"Good boy, Shadow. You're a good dog." He licks my hand in agreement.

I check my watch and realize that Rachel will be home in a few minutes. I don't want to be here when she gets back. She'll pepper me with more questions, questions for which I have no answers. Not yet, anyway. I nudge Shadow aside, and he seems to take it in stride, trotting off to the back door, where he moves through his doggy hatch to the backyard.

For the second time, I rinse my mug and set it in the dish drain, then head for the living room. I grab my tweed jacket from where I hung it on the banister, pick my briefcase up off the floor of the foyer, and leave the house.

The day is bright and sunny, a perfect spring morning. Easter is two days away, and we'll celebrate it here. Ruth is coming, of course, and Rachel wanted me to invite my client Joel Conrad as a kind of setup. I told her I didn't think Easter was an ideal blind date venue, and she gave her typical Rachel look—exasperation coupled with disbelief and amusement. I didn't mention that Joel Conrad is not a suitable prospect for her sister because his idea of the perfect woman is an eighteen-year-old with triple-E breasts.

As I get into the car, I check my watch. I turn the ignition and back out of the driveway. Before I reach the asphalt, a shiny new red Accord rockets past as if the driver is trying to break the sound barrier. Our street is long, with not a single curve, and often drivers step on the pedal, oblivious to the fact that there might be children playing. Our community started a campaign to install speed bumps, but the initiative has yet to reach the city council.

When all is clear, I reverse into the street. Just as I shift into drive, I see the minivan coming toward me. Rachel slows as if to stop, but I only wave at her as I step on the accelerator. I see the look of puzzlement on her face as I pass, and I carry that image with me as I make my way to work.

Toward the possibilities.

THIRTY-FIVE

RACHEL

I drop the kids at the valet and slowly pull away so the cars behind me can move up. As I wait at the exit to make the turn, I glance in my rearview mirror and see Eden and Jonah walking hand in hand toward the kindergarten gate. I've watched them do this every day since the start of the school year, but it still makes me smile. I know that in a few years, when Eden's a teenager and Jonah is in middle school, they won't want anything to do with each other, so I make sure to hold this image in my mind and in my heart where I can cherish it.

I circle to the back of the school, where Lisa Grant is waiting for me by her behemoth Sequoia. I double-park next to her and roll down the passenger window and grab the sheaf of papers on the seat.

"Morning, lady," she says.

"Hey." I hand her the papers. "We've got a ton of donations for the gala."

"Awesome sauce," she says. "Time for coffee?"

Ordinarily, I would accept the invitation. I love coffee with Lisa. We chat about everything and nothing, and because she is snarky and hilarious, I spend a good deal of the time choking on my latte because I'm laughing so hard. But I want to get home and catch Sam before he leaves for the office.

"Rain check?" I ask, and she nods.

"Next week for sure," she says.

I pull away and head for home, hoping my husband will still be there.

Something's going on with Sam, and I can't figure out what it is. He's still the same guy. He isn't acting strangely. He still jokes with the kids and helps Eden with her homework and asks them both questions about school. He still strokes my back in bed and kisses me hello and goodbye and helps with the dishes and talks to me about annoying or high-maintenance clients. But for the past week, I've sensed something, a shift, just below the surface. He's not wearing a sign. No one else would even notice. But we've been married for thirteen years, and I can tell he's not entirely himself.

I hope it's not a midlife crisis. Sam's a little too young for that, but you never know. Maybe his business is in trouble. Maybe he wants to switch careers. Just before I got pregnant with Jonah, we had a conversation about that. I think we'd been drinking, and he told me that he'd always seen himself as a high school teacher, teaching wood shop and coaching the football team. I'd been surprised. In all the time we'd been together, he'd never mentioned anything like that. But I told him I would support him if he really wanted to make a change.

Then Jonah came along and we had a family of four, and when I brought it up to him again, he said it wasn't practical to make a career change, what with two kids and a mortgage. He wasn't angry or resentful when he said it, just matter-of-fact. And then he admitted that he knew he was a good architect and he would probably suck as a high school teacher, and we never discussed it again.

It might not be about work or his age. It might be something small and stupid, like he just discovered gray hair in his pubes or a wart between his toes. I just wish I knew. What's that line from *The Matrix?* It's the not knowing that drives you mad.

Maybe Sam and I need a little alone time. We haven't had a date night in a while. Usually we're good about carving out couple time, but both of our schedules have been crazy lately.

I decide to call Ruth when I get home to see if she can watch the kids tonight. It's their first night of vacation, and we always do something as a family to celebrate, like dinner and a kid-friendly movie or an hour at the nickel arcade. But we can push that off until tomorrow night. Ruth might not be available at such short notice, although I can't imagine my sister having any big Friday night plans. Anyway, I can ask. I just want to give Sam an opportunity to talk about whatever it is that's going on before it gets any bigger.

When I make the turn onto our street, I see Sam pulling out of the driveway. He shifts into drive and I make to stop so we can chat through our open windows, but he doesn't even slow down, just smiles and waves at me as he passes. Disappointed, I pull into my spot on the left side of the driveway.

I don't have a lot of time to worry about Sam. I need to get focused. I only have a few hours before I have to pick up Jonah from school, and I need to do my blog. The kids are going to be on vacation next week, so I want to make sure I have all of my posts for the next seven days ready to go. My sponsors pay me to be consistent, after all. It's not much, but the money I make pays a bill or two and gives me a little extra cash to play with.

Sam was funny about me starting a blog. He thought there were other ways I could more effectively spend my time, and he pointed out that 90 percent of blogs never gain any kind of following to speak of and are mostly just the stream of consciousness (aka masturbation) of people who have too much time on their hands. He didn't tell me not to do it. He would never tell me not to do something I really wanted to do. He told me to go for it. But he was surprised when my blog took off and downright shocked when I started making money on it.

"So, companies pay you to review their products? And women read your reviews? And then, if a woman reads your review on a particular brand of diapers and buys those diapers by clicking on a link from your blog, you get a percentage of the sale?"

"Yep." I tried not to be smug, and to his credit, Sam was happy for me and told me over and over again how proud he was of me.

"I have to do something with my time," I told him. "Lounging on the couch eating bonbons gets boring after a while."

We laughed at that, because we both knew that a mom's life leaves little room for couch lounging and the consumption of chocolate-covered ice-cream bites.

When I walk in the door, Shadow greets me, tail wagging enthusiastically. He kisses my hands, and when I bend down, he jumps up to kiss my cheeks.

"Good boy, good boy."

He circles around me and glances out the open front door, sniffing the air. When I close it, he crosses to the living room window and looks outside, then looks at me and gives me a strident bark. Our usual morning routine.

"The kids are at school, Shadow," I tell him. "Don't worry. They'll be home soon."

He cocks his head to the side as if he doesn't believe me. "They're fine, I promise." He barks again, then trots behind me as I go the kitchen.

I hand him a Milk-Bone, and he carries it to his bed and lies down to eat it.

I set my cell phone on the kitchen table next to my laptop, then boot up the computer. I have the impulse to text Sam about our possible date night but figure I should check with Ruth first. I pick up the cell and call her landline, knowing full well that if she's home, she won't answer her cell. When she doesn't pick up, I try her mobile and when she doesn't answer that, I leave a message.

"Hi, Ruth, it's me. Where the heck are you at eight thirty on a Friday morning? Anyway, give me a call back when you have a minute. Thanks, 'bye."

Sam was good enough to leave some coffee behind. I grab my mug from the dish drain and pour myself a cup, cream and sugar it, and take it to the table. I spend the next thirty minutes checking my personal e-mails and the messages on my blog server. When I'm finished, I glance at my phone, surprised I haven't heard back from Ruth yet. I shoot her a quick text, set my phone down, then open the folder on my desktop that has all my new blog posts for the coming week.

Halfway through the final polish on the third post, my cell phone rings. My sister's face appears on the screen, and I chuckle, as I do every time she calls and I see her picture. Her expression is exasperation and mock disdain. She disapproved of my taking her picture to put into my contacts and would not give me a smile, no matter how much I pleaded with her. I took the pic anyway, and she was so mortified that this was the face I would see every time she called, she offered to smile for me. I refused. She called me a brat, and I stuck my tongue out at her. No matter that we're in our thirties and forties—that sister thing never completely goes away.

"Hi, sis," I say upon answering. "Where are you? I've been trying to reach you all morning."

"It's not even ten thirty yet, Rachel. 'All morning' is a bit of an exaggeration."

I mouth the word *whatever* to myself.

"I had therapy this morning," she tells me, as if I should have known.

"Sorry, Ruth. I thought that was Wednesday."

"It is, usually. Dr. Moore had to switch it this week."

"How was it?" I ask.

"Good," she says. "I think we're making progress."

"I'm so glad," I tell her, as I always do.

I know why Ruth sees a therapist, and I support her 100 percent. She's had a tough time, what with Charlie leaving and starting a new family. I can't imagine how that must have been for her, to be abandoned for another woman, and to know that woman stole her life, the life Ruth was supposed to have. *My* life, if I think about it, or one that closely resembles mine. When it first happened, I wanted to wring Charlie's neck. He was like the big brother I never had, and it felt like he betrayed me, too. But my pain was nothing compared to my sister's.

Ruth has been seeing this doctor for over a year now, but I haven't noticed a discernible difference in her behavior or her actions. She still locks herself away in her apartment night after night, never goes out with friends, and she still hates all men on the face of the planet, including my husband and our father, who's been dead for twenty-five years.

"So, what's up?" she asks. "You called for a reason or just to say hello?"

"Both. Um, do you have plans tonight?"

"No. Just catching up on my TiVo, as usual. Is this an invitation or a babysitting request?"

"Babysitting request. Sam and I need some alone time. Do you mind?"

"Not at all. I'd love to," she says, and I smile. I can always count on Ruth. "What time do you need me?"

"Let's say six? And I'll order you guys a pizza."

"Don't be silly. I'll bring a lasagna. I can make it this afternoon."

"You don't have to do that," I tell her, even though my kids love her lasagna.

"I know, but I will. See you later."

"Thanks, Ruth. I appreciate it."

I hang up and immediately shoot a text to Sam. Fancy a date tonight? Ruth can sit for us.

I watch my screen, waiting for a reply. After a couple of minutes, I set the phone down. He's probably in a meeting. I return my attention to the blog post, which is a review of a new eco-friendly fabric softener with no dyes and no artificial perfumes that doesn't make your laundry smell like dirt, which I'm definitely in favor of. I've even agreed to highlight the product on the top banner of my webpage for a month—for a small advertising fee, of course.

As soon as I move on to the next post, my phone beeps. I swipe the screen and see a text from Sam.

> Was going to call, babe. Carson wants to take a run out to the Hewitt project. He's worried about the deadline. You know the drive. I could be pretty late. Rain check?

I feel myself deflate. I know I can't be upset. This kind of thing happens in the life of an architect. He told me this morning that work was crazy, and I know that makes him stressed, and that's probably all there is to him being a little off this week. His work pays the bulk of the bills and the mortgage, so what can I say, really?

> Disappointed, but I understand. Drive safe. Want me to save dinner for you?

Again, I stare at the phone expectantly. He doesn't text me back.

THIRTY-SIX

RUTH

I don't like lying to my sister, but sometimes lying is a necessity.

I wasn't at therapy when she called. My therapy was Wednesday morning, as always. But I couldn't tell her where I was. She wouldn't understand. *I* don't even understand.

I have a new routine. It began last month with a random occurrence. I was at the pharmacy on Euclid, which I don't frequent, but my usual pharmacy was out of my medication and sent me to their other branch downtown. The pharmacist could have had my prescription sent over, but I didn't want to wait, was down to my last three pills, so to expedite things, I took the option of going myself.

As I was coming out of the store, I happened to look across the street and saw a group of young mothers pushing their strollers into the adjacent park. Charlie's new wife was among them, although calling her his *new* wife is rather inappropriate, since they've been married for over a year. She was pushing a double stroller, and there was another woman who looked like a teenager pushing a single stroller beside her.

I felt nauseated and exhilarated at the same time, and more than that, I felt like my will was not my own. I crossed the street, compelled by some perverse need to see my husband's family up close, and surreptitiously followed the group into the park. I kept at a fair distance, not wanting to be noticed. I've never met Charlie's wife in person—I've only seen her picture on Facebook—and I have no idea if she knows what I look like, but I didn't want to take any chances.

They went straight to the playground, just inside the park gates, and I kept walking, pretended to be interested in something on my phone, ducking my head as I gazed at the lifeless screen. I found a park bench on the other side of the playground from where the group of mothers had stopped and encamped. I watched them, obscured by the jungle gym, these mothers who had the luxury and blessing of coming to the park on a Friday morning. They all looked very much the same: fit, wearing designer jeans and light sweaters, their hair—various shades but predominantly blonde—perfectly coiffed, their makeup perfectly applied, their countenances carefree. Charlie's wife was older than the others, but not by much, and she looked like a magazine image of a mother, with her highlighted shoulder-length locks, button nose, and pink lipstick.

The teenager was clearly her nanny, and I held very ungracious thoughts toward both Charlie and his wife. I don't have children (and never will), but the idea of turning over a great percentage of your child's care to someone else seems like throwing away a gift.

I sat and watched as Charlie's new wife released the twin girls from their confines and let them run free. The nanny pulled the infant boy out of his stroller and handed him to his mother. She set him across her lap and laid a small blanket over him as she covertly fed him from her breast.

I watched and watched, and imagined that this could have been my life if I hadn't been defective, if only my uterus and ovaries had been compliant to my demands. I could have been a part of this group of women. I would have been older by many years, but they would have accepted me and loved me, and we could have shared advice and diapers and stories of wonder of our babies' firsts and complaints of sleeplessness and our impatience to stop nursing so we could drink again.

I left the park that day in complete emotional turmoil, which I couldn't share with my sister or anyone else in my life. I tried to reach my therapist, but it was a Friday, and he was unavailable until the following week.

I've been coming to the park every Friday since then. I tell myself I won't, but then I do. It's almost like an addiction. I know there's no harm in it, except . . . except a part of me dies every time I see her with her three children. Charlie's children. The children I couldn't give him.

It was a blessing when Rachel asked me to babysit. The scene at the park this morning left me feeling sorry for myself and so damn empty and unfulfilled and useless. I didn't know what to do with myself. Just because you are not physically able to bear children doesn't mean your biological clock doesn't tick. The maternal stimulation that Jonah and Eden provide is exactly what I need.

As I pull into the garage of my apartment building, my phone chimes with an incoming text. I park in my assigned slot and pick up the phone. The text is from Rachel.

Sam has to work late. Don't need you to babysit.

My heart drops, and I feel tears threaten. Then the phone chirps again. Want to come over anyway? We can put the kids down early and have a girls' night in.

I take a deep breath and blow it out very slowly. Then I type a response. Sounds lovely. Should I still bring the lasagna?

A moment later, she replies. You supply the lasagna, I'll supply the wine.

I smile through my tears. *Thank God.* I don't think I could handle a night by myself in front of the television. Not tonight. It will be good to be with my sister without Sam around. We haven't had much girl time lately. Maybe I'll tell her what I've been doing these Friday mornings. I haven't told my therapist. I should, but I can't. I'm ashamed.

Maybe I can tell Rachel. She'll probably laugh and make me feel silly, but that might be okay, too, because it is silly. And I need to stop. And telling Rachel might help me stop. Perhaps she and I can make a standing date to have coffee every Friday morning. Except the kids are off next week, so she won't be able to make a date with me until after they're back in school. *Then you have another week of watching.* I'm conflicted by the thought. Angry with myself for having it, and relieved that I don't have to give this up just yet.

Maybe I won't tell Rachel tonight. It can wait.

I get out of the car and walk to the elevator. Just as I press the "Call" button, the doors slide open. Judd Stevens, my downstairs neighbor, steps out. He is in his late forties, tall and lanky with an open, honest face. A professor of literature at the local college. A widower. He smiles when he sees me.

"Hello, Ruth," he says. "Just on my way to school. How are you this morning?"

He holds the elevator door for me, and I step in. "I'm well, Judd. Thank you. How are you?"

"Other than my sciatica, I'm just grand. Say, when are you going to come down and share that bottle of wine with me?"

The first time he asked me down was two months ago. He'd received a wonderful bottle of Château Lafite Rothschild from the dean at the college, and he didn't want to drink it alone. He said only a woman of my character could truly appreciate a wine such as this. I'd asked for a rain check, but I never assumed he would actually wait for me.

"Hmm. I don't know." I feel my pulse rise, but not in a good way, and all I want to do is get up to my apartment where it's safe.

"Come on, Ruth. We've been neighbors for a year and a half. You know my intentions are completely honorable. It's just a glass or two of wine."

My eyes meet his, and for a single moment, I wonder what the hell I'm so afraid of. I was never like Rachel, impetuous and gregarious and reckless. But I was also never the simpering, tragic figure I've become.

Before I can stop myself, I say, "I'm free tomorrow night."

His smile grows wider. "Wonderful. Around seven?"

"Shall I bring some cheese?"

"You'll bring nothing but yourself, if you don't mind." He winks at me. "See you then?" he asks, almost as if he suspects I'm going to cancel at the last minute, which I probably will.

But for just these few seconds, I allow myself to imagine that I am a woman who has actual plans tomorrow night.

"See you then," I say.

When I step into my apartment, I notice that the air smells stale. I take off my jacket and hang it in the closet, then I spend a few minutes opening windows throughout the apartment. The cool April breeze whispers through the cracks, carrying with it the fragrance of sunshine.

I go to the little corner desk in my living room and sit down. I pull out the second file drawer and peruse my recipe folder, then find the lasagna recipe. Luckily, I already have all the ingredients, although the sausage will need to defrost.

I think about Judd Stevens. Maybe I should make a second lasagna to bring tomorrow night. We don't have to eat it. He can put it in his freezer for another night. Then I realize that if I make a second lasagna for him, I'll really have to go. My stomach clenches at the thought. I haven't been alone with a man since Charlie. I don't know if I remember how to behave.

I decide to make a second lasagna for myself. If I happen to keep the date—oh God, did I just say *date*?—I'll take it to him. And if, more likely, I cancel, I'll put it in my freezer and save it for another meal with my sister's family. The kids love my lasagna. Possibly as much as they love me.

I pull the sausage out of the freezer and set it on the counter to defrost. My thoughts shift from Judd Stevens to Charlie's new wife and his new family. They're perfect, those children. Blond and gorgeous, I can tell from across the playground. Of course they are. Why wouldn't they be?

I know it's wrong to resent innocent children, and, really, my resentment isn't directed specifically at them. But they should be *my* children. Not *hers* and Charlie's. *Mine* and Charlie's.

I don't like the direction of my thoughts, but I can't really start the lasagna until the sausage thaws, so I march into the living room and sit on the couch and turn on the TV. I scan all of my recordings and settle on an episode of *Bones* from several years ago that I never watched.

A grown woman watching her TiVo at eleven o'clock on a Friday morning is pathetic. But there are worse things I could be doing. Worse things I've done.

THIRTY-SEVEN

SHADOW

I don't like being alone. I like it much better when my humans are home. I like it best when all of them are here, but if it's just one, that's okay.

My mistress and Little Male and Little Female and my master left the house. I don't know how long I was alone—I can't really tell how the time goes by. But then my mistress came home. She patted my head and gave me a treat and that made me happy because I like treats even better than the food in my bowl.

I'm on my bed now, eating my treat, while my mistress sits at the table staring at the little screen. There's nothing alive on the little screen right now, just squiggly lines, and her fingers are tap-tap-tapping, and more squiggly lines come on the screen with every tap.

I start at the knobby end of my treat and crunch through it. It tastes a little bit like the bendy strips my humans give me sometimes. Those are the best, and my tongue goes out of my mouth and drops of drool fall on the floor when I'm sitting waiting for them to give me one.

I finish my treat and feel my insides move. I get up and go through the small door that's just for me in the big door. I go to the grass and sniff around for a while, trying to find the right place to make. Finally, I find it, over by the fence. I squat. Up on the branch of the tree from the other side of the fence is a bird. It shakes its feathers and looks down at me. I sniff the air and can smell the bird's wings and the worm it ate.

I try to cover what I made with my back paws, but the grass never covers it. I hear something from the front of the house, and I go back inside. My mistress is still sitting at the table, but she isn't tap-tap-tapping. She's looking at her little screen. Her face is not happy.

I go into the couch room, behind the couch, and stand at the window. I see the front yard, the grass that I'm not allowed to make on. I see the sidewalk that sometimes I walk on when my humans put my collar on and attach it to a long rope. I see the dark, wide strip where the cars move back and forth. I see the sidewalk on the other side of the dark strip. I see, sitting on that sidewalk, the cat.

I push my nose against the window, hoping this time I can go through it, but the cold hits my nose and I pull away. The cat sees me, or somehow knows I'm here. It stiffens and turns its furry head in my direction and stares at me and then yawns.

I feel the fur on my back go up, even though I didn't make it so. My ears perk forward. The cat meows, and I hear it through the window. A whine happens in my throat, and then I bark. And then I bark again, and then I'm just barking and barking and I paw at the window and the cat is just staring at me with a face that looks like it thinks it's better than me, which is not so because dogs are better than cats because dogs eat cats and cats can't eat dogs.

I bark and bark and my mistress comes into the room and I hear my name come from her mouth. I stop barking and turn to her. Her hands are on her hips, and she has an angry face.

"Shadow, no!" she tells me, and I whine and sit back on my haunches. I'm a Good Boy and I listen to my humans. But the cat is still there. My mistress says something else, and I don't know what her words mean, but her voice sounds not angry anymore, so I wag my tail at her. She walks over to where I am. She says something I can't understand, and then she says *the cat* and then something else, and I know she saw the cat. She pats my head and calls me a Good Boy, and I want to be a Good Boy for my humans, but I also really want to bark at the cat.

My mistress walks back into the kitchen, leaving me sitting, looking out the window.

The cat arches its back and stretches its paws, turns around and shows me its backside, jerking its tail from side to side, like it knows I'm watching.

I want to get the cat. I don't know exactly why—it's just something inside me. I don't want to eat it. I just want to get it and show it that dogs are better and stronger and just more good than cats.

If I have the chance, I'm going to get the cat.

THIRTY-EIGHT

Jonah

Oh my gosh, oh my gosh. It's time! This day has been so long, the longest day in the history of the world. I don't know why they don't do the spring egg hunt when we first get to school. They make us wait till after lunch, which is like forever. Mommy said it's because the teachers don't like us to have sugar first thing in the morning, but I told her that didn't make sense 'cause I have cereal or pancakes for breakfast sometimes and they both got sugar in them. But Mommy said that cereal and pancakes have other things in them that are good for you and that Easter eggs are, like, 100 percent sugar, and that 100 percent sugar can make you all jumpy and excited and make you not be able to do your work in class. But I couldn't do my work in class anyways 'cause I was too excited thinking about the egg hunt!

When we finally got to have lunch, I was almost too excited to eat the sandwich Mommy packed for me, but I knew I wasn't supposed to eat the eggs unless I had something good for me in my tummy. So I ate the whole thing, and the carrot sticks and the string cheese she sent, and I ate it all real slow, so it would take time. Then we got recess, and I played on the jungle gym with my friend Jesse, and he said he was going to find the most eggs and I told him, no, I was going to. The one who finds the most eggs gets to take home Marco, Mrs. Hartnett's stuffed monkey, for the whole vacation. I want to take Marco home so bad.

After recess, my teacher made us line up by the gate and handed all of us the paper baskets we made yesterday for putting the eggs into. We've been waiting here for five minutes while the fourth and fifth graders are hiding the eggs. Jesse kind of sneaks over to the side of the building and looks around the corner like he's trying to see where the big kids are hiding the eggs, and my teacher calls him back with a real serious voice and tells him now he has to go to the end of the line. He kicks the ground and makes a mad sound, but he goes.

Then all of a sudden, a fourth or fifth grader comes around the side of the building and says they're ready. I jump up and down, but in my place 'cause I don't want to get sent to the end of the line. Then Mrs. Hartnett looks at all of us and repeats the rules. I don't need to listen 'cause she already told us them this morning, and they're just about being nice and respectful, not grabbing or pushing or shoving, and everybody already knows that anyways. Then she tells us that as soon as we hear the whistle, we all need to stop finding eggs and march straight over to the four-square courts and that anyone who doesn't won't be able to win Marco. I'm glad I listened to that last part 'cause I kind of forgot about it.

Then my teacher raises her hand and says, "Happy hunting!" And I dash around the corner toward the big-kid playground, with all my classmates running along with me.

The fourth and fifth graders are all standing in a big circle around the jungle gym, blacktop, and field area, watching us kindergartners find eggs, making sure we're not fighting or anything. I see Eden over by the monkey bars, and I give her a big wave. She must not have seen me because she doesn't wave back, but I don't have time to think about that right now 'cause I got to find my eggs.

While most of the other kids go onto the big-kid jungle gym, I duck underneath it, because I know that's a good place to hide eggs. And I'm right, 'cause they're everywhere. I can't even count how many I put in my basket, but lots and lots, and then, when Jesse and some other kids follow me under, I scramble out the other side and go to where the grass starts. I see so many eggs hiding in the long grass! I get down on my hands and knees and kind of crab walk along the grass, scooping eggs into my basket. I pretend I don't see the ladybugs on the grass—they're called Coccinellidae—'cause if I stop to look at 'em, I won't get as many eggs.

I'm just grabbing a couple more when I hear the whistle. My fingers are already on them, so I scoop 'em up and put 'em in my basket and then I march over to the four-square area. I can't believe how fast that hunt went! And I think I got a lot of eggs, but when I look at other kids' baskets I see that a lot of my classmates have a lot of eggs, too, and I think maybe I'm not going to win Marco after all. I still get to keep all the eggs for eating and sharing with Eden and Mommy and Daddy, and that's good, too, but I sure do wish I could take Marco home.

Our teacher puts us in another line along the four-square lines and tells us to all sit down where we are. Then she tells us to count the eggs in our baskets. She tells us that if we have too many to count, we should put them in little groups of five. I can count to a hundred, so I don't need to make little groups, but I know some of my classmates can't count that high yet.

I dump over my basket and a couple of my eggs go rolling over and one of them hits Cindy in the side of her leg. She grabs it and goes like she's putting it with hers and I tell her it's mine. She sticks her tongue out at me but hands it back, and I'm glad 'cause I don't want to fight, I just want to count 'em all, and what if we had 'zactly the same number of eggs, but her taking that one of mine made her have one more than me? That would be stinky winky.

I count my eggs, all the way up to forty-seven eggs. There's lots of cookies-and-cream for Eden and lots of peanut butter for Daddy and lots of plain chocolate for Mommy. I want to eat one so bad right now, but I know I have to wait until everybody's counted and the winner is picked.

I look around to see what kind of piles my classmates have and whether they look bigger than mine, but I can't tell. Finally, Mrs. Hartnett asks us to raise our hands when we're done counting. Most of us put our hands up, but a few kids don't, so she goes over and helps them count, then tells them how much they got.

"Okay," she says. "Moment of truth." I'm not sure what that means, because you should always tell the truth every moment. "We're going to go down the line and call out how many eggs we found. Ready?"

And so we do. I'm sort of in the middle of the line, and every person up to me doesn't have as many as me. Jody came real close with forty-five, and he's all excited until I shout out, "Forty-seven."

Then I get all scared that someone after me is going to say forty-eight or fifty or something. A few kids have forty and forty-four, and then it's Jesse at the very end of the line, and he looks at me with kind of a mad face and says, "Forty-six."

"Well, that means that Jonah Davenport is the winner!" Mrs. Hartnett says, and she's giving a real big smile and I'm smiling real big right back at her because I *won*!

"Okay, everyone," she says. "It's time to go back to class. Grab your eggs, and let's go."

I pack mine up real fast and as I'm walking toward the kinder area, I see Eden. She's talking to someone, but I'm so excited about winning Marco and finding all the eggs to share, I run over to where she is and give her a great big hug.

"I won, I won, I won!" I yell at her. "Isn't that great, Eden? I get to bring home Marco, and I got so many cookies-and-cream eggs you're not going to believe it!"

Eden isn't hugging back, but that's okay. I must have sort of scared her. She steps away from me, but she's not looking at me, she's looking at one of her friends, and her friends walk away.

"I won," I tell her again.

"Good for you, Jonah," she says, but she's kind of got a mad face on. Then she runs to catch up with her friends, and I think how funny she is that she's not even excited about the cookies-and-cream eggs.

Then I remember that I won, and I race over to the rest of my classmates and we head for the classroom and I start to think about Marco and having him for a whole week.

THIRTY-NINE

EDEN

I walk with my besties, Carlee and Ava. Mr. Libey leads all of us across the blacktop toward the jungle gym and the field to hide the dumb eggs. There's like twenty of us fourth and fifth graders on the spring egg hunt committee. I didn't even want to be on the committee, but Carlee talked Ava and me into it. She told us we get out of class and that we could, like, totally steal some eggs when we were hiding them for the kindergartners. And then Ryan raised his hand to be on the committee, and when I saw him, I kind of raised my hand, too. Not that I like him or anything. I mean, he's kind of cute. He's got blond hair and big blue eyes and he makes jokes that are really funny. Not like Matt. Matt's funny, but he makes jokes that are really mean, like making fun of other kids. Ryan doesn't make fun of anyone; he just says stuff that makes you laugh. But I don't like him, you know, that way. Okay, maybe I like him a little.

"I like the Butterfinger eggs best," Carlee says.

Ava shakes her head. "Not me. I like the peanut butter ones."

Corwin Kwe is walking right behind us, and when Ava accidentally drops her paper bag full of eggs, he picks it up really fast and hands it to her. I think maybe Corwin likes Ava, which is kind of funny because he's really short and she's like the tallest girl in fifth grade. She snatches the bag out of his hand and doesn't even say thank you, just sniffs and turns away, which I think is rude, but I don't say anything because Ava will say something mean to me, like, "Oh, aren't you just Miss Goody Two-shoes, Eden?"

Anyways—oops, *anyway*, the committee spends about ten minutes hiding all the eggs for the kindergartners. Ava and Carlee head to the grass. I'm following them, holding my paper bag full of eggs, but then I see Ryan go to the jungle gym and I sort of turn and head in the same direction. I grip the paper bag really tight, and my hand feels really sweaty all of a sudden and I'm not sure why. I switch the bag to my left hand and wipe my palm on my dress.

Ryan puts a handful of eggs on the swinging bridge, then looks over at me. His bangs are a little bit long over his eyes, but I can see that his eyes are kind of crinkly at the corners like he's grinning.

"You eat any?" he asks.

Mr. Libey told us we weren't allowed to eat any of the eggs, that they were for the kindergartners, even though I know for a fact that Carlee and Ava both scarfed down like four each when nobody was looking.

I think about telling Ryan a lie, 'cause I don't want Ryan to think I'm a geek, or a Goody Two-shoes, or something. I pour some eggs onto the platform next to the slide and shake my head.

"Nah. Me neither." He shrugs. "They're for the little kids. And I guess the committee gets to share whatever's leftover, if there is any. At least, that's what happened last year. Hey, we should hide some underneath, what do you think?"

I look down at the ground under the jungle gym, then back up to Ryan. He's smiling and nodding like he's excited to be doing something no one else thought of. My dress will get totally dirty, and if I rip it Mom will be so mad, but I don't care. I nod back at Ryan, and we both drop to our knees and start crawling along the blacktop, pouring out eggs as we go.

"This is beast," Ryan says, and I can't help but giggle. It's totally beast.

"What're you guys doing under there?" Ava's voice. "Kissing?" I hear Carlee laugh, and then Matt joins in.

"Ryan and Eden are under the jungle gym *kissing?*" Matt shouts. My cheeks go hot again, and when I look at Ryan, he's frowning. And even though it's dark under here, I can tell that his cheeks are red, too. He scrambles out from the other side of the jungle gym as fast as he can. I crawl out on my side, stand, and brush the dirt and pebbles from my dress. Ava and Carlee and Matt are still laughing. I glare at them.

"Shut up," Ryan says. "You guys are total losers."

"Okay, committee!" Mr. Libey calls from the four-square courts. "It's time to bring out the kindergartners. Make a wide circle and keep an eye out for any shenanigans."

I walk over to the monkey bars and cross my arms over my chest, then look over to the kindergarten gate. I pretend I don't see Carlee and Ava come up beside me.

"God, we were just joking, Eden," Ava says. She doesn't sound sorry at all, and that makes me even madder.

Out of the corner of my eye, I see Carlee nudge Ava's arm. Then Ava takes a big deep breath. "I'm sorry, Eden. That was mean."

This time, she sounds like she means it. I turn to her and shrug. "Whatever."

Just then, the kindergartners race across the blacktop and start scrambling toward the eggs. I see Jonah running really fast, a big smile on his face. He waves at me but I don't wave back, because even though Ava apologized, I'm still a little angry and embarrassed. I take a quick peek over at Ryan, who's standing in the circle by the field. He's looking at me, but when he sees me, he turns away real fast like he doesn't want to be caught. My cheeks do that stupid red thing again, and it takes the whole spring egg hunt for them to cool off.

The hunt lasts, like, all of five minutes and then it's over. The teachers take the kindergartners over to the four-square court to count their eggs, and the fourth and fifth graders start wandering back toward our classrooms, but because we got out of doing work for the egg hunt, none of us are in any hurry to go. Ava and Carlee and me are walking side by side, and Ryan and Matt are kind of a little bit behind us. I want to look back at Ryan, but I don't let myself.

Just then, Corwin Kwe runs up to Ava and holds out his hand. I see four peanut butter eggs on his palm. "I got these for you, Ava."

I'm thinking that was really nice of him and how would I feel if Ryan handed me my favorite eggs? I guess I would feel kind of warm and fuzzy. But Ava pulls her lip up in a sneer and looks at Corwin like he's some kind of nasty bug.

"Ew. Like I'd ever eat something that was in your dirty little hand."

Carlee and Matt start laughing. Corwin blinks real fast and looks like he's going to cry.

"I think Corwin likes you, Ava," Matt teases. "I think he *really* likes you."

My stomach turns over, and I feel kind of how you feel before you throw up. I want to tell Matt to stop, that he's not being nice, but everyone else is laughing, even Ryan, so I don't know what to do. Then Corwin stamps his foot and throws the peanut butter eggs on the ground.

"I—I—I would never like you. You're like the w-w-worst person ever. You're bad at math and you're so stuck-up."

My stomach twists again. I can't believe Corwin just said that. Nobody ever talks to Ava like that. I look at her, and her eyes are squinting down at him.

"Why don't you go play in the street, Corwin," she says. Carlee and Matt laugh. Ryan and I look at each other, and this time I don't look away and neither does he. Corwin wipes at his nose, then runs away from us and toward the classroom. I feel totally bad for him because I know what's going to happen. Ava and Matt and Carlee are going to tell everyone what happened, and everyone is going to be laughing at him and making fun of him for the rest of the school year.

We all start shuffling toward class again, and I kind of slow my steps so that Carlee and Matt and Ava can go ahead. Ryan and I are walking side by side.

"What's your favorite egg?" Ryan asks.

"Cookies-and-cream," I tell him.

"Hey, mine, too. What's your favorite kind of candy?" he asks, and now my stomach doesn't feel bad—it just feels kind of fluttery because Ryan's talking to me and asking me what I like.

I think about my favorite kind of candy, and I wonder which candy is Ryan's favorite, and whether he'll think my favorite candy is good or bad, or whether he likes it, too—wouldn't that be cool if my favorite is his favorite, too?—but before I can answer him, Jonah knocks into me and throws his arms around me and starts babbling at me.

"I won, I won, I *won*!"

My friends make sounds of surprise as Jonah squeezes me and jumps up and down.

"How *sweet*," I hear Ava say, but I can tell by the way she says it that she doesn't think it's sweet or nice or good at all. She starts to snicker while Jonah babbles on.

"Isn't that great, Eden?" he says. "I get to bring home Marco, and I got so many cookies-and-cream eggs you're not going to believe it!"

"Kindergartners are so lame," Matt says.

"I know, right?" Carlee says. "I hate my little brother."

I tear Jonah's arms from my waist and step away from him. I look over at Ryan. He gives me a strange look, then trots to catch up with the others. I want to tell him what my favorite kind of candy is, Fun Dip, but now that Jonah interrupted us I won't get to, probably not ever. *Thanks a lot, Jonah!* I glare down at my little brother. He looks so happy and excited, and I just want to smack him.

"I won," he says again.

"That's great, Jonah." I turn away from his smiling face and follow my friends, hoping Ryan will slow down so we can finish our conversation.

He doesn't.

FORTY

SAMUEL

I gather the blueprints and schematics from the conference table and roll them up, heaving an inward sigh of relief. The meeting with Greg Talbot and his partner, Bob Jacobs, went well. Better than expected. We have a few more details to iron out, but I'm fairly sure they'll be signing contracts with us within the week. Carson will be elated. We're a small, boutique firm—up till now, a two-architect operation with only a handful of employees—but recently we've discussed expanding, bringing in some twentysomethings to mentor. As soon as Talbot and Jacobs are a done deal, Carson and I will have to revisit that conversation.

My prospective clients stride from the small conference room. From the doorway, Greta gives me a covert thumbs-up and a closed-lip grin. She crosses to the table to clear away the coffee tray, the cups, and the plates of half-eaten scones. I glance at her as I secure the blueprints with a paper clip.

"Celebratory lunch?" she asks. Her hands are overfull, and I relieve her of three of the plates. "Thanks," she says. She smiles warmly at me, causing a stirring that has become familiar, if not altogether comfortable, at the sight of her smile.

We head to the kitchenette at the end of the floor. She lowers the coffee tray into the sink then takes the plates from me, her fingers brushing against mine. She tosses her head, and I smell peaches and vanilla. I don't know what the fragrance is—Rachel would probably know—but it's soft and subtle and sexy.

"What do you think?" she asks as she turns on the faucet and rinses the dishes. "Orsini's?"

Orsini's is an Italian restaurant about four blocks from here. Pricey, delicious, and *public*. I took Greta to Orsini's six months ago, the day I gave her a raise. Carson was with us. Greta is my assistant exclusively, but *our* employee, and he felt he should be part of the celebration. There was nothing untoward going on between Greta and me. And there still isn't, not really. But the idea of taking Greta to Orsini's today doesn't feel right.

Things have shifted between us since that lunch. The occasional lingering stare, the accidental touch as we pass each other in the hall, the not-so-accidental neck rub at the end of a long day. I'm not certain what these things mean. I don't want to assume or make too much out of what could merely be workplace-inspired flirting and faux intimacy. That happens all the time, right? But it doesn't feel that way with Greta. And I need to find out. No. I *want* to find out. There's a difference. The latter merely signifies curiosity, whereas the former suggests a foregone conclusion. I keep telling myself that, anyway.

"How about sandwiches from Capellini's?" I propose, and she nods.

"Even better. I'll order the usual."

She turns her attention to her task, and I take a last look at her before heading to my office. I carry her image with me as I go. Young. God, she's young. Twenty-three or -four. Long legs; high, ample breasts; full lips; and a lovely pert nose. And her eyes. Green with flecks of gold. Beautiful in and of themselves, but beguiling mostly because of how they look at me. With adoration. No one has looked at me that way for a very long time.

Not that Rachel doesn't love me. But she doesn't look at me the same way she once did. Marriage tears off the rose-colored glasses and forces us to look at each other for who we are rather than who we want each other to be. Rachel accepts me, warts and all. And I accept her for who she is. But I sometimes miss being adored. Which is why I can't seem to stop thinking about Greta.

I am self-aware enough to understand that as I careen toward my golden years, I reminisce more often about my younger days, about the high school quarterback and cheerleader magnet I once was, when a forty-yard pass was all it took to fulfill me. I know it's ridiculous and borderline pathetic, especially considering the life I have now. But despite the knowing, I find it impossible to bury my attraction—lust— for my assistant.

I grab my cell phone from the inside pocket of my suit jacket, then remove my jacket and hang it on the hook of my office door. I glance at the screen and see the missed text from Rachel. Disappointed, but I understand. Drive safe. Want me to save dinner for you? I reread the earlier text asking if I fancied a date tonight and the response I'd sent just before my meeting. Was going to call, babe. Carson wants to take a run out to the Hewitt project. He's worried about the deadline. You know the drive. I could be pretty late. Rain check?

It's not exactly a lie. Carson wants me to check on the project today because we're a week behind schedule. However, my partner has a din-ner event with some local muckety-mucks, so he will not be joining me.

I sit at my desk and wake my computer. The machine whirs to life, and the familiar screen saver materializes on the monitor. A Davenport family selfie Rachel took during a trip to the mall over the holidays. Our faces are smashed together, and we're laughing.

Through my office window, I see Greta sashaying to her desk. She cocks her head to the side and peers at me, catching my stare. She winks, then shakes her mane flirtatiously and sits down. A moment later, Henry Beecham, our bookkeeper, approaches her with a file folder and sets it down on her desk. I watch them interact for a few sec-onds. Greta is completely professional, no winks or grins or coquettish mannerisms of any kind, and I am relieved that she reserves that behavior for me alone. Relieved and ashamed. Ashamed that I am relieved.

I manage to force her and Rachel—because thoughts of Rachel are always intertwined with thoughts of Greta—from my mind in order to focus on my work. I open a current file, which wipes the family selfie away and replaces it with digital schematics. I'm working on a 3-D rendering for a restaurant just off I-5. My father would have hated this software program, which allows me to move walls and windows and alter the structural elements with a few taps on the keyboard. Dad was old-school all the way, and his favorite part of the business was making models. But I have fully embraced the digital world and welcome any tool that will streamline my workload. Within minutes, I'm happily immersed in my design.

As usual, I lose track of time. I'm just saving my changes when I hear a knock. Greta stands at the open office door and holds up a large paper sack. I glance at the clock on my computer, then through my window to see that the rest of the office is empty. Everyone is already at lunch.

"Should I come back? I can stick these in the fridge."

"No," I tell her. "Your timing's perfect."

She grins at me. "Always has been."

She walks to my desk and sets the sack down, then takes a minute to shuffle some of my papers out of the way. Her fingers are long, the nails medium length and painted coral red, and for a brief moment, I imagine them raking across my skin. I stifle the thought quickly, before it can betray me. I close the restaurant file, and Rachel's and the kids' faces reappear. Rachel's smile looks accusing. I put the computer to sleep as Greta sets out the food. She grabs the chair across from me and scoots it next to the desk, then sits.

"Italian combo, the works," she announces as I unwrap the sub from its parchment paper encasement. "And don't worry." She grins. "I've got Altoids in my desk."

"You think of everything," I tell her as I take a bite.

"Yes. I have."

I look at her. She is watching me closely, a small smile playing at the corners of her lips.

"You were great this morning," she says. "Your enthusiasm is really contagious. I could tell by their faces. Jacobs and Talbot could actually see your vision."

"The blueprints and 3-D rendering help."

She shakes her head and looks down at her own sandwich, tuna on whole wheat. She picks at the crust. "No. Anyone can show a rendering. It's still just a blank image. The way you bring the image to life, as if it already exists in reality—I mean, how you have them close their eyes and imagine walking through the lobby and taking in all the details, the floors and walls and windows, how the sun will light the space at various times of the day. You're so good, Samuel."

I feel a tightening in my chest. "Thanks, Greta. I appreciate that."

"I'm so glad you took a chance on me. I'm learning so much. And I . . . Well, you know how I feel."

My eyes meet hers. "You have become completely invaluable to me, too, Greta."

She grins. "Good." She glances out the office window to the empty room beyond, then slowly places her hand over mine. Her fingertips softly stroke my flesh. "I wouldn't want to be replaceable."

"That could never happen."

"I'm glad."

My skin has grown hot where her hand lies, and my dick is twitching. A vision slams into my mind, of me rushing to her, lifting her out of the chair, turning her and bending her over the desk, pushing up her skirt and yanking down her panties—red lace, I'm guessing—and shoving my stiff erection deep inside her.

I use the pretense of taking another bite of my sandwich to pull my hand away. She smiles and lifts her sandwich, nibbles daintily at the edge of it, then sets it back down. Rachel eats with gusto, practically inhaling her food. Her zest for eating was something that attracted me when we first started dating. Now, I find it humorous and endearing.

"Still planning on going out to the Hewitt site this afternoon?" Greta asks, pulling my thoughts away from Rachel. I nod and try to chew my mouthful politely. "Still want me to come with you?"

She remembers the invitation I'd thrown out yesterday. I said it would be a good learning experience for her, but now I realize it was a bad idea. I should not be alone with this woman outside the office. Here, it's safe. We must adhere to the rules of decorum. We can flirt and wink and place our hands over each other's hands and not worry that it will lead anywhere. But in the outside world, alone, with miles of land between us and anyone who might notice or care . . . anything might happen.

Oh, who am I kidding? Certainly not myself. That situation is exactly why I invited her. To find out, once and for all, what this is between us.

It's a bad idea. And still, my heart beats rapidly in my chest with the knowledge that she will be joining me.

"Absolutely," I say, but my inner voice is screaming at me. I listen to it. "But look, Greta," I say. "It's Friday night. You shouldn't be working. You should be out on a date or drinking with friends. You shouldn't be with your middle-aged boss checking on a project. Really."

Her eyelashes flutter, and her lips turn down. "I thought you wanted me to come."

"I do. It's a long drive, and the company would be appreciated." I try to sound professional. It's bullshit. "And I think it would be good for you to see the project at this stage. But you're young, Greta. You should be out having fun on a Friday night. With people your age."

She looks at me straight on. "I don't like people my age," she says. "I never have."

"Well, then . . ." I don't know what to say. Thankfully, I see Carson push through the front door. A moment later, he appears at my office.

Carson turns fifty in two months. His hair is thinning on top, and his jowls have started to succumb to gravity, but his youthful energy is a counterbalance to his looks.

"Heard it went great with Talbot and Jacobs," he says, then gives me the Richard Nixon victory sign, a long-standing joke between us.

"Yeah, they'll sign," I reply. Carson nods at Greta, and she smiles back at him.

"Mr. Davenport was great."

"Always is, dear," Carson says. "That's why I keep him around." He looks at me. "You going out to Hewitt?"

I nod.

"We were just talking about that," Greta says. "It's on the schedule for this afternoon." I'm relieved she doesn't mention the fact that she's joining me.

"Great," he says. "Let me know how it looks."

"We will," Greta says. I cringe inwardly as Carson shoots me a strange look. He nods his head once and shrugs.

"Good. Great. Yeah, okay, so call me tonight when you're done."

"Don't you have that dinner thing?"

I don't want to call him tonight. I know why he's asking me to, and I resent it.

"Yeah, no, I do. Dinner with four members of the city council. Going to be about as much fun as a root canal. Call me if for no other reason than to give me a break from those jerk-offs."

"Okay."

Carson nods again, then heads for his office.

Greta turns to me and smiles. "Leaving at four?" she asks.

"Yes. Traffic will be bad, but I don't think I can get out of here any sooner."

"That's okay. I don't mind traffic. That'll give us time to talk."

"About what?" I ask, even though I'm not sure I want to know the answer.

"About anything," Greta replies. She takes another nibble of her sandwich and grins playfully at me.

I set down my sandwich, my stomach suddenly uneasy. *What the hell have I gotten myself into?*

"Might be better if we caravan," I suggest. "So we can both head home from there."

She tries not to look disappointed. "You're the boss."

FORTY-ONE

RACHEL

I arrive at the school five minutes after kinder pickup, cursing myself for being late. Jonah is one of the last kids remaining behind the gate. When Eden was in the lower grades and I arrived late, she would be angry and unforgiving, glaring at me as I waved to her teacher and punishing me long into the evening. But Jonah is happily chatting with another kindergartner, gesticulating like an Italian mama and clutching a stuffed monkey to his chest. He doesn't even notice me as I toss a greeting to his teacher. When Mrs. Hartnett calls to him, he turns toward me and gives me a beatific smile, and my heart seizes in my chest.

"I won, Mommy! I won! I won the egg hunt!" He barrels into me, throws his arms around my waist and squeezes me tight while managing to keep a firm grasp on the monkey. "I get to keep Marco for the whole vacation!" he tells my stomach.

I peel him away, then kneel down and grasp his face in my hands. "Congratulations, my guy! That's amazing!"

"I found forty-seven eggs!" he cries. "Forty-seven! Jesse found forty-six. I thought he found more than me when I looked at his pile, but I found one more than him and I won and I get to keep Marco! Mrs. Hartnett said I should take pictures of Marco and us and then I can share them with the class when vacation's over."

"I think that's a great idea," I tell him. I stand, and he instantly laces his fingers in mine. "I'm sorry I'm late, honey. I was working."

"You're not that late," Jonah says. "It's okeydokey, artichokey. Work is important."

I smile down at him. "Not more important than you."

"Oh, sure. I know that. Nothing's more important than me, right?"

"Right!" I lead him to the minivan.

"But I knew you'd be here and anyway I was talking to Joey M. about vacation and he said his family is going skiing and he thought that was the best way ever to spend vacation, and I think it is, but then he told me his dad isn't going and that his mom's friend is going instead and his brother is going somewhere else, and I thought maybe it wasn't that great because he's not going to be with his whole family, and I told him I didn't know what we're doing for vacation and he said that was stinky, like that we weren't doing anything, and I told him it didn't matter 'cause we were going to be together as a family so whatever we do will be the best 'cause we'll all be together."

Finally, Jonah takes a breath, and I use the break to strap him into his car seat.

"We're all going to be together for vacation, right, Mommy?"

"Absotively," I say.

"Posolutely," he finishes.

"So, wow, forty-seven eggs, huh?" I ask.

"Oh my gosh, yes! And lots of each kind. I got . . ." He scrunches up his face and thinks hard. "Fifteen cookies-and-cream—Eden's going to be so happy. She said we'd split 'em fifty-fifty, but I'm going to give her more because I don't need them all. And I got thirteen chocolate ones and nine Butterfinger ones and ten peanut butter ones for Daddy."

"He'll be so happy," I say.

"I can't wait to give them to him," Jonah says as I pull out of the parking lot.

"Well, unfortunately, Daddy has to work late tonight," I say, "so you'll have to wait until tomorrow."

I glance in the rearview mirror. Jonah is frowning.

"Can't we go to his work now, Mommy? So I can give 'em to him? If he has to work late, he might need the eggs to help him have energy."

I bite my lip and watch the road. My five-year-old son has more compassion and caring than most people I know. It makes me proud—I must be doing something right. But also, I recognize that he is a force unto himself, and perhaps I only deserve partial credit. He came out of my womb a smiling, effervescent, joyful presence. Perhaps Sam and I can only take credit for not squashing that energy, for not suffocating his innate goodness.

"If we go see Daddy, we won't have time for the playground."

Jonah gets out of school exactly one hour before Eden. Our routine is to go to the park on the next block, where he can play for forty-five minutes. The younger students who get out early aren't allowed on the school jungle gym due to some ridiculous district mandate, but the park is close by and has an even better play area than the school. Usually, other kinder moms are there, waiting for their older offspring, and Jonah and I both enjoy the camaraderie of our individual age groups.

"I think giving the eggs to Daddy is more important. What if he doesn't have time for dinner?"

I check the clock on the minivan. Sam's office is ten minutes away. Ten-minute return trip.

"Okay, but we can't stay long. We don't want to be late picking up Eden."

"No, we don't," Jonah says. "She'd be way mad at you."

I punch the button for the CD, and Jonah and I sing "The Green Grass Grows All Around" together—his favorite. I forget where I am in the lyrics nearly every verse, but Jonah patiently corrects me.

"No, Mommy, the *wing* . . ."

"Oh, right. *And on the bird, there was a wing/the prettiest wing that you ever did see . . .*"

After two rounds of the song—I did better the second time, according to Jonah—we pull into the parking lot of Sam's building. It's a nondescript two-story office building with cream stucco and blue-tinted windows. Sam's company shares the second floor with an insurance agency, a mortgage broker, and an escrow firm. Jonah and I alight from the minivan and head for the entrance. He carries his paper sack containing his spring egg hunt bounty and Marco the monkey. I let him push the button for the elevator, and he smiles when he hears the ding and the elevator doors slide open.

"Modern technology," he says, and I laugh.

We alight onto the second floor and head for the door at the far end of the hallway. Sam's building reminds me of the dentist's office we frequent, with tired gray carpeting and wood-paneled doors. At Davenport and Gregson, I twist the knob and enter the modest office space. There is no reception area, just one long space with two offices and a conference room on one side and desks and drafting tables on the other side. A young man . . . well, younger than me by a decade—sits at the first desk, typing into his computer. I recognize him as Henry Beecham, the bookkeeper for my husband's firm. He looks up and smiles when he sees Jonah. He pushes his black-rimmed glasses up to the bridge of his nose, then holds up his hand for a high five.

"Hey, my man," he says. "How's it going?"

Jonah complies with the high five, then proceeds to regale Henry with the story of his egg hunt and Marco. Henry looks genuinely interested, listens intently, and asks questions. I like Henry. He's worked for Sam for almost a year, and I hope he stays.

"How's it going, Mrs. D?" he asks. "Haven't seen you much lately."

I nod. It's true. I rarely visit Sam at work nowadays. Not since the blog. I used to bring him lunch or stop by after shopping, always bestowing upon him a little insignificant gift, like the Sriracha boxers

I'd found at Target, or the "365 Ways with Duct Tape" calendar I'd happened upon at Barnes and Noble, just to let him know I was thinking about him. But my free time has become rare. I know Sam understands.

"Is he here?" I ask, and Henry nods and jerks a thumb toward Sam's office.

"You want an egg?" Jonah asks. "I got lots. I'm saving the cookies-and-cream for Eden, and the peanut butters for Daddy, but I got some Butterfingers and some chocolates." He looks up at me questioningly. "You like the chocolate ones, Mommy, but is it okay if I give Henry one?"

I nod. "Of course. I don't need that much chocolate. I'm bulging too much these days." I pat my stomach to prove the point, but Henry scoffs.

"You look fantastic," he says. "But I will take a chocolate egg, if you're sure."

Jonah's head bobs up and down. "How about two? 'Cause one is never enough."

"Mrs. Davenport." I hear my name and look up to see Sam's assistant staring at me from a few feet away.

"Hi, Greta. I've told you, please call me Rachel." She looks uncertain, uncomfortable. Sam told me that when she came to work for him, she refused to call him Sam. "Mr. Davenport" this and "Mr. Davenport" that. Almost drove him crazy until she finally agreed to call him Samuel. For some reason, that bothered me, although I couldn't figure out why.

"Rachel," she says, looking at the carpet. "This is a surprise."

"Jonah won the spring egg hunt at the school and wanted to bring Sam his winnings."

"I got ten eggs for Daddy that are his favorite," Jonah says proudly.

Greta bends down to smile at Jonah. "Let me guess. Peanut butter."

"Yeah!" Jonah exclaims. "How did you know?"

"I'm his assistant," she says. "I know everything there is to know about your daddy."

She is talking to Jonah on his level and being effusive in a manner that five-year-olds respond to, but something about the way she says that—*I know everything there is to know about your daddy*—rubs me the wrong way. She stands and winks at me.

"Obviously not everything," she whispers.

Somewhat mollified, I follow Jonah to Sam's office. Greta falls in step beside me.

"He is so adorable," she says, giving Jonah an adoring look.

I nod in agreement. "He is." I smell vanilla and peaches on her. "Is that Chanel? Coco?"

Greta blushes. "It is. You're good."

"It's lovely," I tell her.

"Thank you."

"Daddy, Daddy, Daddy!" Jonah shouts. He runs into Sam's office and rushes to him. Sam stands behind his desk and glances over at me. I know it's crazy, but I can't help but think Sam looks alarmed, as if he's been caught at something. A fraction of a second later, the look of alarm is replaced by an expression of sheer joy as he wraps his arms around his son and lifts him into the air.

I stand at the office door and gaze at them, my two men. I glance back at Greta. She watches them intently, but when she feels my gaze upon her, she immediately looks away, takes her seat at her desk, and busies herself with some paperwork.

Sam crosses the office and looks at me, puzzled. I shrug.

"He couldn't wait," I say.

"I've got ten whole peanut butter eggs for you, Daddy," Jonah says, still suspended in Sam's arms.

"Ten?" Sam asks, feigning incredulity.

"I found forty-seven! And I get to keep Marco. Oh, this is Marco."

"Nice to meet you, Marco," Sam says.

"He says it's nice to meet you, too," Jonah tells Sam.

Sam kisses my cheek. Awkwardly. I know I haven't been here in a while, but Sam's demeanor feels stilted.

"Sorry about tonight," he says, and I realize he feels bad about working late on a Friday.

"It's no problem. We'll do it another night. Ruth's always available, as you know."

Sam puts Jonah down, and he immediately reaches into the bag, pulls out eggs one by one, inspects their wrappers, and sets aside the peanut butters. I check my watch.

"Okay, my guy, we have to go. We have to pick up your sister."

"Can't be late for Eden," Jonah says. "Or she'll make Mommy pay."

Sam and I exchange a look, then both of us chuckle. He kisses me again, chastely, on the cheek. "See you later?"

I nod. "I'll save you some of Ruth's lasagna." I feel his eyes on me the whole way out.

FORTY-TWO

RUTH

The lasagna took an hour to make.

I watched a couple of recorded shows on my TiVo while I waited for the sausage to defrost but realized I wasn't really paying attention; my mind was wandering and I needed an active occupation. So I decided to urge the sausage along in the microwave. The corners cooked too much, but I cut them away and went about the task of putting the lasagna together.

Judd Stevens has taken up space in my thoughts, which is only marginally better than me fixating on Charlie and his new family. I try to banish Judd, but I can't. I don't want to think about tomorrow night and our shared bottle of wine. And yet, as I lift the pasta sheets from the boiling water, I find myself dreaming up possible scenarios. One, we could sit side by side on his couch, our wineglasses on the coffee table, my mouth frozen as I desperately attempt to come up with something fascinating to say, him working to mask his embarrassment at having ever thought it was a good idea to invite me down. Two, we could sit across from each other at his dining room table, the wine—delicious, of course—a lubricant for easy conversation and meaningful glances that will pave the way to his bedroom. Three, I could cancel and thereby nullify both of the above possibilities.

Number three is the most likely scenario, and the one I would ordinarily choose. But a part of me craves scenario number two. I haven't been with a man since Charlie. I have my physical challenges, obviously. And I have my trust issues concerning men. But I am also a woman, with needs and desires and . . . oh, God, to be intimate with someone again. To lie in someone's arms, to be held, to be touched and kissed and adored. I proclaim to anyone listening—my sister, mostly—that I don't want that, I don't need that, I'm fine without it. But I'm not.

I place the long pasta strips along the bottom of the greased pan, then sprinkle ricotta, mozzarella, the crumbled sausage, and my homemade marinara. The process is meditative. I am anal-retentive about it. Can't leave any holes. Must have all the ingredients evenly parsed. It takes a while. I think of Judd. I think of the lasagna I tell myself I'm making for me, but really it's for Judd, if I keep our date. Does he even eat lasagna? Maybe he's gluten-free. Maybe he's a vegetarian or a vegan.

What the hell am I doing?

On the second lasagna, the one for me, or for Judd, I haven't decided yet, my knuckles start to seize, then my hands. I've already taken my pill this morning, and the sudden pain in my extremities surprises me.

I walk on shaky legs to my bathroom and open the medicine cabinet. I pull out the ibuprofen, open the lid with trembling hands, and shake three gelcaps onto my palm. I pop them into my mouth, return the bottle to the cupboard, and bend over the sink, where I cup my hand under the tap and sip enough water to swallow the pills.

I should cancel tomorrow night. What would a healthy, vibrant, attractive middle-aged widower want with a pathetic sack like me?

I stand and close the medicine cabinet, then gaze at my reflection in the mirror, trying to be objective about what I see. I am not unattractive, not for a middle-aged woman. Although I have crows'-feet in the corners of my eyes and lines that pull down at the corners of my mouth and a crease across the middle of my neck—all signs of my age—I still have high cheekbones and only one chin. My eyes are a striking blue, and the skin of my eyelids has yet to start a downward journey. My lips are still full, not chapped thanks to the nonpetroleum jelly I put on every night. My hair has gone very gray, but I could take care of that with a trip to the drugstore, should I choose to do so.

I watch my reflection as I reach up and place my hand under my right breast. I've had no children, have never endured the voracious suckling of a babe. My breasts are not those of a twenty-two-year-old, firm with nipples pointing skyward, but neither are they the bosoms of a mother thrice over, tired and sagging and deflated by time and an infant's unquenchable thirst. They are breasts a man could still revere. I think of Judd, downstairs, and red splotches appear on my cheeks.

Charlie loved my breasts, paid homage to them regularly, told me they were spectacular. Until he didn't. Until he found another pair that could provide milk, breasts that were attached to a uterus that could manage a fertilized egg.

I continuously tell myself that Charlie deserves to be happy. My therapist is helping me along with that mantra. But he also tells me that I deserve to be happy, too.

I deserve to have my breasts revered. I deserve to enjoy a glass of Château Lafite Rothschild with an attractive widower. I just wish I knew whether or not I could actually handle it.

I splash cold water on my face. The ibuprofen has yet to take effect. My hands feel like claws, my fingers like cylinders of lead.

The apartment around me feels like a cell, the walls closing in.

I hurry to the kitchen, fumble through my purse for my cell. I swipe the screen to bring the thing to life, then click on my texts and swipe at Rachel's name. I type without much thought or contemplation.

I know it's early, but is it okay if I head over now?

I rest my arms on my minuscule Formica counter, counting in my head as the seconds tick by. On forty, I get a reply. Just heading to school to pick up Eden. Come any time. Use your key if we're not there yet.

I sigh with relief. Saved again. I need to see Rachel and her children. I know they will ground me, as they always do. Maybe I'll mention Judd to my sister. She'll tell me to go for it—I know she will. Maybe that's exactly what I'm looking for. A nudge. A cheerleader.

Permission.

I wrap the first lasagna in loose foil; the second, I wrap tighter and place on the top shelf of my freezer. I wonder where that lasagna will land. But I don't give it much more thought. I grab the first pan, sling my purse over my shoulder, and head for the door.

FORTY-THREE

SHADOW

I'm alone. The humans are all gone. My mistress left . . . I don't know when or how long ago, but the house is empty and I don't like it. I am a Good Boy and I like to protect my humans, Little Male and Little Female and my master and mistress. But I can't protect them when they're not here.

I go to the front window and look out. I don't see the cat. But I can smell it. I watch the outside for a while, waiting to see the cat. It doesn't come out from wherever it's hiding. Sometimes my little humans play the hiding game with me. Little Male will throw the ball into my yard from the door, then run away with Little Female. Then I run into the house and look for them. They don't hide upstairs, because they know I'm not allowed up there. Sometimes they hide behind the couch or in the little room with the coats and the shoes or under the table in the back room. I always find them, because I can smell them wherever they go. And when I do, they smile and laugh and pet me and tell me I'm a Smart Boy. I don't know what *smart* means, but I know it's like good, because they look happy like when they say "Good Boy."

The cat is still not anywhere I can see it. I pad to the food-smelling room and sniff the ground. Maybe one of my humans dropped something. I think I already checked, but I can't remember, so I check again. But I don't find anything.

I wander over to my bed in the food-smelling room and lie down. My eyes start to close. Then I hear it. My ears go up, and the fur on my back straightens. From outside, there is a loud mewling sound that I know is coming from the cat. I stand up and run to the front window. And there it is again, only now, it's on the sidewalk right in front of me, staring at me through the window. I press a paw against the glass, then I'm up on my back legs with both paws on the front window and I'm barking and barking and I can't stop, I won't stop, I couldn't stop, not even if my humans were here telling me, "No, Shadow!"

The cat walks on its short legs to the grass, not looking at me. It wanders around for a while, pawing at the grass, then it turns so that it can see me, crouches, and starts to make.

I hear the whine deep in my throat, and I let it out and it sounds like a howl. The cat is making on grass that I'm not allowed to make on. I paw and paw the window, barking, whining, pawing—I need to break through the glass so that I can get the cat.

I hear Dark Female's car before I see it. It stops next to the sidewalk, creaks and shudders, then goes still. Dark Female gets out, and I hear the hollow car-door slam. The cat runs away and crosses the wide dark strip. It sits on the sidewalk and starts to lick its back.

I lower my front paws to the ground, because I know if Dark Female sees me against the window, she will call me Bad Boy with her mad-looking face. She goes to the back of the car and pulls something out. I sniff the air and smell something, very faint but good smelling. As Dark Female comes closer to my house, my tail wags. I don't make it wag—it just does.

I hear the key in the front door, then the door opens and Dark Female walks in carrying something in her hands that is definitely food. I know it's not for me, but my tail wags and wags just the same. Dark Female tries to close the door with her foot.

"Hi, Shadow," she says. She isn't smiling or happy sounding, but she doesn't have mad face, either, so I trot over to her. She can't pet me because of the thing she's holding, but Dark Female never pets me. "Good boy," she says, but her voice sounds flat and tired, not like when my humans say it.

She walks toward the food-smelling room just as the front door starts to roll open. I see outside, to where I'm not allowed unless my humans have me tied to the long rope. And outside, across the dark strip, is the cat. I take a few steps past the door, knowing I'm being a Bad Boy, but I can't help it. I chuff. The cat's ears jerk in my direction, then flatten on its head, like it knows there's nothing between us now, no window to keep me in, to keep me from getting the cat. It snarls and scurries away and I start to run, but before I can get down the stairs to the walkway, I feel my collar tighten on my neck.

"No, Shadow! Bad boy!" Dark Female is holding my collar. I know I could pull away from her—her hand isn't strong like my neck. But I don't like her calling me Bad Boy, even though going out of the front door is a Bad Boy thing. I chuff and snort and whine at the cat, then I let Dark Female lead me back into the house.

She closes the door and lets go of me, then looks down at me with mad face. She says something I don't understand, but her mad face is getting less and less. She turns and walks toward the food-smelling room, and I follow her. Maybe something will drop out of the thing she was carrying. That wouldn't be as good as getting the cat. But pretty good.

FORTY-FOUR

JONAH

I never noticed before, but Marco has strips of Velcro on his paws, just like my sneakers from when I was in preschool. I learned to tie my shoes over summer vacation and Mommy and Daddy were real proud. Eden taught me. She spent every morning showing me how, first with both the ties being bunny ears and then just one of the ties being a bunny ear and the other tie kind of looping around the bunny ear and pulling through. I like how she was all patient with me and didn't get all mad when I couldn't do it.

Anyway, Marco has Velcro on his paws so you can wrap him around your neck and stick his two paws together and he'll hang on you like he's giving you a hug. I have him hanging around my neck as I climb down from the car. It's good because I can hold my egg bag with one hand and my backpack with the other.

Eden isn't very talky right now—she's kind of got a frown on her face and every time Mommy asks her a question, she only answers with like one word or something. Eden is a great sister, but sometimes she can be grumpy, like now. She didn't even smile or anything when I told her how many cookies-and-cream eggs I got. She just kind of gave a little snort, like Shadow does sometimes, and looked out the window at the street.

Sometimes when she's grumpy, it makes me grumpy, too. But not today. Because I won the spring egg hunt and I got to take home Marco, and nobody and nothing could make me grumpy today.

Auntie Ruth's car is on the street in front of our house, and I'm kind of excited because Mommy said Auntie Ruth was bringing over lasagna and I really like Auntie Ruth's lasagna. Eden got all mad and said it was the first night of vacation and it's supposed to be family night and where's Daddy? And Mommy said it's still family night 'cause Auntie Ruth is family, and Daddy has to work late and that happens sometimes.

I'm a little bit sad that Daddy's not going to be home, but I gave him his eggs for his working-late night, so he'll be okay. I'm going to give Auntie Ruth all of my Butterfinger eggs 'cause I know she likes 'em—at least, I think so. I think it's really nice of her to bring over lasagna, so I want to do something nice for her, and even though I like the Butterfinger eggs really a lot, I like the other ones, too, and I don't mind giving the Butterfingers to her.

Mommy gets out of the car, then helps me out of my seat and I follow her up the path. She stops kind of all of a sudden and I bump into the back of her legs. She's looking at the grass and I think maybe she sees a bug, but when I look where she's looking I see a poop instead.

Mommy looks down at me and scrunches her nose. "Cat poop."

I nod and we both look over at the sidewalk. Gigi, the big fluffy kitty from across the street, is sitting on the edge of the grass, her tail going back and forth. I know she's a cat, and cats aren't like people, but Gigi looks like she's grinning or something, like she knows she did a bad thing but she's happy about it. I feel the corners of my mouth twitch, 'cause it's kind of funny, but I don't let myself smile.

Mommy blows air out real loud. "I'll get it in a minute."

Eden kind of stomp-stomps past us up to the house, and Mommy follows her. I look at Gigi, and she slowly walks over to me and rubs her side against my leg. It tickles real bad, but also feels nice and soft. I bend down and pet her, but then I hear Shadow start barking his head off.

"Don't let Shadow out!" Mommy shouts to Eden, then she runs up to the house and grabs the door before Shadow can sneak outside. "Come on, Jonah. Let's go."

Mommy goes inside and shuts the door so Shadow can't get out. I look down at Gigi.

"You shouldn't make poops on our lawn, Gigi," I tell the kitty, but I know she doesn't understand what I said, and even if she did, I don't think she'd care too much. "If Shadow gets out, he'll eat you." She meows at me, all lazy and stuff, like she's not afraid of a big old dog. Then she scampers away from me and trots across the street, back to her own yard.

I go inside just as Eden is stomp-stomp-stomping up the stairs. Mommy calls her and tells her to say hi to Auntie Ruth, and Eden does that snorting thing again but comes back down the stairs so she won't get in trouble.

Shadow runs over to me just as I drop my backpack on the floor. He starts sniffing me, and at first I think he wants the eggs, but then I realize he's sniffing Gigi the cat, and maybe Marco, too, 'cause I guess Marco has lots of smells on him since he's been going home with kindergartners for like years and must have picked up a ton of different smells from all the kids and their houses and pets and stuff. I pat Shadow on the head, then follow Mommy and Eden into the kitchen.

"Hi, Auntie Ruth," Eden says, still frowning, and I hope Auntie Ruth doesn't think Eden's frowny because she's here. I want to say something like, "Don't worry, Eden was frowning like that the whole way home in the car." But I don't. Instead, I give Auntie Ruth a hug and let her pat my back like she usually does, and then I tell her I won the egg hunt.

"Well, well," she says, smiling big at me. "Congratulations. Jonah, master of the spring egg hunt. And who do we have here?" She's looking at Marco, and I kind of stand up straight 'cause I'm kind of proud of myself.

"This is Marco," I tell her. "He gets to stay with us the whole vacation!"

"Isn't that something?" Auntie Ruth says, and I can tell she's excited, too, not just pretending to be. "Nice to meet you, Marco."

I look up at my auntie. She's holding one hand in the other and kind of rubbing her fingers. Her knuckles look kind of puffy, like when I fell off my bike on my knee and it blew up like a balloon.

"If you want, Auntie Ruth, you can take him home with you for a couple nights. So you won't be lonely."

Auntie Ruth's eyes go all wide and start getting shimmery and stuff, and behind her, Mommy makes a worried face.

"That was a stupid thing to say, Jonah," Eden says.

"Eden," Mommy says in her stern voice.

I feel like I've done a dumb-dumb thing, but I don't know what it is. Mommy looks upset and Eden looks cross and Auntie Ruth looks like she's going to start crying. Then she bends her knees and puts them on the floor so her face is right there with mine. Her lips are kind of white, like it hurts her to go down on the floor, but she does it anyway. She takes my hand, the one that isn't holding the bag of eggs, and looks at me really hard.

"Jonah, that is, I think, one of the nicest things anyone has ever said to me." She kisses my hand, then her white lips go into a smile. "You are a very special guy. And I want you to know how much I appreciate your offer, but I wouldn't dream of taking Marco away from you. However, maybe you could bring Marco over during vacation, for a sleepover?" She looks over at Eden. "Maybe your sister could come, too?"

"Could we watch *Dancing with the Stars*?" Eden asks, and she looks happy for the first time since she got in the car after school.

"I have about two dozen shows on my TiVo," Auntie Ruth says with a nod.

"Awesome," Eden says. "That's totally beast." I look at Eden, and her smile suddenly leaves her face.

"We can, Mommy, right?" I ask, and Mommy nods.

"Absolutely. Auntie Ruth and Daddy and I will work it out."

I take my bag over to the kitchen table and climb into one of the chairs, then dump the eggs onto the tablecloth. They roll across the table, but none of them fall on the floor, which is a good thing 'cause Shadow is right there, waiting, and I know chocolate is bad for doggies. Mommy helps Auntie Ruth up and they start talking about lasagna and garlic bread. I look over at Eden and she's standing by the wall kind of giving me a frowny face.

"Hey, Eden," I say to her. "Look at all the cookies-and-cream I got. Here, take 'em. Fifty-fifty." I count out the eggs; there's fifteen, I know, because I counted them before, and fifteen's an odd number—Mrs. Hartnett hasn't teached us about odds and evens yet, but Daddy told me about them and showed me on my whiteboard, so I already know there's going to be one egg extra. I grab 'em one by one and set 'em apart. One for Eden, one for me, one for Eden, one for me. Pretty soon, I have two piles that have seven eggs each, and sure enough, there's one extra. I push it into Eden's pile.

"You can have the extra one," I tell her.

She comes over to the table and scoops up her eggs, then turns around and heads for the stairs without even thanking me. I think that's kind of not nice. But then I think of all the times Eden helped me and maybe I forgot to say thanks, like when she helped me color my shapes for my school poster, or when she helped me pass my kinder-reader test, or other times, too. I'll forgive her for not saying thanks this time, 'cause I know that even though she's not smiling or anything, the eggs made her happy, 'cause the cookies-and-cream ones are her favorite.

FORTY-FIVE

EDEN

I know it's not his fault. He's only five, so I really can't blame him. But I swear, sometimes having a little brother is like a total bummer. Ryan Anderson didn't talk to me or even look at me the whole rest of the day, not even once, not after Jonah came running over and hugged me in front of my friends. Even when Mr. Libey assigned groups for Language Arts and Ryan was in my group, he totally ignored me, even when I asked him a question. He pretended not to hear me and started talking to Dustin Schulman about some stupid baseball thing.

I'm up in my room, sitting on my bed, with the cookies-and-cream eggs scattered in front of me. We're not allowed to have food up in our rooms, but Mom was busy talking to Aunt Ruth and didn't even notice me taking them from the kitchen table. I didn't thank Jonah, and I do feel kind of bad about that, especially because he gave me the extra one, but I just couldn't seem to form the words, because even though it's not his fault, I'm still mad at him. My friends didn't make fun of me or anything, but I knew they thought it was totally lame, what Jonah did. But they had more important things to do, like make fun of Corwin. I felt bad for Corwin getting all teased just because he likes Ava. Not that he likes her anymore. And I'm kind of glad for him because even though she's my friend and all, she can be really mean, and Corwin should like someone who's nice to him because he's nice, too.

Carlee likes Matt, and she says that he kissed her behind the portables right before Christmas break. Not with tongue or anything—*gross!*—but I don't know if I believe her. Matt doesn't act like he likes her at all, and Carlee made us do a double cross-your-heart swear that we would never bring it up to him.

Ava doesn't like any of the boys at school. She says she has a boyfriend back in Texas, where she lived before her family moved out here last year. His name is Tim and he's in sixth grade, and she says they've done all kinds of things, like kiss on the mouth, with tongue—*gross!*—and hold hands and play doctor. I didn't know what that game was, and when I asked her, she kind of laughed like I was the stupidest person ever, but then Carlee told me she didn't know what doctor was and I felt better. And then one day, when Carlee and me were at her house for a playdate, we googled *doctor* and found out that it's a game where you look at and maybe even touch each other's privates. And even though I don't want anybody, especially a *boy*, looking at or *touching* my privates, and I was a little bit freaked out that Ava had maybe done that, I kind of also thought she was a little bit cool and totally grown-up for doing that.

I unwrap a cookies-and-cream egg, pop it into my mouth, and wad up the foil wrapper. I think about Ryan and what I would have told him if Jonah hadn't interrupted. Fun Dip is my favorite candy, not just the powder, but the sticks you dip with. I wonder if Ryan likes Fun Dip, too. Now I'll probably never find out.

With the white chocolate melting on my tongue, I lie back against my pillow and think of Ryan. His big blue eyes and blond hair and the curvy way his lips grin. For just a small minute, I think about playing doctor with Ryan, but then my stomach gets fluttery, but not in a good way, more like an "I ate way too many corn dogs" way, and my face gets hot and I feel super embarrassed even though I'm all alone.

I sit up again and roll the eggs back and forth across my bedspread, then I gather them up and take them to my desk and hide them in the top drawer. I know Mom comes in here every so often and looks through my things. I don't know what she thinks she'll find. I'm only ten. What could I be hiding? If she finds the eggs, she'll probably get all mad and say something like, "That's how you get bugs upstairs!" and Jonah will get all excited because he *loves* bugs and would be happy if a bunch of them creepy-crawlied into his room.

There's a knock at my door that makes me jump, and I slam the drawer shut real fast, just in case it's Mom or Aunt Ruth. I know dinner won't be ready for like another hour, so it's probably Jonah. Yup. He swings the door open before I even tell him it's okay to come in.

"Hi, Eden," he says. The dumb monkey is hanging around his neck. "Wanna play with me and Marco?"

Oh, sure. I really want to play with my little brother and his stuffed animal. I mean, I still have stuffed animals—they're on my bed—but I don't play with them anymore.

"No," I tell him. "I don't."

"Oh, come on, Eden, it'll be real fun, I promise. We could pretend Marco's an alien from another universe and he's come to eat our brains and we have to make an army to protect ourselves, but then Marco starts to turn into a good alien and doesn't want to eat our brains anymore but wants to help us fight his very own people. *Alien* people."

I slap my hands over my ears. "Shut up, Jonah! Don't you ever take a breath?" Mom says that to him sometimes, not the shut-up part, but the taking-a-breath part. Only she always says it with a smile on her face, not like I just did in my mean voice.

"You said *shut up*, Eden. That's not 'llowed."

"What're you gonna do? Tattle on me?"

He bites his lower lip, then slowly shakes his head. "I wouldn't tattle on you, Eden. 'Cause you're the best sister."

I drop my hands and stare at my nails. Ava got a Jamberry for Christmas and she always has these cute patterns on her nails. Mine don't even have clear polish. Mom said she'd take me for a manicure, but she won't buy me a Jamberry because they cost like a hundred dollars.

I finally look up and see that Jonah is still there. I'm not going to apologize to him for saying *shut up*. I'm not. I'm mad at him. He ruined things with Ryan. But he doesn't know any of that.

"I don't feel like playing with you right now, Jonah, okay?"

"Sure, it's okay, Eden," he says, then his face gets smiley again, like he's just happy that I'm talking to him without yelling. "Maybe later, huh?"

Not. I shrug, and he smiles at me like I told him yes. He looks at Marco.

"Maybe Eden will play with us later, alien monkey from another universe."

He runs out of my room, leaving my door wide-open. I sneak another egg out of the desk drawer, and while I'm looking at the pink-and-purple wrapper, I suddenly feel really bad about being mad at Jonah. I am not the best big sister. But he is probably the best little brother I could have. Especially compared to Carlee's little brother who, like, bites her almost every single day, or Matt's little brother who steals his toys, then breaks them and doesn't say sorry or feel bad about it at all.

I put the egg back in the drawer. I don't want it anymore. Maybe I'll go find Jonah and play that stupid alien game with him.

I shake my head, which I know is kind of silly because there's nobody looking, but I do it anyway. I don't want to play with Jonah. I really don't. Not even just to be nice. Tomorrow I probably won't be mad at him anymore and I'll play with him then.

I want to FaceTime with Carlee and Ava, but Mom said I couldn't before dinner. I don't know why not, but I didn't bother arguing with her because she used that voice that means she isn't going to change her mind. Dad calls it her nonnegotiation voice. Maybe I'll read for a little while. I just started the Percy Jackson series. Dad said I was finally old enough, and I like it, and I don't even mind that there's a boy as the main character.

I get down on the floor and crawl over to my bookshelf, find Percy Jackson, trail my fingers over the outside part where it says the name. Mom told me what that part's called, but I forgot. No, wait. The spine. That's it. But I don't pull out Percy Jackson because right next to it is my school yearbook from last year. I pull that out instead, then sit cross-legged on the floor and open it to Mrs. Bertrand's class page.

I wasn't in Mrs. Bertrand's class last year. But I know a lot of people who were. Like Carlee and Corwin and Aimee. And Ryan.

FORTY-SIX

SAMUEL

The Hewitt project is situated on the outskirts of a new suburban development about thirty minutes outside the city. Thirty minutes when there isn't traffic. But at four o'clock on a Friday afternoon, the freeway is the usual crawl, commuters ending their workweek, sitting behind the wheels of their cars, imagining the taste of their first cocktail, checking their phones to see if their wives have texted them last-minute needs, which they won't be able to fulfill for an aeon due to the gridlock.

The carpool lane moves a little more quickly. My idea to caravan was squashed when we met in the parking lot forty minutes ago. Greta hopped into my car, telling me it would be better to carpool. She was right. We'll cut fifteen minutes off our time in this lane. But it probably wasn't a good idea.

Her perfume isn't cloying, it's lovely—reminds me of peach cobbler. And her long legs stretch out into the shadows beneath the glove compartment. I keep my eyes studiously on the road, but every so often, when I catch her looking out the passenger window, I steal a glance at the smooth porcelain skin of her thighs. I am not an adolescent. I am able to control myself. But I am a man.

Fuck. This is wrong.

And yet, I have willingly stepped into this situation. Ha, no, I invited this situation, orchestrated it. But why? *Why?*

Greta has undertaken to act as DJ for the ride, switching stations and choosing songs she likes, singing along with them in a soft but perfectly pitched voice. She hasn't launched into conversation, save for the occasional question about whether or not I know the song playing, and if I do whether or not I like it. Every once in a while, I feel her gaze on me, and when I glance at her, she wears an inquisitive or intense expression, as though she wants to *talk*. But so far, thankfully, she hasn't broached any taboo or uncomfortable subjects, like, for example, why did I ask her to join me on this trip?

The answer to that question is as complex as it is simplistic. The answer is, I don't know.

I am happy. I have a good, solid marriage. I have wonderful kids. I have an existence that would be envied by half the population on the planet, at least. So what on earth compelled me to introduce chaos into the otherwise perfect landscape of my life?

Again, I am a man, and we are ruled by base urges, dominated by our dicks. And don't forget about our egos. Monstrous, fragile egos.

But those are excuses, and poor ones at that.

What's interesting and ironic, equally, is that I wish I could talk to Rachel about this. She is my best friend and my sounding board. She listens thoughtfully to me when I spew to her about work problems, or complain about age-related challenges such as the bursitis that plagued me most of last year and wreaked havoc on my already mediocre golf game, or my frustration with the predominance of stupid people in service positions these days. She listens and offers me clarity. She gives me insights into my own character, and those insights are often laced with humor. She helps me to laugh at myself.

I have friends. Buddies, acquaintances. Carson and I are fairly close. Frank DiSilva is my oldest friend, lives back east, and we talk every month or so. But Rachel is the one I turn to regularly.

Rachel, whom I'm about to betray. If Sister Johnna from eighth grade is correct, and the thought is as bad as the deed, I have betrayed her already.

We reach the turnoff just after five. I drive through the newly minted downtown area—a patch of strip malls and fast-food restaurants built rapidly to accommodate the quickly rising population of this suburb, the paint barely dry on most of the buildings.

"Oh, a Ross Dress for Less," Greta chirps. "My mom loves that store. *Ooh*, and a Raising Cane's. Yum!"

I have never seen my assistant like this. At work, she is a consummate professional, always meets her deadlines, goes the extra mile, stays late and arrives early. She comes across older than her years. But now, she stares out the passenger window with excited anticipation, like a child visiting Disneyland for the first time.

She is *a child, Sam.*

I follow the directions of the GPS to an as-yet unmarked street. The Hewitt project stands at the end of the street.

When Marshall Hewitt came to me with the idea last year, I declined. The location was outside Carson's and my geographic perimeter, and the job held little appeal. Architecture has been good to me. But over the past few years, I've found less fulfillment in it. With two kids and a stay-at-home wife, a career change would be impractical, so I resolved to only take on projects I was passionate about.

The approach to the rehabilitation facility was cookie-cutter at best—private lodging, a gym, a theater, a cafeteria, and half a dozen conference rooms for AA and NA meetings, seminars, and lectures. The board wanted simple, industrial, practical, user-friendly. Although I wasn't interested, I was moved by Marshall's speech, by his passion to give something back to the world, his entreaty that we should use our gifts for the betterment of humanity as a whole. Then Carson signed on. He had a sister who overdosed many years ago. So I took the assignment. And here we are.

This is not my most creative design. I don't take great pride in the edifice before me. But hopefully, it will be a safe haven for those willing to repair and rebuild their demolished lives.

A dozen or so men loiter outside the building, shooting the shit, all of them wearing the regulation construction helmets. I recognize Javier, the foreman, and throw him a wave. He straightens his posture and walks toward me.

"Mr. Davenport. *Como estas?*"

I put out my hand. "*Bien, gracias.* How's it going?"

Greta stands beside me, and Javier is careful not to ogle her. His eyes shift quickly from her back to me.

"Good, you know? Really good. I know Mr. Hewitt's worried—he's out here like every couple of days. But we're on schedule, swear to God. Most of the drywall is finished, and Marcello should be done with the electrical by end of next week, latest. Rodney's crew's working on the pipes. Another few days. We got the inspectors coming the week after. We'll be ready."

"That's great, Javier. Terrific." Hewitt wants a May Day grand opening. Shouldn't be a problem if Javier stays on schedule. "Mind if we take a look around?"

Enthusiastic nod. "Go for it. We're done for today, but I'll hang out."

I smile at him and slap him on the shoulder, glance up at the luminaires that are blazing even though daylight savings has rendered them ineffectual. "You can take off, Javier. I'll make sure everything's dark before I go."

The man gives me a sideways look, then turns toward Greta. Glances back at me with a knowing expression that I resent only because he's not wrong.

"Yeah, sure, Mr. Davenport. Okay."

"Javier, I've told you before to call me Sam."

"Yeah, I know, that's right. *Sam.* Okay. We'll be back first thing Monday. And like I said, no worries. Okay? We're on this."

I nod and watch as he gathers his men with hand gestures and quick, staccato phrases in Spanish. They move in a herd toward the parking lot, which has been paved but has yet to be marked for individual spaces.

Greta looks over at me, and a slow smile spreads across her face.

"Alone at last," she says.

I chuckle. "We were alone in the car all the way here," I say.

"Can't do much in an enclosed space, *Mr. Davenport.*" She takes a few steps and narrows the gap between us. "Care to show me your building?"

She closes her hand over mine, then slowly licks her lips. My arousal is swift. I think of Rachel and what she would say about this.

Greta squeezes my hand and pulls me toward the building. I go willingly.

FORTY-SEVEN

RACHEL

My call goes to voice mail, and I leave a quick message, then plug my phone into the charger. I carry the last of the plates to the sink and lower them into the sudsy water, then retrieve my wineglass and set it on the counter next to me. Ruth walks in, grabs a dish towel, and moves in beside me, at the ready. I feel her eyes on me but don't meet them. I run the sponge over a plate, scrubbing at the bits of melted cheese and red sauce that adhere to it.

"Kids okay?" I ask.

"Watching a cartoon in the big bed," she says.

Despite the fact that we have a fifty-inch screen in the living room, the kids prefer stretching out on Sam's and my bed and watching a show on the twenty-seven-inch TV mounted above the dresser. If Sam isn't home, like tonight, I'll allow them two before bed. When he's home, he'll give them one show, even watch it with them, then shoo them from the room so he can put on one of his favorites on Netflix.

"You okay, Rach?" Ruth asks. She takes the plate from me, dries it, and carefully places it in the dish rack. I know her hands are bothering her, but she doesn't complain, doesn't moan or whimper, which she usually does.

"Yes, of course," I tell her. "What about you? Hands okay? You know you can just leave the dishes in the rack and let them air dry."

"My hands are fine. You've been pretty quiet tonight."

"I was too busy eating your delicious lasagna to talk." She chuckles. Ruth loves flattery, and I suppose that's because she doesn't get very much in her life. I set the plate I'm washing back in the sink, then reach over and give her a soapy squeeze. "Thanks for dinner. And for coming over tonight on such short notice."

"I'm glad I'm here," she says, then glances at the remaining dirty dishes. "What do you say we leave these to soak and go sit and finish our wine?"

I consider her suggestion. I hate leaving dishes undone. I'll only have to do them later. But I might enjoy doing them more if I'm a little buzzed. Although the probability of breaking a few plates will increase proportionally to the amount of wine I drink. But, whatever. I nod to Ruth, and she smiles and sets the towel on the counter.

I grab my wineglass and the bottle of red and trail Ruth into the living room. Her gait is halting, as though her knees aren't fully cooperating, and my heart goes out to her. I don't know what I'd do if I couldn't jog or swim in the ocean or get down on the floor with my kids. I know Ruth feels less than because of it. She shouldn't, but she does. I want to say something, to ask if she's okay, but sometimes she reacts to my sympathy as though *I'm* the one making her feel less than. So I say nothing and slow my pace.

Shadow's nails clack on the wood floor as he follows us from the kitchen. He pads to the window, pushes aside the sheer curtain with his nose, and takes several strident sniffs of the air. Finally, he moseys to his bed and curls up in a big charcoal ball.

The wine is good, a cabernet recommended to me by the guy at Trader Joe's. I top off Ruth's glass, then my own, then settle next to her on the couch. I take a sip, then another. Every now and then, we hear giggles coming from the master bedroom, and the sound pleases me. Eden has been a sourpuss all afternoon. I'm not sure why. She isn't talking. But her moods always carry over onto her little brother, even when he has nothing to do with them. I'm not looking forward to her rapidly approaching adolescence. What the hell am I going to do with her when she's having her period? God. The idea frightens me.

Still, her grumpiness didn't get in the way of her appetite; she ate an enormous helping of Ruth's lasagna and asked for seconds, then topped it off with a scoop of ice cream. Ah, to have a ten-year-old's metabolism.

"Sure you're okay?" Ruth asks. If it weren't for the mellowing effect of the wine, I'd be irritated with her. "You seem a little distracted."

"I was going to say the same thing about you," I reply. And it's true. Since Jonah's lovely, heartbreaking comment about Ruth's loneliness, she's been quieter than usual. Ordinarily, she would correct my children's table manners, or scold Shadow when he begs for food, or, again, complain about the pain in her hands. She has done none of those things this evening.

"Just a long day, I guess."

"I don't know how you can have therapy first thing in the morning, sis. I can't even speak in full sentences before noon."

Ruth shifts beside me. She looks uncomfortable. "Yes, well, Dr. Moore is extremely busy. I take what he has available."

"It's helping you, right, Ruth?"

She stares at me for a moment, as if contemplating. Then she nods slowly. "It is. Maybe you should try it."

I force a laugh. "What do I need therapy for?"

Her gaze is unwavering. "You tell me." She reaches her hand out and places it on mine. "I'm your sister, Rach. I can tell when something's up."

"Nothing's up," I say, a little too quickly, and she arches her brows. "Honestly, Ruth, it's nothing. Sam's been a little off lately, and I . . . I'm not sure what it is."

"Is he having an affair?"

I roll my eyes, even though I'm not surprised by Ruth's instantaneous response. Adultery is her go-to problem when a man is in the equation. I don't blame her, after what she's been through with Charlie. I don't even allow myself to be annoyed by the question.

"No. It's not that."

"Are you sure?" she presses.

I laugh, this time with genuine humor. "Well, I don't suppose we can ever be one hundred percent sure, can we?" A sudden image of Sam's assistant comes to mind. The lovely Greta, a temptress, certainly, and she adores my husband. But no. No. Sam would never cheat. He might think about it. Haven't we all thought about cheating at one time or another? But he would never go through with it.

"As much as I can be sure of anything, I'm sure it's not that, Ruth."

She sighs, clearly not convinced, but she doesn't argue the point.

"I'm thinking midlife crisis," I say. "I just hope he buys himself a damn Ferrari and gets over it."

Ruth grins at me. "Can you afford a Ferrari?"

"If we sell the house." We both chuckle. I watch her as she takes a sip of wine. "And you? What's up?" She doesn't respond. "You said it yourself—we're sisters. Sisters can tell."

She lowers the wine into her lap and thinks for a long moment, then looks into her glass, as if the answer is there. "My neighbor."

"Your neighbor." I have no idea where this is leading. "Your neighbor, what?"

"He asked me out." She shakes her head. "No, he asked me in. He has a wonderful bottle of wine he wants to share with me. He's a very nice man. Widower."

Whoever he is, she likes him—that's clear. I try to wrap my mind around the situation, but I admit, I'm completely blown away. Ruth's never mentioned a neighbor to me before. Never mentioned any man other than Charlie. I have the urge to spring off the couch and jump up and down with glee. But I can tell by her expression that Ruth is conflicted. I keep my voice even.

"That's great, Ruth. When?"

"Tomorrow night."

"And? What did you say?"

Her voice is quiet. "I said yes."

I tamp down my excitement. "Wonderful."

"I'm going to cancel."

"Why?"

"Sunday is Easter. I have to make the pie."

I tsk. "Oh, please, Ruth. You can make banana cream pie in your sleep. Make it early. Don't make it at all. I'll buy one at the market." She looks at the floor. "What? What is it?"

"I don't know if I'm ready."

I gape at her. "Ruth, it's been eighteen months. How much longer do think you'll need to be ready? I'm sorry, but you're not getting any younger. None of us are." She winces, and I soften my tone. "You're a beautiful woman who deserves a little happiness. Or a lot of happiness. But you have to stop closing yourself off from it."

"I don't want to get hurt again." The confession costs her. Her eyes start to well up.

I put my hand on her shoulder. "It's just a bottle of wine, sis. It's not a marriage proposal. Have a little fun. Drink some wine. Talk. Get naked."

Her eyes go wide even as she starts to laugh. "Rachel!"

I shrug, glad to hear her laugh. "Okay, don't get naked. But it might be nice for you to get laid sometime before you die."

"You're terrible."

"Yes, but I'm also right." I pull my hand away and pick up my wineglass, take a sip. "Not all men are liars and cheaters, Ruth. Seriously. I mean, look at Sam."

She cocks her head to the side as if she still doubts Sam's innocence. I let it slide.

"Keep the date?"

After a slight hesitation, she nods. "Okay. I will. On one condition. I need you to dye my hair."

I grin at her and nod. Just like when we were kids, only back then, we dyed our hair only to try crazy colors, not to hide the gray. "Tomorrow morning?"

"I'll pick up the color at Target. I have to get the ingredients for the pie anyway. Then I'll swing by?"

"Perfect. Now, tell me all about him. Your *neighbor*."

"I don't know that much," she says.

"Then tell me what you know."

I sit back and listen to her describe her neighbor, feeling a little giddy on her behalf. My sister has a date. I know I shouldn't get too excited, but I can't help it. Plus, it gives me something to focus on other than the fact that my cell phone has remained maddeningly silent. Sam hasn't returned my call.

FORTY-EIGHT

RUTH

When Rachel goes upstairs to tuck the kids into bed, I slip into the kitchen and finish doing the dishes. I know I will pay for my kindness with a thousand daggers of pain tomorrow morning, but I'm feeling a little tipsy. Not from the wine, but from the conversation about Judd. Talking with Rachel about my neighbor has elevated my spirits to heights they haven't reached in a long time. Too long. And I hardly know the man! But when she and I were on the couch, and I was telling her about Judd's salt-and-pepper hair and his lean physique and the way his eyes sparkle when he talks to me . . . well, I felt like I was sixteen again.

Which I am not.

As I dry the last of the plates, a cloud skirts across my mind. I didn't tell Rachel about my weekly pilgrimage to the park to spy on my ex-husband's wife and children. I decided earlier not to share that information with her just yet, but I feel guilty about keeping it from her. At one point, when she asked me what was wrong, I almost spilled the whole thing, but then we got to talking about Judd—I feel my cheeks grow hot at the mere thought of him. There was no organic way to introduce the subject of the park after that. And it was so enjoyable to just be sisters, sitting, talking about a boy. I didn't want to spoil it.

"Oh, Ruth. You shouldn't have. Your hands." Rachel crosses to me and takes the dish from me, the last dish, as though this final one will be the straw that broke the camel's back, or the plate that broke her sister's hands.

"It's okay, Rach. I took Advil earlier."

"But they'll be sore tomorrow."

"Then I'll take more."

"Thank you. That was really nice." Since I told her about Judd, she's been wearing a perpetual grin. Rachel is excited for me. Probably more so than is warranted. I am excited, too, but seeing that grin on her face makes me nervous.

I dry my hands on the dish towel and glance at my watch. "I should get going. It's getting late."

"The kids want you to say good night before you leave," she says. "Do you mind?"

My heart swells. "I'd be delighted."

I walk to the stairs and place my hand on the rail, then hoist myself up the first rise, my knees protesting. It gets easier with each step, or I tell myself that. Once at the top, I head down the hall to Eden's room and knock softly on the open door.

"Hi, Aunt Ruth."

I enter and walk over to the bed, then sit down upon it. My niece, who during the day is so full of bluster and bravado, looks very small and very young lying beneath her pink floral comforter. The soft amber glow of the night-light illuminates her face. I can't help but see the beauty she will someday become. She looks so much like my sister, but her features are sharper, likely thanks to Sam, and those will render her even more striking than my sister.

"You wanted to see me?"

"Um . . ." She scrunches her nose up. "Well, Mom said she'd send you up we could say good night and thanks for the lasagna."

I deflate. So this wasn't the kids' idea, but Rachel's. *Poor lonely Ruth. Let's make her feel important and needed.* I wish I could bring myself to resent my sister's puppeteering, but I don't have the energy.

"It was really good," Eden says. "The lasagna. It's always really good, Aunt Ruth. So, thanks."

"You are very welcome," I say, lifted a little by her praise. "My mom, your grandma, taught me to make it. Maybe someday, I can teach you."

"That would be totally beast," she says.

I make a show of narrowing my eyes at her. "Beast? Is that a good thing?"

She smiles and nods. "Totally."

I lean over and kiss her forehead, then push myself off the bed and head for the door.

"Aunt Ruth," Eden calls to me. Her voice is soft, almost a whisper. "Did you ever like a boy who didn't like you back?"

I take a quick breath, then clear my throat to mask my discomfort. I cross back to the bed and peer down at her.

"As a matter of fact, I have." I think of Charlie, and the men and boys who came before him. I think of my college years, when unrequited love was the norm.

Eden sighs. "It's kind of a bummer, huh?"

"Totally," I say. I sit back down and gently run my fingers through her strawberry-blonde locks. This is a moment I'll treasure, a private, quiet interlude between my niece and me.

"But, you know, Eden. Any boy that you like, who doesn't like you, well, that boy isn't the brightest watt in the bulb. Not very smart, if you ask me. Because you are amazing."

"You have to say that because you're my aunt."

"I don't have to say any such thing," I tell her. "I say it because it's true."

"Thanks, Aunt Ruth," she says.

"Feel better?" I ask.

She gives me a half smile. "Not really."

I chuckle and tweak her nose. "That's okay. You will. I promise."

I kiss her again, then get up and move to the hallway, then head for Jonah's room.

My nephew's night-light is Thomas the Train and casts a blue hue over his skin, making it look deathly pale, almost translucent. The stuffed monkey is firmly in his grasp, its head tucked into the hollow of his neck. Jonah's eyes are closed, and his breathing is so deep and steady that I think he's asleep. But when I bend over to kiss his cheek, his eyes pop open.

"Hi, Auntie Ruth. We were waiting for you. Marco wanted to say thanks for the lasagna. He told me it was the best lasagna he's ever had, like, in the entire world."

"Well, I'm so glad to hear that." I sit on his bed, as I did in Eden's room, and stroke Jonah's forehead. He looks so much like Sam, barely a trace of Rachel in him. I wonder, as I gaze at his dark curls and dark-brown eyes, what my son would have looked like, if Charlie and I had been blessed with one. Would he have taken all of his father's attributes? Or would I be able to see some of myself in him?

Useless questions. Worse than useless. Masochistic.

"I can't wait for Marco and me to stay over at your house," he says, his voice thick with fatigue. I don't correct him by pointing out that my home is an apartment, not a house. Children are forgiving and easy-going and accepting. Until they're not. So I've heard.

"I think Marco would like your tuna melts." He yawns.

"Well, everyone else does."

"Got any bugs at your house, Auntie Ruth? Marco likes bugs almost as much as me."

I smile down at him and pat his arm. "I think I might have a few cockroaches."

His eyes go round at that. "Cockroaches are super cool. They got an *exoskeleton*, and that means their bones are on the *outside*. And if the world blew up, cockroaches would live through it and you can, like, put 'em in the microwave for like five minutes, and they'll be just fine and dandy."

I stifle a shudder. "Isn't that interesting."

He yawns again. "Okay, night-night, Auntie Ruth."

"Good night, little man." I kiss his cheek for the second time, then pull his covers over his chest and tuck them around him.

I stand and gaze at him, marveling at his preciousness. I think of my few cherished minutes with Eden.

I am not a mother, nor will I ever be. This is the closest to motherhood I will ever get.

I soak it in, revel in it, and cloak myself with it, as though it is armor, as though it will protect me and bolster me for the moment so soon to come, when will I return, alone, to my empty apartment.

FORTY-NINE

SHADOW

I like this time of night, because my ears get to rest. Not that they don't hear things. They hear everything. They hear the buzz of the poles on the sidewalk outside the house, and the cars—not just the ones that pass on the dark strip outside, but farther away. And they hear the critters outside and the hum inside the walls of the house, and sometimes a big roaring sound from the sky. But at this time, there's less for my ears to hear, and that means I can sleep good.

I'm not sleeping now because I can't. My master isn't home. And usually he's home this time of night, when the light leaves the sky and it's black outside and the sounds get less in my ears. But he's not here now, and I won't go to sleep until all my humans are here.

Little Female and Little Male are upstairs. When I sniff the air, I can tell that they are both not sleeping. Their smell is awake. But they are quiet. I smell them being tired.

My mistress sits at the table in the food-smelling room. I am in the couch room because that room is closest to the door, and I can greet my master when he comes in. But my mistress smells different tonight. Usually, she smells like happy face and outside air. But not now.

I get up on all my paws. I am going to the food-smelling room, but first my paws take me to the window. I look outside the glass, but I can't see when it's black outside. I sniff the air, but I can't smell the cat.

I trot into the food-smelling room and go to the table, where my mistress sits. She looks down at her little screen. Her face is not mad and it's not happy, but her eyes are frowning. She puts the little screen thing on the table and picks up a glass bowl with a long glass leg, filled with something that smells like I wouldn't think it's tasty. She drinks it down, then looks at me. She pats my head and scratches under my chin and tells me I'm a Good Boy. But the sound of her voice makes me think that even though she said it, she's not really thinking about me.

I sit next to my mistress's feet, then slide into down, even though my mistress didn't tell me *down*. I roll over so that my belly is facing my mistress. When I do this, my humans always reach over and scratch my belly, like they can't help themselves. But my mistress isn't even looking at me.

I roll back to down and look up at her. She empties the glass bowl with the glass leg and sets it on the table, then looks at me. She smiles, and it is a good smile. It's the smile that tells me she's about to get down on the floor with me. And she does, putting each leg on either side of me and her arms around me and scratching me until my back paw starts shaking without me wanting it to.

A part of me wants to go back to the couch-room bed to wait for my master, but I can't leave the scratching and tickling and lovies from my mistress. My mistress is the best human when it comes to lovies. I think I like her lovies better than food. Maybe.

When she stops, I'll go back to my couch-room bed. And even though I can't tell how the time passes, I hope she doesn't stop for a long while.

FIFTY

JONAH

"Marco. Tomorrow we're going to find bugs."

Marco doesn't say anything. I really don't expect him to 'cause he's not real, he's just a stuffed animal. But even though I know that, I kind of think maybe he's more than that. Marco's been to a lot of places, to lots of different houses with kids like me and their families.

Mommy read me a story a little while ago, a story she said her mommy read to her when she was little. It was called *The Velveteen Rabbit*, and it was about a stuffed animal who got loved on so much that he became totally real. I think maybe Marco is real, but only when the lights are out and everyone's asleep. Kind of like Santa Claus, 'cause he only comes when all the kids are sleeping.

"I think you're real, Marco. I know you are," I tell him. "And I know you're not going to come to life until after I fall asleep, but that's okay. I got real awesome books you can read, like *Goodnight Moon* and *Where Do Balloons Go* and *Alexander and the Terrible, Horrible, No Good, Very Bad Day*. I can't read that one by myself, but I bet you can. And I got a big 'cyclopedia of bugs—it's on the bottom shelf and Auntie Ruth gave that one to me, and that one would be really good for you to read tonight while I'm sleeping so you're ready to find bugs tomorrow morning."

Marco doesn't move. His skin is like the blanket my nanny made for me when I was born, all knitted with yarn. It's brown on his arms and legs and back, but then on his face, his nose and mouth are a lighter color, like sand, like the color of Mommy and Daddy's bathroom. And then there's a red stripe across the middle of his mouth, I guess for his lips. They're kind of curvy up, like in a smile, and his eyes are shiny black buttons.

He's smiling at me, and I squeeze him tight and think about all the eggs I found today, and counting them. And then, when we got back to Mrs. Hartnett's classroom, how she went over to the big cabinet and pulled Marco down off the shelf and handed him to me with a really serious face, telling me what an honor it was for me to have Marco for the whole break and how important it was for me to take real good care of him. I already knew that, but I nodded anyway so she'd know I knew.

I'm so excited that I get to keep him for a week—nine whole days, if you count the weekends. I already love him lots, and I know I'm going to be sad when I have to take him back to Mrs. Hartnett, but I'm not going to think about that. I'm just going to have the best time ever. Starting tomorrow.

I pull on Marco's arms and bend them up and down, and then I think maybe he won't be strong enough to get the 'cyclopedia off the shelf. Maybe when he comes alive he gets all strong and stuff, but what if he doesn't? I push off my covers and get out of bed and go to my bookshelf, then I drag the big 'cyclopedia off the shelf and put it on the floor. I open it to the middle of the book. I can't see the pages real good 'cause it's pretty dark, but I can tell by the shape that the bug on the page is from the order Coleoptera. Beetles and weevils. I think it's a Buprestidae. I know most of the orders and suborders, and Daddy and Mommy think I'm a genius when it comes to bugs, even though Mommy gets all icked out when I talk about some of them.

I kind of want to turn on my light and look through my 'cyclopedia, but I know I need to go to sleep so I can have lots of energy for tomorrow.

I leave the 'cyclopedia open for Marco, then crawl back into bed and pull my covers up over me and him, then pull him into me.

"Tomorrow's gonna be the best day ever, Marco."

FIFTY-ONE

EDEN

I feel tired, but my stomach is still really full, so it's hard to get comfy. I probably shouldn't have had seconds at dinner, but Aunt Ruth's lasagna is so yummy, I couldn't help it.

I like what she said to me before, about me feeling better soon. I hope she's right. I try to tell myself over and over that I never really liked Ryan Anderson that much, but it feels like a lie. I should have read Percy Jackson before dinner instead of looking at my yearbook from last year. I kept reading what Ryan wrote. I read it so much, I know it by heart.

Ur 2 good 2 B 4gotten. Have a gr8 summer. Stay awesome. RyAn.

Ryan Anderson.

Stay awesome. He thinks I'm awesome. Well, he did at the end of the school year last year. I don't think he thinks I'm awesome now, not after Jonah attacked me with hugs today. But he used to think I was awesome.

Fuck Jonah, I think. And then my cheeks get really hot because even though I didn't say the f-word out loud, which would mean I owed, like, twenty dollars to the curse jar, I *thought* the f-word, and that's bad.

Especially because I thought it toward my little brother. And that's a big-time no-no.

The night-light in the corner of my room makes a shadow dance on the ceiling. I told Mom and Dad that I didn't need a night-light, that I was too old for one. But they said it was for them, so that they wouldn't trip over anything when they came to check on me. I know they only told me that so they could keep the light on for me, and I was kind of mad, like I thought maybe they were thinking I was a baby who needed it. But I'm kind of glad they kept it. It's not that I'm afraid of the dark, or anything, not like Jonah, who wants Mom and Dad to keep the hall light on. I don't like the hall light being on, because it's too bright and I can't sleep. So Mom told me I could close my door—almost all the way. But the night-light is okay because if I need to go to the bathroom— and sometimes I do in the middle of the night—I can see my way.

And also, the night-light helps keep the monsters away.

I don't believe in monsters, not really, but I know that bad things can happen, and sometimes they happen in the middle of the night, and sometimes when they happen, if only a light had been on, then the bad things might not have been *too* bad, because you could see your way out of them.

I know I should be real happy. It's the start of spring break, and I have a whole week of sleeping late and not going to school and not doing homework. But I won't get to see Ryan, either, and that sucks big-time. *Uh-oh.* I owe the curse jar, like, twenty-*five* dollars now, but I can't help what I think.

It's okay. It's spring break, and maybe by the time we go back to school, Ryan will have forgotten about Jonah's hug, and he'll start acting normal again, like he knows I exist, that I'm there, and we'll talk about favorite candies and things.

It's going to be a fun vacation. Mom and Dad haven't said anything about plans to go away or anything. But that's okay. It's better, really, because then I can spend more time with my friends. I think I'll

FaceTime Carlee in the morning. Maybe Ava, too. Maybe we can have a playdate. I know Mom will let me.

My eyes start feeling really heavy and tired. I like watching the dancing shadow on the ceiling, but I can't keep my eyelids open any longer. I close them and see Ryan Anderson in my brain. He's smiling, and I can't help but smile back.

FIFTY-TWO

SAMUEL

What the hell am I doing?

Greta and I have traversed the entire building. She has boosted my pride by oohing and ahhing at the appropriate moments, but when I remember her enthusiasm for the nearby Ross Dress for Less and Raising Cane's, my own gratification is somewhat tempered.

We are now in the sleeping quarters of the center. There are no beds—thank God. The square cutouts in the walls where the windows will be let in the cool breeze of the April night. The rooms are small, dormitory-style, only large enough to accommodate two beds. The center will have the capacity to house fifty-two people at any given time, based on need. The occupancy is not my purview, however. I designed the space as per my client's instructions. Once the center is complete, it will merely be another entry on my résumé, another group of photos in our catalog.

"This is phenomenal," she says. *Phenomenal* is her word of choice. The first time she said it, my loins stirred. Now, on the eleventh usage, I feel my scrotum shrivel.

Greta walks the length of the room, away from me, then turns on her stiletto heels, and walks back toward me. She smiles like a Cheshire cat. "You really are amazing, you know."

I shake my head. Her smile has brought my lower region back to life.

"This isn't the Twin Towers, or the Chrysler Building or the Eiffel Tower," I say.

She looks down at the concrete floor, which a month from now will be covered with laminate masquerading as hard wood.

"No, it's none of those things," she says. "But this place, it has a purpose. An honorable purpose. And you have created a space that will give dignity to those poor souls who need to be here, who've come for redemption."

Her assessment causes me to take a step toward her. Despite my ambivalence about this project, nothing is more seductive than a beautiful woman's idolatry.

"I've learned so much from you, Samuel," she says, her luscious lips turning up into a smile.

"I'm glad." I can't think of anything else to say.

"And I really appreciate the interest you've taken in me. You're so patient. You take time. You've really helped me to understand the whole process." Another step toward me. A mere eighteen inches separate us.

My brain suddenly suffers from lack of circulation due to the fact that all the blood in my body is rushing to my dick. "A part of me always wanted to be a teacher."

Her eyes go wide with glee. "You'd make a wonderful teacher."

"You think?" I ask. Ironic, because I've lost the ability to form coherent thoughts.

"Definitely."

I clear my throat, hoping to clear the fog from my head. "Well, teachers are paid a lot less than architects."

Her gaze is direct. "Money isn't everything." She closes the space between us. I can feel her breath on my neck. "Can I tell you something?"

I nod, unable to trust my voice. She grins. "I think you know what I'm going to say, Samuel. I have a crush on you."

I take a deep breath and exhale slowly as I quickly ponder the ramifications of her words. I knew it, of course I did, but confronted with her confirmation, I find myself at a loss. What now? My dick is hard, twitching, craving, ready. But my brain is full of noise.

"You have a crush on me, too, don't you?"

I can't bring myself to give her an answer. She doesn't need one. She wraps her arms around my waist and presses herself against me. I don't reciprocate, but my erection gives me away. She pulls away slightly, glances down, then back up again. Her grin has become feral.

"I knew it." She rests her head against my chest and starts to slide her hands across my back. I remain paralyzed, unable to act or react, but Greta appears unfazed.

"It's okay, Samuel. I know you're conflicted. I am too. I *like* Rachel. She's phenomenal. She gives me lovely gifts for my birthday and for Christmas. And the way she is with your kids. Fantastic."

I want to yell at her to stop talking about my wife, especially while she rubs herself against me. It would be comical if it weren't so grotesque.

"We don't have to do anything," she whispers, and the soft, throaty timbre of her voice almost sends me over the edge. I see myself grabbing her by the shoulders, shoving her against the wall, turning her around so that her ass is mine to own, to violate, to ram into until I explode inside her. This vision fills me with shame, but also with a sense of longing so excruciating, I can barely stand it.

Greta reaches up and grasps my neck with her hands and pulls my face toward hers. An instant later, she gently grazes her lips across mine. When I don't protest, she tilts her face to the side and aggressively takes my mouth.

I could kiss her back. I *would* kiss her back, but I'm suddenly besieged by vivid images of my family. If a person on the brink of death sees his life flash before his eyes, a man on the brink of cheating might also see his wife, his children, his entire familial existence flash before his eyes.

Rachel on our wedding day, smiling, eyes dancing, beautiful. Rachel in labor with Eden, a fierce warrior; stitching a Halloween costume by hand, grinning as she sucks on her punctured thumb. Eden on the monkey bars, at her ballet recital, proudly displaying an academic award at school. Jonah riding his Big Wheel, writing his name for the first time, joyfully finding a wasp's nest in the neighbor's yard. The four of us on the beach, at Disneyland, at the fair, at dinner, laughing, holding hands, all of us together.

With those pictures of Rachel and Eden and Jonah crowding my mind, I realize that Greta's lips, which I once thought sensual and imagined would be sweet like strawberries, taste bitter on my tongue. Her caress feels like dry ice scraping across the skin of my neck; her breath smells fetid. Bile rises from my stomach and burns my esophagus. My erection deflates, once and for all.

Even as Greta continues to grind against me and plant warm, wet kisses on my neck and nibble on my ear, I consider how best to disengage from her. She is a lovely young woman, and I don't want to hurt her feelings or alienate her. Selfish bastard that I am, I don't want to lose the best assistant I've ever had.

My ringtone chimes from my breast pocket, and Greta freezes. I take the opportunity to pull away from her. She steps back, grinning at me and breathing heavily, unaware of my complete withdrawal from the situation. I grab my cell from my pocket and stare at the screen, which is filled with the picture of my beautiful, smiling wife. *Rachel.*

How could I have allowed this to go so far?

I'm sorry, Rachel.

I can't go through with it, though. Doesn't that count for something?

I will never let anything like this happen again, I swear to you, Rachel.

"You can answer it if you need to," Greta says, even as I let the call go to voice mail.

I shake my head and look down at the concrete floor. "I should get home," I tell her, forcing a tone of regret. She nods and smiles, not sadly, but knowingly, as though this night—here at the center, where she pressed her lips against mine in a cold, nondescript, unfinished room—this was only the first time, that there will be more stolen kisses, more covert rendezvous, that a series of secret liaisons lie ahead for us. That there is and *will* be an *us*. I don't disabuse her of that fantasy, but a fantasy is what it is. I will never stray from my wife. I will never, in any way, put my family in jeopardy. I will not lose the amazing, blessed life I have.

The drive back is interminable. I can't wait to get home.

FIFTY-THREE

RACHEL

The kids are asleep. Eden's chest rises and falls; her eyelids flutter as though she is dreaming I gently brush errant strands of hair off her face, then kiss her forehead. I close the door almost all the way, then walk to Jonah's room. He snores lightly, and I smile at the familiar sound. Marco is tucked in the crook of Jonah's neck, his long stuffed arm draped across Jonah's middle. I move to the bed and repeat my ritual, smoothing Jonah's curls and kissing him softly on his cheek.

As I retrace my steps to the door, my toe catches on something, and I stumble. I look down and see Jonah's bug encyclopedia lying on the floor, open, pages fluttering from where my foot hit it. The pages come to rest. In the low light of Thomas the Train, I can barely make out a glossy picture of some horrendous creature. Jonah loves the book, a huge score for Ruth. She gave it to him for his last birthday, having chosen it without any help from me. She was delighted by his reaction.

I consider closing the book and returning it to the shelf, but I'm fairly certain that Jonah left it out for a reason. Probably, he wants it to be waiting for him when he jumps out of bed in the morning. Likely, he had it open to a particular page, but there's nothing I can do about that, since I have no idea which disgusting bug he chose to greet him.

I leave his door open so that he can see the hall light if he wakes up, then I wander back downstairs. Shadow lies on his bed in the living room. His head is down, but he's wide-awake and gazing at the front door.

"It's okay, boy," I tell him, and his ears flop toward me. "Daddy will be home soon." *I hope.*

I take a minute to straighten the pillows on the couch, then shuffle into the kitchen. I check my phone to see whether or not Ruth has texted—she usually does to let me know she got home safely. There's a text from her: Safe and sound. Thanks for tonight. See you in the morning.

There's also a text from Sam: On my way. Home soon. Need anything? xxoo.

A sigh escapes me. I reread the message and feel my shoulders loosen for the first time since this morning. Sam's text is the usual, nothing extraordinary about it. And its ordinariness gives me relief. Everything's fine. Sam is fine. Sam is Sam, green eggs and ham. Maybe he's a little stressed about work or his upcoming birthday or . . . whatever. But he's okay. We're okay.

I send him a quick response. Don't need anything but you. xxoo

I've probably been paranoid these past few weeks, reading into every little thing he does, every one of his gestures, every word out of his mouth. With that kind of scrutiny, how could I not suspect something was going on? Our lives shift daily. Our moods, our outlooks. Mine do, for sure. If Sam looked a little too closely at me for a little too long, he might think I was schizophrenic. I don't share with him all of the thoughts and feelings I have over the course of the day, how some mornings I wake up worried about my sagging boobs and widening ass, or obsessing about the trash island in the South Pacific, or wondering whether or not one of my children will turn out to be transgender. Sam doesn't need to know these things, nor do I need to know every little thought or concern or dilemma he's having every moment of every day.

As I move through the downstairs and turn off most of the lights, I make a decision to stop looking too closely at Sam and just be here for him when and if he needs me. He always comes to me when it's important. Always.

"Good night, boy." I pat Shadow on the head, then check to make sure the porch light is on, even though I know it is. I cross to the stairs and head up.

I get ready for bed, then put on my favorite cotton nightie, mint green with little blue daisies. It's a bit old-lady-ish, but Sam swears he thinks it's sexy on me. I pull back the covers and climb into bed, then reach for the novel on my nightstand.

For a few minutes, I just stare at the book cover and think about Ruth and her date tomorrow night. I send up a quick prayer that she has a good time with her neighbor. What I told her was true. She deserves to be happy. She deserves the attention of a nice man. It would also be nice not to have to worry about her as much as I do.

I open the novel to my bookmark and start to read. As much as I want to be awake when Sam gets home, I can barely keep my eyes open. *How pathetic!* I think with a laugh. In bed and exhausted by nine fifteen on a Friday night.

I suppress a yawn only to give in to another. I try to focus on the page, even though I doubt I'll get to the end of the chapter. Still, I make a valiant effort.

I don't want to waste the nightie.

FIFTY-FOUR

RUTH

I go about my nightly ablutions with the same enthusiasm as always, only tonight, I'm actually hoping the wrinkle erase and the firming cream and the whitening toothpaste will do their jobs. Laughable, really. I know in the morning I will look exactly the same as I do now.

I bend down and peer into the small four-times magnifying mirror on the vanity and inspect my eyebrows. I haven't tweezed them in far too long, and I am starting to resemble Frida Kahlo. I decide to wait until just before my date tomorrow night so I won't be surprised by any last-minute hair eruptions that might occur between now and then.

My date tomorrow night. My stomach tightens, although I'm not sure if I'm feeling dread or anticipation. Probably both.

I stand and look at my reflection, and for a brief moment, I wonder how Judd sees me, how he will look at me tomorrow night. I hope his lighting is soft. I'm not being negative, just practical. I am a middle-aged woman. Not unattractive. But not twenty-five.

The hair dye will help. I always feel better, *younger,* when the gray is banished.

Rachel thinks I close myself off, and she's right. She also thinks that I don't care what I look like, that I don't put more than the most minimal effort into my appearance. But she's wrong on that score. If she took a minute to investigate the creams and toners and lotions I've accumulated, if she saw the amount of money I've spent on these products, she'd realize her mistake.

I let my roots grow out and I forget to pluck my brows, and I wear comfortable clothing as opposed to stylish and flirty. Because I haven't been interested in drawing attention to myself, especially from members of the opposite sex. But I've always known, at some point, that would change. Hoped, anyway. Hoped there would come a time when my grief over Charlie would reduce itself to a more manageable emotion, and I would get past my persecution of the entire male population if only to have the companionship and comfort that all human beings crave. To stave off the ever-present loneliness. It hasn't happened yet, but I still cling to the idea, in the deepest corner of my heart where no one else can see it.

Thus the skin products and nightly regimen.

I don my flannel pajamas and sit down on my bed and turn on the little thirteen-inch TV on my dresser. My bedroom is small enough that I can touch the dresser from the end of my bed, but I don't mind much. If the room were larger, the TV would be farther away, and I wouldn't be able to see it.

As I surf through channels, my thoughts settle on Judd. I won't get my hopes up. But I will allow myself to look forward to our date. For eighteen months, I've been living a kind of half life, unable or unwilling to look to the future with optimism. Whether or not the evening goes well, I must change my perspective. I must stop going to the park. I must stop obsessing over Charlie and his wife and children. I need to let go of him, wish him well, accept the fact that he has a new life and let him live it. And I need to live mine.

Perhaps tomorrow will be the beginning of a new chapter for me. A new and exciting adventure.

Perhaps *after* tomorrow, my nephew will no longer see me as his lonely old aunt who needs a stuffed monkey to keep her company.

Wouldn't that be nice?

FIFTY-FIVE

SHADOW

I hear my master's car outside, and my tail thumps against my bed. His footsteps get louder until I can smell him by the front door. I stand up and step off my bed, and my nails make a clack on the floor. I stretch my legs forward, then I shake myself and my collar jingles. The front door opens and I see my master, and my tail wags faster and faster and thumps against the wall. I am happy to see him and also happy that all my humans are home where I can protect them and keep them safe.

The smell on my master is strange and strong and feels funny in my nose. It smells like something I know, something food-smelling and sweet, but I know if I tasted it, it would burn my mouth. The smell makes me sneeze.

My master seems tired, but he makes a small happy face at me and scratches my neck, but not for very long. He says my name and calls me a Good Boy, then walks past me to the stairs.

He looks up to the second floor, where I'm not allowed, stands there for I don't know how long, but for longer than he scratched my neck. He turns his head like he's listening, so I listen, too, but all I hear are my sleeping humans.

My master turns back around and makes a frown face, then sniffs his jacket. He can smell that strange smell—not like I can, because dogs' noses are better than human noses, but I can tell my master doesn't like that smell. He takes his jacket off and carries it down the hall, then comes back without the jacket. He walks to the food-smelling room, and I follow him so he'll give me a treat, but he doesn't. He goes to the sink and washes his hands, then splashes water on his face.

I can still smell the strange smell from the jacket down the hall, but it's much less, and my master barely smells like it at all now. I want a treat, so I let out a whine and a small bark.

"Quiet, Shadow," my master says, and I know I'm not supposed to bark when my humans are sleeping, but I really want a treat. I feel a whine in the back of my throat and try to stop it. My master looks at me and smiles, then gets a treat for me and tosses it in the air. I jump up and snap my jaws around it before my paws hit the floor. I hold the treat in my mouth and take it to the bed and start to eat it.

My master goes to the big cold box and opens the door and brings out a bottle. He pulls the top off and drinks from it. I watch him walk slowly to the table and sit down, and I know better than to go to his feet and beg because he doesn't have anything that I would like.

He drinks from the bottle again, then sets it down. He rests his arms on the table, with his hands up by his face. He rubs his face with his hands, harder than when he pets me, then stares at the kitchen door. I hear him breathe very big and long, and the air whooshes out of him. He makes a happy face, then finishes the liquid from the bottle. He stands up and sets the bottle next to the sink, then walks out of the food-smelling room.

I get up as fast as I can and follow him to the stairs. He looks down at me, then sits on the stairs and gives me a few good scratches and belly rubs, even tickles me until my leg starts moving all by itself, just like it did when my mistress petted me. He tells me Good Boy again, and I see and smell happy on my master.

He tells me, "Good night, Shadow," and I know this means that I won't see my humans until the sky is light again. But that's okay, because I can still hear them and smell them, even from down here. My master goes up the stairs. I watch him until I can't see him anymore. Then I go to my couch-room bed. I don't lie down, because a smell just came to my nose. The smell that makes me whine and bark, but I don't because I don't want to wake up my humans.

I walk over to the window and sneak my nose through the fabric, then sniff. I look through the glass, but there's only darkness. I can't see anything.

But I know the cat is there. I can smell it.

PART FOUR:
ANOTHER DAY WITH
DR. MEYERS

FIFTY-SIX

MADDIE

I've seen the Davenport family twice a week for the past two weeks, and we've come to an impasse. Grief counseling can be a long process, and as a therapist, I must be patient. But something about the Davenport family's plight has captured my imagination and caused me to become nearly obsessed with them. Since getting my PhD and setting up my practice, I've always been aware of the dangers of getting too close to a patient or to a specific situation. It colors the therapist's judgment and devaluates their treatment. But the truth is, I can't help myself.

Every night over the past two weeks, I have removed the photograph of Jonah Davenport from the file and allowed myself to gaze at it for long moments. I'm not sure exactly why I do this. Perhaps I see in him the child I decided not to have, although his coloring is a little too light to be sprung from my loins, even with Peter's donation.

Jonah Davenport has become real to me, this child. Alive. He has begun to haunt my dreams. When I close my eyes, I see him running across my lawn, chasing a bug, his dark curls bouncing about his neck, his laughter floating through the air.

I like this family. It is not my job to like or dislike my patients. My job is to help them. These are good people. Not perfect, but good. I feel their goodness instinctually, and I want them to get past their grief so they can go on to live fulfilling lives and spread their warmth and generosity and kindness to others. Like most of my patients, each member of this family has the ability to have a positive impact on the world around them, whether they know it or not.

Yet each of them is paralyzed by his or her guilt, unable to break free and move forward. I have not been able to get to the root of their guilt. I have not been able to coax any clear admission from any of them. They hold tight to their own roles, or *supposed* roles, in Jonah's death.

My next appointment with them is tomorrow morning.

After a light meal of leftover poached salmon and asparagus, I run myself a bath, take one hit from the joint I rolled a few nights ago, then soak for thirty minutes. I try to think of anything but the Davenports. I try to think of nothing. It doesn't work.

I wrap myself in my terry-cloth robe, then carry my iPad to the bed and make myself comfy. I check the clock on the nightstand, then open the FaceTime app and call Peter. He answers immediately, as if he's been waiting for my call. He looks tired.

"You're a sight for sore eyes," he says.

"Back at you," I tell him. "Long day?"

"Definitely earned my paycheck today." He narrows his eyes at me. "What's up? You have that look."

My husband knows me well. Even through the screen, he is able to sense my mood. I love that about him—most of the time, anyway.

I tell him about the Davenports. I am discreet, only giving him the broad strokes, no names, and although he is exhausted, he listens quietly and patiently before offering me his objective advice.

"Have you spoken with them about the day it happened?" he asks, and I shake my head.

"I've tried. I've brought it up to each of them and introduced the subject to them as a group, but they resist. I haven't wanted to push. It's all about building trust right now."

"And do you feel you've done that? Built trust?"

"With the daughter, yes. The wife doesn't seem to trust anyone. The husband is trying, and the sister . . . well, she trusts me, I think."

I stare at my husband's image on the iPad. Peter's face is smaller than in real life, but just as handsome. His blue-eyed gaze is direct. "If this initial part of therapy is about building trust, why are you pushing for revelations?"

I don't tell him about my latest dream, in which Jonah Davenport came to me. I don't tell him that a dead little boy implored me to help—and fast. Those were his words. *You gotta help 'em, and fast.* My husband is a numbers man, left-brained, practical to a fault. An atheist, as opposed to my fence-sitting agnosticism. He wouldn't understand. He would tell me my dreams are a projection of my desire to help the family. He'd be right. And yet, they feel more like visions, as though if I were to awaken, Jonah would be sitting beside me on my bed. His *ghost.*

"I just . . . If they don't get past the guilt, they won't be able to fully grieve and let their loved one rest. The longer they carry it, the more likely it is to destroy them. The family unit is in a precarious position at best. Every day is like a ticking clock counting down to an atomic bomb that will blow them apart."

"Hmm." He considers my words for a moment. Then, "Well, my love, your only option is to press the issue. Make them talk about that day."

I release a pent-up breath. His words mirror my own conclusion. "It could be too soon."

"Better than too late," he says.

I nod. "I miss you, tonight especially."

"I miss you, too. I trust Cleopatra is keeping you company." He grins at me, knowing how fickle our cat is. Then he grows serious again. "Look, Mads. Your instincts and your compassion are two of the qualities that make you extraordinary at what you do. Use them. They won't let you down."

Our conversation shifts focus, and he tells me about his day. I force myself to listen actively, as he did for me. It's difficult, as my thoughts are elsewhere, but I manage. When he's finished with his story, I ask him if he would like to partake in a little FaceTime naughtiness, but my offer is more obligatory than sincere. If he wants to, I will, and I will enjoy it—it actually might help take my mind off the Davenports for fifteen minutes. But I'm relieved when he begs off.

"Sorry, darling. I don't have the energy tonight. Mind if we save our strength for the weekend?"

A few minutes later, we sign off. I shut down the iPad and lean back against the headboard, glance at the eight-by-ten glossy of Jonah Davenport resting on top of the file folder on the nightstand.

Cleopatra wanders in from the hall, languidly walks across the floor, and comes to a stop a few feet from my side of the bed. She sits back on her haunches and regards me with wary green eyes. She cocks her head and seems to stare at the nightstand, then returns her gaze to me.

On the nights Peter is away, Cleopatra sleeps with me. She jumps onto the end of the bed and makes a show of ignoring me, paws the comforter, then collapses into a fluffy white ball and falls asleep. Over the course of the night, she worms her way ever closer to me and ends up curling into the crook of my neck and staying there until I awaken in the morning.

From the first night I dreamed about Jonah Davenport, and for all subsequent nights, she has stayed away, preferring a perch on the couch or the easy chair in the living room. My rational brain knows this is only coincidence. Of course it is. Any other supposition would be ridiculous.

My junior year in college I took a parapsychology course as an elective. Ghosts and apparitions, demonic possessions and other unexplained phenomena. I'd listened politely to the professor, whose mismatched, obnoxiously colorful fashion choices were another unexplained phenomenon. He was very passionate about the subject. He was a believer.

I did well in class, but I was not swayed. Quite the opposite. With each sighting or fantastical occurrence, I psychologically analyzed those persons involved with the experience. Asked questions. Why does this granny need to see the ghost of a young Victorian girl in her garden? Why did that teenager need to see inexplicable lights in the sky? What suppressed torments did this prepubescent girl endure that she felt she must conjure a demon to overtake her?

And yet, even as I rejected the material presented to me, I admit there was an infinitesimal part of me—perhaps the agnostic in me who *just doesn't know*—that was persuaded to *allow for the possibility* that some things are beyond our understanding.

Rachel Davenport claims she has seen Jonah. She grows more coherent and less medicated with each session, yet she has never rescinded her statements. In fact, she says he's come to her again. I have no doubt that she *believes* she sees him. And the mind is capable of creating powerful illusions.

Cleopatra hasn't moved. She remains where she is and watches me closely. I pick up the photograph of Jonah, and she mewls softly. A shiver runs down my spine, and my arms are suddenly covered with gooseflesh.

I look at the photo and think about the vivid *realness* of Jonah's presence in my dreams—Jonah, a boy I have never met. Cleopatra swishes her tail rapidly.

I set the photograph back down, and she mewls again. I stare at her unblinking green eyes. *Is it possible?*

Cleopatra yawns, then jumps up on the bed. I laugh out loud and shake my head with self-mocking. It must be the pot. I don't believe in ghosts. My dreams are just dreams. And I can't let all this worthless mental exercise cloud my prime objective—to help the Davenports move on.

FIFTY-SEVEN

The Family

On the first of our biweekly sessions, I meet with the family as a group before splitting off and speaking to them individually. Not much has been accomplished during this time—each family member seems reluctant to share anything of significance—but I feel it is necessary, since my ultimate goal is to restore them to a whole unit.

This morning, they are all in their usual places. Ruth and Rachel sit side by side on one couch, Sam by himself on the other. Eden occupies the easy chair next to mine and Shadow sits at attention in front of her. She has brought the dog to each of our sessions, and he has a calming, comforting effect on her. I can tell he is a good dog, gentle and loving, with warm brown eyes that take in everything. Sam and Rachel are indifferent to his presence, but Ruth's disdain for the canine is evident.

Ruth holds a mug in her hand, as per usual. She makes green tea as soon as she walks in and leaves the tea bag in the water for the duration of the session. By the time her individual slot is finished, the remaining tea is the color of moss. Sam brings his own travel mug filled with coffee and sips it until it's empty, then rinses the mug in the sink. Rachel sits with her hands in her lap, often worrying them or picking at her cuticles. Ruth always offers to make her tea or a pot of coffee or to bring her juice or water, and Rachel always declines. When Eden arrives, she scurries to the fridge and pulls out a juice box, drinks it down immediately, then tosses the empty in the trash and cements herself to Shadow.

Dark crescents bruise the skin below Sam's eyes. The line between his brows is as deep as a trench. He appears to have lost weight since our initial meeting, and his stoop is more pronounced than it was. Ruth's hair is pulled into a loose, disheveled knot with at least six inches of gray winding down from her scalp. She wears an oversize knit sweater, old and peppered with holes. Her lips are pinched with tension. Rachel stares at her hands. Her color is better; gone is the sickly pallor she had when we met, although her cheeks are far from rosy. The vacant look is gone from her eyes. But now, she looks completely present and unmistakably haunted. Eden seems tired, world-weary beyond her years. She pets Shadow slowly, rhythmically, staring past him with an ambivalent expression on her face.

"As I'm sure you all know, we are beginning our third week together," I say. "I'm glad you're here and that you have decided as a family to move ahead with our sessions."

"Did we have a choice?" Rachel asks, and when I look at her, I'm surprised to see a sardonic grin touching the corners of her mouth. She doesn't generally speak much, and never with humor. Perhaps a bit of the old Rachel has begun to sneak through. I take it as a good sign despite the fact that her grin instantly vanishes and is replaced by a frown.

"You always have a choice, even when you think you don't."

Rachel makes a noise of dissent, then looks away.

"I like to meet with all of you together, because you are a family unit and I believe it's important to respect that unit, to preserve and protect it. I know that your unit has suffered a catastrophic blow, one that you have each felt individually, and that your family will never look or feel the same again. But my hope is that at some point, your family unit, although different now, will feel good and whole to you again.

Rachel turns toward Sam just as he looks at her. A meaningful look passes between them. Rachel's eyes shimmer, and she is the first to look away. Sam gazes at his shoes.

"As a family, it's also important that each member knows what's going on with the others. Sam, you mentioned that before the accident, you had family dinners, that often Ruth was present, and that you all talked about your days and asked questions and shared information. I know you haven't resumed this tradition, which is another reason I like to meet with all of you. So you can share with one another."

I pause and look around the room. The adults studiously avoid eye contact with me. Eden looks right at me.

"How's school, Eden?" I ask her, and her shoulders tense.

"Okay."

"Is it?"

She glances furtively at her parents, then shrugs. Eden told me last week that she hates school, that it wasn't getting easier, that the other kids were still treating her like an outcast. I won't betray her confidence and share that information with her parents or aunt, but I want them to know what she's going through.

"There's nothing you'd like to talk about?"

Her lower lip trembles. "Not now. Maybe later. With you."

"What is it, Eden?" Sam asks. "You can tell us."

"I don't want to talk to you about it, Daddy. You're super upset all the time anyway, and I don't want to make it worse."

Sam's cheeks flame, then he disguises his shame with anger. "I want you to tell me what's going on in school, Eden. Now."

"Sam," Ruth says, her voice stern. "Leave her alone."

"Stay out of it, Ruth," Sam warns.

"Don't talk to my sister that way," Rachel says.

Eden sits up straight in her chair, the cords in her neck straining. "Don't fight!" The grown-ups go silent. "School sucks, okay? It totally sucks and I hate it. The kids all think I'm a freak. None of my friends talk to me anymore—*no one* talks to me 'cept Corwin Kwe and Aimee Joyce—and the teachers hardly even look at me, and when they do, they have this really sad look on their faces, like, 'Oh, poor little Eden, what a tragedy.' It's totally awful, and you guys don't care because you don't care about anything anymore."

Shadow, sensing Eden's distress, emits a guttural whine, then begins to lick the tears from her cheeks. Rachel's mouth forms an O of surprise, and she blinks rapidly. Sam leans forward in his seat as though he is going to go to his daughter, but something holds him back.

"Of course we care," he says, although his tone lacks conviction. Eden shakes her head but says nothing.

"I know she's been having some trouble," Ruth says. "But what can we do? It's not like she can just drop out of fifth grade."

"I'm not suggesting we come up with a solution right now, Ruth. I just want you all to know what's going on with each other. How about you? How are you doing?"

Ruth takes a breath, blows it out. "I'm all right. I mean, terrible, but all right. Busy, what with helping out." Sam chuffs derisively, and Ruth glares at him. "I'm happy to do it, as you well know, but sometimes I don't feel appreciated by my brother-in-law. My joints ache all the time, but I'm still there, cleaning and doing laundry and cooking. But Sam treats me like I'm overstepping."

"I don't," he counters.

"You do and you know it."

"Okay, Ruth," I interject before tempers escalate. "Thank you for sharing." Ruth crosses her arms over her chest and harrumphs. I ignore her and look at Sam. "Sam, how's work?"

"Fine. We've made some changes internally, brought in some new people, a few junior architects. I have a new assistant." He glances at Rachel, and I follow his gaze. Rachel's posture stiffens, but she doesn't look at him. "We have a couple of projects about to kick into high gear."

"Sounds like things are moving along for you in that area."

"I have to pay the bills, don't I?"

"It's a good thing, Sam, to have your work."

He nods but says nothing. I turn to Rachel. She is ready for me, doesn't even let me ask the question.

"My turn?" Her voice is quiet but intent. "How am I?" She laughs without humor. "I'm here, Dr. Meyers. That's all I can tell you."

I nod, knowing she will say no more.

"Yes, you're here. You all are here. And that's a good thing. I would like to suggest an exercise for you to do as a family over the course of the next week. I would like you to have a meal together. It doesn't have to be dinner. Lunch or breakfast would be good, too. I'd like you to sit down around the table and share with each other. Ask each other questions, interact. I understand that doing this at home might present difficulty, as Jonah's seat will be empty. At some point, you will have to deal with that, but for now, a good solution would be to go to a restaurant."

Samuel releases a staccato cough. I turn to him.

"Yes, Sam?"

"A restaurant? Rachel barely leaves her room and you want her to go out to a restaurant?"

Rachel's eyes are closed, her face a mask of pain.

"Would you consider it, Rachel?"

She shakes her head from side to side. Ruth takes her hand, but Rachel yanks it away. "I can't. Not yet."

"What about a family dinner in your home?" I ask gently.

Her eyes fly open. "Without him? You want me to sit at the table and stare at his empty chair. You just said we weren't ready for that, and now you're asking me to do it?"

"What about the counter?" Sam asks, and all eyes turn to him, including Rachel's. He looks at me. "We have a counter in the kitchen, on the island. Rachel and I have talked about putting stools around it and eating there sometimes. I could get some stools at Target."

Rachel's gaze returns to her lap. "Would you consider that, Rachel?" I ask her.

Her voice is flat. "I'll consider it."

"That's a start. Okay. We're going to split off into our individual sessions, but before we do that, I want to let you know that I'm going to ask each of you to discuss the day of the accident." The tension is immediate and thick. I feel it rather than see it, and so does Shadow. He lets loose a loud bark.

"I don't want to talk about that day," Eden says, her eyes wide and glassy.

"I understand."

"No. You don't understand." Rachel's go-to phrase.

I train my gaze on her and keep it steady. "We have had seven sessions in total, Rachel. Three group sessions, including this one, and four private sessions with each of you. We have yet to discuss the day of the accident in any detail whatsoever."

"You know what happened," Ruth says, her voice hoarse and wavering. "Why do we have to talk about it?"

"That day is why you're here, Ruth. Not the events before or the events since. But that day. I'm certain that until we talk about it, until you each tell me what happened the morning Jonah died, I will be unable to help you move through and past your grief, and you will be unable to help yourselves. You're here because you want to move forward. This will be painful. But I believe it's an imperative step toward your goal."

Silence fills the room, save for Shadow's panting. Everyone is lost in his or her thoughts, his or her recollections. After a moment, Sam pushes himself to his feet. "All right. Let's get this over with."

FIFTY-EIGHT

Samuel Davenport

He paces. His usual.

"How are you doing, Sam?"

"I already told you." He jerks his thumb toward the family room. "Out there."

I smile and nod. "You told me about work. Not about you personally. How are things between you and Rachel? Have you moved back into the master bedroom yet?"

He shakes his head. "No. And I don't think I will be any time soon."

"Is that your decision?"

"Hell, no."

"Do you and Rachel talk? Communicate at all? Is there any interaction between you two?"

"Barely. I mean, she's coherent now that she's off her meds. She's coherent, but still withdrawn. She watches TV in the bedroom, all day, all night. Cries still, but tries to hide it. She rarely talks to me except out of necessity. She's a little better with Eden, but not much."

"Do you think all of this is a result of Jonah's death?"

Sam is quiet for a moment. I know the answer before he gives it. "No."

"Was it something that happened before he died?"

Sam looks at me, sighs. "The night before. Well, it was something I did the night before, but it didn't come to light until the morning Jonah . . ."

Pity is useless in terms of therapeutic value. But the expression on Samuel Davenport's face is so utterly devastated, so full of remorse, that I can't pretend it doesn't touch my heart.

"I was with another woman. My former assistant. We didn't have sex. She kissed me. I didn't kiss back, not really. By then, I knew it was a mistake. I'd taken her out to a job site, knowing it was going to be empty, that we'd be alone. I could tell you that I had no intention of fucking her. Sorry."

"It's okay, Sam. You know the rules." He nods. "And did you? Have every intention of having sex with your assistant?"

"I certainly allowed for the possibility. And honestly? Yes, probably deep down, I did. I'm sure you think I'm an awful person, but that's okay. I am. I'm an idiot."

"But you stopped. You didn't have sex with her."

"Yes, but just being there with her in the first place . . ."

"Why did you stop?" I ask him.

"Because I love Rachel. I love my kids, my family. Their faces kept flashing in my head, and I knew if I went forward with Greta, I'd risk losing them, forever."

"Sam," I say, gently but forcefully. "The fact is, you did stop, and for the right reasons. Does that sound like something an awful person would do?"

"I think a good person wouldn't have put himself in that position in the first place."

"Sam, in my experience, truly bad people don't question their intentions and worry about their choices and feel guilty even when they make the right choice. You made a brief error in judgment."

"And I've paid for it, haven't I?" He rubs his forehead, then swipes at his eyes, continues pacing.

"Do you think Jonah's death was some kind of karmic retribution meted out to punish you personally?"

"I don't know." He thinks for a moment. "No. But it was my fault."

"Because of what you did the night before?"

"Because of what I did the day it happened." He collapses onto the chair and stares at me. His eyes are bloodshot with unspent tears and fatigue.

I sit in the chair across from him. I don't pick up my notepad, just lean forward and give him my full attention. "Tell me about that day."

And he does.

FIFTY-NINE

RUTH GLASS

"She's getting better," Ruth says, as if the family's inability to move forward is all about Rachel and not remotely to do with her. This is partially true. Rachel is the "Power" button. But all the parts of the machine have to work in order for it to function.

"I'm glad," I reply.

"I mean, not much. She's still in her room most of the time, but she's not out of it like she was."

"And how are you, Ruth?"

"Oh, well." She clears her throat. "You heard me in there. That's basically still my life. Taking care of them. Hasn't changed over the past two weeks."

"Are you still staying with them?" I ask.

"Most nights. I think I should start weaning them, and myself."

"That's probably for the best."

"Yes. I know, ultimately, things will have to go back to normal. Well, back to a new normal, at least."

I nod. "Absolutely."

"I admit, I don't like it much, being alone in my apartment. It's not a bad place, but I get lonely." She says this last as though admitting to a ridiculous sentiment.

"Loneliness is something we all experience. It's natural when you live by yourself, and it can be especially intensified when tragedy occurs. Have you dated at all since your divorce, Ruth?"

I catch the thoughtful expression on her face before she can wipe it away.

"No."

"Not one date?"

She chuckles sadly.

"What is it, Ruth? What's funny?"

"Honestly, it's not even remotely humorous. Ironic is what it is. I had a date. Was *supposed* to have a date. The night Jonah died. Obviously I had to cancel." She raises her eyebrows, then immediately frowns. "I'm sorry. I didn't mean to sound irreverent."

"You didn't. So, you had a date scheduled for that night . . ."

"Yes. My first date since my divorce. With my neighbor. Nice man. Widower." She thinks about him for a moment, and a small smile plays at her lips, then fades away. "That's why I was at Rachel's that morning. She was going to color my hair." She yanks at a few errant strands that have escaped the knot. "We never got to it."

I nod. "Tell me what happened."

She shakes her head slowly. "I don't want to talk about it." But, after a moment or two of silence, she recounts the events of that day.

SIXTY

Eden Davenport

Eden sits on the floor, crisscross applesauce she calls it. When I was a child, we called it Indian style, but that moniker is no longer politically correct. Shadow lies on the floor in front of her, his head down, but his eyes open and watchful. Her hands never leave his coat. They move continuously, stroking his fur, coming to rest, scratching his ears, resting again. But her young, unblemished, ivory face is a mask of worry. Her brow is furrowed, and in that instant, she reminds me of her father.

"You said before you were going to make me talk about the very bad day," she says, keeping her gaze directed at Shadow.

"Yes," I reply. "If that's okay with you."

She shakes her head. "It's not. I don't want to talk about that day."

"Why don't we start with yesterday," I suggest. "What did you do?"

She relaxes a bit. "Yesterday was Monday. I went to school."

"How was it?"

"I told you already!" Her voice is loud and uncharacteristically angry.

I bow my head and apologize. "I just wondered whether you might share some specifics with me. About your day."

"Everyone thinks I'm a loser. It's like, they think having a dead brother is contagious or something. Like if they talk to me or hang out with me, then their brother or sister or someone will die."

"But you know that's not true, right, Eden?" This girl is hurting. Her sorrow makes me hurt. I want to erase her sorrow, but I know this is not a magic show. I can't snap my fingers and make her hurt disappear. I can only provide her with tools. "You know that you are not contagious in any way."

"I feel like I am. Not contagious, maybe, like when you get the flu. But I feel like maybe I'm . . ." She struggles for a moment. "Tainted."

"That's a very big word," I tell her, wondering who called her that.

"Not so big," she says. "Only two syllables."

"You're right. But it's big in meaning," I say.

"It was in a book I chose from Accelerated Reader. It means 'a trace of something bad, offensive or harmful.' I looked it up."

I abandon my chair and kneel down in front of her, choosing to ignore the therapeutic directive to maintain distance. I reach out and still her hands on Shadow's coat. The dog turns his head toward me, as if he is paying close attention to my words.

"Eden. Please listen to me. You are not tainted. Are you hearing me? Please, really. You are a lovely, smart, and amazing young woman. You are not tainted in any way, shape, or form."

Eden's hands tremble beneath my grasp. She shakes her head. "You're wrong, Dr. Meyers. I *am* tainted. It's my fault Jonah's dead. I said something to him that . . . d-d-day." She bites her lip as tears stream down her face. "I said something really mean, I told him to do something, and that's why he died. It's my fault."

I maintain a firm grip, subconsciously conveying the message *I'm not going anywhere.*

"Tell me, Eden. What did you say to Jonah? What happened that day?"

Shadow whines, kisses my hands, my face, any part of me he can reach. Eden must see this as a sign of trust. She starts to talk to me. And doesn't stop until she gets everything out.

SIXTY-ONE

RACHEL DAVENPORT

Rachel doesn't want to talk today. She never wants to talk, but today she's even more reluctant.

For the past two weeks, I've watched her emerge from her drug-induced haze. Her eyes are clear and focused, and her energy level is higher. But these positive changes have not inspired her to fully participate in this process. She doesn't trust me yet.

I have Sam's account of the events of that morning. Sam and Rachel were together when the accident happened. I can intuit Rachel's perspective and the reasons why she bears the blame. But she needs to be the one to tell me, in her own words. And I'll do whatever it takes to make that happen.

She reclines against the back of the couch, feigning comfort, but her rigid shoulders and clasped hands betray her.

"You look well," I say, positioning myself in the chair opposite her. She snickers.

"Right."

"You don't believe me?"

"I know what I look like," she says, picking at a cuticle.

"Do you know what you looked like the first day you came in? Trust me, you look much better now."

She snaps her head toward me and lets out a surprised laugh. "That was direct."

I meant it to be. "Well, Rachel, the soft touch doesn't seem to be working with you. Thought I'd try something new." I stare at her, hard.

"So the gloves are off now?" she asks.

"This isn't a boxing match. But you are fighting me at every turn. Do you want to move forward past your grief? Because I see no evidence that you do."

"Maybe I don't. Maybe I don't deserve to."

"That's bullshit, girl," I snap, suffusing my voice with what I call street edge. Rachel's mouth drops open. As a therapist, I don't lecture. Lecturing is frowned upon in my profession. We're supposed to ask questions, let our patients come to the right conclusions themselves. But with Rachel, my instincts compel me to abandon my training.

"I'm gonna tell you what isn't bullshit," I say. "You are in the driver's seat here. You get to decide. No one can do it for you. Not me or Sam or Ruth or Eden. Just you. You want to bury yourself in your grief and shrivel up and die before you're dead, that's your choice. But you'll end up dragging your whole family down with you, Rachel. They're grieving for Jonah, but they're also grieving for you."

Her lower lip trembles, and in that instant, she looks just like her daughter. Her voice is hoarse, thick with emotion. "I don't deserve to move forward."

I shake my head for emphasis. "So we're back to this now?"

"You don't understand."

"We're back to that now, too? Then help me to understand."

Rachel is silent. I try a different tack. "What about Eden, Rachel?"

"What about her?"

"Does she deserve to move forward?"

"Of course, she's a child," Rachel whispers.

"What about Ruth?"

Rachel seems to getting the gist. She nods. "Yes."

"Sam? Does he deserve to move past his grief?"

Her answer is quick. "No. He doesn't."

I lean forward. "Why not? Because of what he did the night before the accident?"

"He told you?"

I don't respond to her directly. "Let me see if I'm following you. Sam made an error in judgment, and for that one misstep he should be forced to grieve over the loss of his beloved son forever? Do I have it right?"

She blinks a couple of times, then looks at me. Opens her mouth, closes it, swallows. "Sam deserves to move past his grief. I just, it's hard for me to let go of . . . If Sam hadn't done what he did, I wouldn't have done what I did, and Jonah would still be alive."

"What did you do, Rachel?"

She doesn't answer me, changes the subject. "He came to me yesterday."

"Jonah?" My mind flashes back to my dream and Jonah's imploring brown eyes.

"I thought I was dreaming," she says. "I mean, I haven't seen him for a while. I thought maybe, without the meds, I wouldn't see him at all, but there he was, sitting on the end of my bed. It was different, though. He was . . . faded."

"Did he talk to you?" *You gotta help 'em, and fast.*

She frowns at the memory. "Yes. But I couldn't understand what he was saying. It's like he was speaking English, but I couldn't compute the words."

I pause for a moment. Then, "Do you think it might be possible that he wants you to let him go?"

She jerks her head from side to side, her anxiety mounting. "No. He was upset and crying, and he looked really angry, like the time I took him to the doctor for shots—that was the only time Jonah was ever really angry with me. The way he was looking at me, I could tell he blamed me. I asked him to forgive me, but he just shook his head, because he can't forgive me. And why should he forgive me? I can't forgive myself."

"For what, Rachel? What can't you forgive yourself for?"

She springs from the couch. "For fucking killing him! Don't you listen? It's my fault he's dead!"

"I know you believe that."

"Because it's true." Suddenly drained, she drops her head to her chest and returns to the couch. She sits perched on the edge as silent tears slide down her cheeks.

"Tell me what happened," I say gently.

She nods, stares at the floor. "Okay. But it won't change anything."

When she begins, I sit back in my chair and take a quiet breath. Rachel Davenport is finally talking.

PART FIVE:
THE VERY BAD DAY

SIXTY-TWO

JONAH

I'm the first one up. I love vacation 'cause you get to sleep in, but I never do. Sometimes I lie in my bed for a long time and listen to the outside wake up. It's always the birds first. The crows, mostly. They're loud and squawk like crazy, but then other birds start making tweet sounds and I like that sound better, even though I don't know what kind of birds those are. If they were insects, I'd know.

Marco is kind of smooshed under my back, and I roll to my side and pull him out from under me. He's still got that big yarn smile, so I guess I didn't hurt him or anything. I put his arms around me and bring his Velcro hands together, then we hop out of bed and get down on the floor.

I scooch over to my 'cyclopedia, only it isn't open to the page I left it at. That page had a Buprestidae on it. Those're called jewel beetles, too, 'cause they're shiny green like a emerald. Mommy thinks they're creepy, and this one time, one flew into the car and started flying around with that loud kind of buzzing noise it makes, and Mommy started screaming and pulled the car over to the side and got out and opened all the doors and just stood there until the beetle flew out of the car. I was kind of mad a little bit 'cause I wanted to see it up close, but Mommy said no way, olay. I didn't stay mad at Mommy 'cause Daddy told me that girls don't like bugs—that's just how they are and you can't blame 'em for that.

Now the 'cyclopedia is open on the katydid page. Katydids are in the order Orthoptera, and they're really neat. They can be as big as five inches, and their antenna can be twice as long as their whole body. But I still don't know why the book's open to that page. I look down at Marco, and my mouth kind of opens by itself.

"No way!" I say to Marco. "You didn't, not really, did you?" I mean, I like *The Velveteen Rabbit* and all, but deep, deep down in my heart of hearts, I know Marco's stuffed and isn't real and couldn't have gotten off the bed and looked in my 'cyclopedia, even if I pretended he could. But now . . . I mean . . . it's like Daddy says, the proof's in the pudding.

"You wanna look for katydids today, Marco? They hatch in spring, but I guess you already know that since you were reading about them. Let's get some chow and then we can start looking."

I put on clean unders and throw my dirty ones and my pj's in the hamper, then put on some shorts and a T-shirt that has the Avengers on it. I'm not old enough to see that movie yet, but Daddy says he can't wait until I am, 'cause he thinks I'm gonna love it and he's gonna watch it with me.

Mommy and Daddy's door is closed all the way, and Eden's is mostly closed. I tiptoe down the stairs. Shadow is at the bottom, tail wagging, happy to see me, like he always is. I tell him, "Good boy," and scratch his neck. He licks my hand and my face, then sniffs at Marco and even gives him a kiss.

I go into the kitchen, and Shadow follows me. He sniffs at me, then trots back to the living room.

I'm not 'llowed to cook anything—the stove is off-limits—but that's okay, 'cause Mommy makes the best eggs ever. But since she's still sleeping, and my tummy feels kind of growly, and Marco and me wanna get started on our bug hunt, I'm gonna have to find something to eat that doesn't need to be cooked.

I carry Marco to the fridge. The door is hard to open, but I finally do it. Then me and Marco kind of just stare at all the food inside. There's a plastic tub with leftover Auntie Ruth lasagna, and it's so good I'd eat it, even cold, but I'm not sure about lasagna for breakfast. I pull the orange juice carton from the door and set it on the counter. A bag of bread is on the second shelf, but I'm too short to get it. I wish Marco would turn real right this minute so he could climb up and get the bread. I ask him if he will, but he just smiles at me, and I know that he won't turn real until I'm asleep, if he even really did, which I don't know if I believe for sure, but then how did my 'cyclopedia pages get turned?

I grab the step stool from the pantry and put it in front of the fridge, then Marco and me climb on it and I grab the bread. I'm not 'llowed to use the toaster, either, at least not without a grown-up in the room. But that's okay. I can just eat the bread without toasting it. Toasting takes time, and Marco and I are in a hurry.

I'm also not 'llowed to go out front of the house if Mommy and Daddy are asleep upstairs. But that's okay, too, 'cause Marco and me can start in the backyard. But, for sure, if Mommy and Daddy aren't awake by the time Marco and me finish scoping the backyard, I am gonna start to make some real big noise.

SIXTY-THREE

EDEN

Wouldn't you know it? Every morning Mom has to wake me up to get ready for school, but the first official day of vacation, I'm awake at seven thirty. I so do not want to be up right now. I'm supposed to be sleeping in. That's one of the vacation rules.

Jonah's up already. I heard him leave his room a few minutes ago, whispering to that silly stuffed monkey like it's real. Duh. That is so kindergarten.

I feel a teensy bit bad about how mean I was to Jonah yesterday. Mom and Dad always say that if you feel bad about something, you should apologize. Maybe when I get up, I'll go downstairs and tell him I'm sorry. Mom and Dad also say "there's no time like the present." I groan and pull one of my pillows over my head. It's dark under the pillow, but after a few seconds I, like, can't even breathe, so I shove it away. I groan again, big and loud this time, then shove my covers off and get out of bed.

The good thing is, even though it's only seven thirty, I don't have to get dressed. I can stay in my nightie all morning if I want. That's a Saturday rule *and* a vacation rule, so it's a double rule.

I go into the bathroom and pee, and even though I didn't think I really needed to, I pee for a really long time. I brush my teeth and look at myself in the mirror, and after I spit out the toothpaste, I start making funny faces at myself. I like doing that. It's fun. Dad likes to make funny faces at me, but I don't know if he practices them in the mirror. That doesn't seem like a very Dad thing to do, but he can be really weird and silly and even though it's kind of embarrassing, I like it. I would totally die if he made one of his faces in front of my friends, but in private, it's okay.

When I'm done with my teeth, I go back into my room and take off my undies, get a fresh pair, and put it on. This pair is my favorite—pink and yellow with little blue stars—and I'm glad Mom washed it because it is the perfect pair of undies for the first day of vacation. I know that sounds dumb, but it's true. These ones are comfy and totally cute; they don't ride up or cut across my waist or anything.

I could probably get dressed, but, no, it's Saturday *and* vacation, so I'm not going to, just on principle.

I walk down the hall and see that Mom and Dad's door is shut. I go down the stairs and see Shadow standing by the window in the living room, his head covered with the curtains, staring outside. When I get to the bottom of the stairs, he turns and sees me, then snorts, like he always does, and races over to me.

Carlee has a Chihuahua, a little dog named Cretin who looks kind of like a rat. Ava doesn't like dogs at all. She says she got bit by one when she was three, but I kind of don't believe her, because I don't remember anything from when I was three. I think she just doesn't like dogs, and I can't wrap my brain around that, because how can you not like dogs?

Shadow kisses my face and my arm and puts his paw in my hand. I pat his head and stroke his fur and tell him I love him. I used to tell Mom and Dad I loved them, like, all the time, but I kind of stopped doing that. But I always tell Shadow I love him. I don't know why I stopped with Mom and Dad. Maybe because my friends made fun of Isabelle Cook because she told her mom she loved her right in front of everyone in line for class

I realize that's pretty stupid, that I should tell Mom and Dad I love them, because I do, and I think it would make them happy, even more happy than it makes Shadow, who doesn't really understand the words but kind of understands the meaning.

I'll tell Mom and Dad I love them as soon as they come downstairs.

I go into the kitchen, and Shadow trots next to me. Through the window of the back door, I see Jonah outside. He's over by the fence, bending down and pointing to something on the ground, telling the monkey something—probably something about bugs. He reaches down and picks something up. *Gross.* I do not like bugs, not any kind, except for ladybugs. Ladybugs are beast. They're pretty and Aunt Ruth says if one lands on you, it's good luck. Last year, Carlee and I spent every recess in March searching the field for ladybugs. We didn't do it this year because Ava thinks it's totally immature.

I'm not going out there to apologize, especially not if he's holding some icky spider or worm. Forget that. I'll just wait for him to come back inside, but I'm not going to apologize until after he washes his hands, because I know when I say I'm sorry, he's going to want to hug me and stuff.

I go to the pantry and pull out my cereal, then grab a bowl from the cupboard. Jonah is creeping along the grass now, and I really hope he watches out for Shadow poop. Mom usually picks it up first thing in the morning so the grass is okay for playing on, but she's still asleep, so there must be some poops out there. Mom and Dad offered to pay me to pick up the poop, add it to my allowance. Fifty cents a pile. Shadow poops *a lot*, which means I could totally be rich by summer, but I told Mom and Dad *not on your life, no way, not gonna happen.* I wouldn't even do it for *a dollar* a poop.

Thinking about Shadow's poop makes me not really hungry anymore, so I set the bowl and cereal box on the counter and wander to the back door. I open it and watch for a minute while Jonah crab walks across the grass, hunched over and staring at the ground.

"Be careful of Shadow poop," I call to him. He looks up at me and smiles real big.

"Hi, Eden! Happy first day of vacation! Marco and me are finding bugs. Wanna hunt with us?"

Like, *not a chance.* "No, thanks. I'm gonna watch *Young Justice.* Want to watch with me?"

He scrunches up his nose like he's thinking about it, but then shakes his head. "I'm gonna keep hunting. But thanks for asking, Eden."

I almost apologize to him right then and there. I probably should, but I know he'll just run over and touch me with his skody bug hands. *Shudder.*

I go back inside and head into the living room. Shadow is looking out the window again and whining. His tail thwap-thwaps against the back of the couch. I grab the remote from the coffee table and fall back onto the couch cushions, then turn on the TV.

I hear laughter from upstairs. Mom and Dad must be awake. I quickly turn the TV back off. We're allowed to watch TV on Saturday mornings and on vacation mornings—another double rule, but never before we eat breakfast. I jump up and run into the kitchen, pour some cereal into my bowl, add milk, then scarf it down as fast as I can without choking.

Back on the couch, I turn the TV back on and find *Young Justice* on Netflix.

By the time the show is over, Mom and Dad still haven't come downstairs. I didn't need to scarf my cereal down after all.

I start another show.

SIXTY-FOUR

SAMUEL

I lie awake half the night, alternating between self-flagellation and self-congratulation. Flagellation for the obvious reasons and congratulation for not letting the situation with Greta go any further.

When I dropped her at her car last night, she stood there, waiting for me to alight from the driver's seat. Possibly she expected a good-night kiss, or a hug, or some other form of intimacy. I stayed where I was, anxious to put my foot on the accelerator and get myself home. Greta gave me a puzzled look, then glanced back at our building, and I could see the wheels spinning in her brain. She assumed my inertia was because I didn't want to be caught in a suspicious embrace by someone still at work. It was too late in the evening for that to be a possibility, but I let her think her assumption was correct.

Another thing that kept me awake was knowing I need to talk to Greta. Sooner rather than later. Staring at the darkened ceiling, with my wife asleep beside me, I tried to come up with a script for what I would say to her. Nothing sounded right in my head.

I finally succumbed to sleep sometime after three. My dreams were vivid and loud, the scenery and secondary characters constantly changing. But when I woke at six, I couldn't remember a single detail from any of them.

I awaken again at 7:59. I roll over and gaze at Rachel. She sleeps on her side, facing me. Her reddish curls cascade around her face and stream across her pillow. Her lips are parted, and she creates a soft whistle as she slowly, rhythmically breathes in and out. Her expression is peaceful, her skin ivory with little splashes of rosiness across her cheekbones. She has never looked more beautiful to me, nor more precious.

Watching Rachel sleep, I chide myself again. Then make promises that will not be difficult to keep.

I will be good to you, Rachel. I will never hurt you, Rachel. I will cherish you and Eden and Jonah. You and the kids are my life.

I think these things, rather than give them voice, but Rachel stirs as though she can hear me. Her eyelids flutter open, close, open again. A lazy smile spreads across her face.

"Watching me sleep?" Her voice is low, raspy with the remnants of sleep. Sexy as hell.

"As a matter of fact, I am."

"Stalker," she singsongs in a throaty whisper.

I smile at her. Reach for her. "I love that nightie."

"I know." She scoots toward me, then turns and nestles against me, her head in the crook of my arm, her back against my chest. "Mmm. You feel good."

I reach my hand around her waist and pull her even closer. "You, too." I trail my fingertips across the soft cotton of the nightie, lingering over the generous swell of her breasts. Instantly, I'm hard. Rachel laughs.

"Wow. You really do like this nightie."

"I'd like it better if it was on the floor."

She laughs again. "Romantic."

I cup her chin in my hand and turn her head toward me, then close my mouth over hers. She tries to shrink away from me. "My breath."

"No worse than mine," I murmur.

She places her hand on my chest to still me. "Let me brush. I promise, I'll be right back."

I throw back my head. "Oh, fine. I guess I'll brush, too."

Rachel throws off the covers and climbs out of bed. I follow her to the bathroom. My dick is standing at attention, creating a tent of my boxer shorts. She sees my erection in the mirror and laughs. I feign shock and shake my head.

"You're never supposed to laugh at that." She laughs harder and I drink in the sound, then laugh along with her. I realize we haven't laughed together like this in a long time.

We brush quickly, Rachel's gaze rarely leaving my crotch. "Don't worry," I assure her. "He's not going anywhere."

She raises her eyebrows and grins. "Oh, yes, he is."

She makes a mad dash to the bed while I detour to the door. I open it a crack and hear the familiar sound of one of the kids' shows from the TV downstairs.

I glance at Rachel. "God bless the boob tube."

"I've got another kind of boob for you over here, buddy. Two, actually."

"God bless that kind of boob." I lock the door and cross to the bed. I climb under the covers, and Rachel meets me in the middle. For a moment, we lie side by side, our arms across each other. She looks at me, and her expression has lost all traces of humor.

"Are you okay, Sam?"

I try for a joke to recapture the levity we shared only a minute ago. "Better than fine, can't you tell?"

A ghost of a grin. "Yes. You're better than fine. *Down there.* Always have been. What about up here?" She reaches out and taps a fingertip against my forehead. "Everything okay?"

I take a breath, exhale on a sigh. "I know I've been a little distracted lately. I'm sorry."

She shakes her head. "No, you don't have to be sorry. You don't even have to tell me what it's about. I just want to make sure you're all right."

I'm here, with you, the love of my life. Our kids are downstairs. Tomorrow is Easter. It's the first day of spring break.

"I've never been better."

Finally, she smiles. "Good."

She closes the small distance between us and kisses me, gently at first, then more passionately. For a split second, I think of Greta and those lips that felt foreign against mine. Rachel's lips feel like home. I push Greta from my mind and sink into my wife's embrace.

SIXTY-FIVE

RACHEL

I fall back against the pillows, my heart pounding. God, that was good. And we both needed it, desperately. Sam's breathing is ragged. I turn to see him smiling broadly at me as he gulps for air.

"You're lucky the kids watch really loud shows," he says.

"Me? What about you? I thought your head was going to explode."

"One of them did."

I roll my eyes, then laugh. "That was fun."

"Fun? Just fun? That was amazing."

"Okay, that, too." I shimmy to the side of the bed.

"Hey, where are you going?"

"To shower, get dressed. Seize the day."

He grins. "I've got something else you can seize."

"What are you, sixteen?"

"Not interested in round two?" He makes an exaggerated sad face.

"You look like an emoji," I tell him. "And, yes, I would love round two, but we'll have to postpone. Tomorrow's Easter, remember? I have to clean the house. Prep the dinner. Little things like that."

"It's just Ruth. It's not like we're entertaining the queen."

I push myself to my feet, relishing the tenderness in my female parts. Just thinking about what we did moments ago makes me shiver with delight. Our sex life has always been really good. Even when busy schedules, kids, work, commitments get in the way, we manage to carve out time. But we haven't made love for several weeks, maybe longer. Too long. I make a mental resolution to take Sam up on his offer of round two before the weekend's up. Is sex on Easter Sunday considered blasphemous?

I walk to the bathroom and turn the shower on, shoving the lever to hot. As I brush my teeth for the second time, Sam comes up behind me and slips his arms around my waist. He kisses my neck, then looks at me in the mirror.

"I'll help with the chores."

"Deal," I say around my toothbrush. "Shadow needs a bath."

"The kids can do that."

"No way. Talk about an even bigger mess to clean up."

He nibbles at my ear. "Okay, I'll do it."

I can feel his penis poking against my butt. I put down my toothbrush and turn around, then point at his nakedness. "Um, you might want to put that thing away and get some clothes on. Ruth's coming over this morning."

He nods sheepishly, as he always does when I tell him Ruth is dropping by. "To help with the prep?"

"I'm dyeing her hair." I grin. "She has a date tonight."

His eyebrows waggle. "Really?"

"Don't mention it to her, okay? I don't want her to think we're talking about it behind her back."

"My lips are sealed," he says, then chugs some mouthwash.

I leave him at the sink and step into the shower, adjust the spray. The hot water feels good. I stand for a moment and let it run over me, then begin to lather up.

"How did it go last night?" I call to Sam. He doesn't answer. Probably can't hear me.

When I step out of the shower a few minutes later, he's already gone downstairs. Hopefully to make coffee. I towel dry my hair and get dressed.

Shadow greets me at the bottom of the stairs. Eden's on the couch—all I can see of her is the back of her head. She doesn't turn around. Jonah is nowhere in sight.

"Good morning," I say.

When she hears my voice, Eden jumps off the couch and rushes at me. I'm expecting a hug. Ha.

"Mom, Mom, can I use your iPad? I want to FaceTime with Carlee and Ava."

"I said, 'Good morning.'"

"Oh, yeah, right," she says contritely. "Sorry. Good morning, Mom."

"And happy first day of vacation," I add.

"Yeah, that too. Can I use your iPad?"

I detect the aroma of coffee in the air and silently sing my husband's praises. "In a little bit," I tell her.

"When, Mom, when?" she presses. "I want to invite Carlee and Ava for a playdate, too. Can I? Please, Mom? I asked Dad, and he said it was up to you."

I take a deep breath and march toward the kitchen. Too many requests before coffee. Eden trails me.

"Tomorrow's Easter, Eden. I'm sure your friends are busy."

"Coffee's ready," Sam says, and I mouth the words *I love you* to him.

"No, Mom, they're not busy. Can I have them over? I promise we won't make a mess. We'll just play in my room or outside or in the garage. We totally won't even get in your way."

"Where's your brother?" I ask her, and she makes a disgusted face, which is entirely at odds with her prettiness.

"Ew. He's out back looking for bugs."

Crap. I haven't picked up the poop yet.

Sam hands me a cup of coffee. I glance out the window before I take a sip. As if reading my mind, he says, "I picked up the poop." I smile at him, and he leans in and whispers, "I thought it was the least I could do for you after what you did for me this morning."

I whisper back, "What do I get for round two?"

He smiles. "We'll just have to wait and see, won't we?"

"Mom!" Eden's piqued voice cuts through the kitchen. "Can I have my friends over? It's the first day of vacation. Please?"

I take a sip of coffee, then smile sweetly at my daughter. "Yes, honey. You may invite them over. But wait till nine to call them, okay?"

She squeaks with joy, then runs over and gives me a hug. Totally worth saying yes to her. She gives Sam a squeeze for good measure. She heads out of the room, but stops suddenly and turns back to us.

"Oh! I forgot." Her cheeks go rosy. "I love you, Mom. I love you, Dad." Before we can respond, she races back to the living room to finish her show.

I glance at Sam. "What was that about?"

He shrugs. "Buttering us up for something? A car, maybe? Nice, though, huh? Don't hear it much anymore from her."

I refill my mug, then lean against the counter and watch Sam put a couple of slices of bread into the toaster.

"So, how did it go last night? I asked before, but you didn't hear me."

He concentrates on the toast. "Good. The center's coming along. Should be ready for May Day."

I know he likes his toast a certain color, but the way he's watching it, staring down into the slots of the toaster, makes me laugh.

"What?"

"Are you waiting for Jesus to appear on the toast?"

He grins at me. "An Easter miracle."

The back door slams open, and Jonah appears, Marco the monkey sprouting from his side. His hands are brown, and his shirt and shorts are caked with mud. He is beaming. "Happy first day of vacation!" he cries.

"And to you, too, my guy." I set down my coffee as Jonah bounds over to me. I put up my hand to halt him. "Wash those hands, mister."

He giggles then goes to the sink. Sam grabs the step stool for him and he goes to work washing off the grime, talking excitedly. "We found some ladybugs and a big fat caterpillar that I think was trying to find a place to make a chrysalis and we found some ants and spiders by the fence."

I nod and feign interest, grateful that he's using the laymen's names for the bugs. Jonah used to call them by their scientific names until I told him I had no idea what he was talking about. Thank goodness he's dumbed it down for Mom.

"That sounds fascinating," I tell him. Behind him Sam gives me an exaggerated nod.

"Marco and me want to go out front and search the hedge. Can we, Mommy?"

"Marco and *I*," I tell him, and he screws his face into a look of puzzlement. "Marco and I, not Marco and me." He shrugs and I laugh. The hedge runs between our property and our next-door neighbors', from the house to the street. It's three feet thick and six feet high and apparently akin to the Amazonian rain forest in terms of exploring.

"Did you brush your teeth?" I ask.

He frowns. "I forgot."

"Did you wash your face?"

"I forgot that, too."

"Clean unders?"

His expression brightens. "That I didn't forget."

"Okay, upstairs, brush your teeth, wash your face, change your shirt."

"Then the hedge?"

I nod. He jumps off the step stool and throws his wet hands around me. I bend over and hug him tight, squashing Marco. "Love you, Mommy."

"Love you too, Jonah bologna."

He starts to run out of the room, then stops and turns back around. "Oh, love you, too, Daddy."

Sam makes a funny face. "Back at you, ham sandwich."

"I'm not a ham sandwich, Daddy. You're silly. But I still love you." He wheels back around and heads for the stairs. I turn to Sam.

"He's something, huh?" I say.

Sam nods and grins at me. "Yeah, I guess we'll keep him."

I take my coffee to the table, along with my notepad and a pen, then I sit and make my to-do list while the caffeine takes effect.

Laundry. Sweep. Market. Sweet potatoes. Wash platters. Oh, right. *Ruth's hair.* I glance over at Sam, then write: *Round two.*

I underline the last entry, then put down the pen and finish my coffee.

SIXTY-SIX

RUTH

I wake up with a stomach full of knots. It's not an entirely unpleasant feeling based on the reason. I admit, I'm actually looking forward to this evening, and as I go through my morning routine, I don't consider canceling. Well, maybe once or twice I do, but not with any real conviction. I am going to keep my date with Judd, and I'm going to enjoy myself. Rachel is right. It doesn't have to be a big deal. The big deal is what the date represents. A new start. Opening myself up. Allowing myself to be happy.

I sip tea at my tiny kitchen table and make an ingredient list for the banana cream pie, doubling the quantity of each item. Might as well make two. Rachel's family loves my banana cream pie and would welcome leftovers. Or I could give one to my neighbor as a happy-Easter gift. I wonder what Judd is doing for Easter. Obviously, it's too soon to invite him to Rachel's. But perhaps I'll inquire about his plans tonight. If things go well. Anyway, best not to get ahead of myself.

I eat an egg and some toast, then take my medication. I'm timing my doses to the minute today so my fibromyalgia won't rear its ugly fangs during my evening. I throw on a pair of jeans and an old, tattered long-sleeve T-shirt—the one I always used to wear when I dyed my hair. One look in the mirror, and I quickly take it off, roll it up, and shove it in my carry sack. I don't want to look like a homeless person. I pull on a light-peach cotton sweater. Better.

A month ago, last week, even, I wouldn't have thought twice about going out in that ratty old shirt. I laugh to myself in the empty apartment. Come to think of it, it's hard to imagine what Judd sees in me, when I often go out looking like a bag person.

A thought whispers through my brain. *Maybe he doesn't see anything in you, Ruth. Maybe this isn't a date. Maybe it's just a friendly invitation. Maybe he feels sorry for you.*

I shake my head. *You know what? Even if that's the case, so what? I'm going.*

Good for you, Ruthie. You go, girl. This last thought isn't my voice. It's Charlie's.

For a brief moment, I think about Charlie and his Easter plans, what they might include. Up until eighteen months ago, his plans were my plans, meaning he spent every holiday with the Davenports. I wonder where he'll be tomorrow. Is his wife's family local? Will he go to her parents' house? Will he and his new wife host? More likely, what with the new baby. Will his wife be the perfect little hostess? I'd like to imagine that she can't cook a lick and that Charlie will think of me fondly when he tucks into his meal of dry, overcooked ham and mushy green-bean casserole.

I can't do everything, but I sure can cook.

I force myself to stop thinking about Charlie and his wife and their Easter. I have to break the habit of obsessing over them. Might as well stop today, on this day of new beginnings.

I grab my purse and my list, then head out.

I generally avoid Target for shopping excursions. I don't like the place. Not because they don't carry everything in the world a person might need—they do. But it's all those moms, pushing their carts with two, three, four kids clinging to them or sitting in the cart, or scurrying through the aisles. They unknowingly taunt me. They remind me of my inadequacies. Occasionally, I'll see a mother completely snap, berating her kids for their behavior, rolling her eyes, painting on a long-suffering expression as though she would give anything to be relieved of her burden. I want to shout at her. I want to tell her to appreciate what she has, to count her blessings, to thank her lucky stars for that burden.

Mostly, I shop at Vons. Much more eclectic patrons. But this morning, I'm going to brave Target. Their prices on hair dye are much better.

The elevator descends toward the parking garage. It opens on the floor below mine, and the doors open, revealing Judd standing on the threshold. Surprise renders me speechless. Judd sees me and smiles, and I quickly smile back. His hair is still damp from a recent shower, and his eyes twinkle.

"Well, good morning!" he says brightly. "What a lovely surprise. You weren't coming down to cancel our date, were you?"

I shake my head. "No, I'm on my way out. To Target. I'm making pies for Easter, and I need some ingredients." I don't mention the dye. Hopefully, tonight he won't notice that my hair is a different shade than it was this morning. Charlie never noticed my hair when I had it done. Rachel complains that Sam doesn't notice hers, either. That would be one male trait I wouldn't mind Judd having.

He steps onto the elevator, bringing with him the scent of soap and a subtle masculine cologne. His proximity makes me almost dizzy, and I tell myself to calm down.

"I'm heading to the store myself," he says. "Thought I might get a few nibbles for this evening." The elevator continues its course. "Anything you don't eat?"

"I'm pretty easy to please," I tell him, then groan inwardly at my choice of phrase. "I mean, I'm not a vegan or a vegetarian or paleo or Atkins. I eat pretty much everything."

"Wonderful," he says and winks. "I'm not too keen on all those restrictions. Makes something that's supposed to be pleasurable too damn complicated."

"I agree."

"I thought prosciutto, cheese, maybe some olives. To go with the wine?"

"Sounds lovely."

The doors slide open at ground level. Judd walks me to my car.

"I made lasagna. I mean, I made one for my sister, and I made an extra one to freeze. I could bring it, but that might be too . . . much . . . with everything else?"

He smiles down at me, and I force myself to meet his eyes, which is one of the most difficult things I've done in recent times. My cheeks flame, but I don't look away.

"Why don't you save it," he says. "For next time."

I nod and get into my car. He closes the door for me, like the gentleman he is, then mouths the words *See you tonight.*

I exit the garage with a smile on my face. If I could get through that encounter, Target is going to be a piece of cake.

SIXTY-SEVEN

Shadow

All my humans are awake, and they all seem excited. If they had tails, they'd be wagging them. There is a hum of energy in the house that only I can hear and feel, and my nose sniffs the smell of happy.

My nose also smells the smell of dirt on Little Male, and he is the tail-waggingest of all of my humans.

I can also smell the cat. I can't see it. I go to the window, then back to my bed, then to the food-smelling room, then back to the window. But I don't see the cat. But I know it's somewhere out there.

Little Female is on the couch watching the big screen on the wall. Little Male runs from the food-smelling room and goes up the stairs. I hear my master and mistress laughing in the food-smelling room. They smell like something else. They smell like clean, but under that, a very human musky scent that doesn't wash off. I smell that on them sometimes, mostly when there's darkness outside and all my humans are upstairs. Their laughing makes me happy.

The big screen on the wall goes dark, and Little Female jumps off the couch and goes fast into the food-smelling room. Then she comes out holding my mistress's small screen, not the very small one and not the medium one that she makes tapping sounds on. Little Female is smiling and that makes me happy, too. She goes up the stairs just as Little Male comes down. She stops and says something to him, but I don't understand the words. But what she says makes him happy. Then she goes up to the place I'm not allowed, and he comes down and goes out the front door.

I trot to the window so I can see where my little human has gone. I hope he hasn't gone too far, because then I can't protect him.

But I see him on the grass outside the window. He has that thing on him, a human toy that's full of smells from other humans, and Little Male talks to the toy and smiles. Then Little Male goes to the big long green thing that isn't a tree and isn't a plant but goes all the way to the sidewalk. I watch Little Male. He has happy face. His toy has happy face, too, but even I know that the toy isn't real like a dog.

My nose catches the scent of the cat, and I look across the wide black strip to the sidewalk on the other side. At first, I don't see anything, but then there is movement and my eyes that see near and far focus on the movement and the movement is the cat.

My tail wags, but not a happy wag. It almost hurts me. And the whine starts deep inside my throat and comes out as a bark, loud in my own ears. No humans hear me. If they did, they might tell me, "Quiet, Shadow," but my master and mistress are still in the food-smelling room, talking and laughing, and Little Female is upstairs and Little Male is outside and can't hear me through the window. I bark again, then whine, then put my paw on the glass.

The cat is looking at me from where it sits. I don't know how cats see, if they can see like dogs, but it definitely knows I'm here. Maybe it can smell me. It swishes its tail, then stretches its mouth open, like I do when I'm tired or just waking up. Then it *meows*. And I can hear it even through the window, even from inside my house, and the sound makes my ears flat. It's the worst sound I've ever heard, and I want it to stop. But the cat keeps going. Meow meow meow.

The cat and its meow is like an itch I can't reach with my paws, and it's making me upset. Then it starts to move toward me, slowly. It stops at the grass in front of my house. And meows again.

I have to stop that sound.

SIXTY-EIGHT

JONAH

"Marco, look! A monarch! Isn't it so pretty?"

The hedge is the best place for looking for bugs. I don't know what kind of plant it is, but it's got big bright-pink flowers on it, and the bees and butterflies like to get the pollen from the big yellow stamens in the middle of them. My teacher, Mrs. Hartnett, said that *stamen* was a very big word for a kindergartner to know, but I told her that I only know it 'cause of the insects who gather the pollen. Mrs. Hartnett is a girl, but she likes hearing about bugs. Maybe 'cause we're just talking about them, not looking at real ones.

Anyways, the hedge has lots of bugs in it. Some of 'em hide from the sun, and some of 'em like the sun, like the black-and-yellow garden spider, or *Argiope aurantia*. The baby spiders leave their egg sacs in springtime, but they're hard to see until they're all grown-up. I prob'ly won't see them till summer, but I still look for them, just in case.

The monarch is sitting on one of the flowers just above my head. I watch it as it opens and closes its wings, like it's stretching or getting ready to fly. I get as close to it as I can. I don't want to scare it or make it fly away. Its antennae twitches, then it rubs its legs together. I like monarchs. There's a *Little Einsteins* episode about them, how they migrate to South America and, like, all the trees in this forest are covered with them. I think that would be so neat, to see them like that, but when I asked Mommy and Daddy if I could go to South America to see them, they kind of laughed and said maybe when I was a grown-up.

The monarch flaps its wings and suddenly it's floating up and up and up, above the hedge and over into the Martins' yard.

I look over to the sidewalk and see Gigi sitting there. She's watching me, almost like she's curious.

"Hi, Gigi," I call to her. She swishes her tail and I turn back to the hedge.

The leaves of the hedge are real green. Mommy says Mr. Escalante feeds the hedge real good food to make it healthy and stuff. He used to use this thing with a really sharp blade and a loud buzzing motor to trim the hedge, but I told Mommy that would kill lots of bugs, or at least, scare 'em away, and she kind of looked at me funny when I said that, but the next time Mr. Escalante came, she talked to him, and now he trims the hedge with clippers, which is much better.

I walk along the hedge toward the house. I look up at the window and see Shadow. I wave to him, but he's not looking at me—he's looking at Gigi for sure. He barks and paws at the window, then whines and barks some more. Lucky he's not out here, 'cause he would definitely scare the bugs.

Closer up to the house, I see some bugs that look like ants with wings, and I know that those are termites, and I also know that Mommy and Daddy don't like termites because they eat the house. Well, the wood of the house, and Daddy says that's not good for the structure. I don't know how they could eat the whole house, though. That would take like a million trillion gazillion termites.

Anyway, I'm okay with termites, 'cause they're bugs, after all, but not as interesting as other ones, so I keep going. Marco seems interested, too.

As I'm walking along, I see something a little ways away on the outside of the hedge, kind of in the middle. It's kind of shimmery, and the closer I get, I squint my eyes really tight.

It can't be. No way, olay.

If that is what I think it is, this might just be the best day ever, even better than winning the spring egg hunt and bringing home Marco.

"No offense, Marco. But just wait till you see this."

SIXTY-NINE

EDEN

I'm FaceTiming with Carlee and Ava. The screen on Mom's iPad is split three ways, with Carlee and Ava's faces on either side and my face in a smaller box on the bottom. I made sure to change out of my nightie and into my yellow shirt and Juicy vest so I'd look cool, because Ava and Carlee always look cool when we FaceTime. I closed my door all the way so that Mom and Dad can't hear my conversation. Not that I'm going to say anything bad, but I don't know what my *friends* are going to say. Not everyone has a curse jar.

"We're having Easter here," I tell them after Carlee asks us what we're doing on the holiday. "Just us and my Aunt Ruth."

"We're here, too," Carlee says. "My cousins are coming. There's going to be like twenty-five people here. My mom's totally freaking out, like, yelling at us to stay out of her way and make sure our rooms are clean. Mine's totally clean already, but she keeps coming in and throwing stuff at me, like 'put this away' and 'clean up this mess.' Total dragola."

"We're going to Mammoth," Ava announces. She smiling like she thinks it's totally beast to be going away, and I guess it kind of is.

"When are you going?" I ask.

"We're getting up at, like, five o'clock tomorrow morning and driving up. We're going to have Easter dinner at this totally swaggy club where they put your napkins in your lap for you."

"That sounds beast," I say, and Ava nods.

"Totally," Carlee agrees.

"Hey, guys, you wanna come over for a playdate today? Mom said it was okay as long as we don't make a mess."

My friends don't answer. They kind of start to look uncomfortable. "What?" I ask.

Carlee bites her lip and looks down and Ava makes a weird face—not exactly mean, but close.

"Um . . ." She frowns. "Is your little brother going to be home?"

"Well, yeah, but he's not going to be playing with us or anything."

"Are you sure?" Ava asks, and now she does sound mean. "Because he seems like he really *likes* you, Eden. Like, yesterday, when he totally hugged you in front of all of us. Even Ryan thought it was totally creepy."

My heart goes all thumpy in my chest and I feel sick to my stomach, like when I watched Dad clean a fish last summer and pull out the guts. Only it feels like *my* guts are being pulled out.

"What—" I clear my throat so I don't sound so croaky. "What did Ryan say?"

"Just that he was glad he didn't have a geeky little brother like yours."

Carlee looks like she wants to say something, but she doesn't.

"Is that true, Carlee?"

She looks down again, then kind of nods.

"We don't want to come over if your stupid little brother is going to be there hanging all over you, do we, Carlee?"

My head hurts. I know why. Because my best friends are totally bagging on my little brother, and I feel like I should defend him, say something about how cool he is, how he gave me more than half of his cookies-and-cream eggs and that he's totally funny, and cute and sweet, but at the same time, I'm so mad that he's embarrassed me, and that because of him, Ryan thinks I'm a loser, and I don't want my friends to think I'm a loser.

My door slams open. "Hey, Eden!" Jonah's voice makes me jerk my head around. And I wish, not for the first time, that I had a lock on my door so no one, especially my little brother, could come in if I didn't want them to. Jonah's all fidgety, totally hyper, probably excited to see me. "You gotta see this, Eden! It's amazing! Come on!"

I turn back to the iPad screen. Ava is smiling that nasty smile of hers. "Speak of the devil," she says. "Widdle baby bwother wants his big sistew."

All of a sudden I feel like I'm gonna explode.

"Get out of here, Jonah!" I scream. "Why don't you just go play in the street!"

When I turn toward my door, Jonah is gone and I get that sick feeling again.

"Wow, you told him, didn't you?" Ava says and giggles madly. I'm relieved, but at the same time, I want to punch her in the face. "You got that from me, didn't you, Eden?"

I don't answer. Carlee has that same weird look on her face.

"We could probably come over for a little while, couldn't we, Carlee? As long as *he* won't be a problem."

Carlee nods but still doesn't look in the camera.

"He won't be," I tell them. "I promise."

SEVENTY

SAMUEL

I'm still buzzing from the sex, can't wipe the smile from my face. I'm glad my kids are too young to suspect anything, although I know Eden's close. Still, Rachel and I were helped this morning by spring break and all its perks. I know there will come a time, and soon, when we will have to be more circumspect. But not yet, thankfully.

I finish my toast, then set my plate in the sink. My plan is to get some paperwork done before I start helping Rachel with the chores, but when I look out the window and see how glorious the weather is—bright-blue sky, not a cloud in sight—I reconsider. Maybe I'll go outside and hunt bugs with Jonah. I know my son would love that, and I can always do paperwork another time. I smile to myself. Good decision.

As I head for the stairs, Rachel calls to me from the garage, and I freeze.

There is no mistaking the tone of her voice. Stern voice, is what the kids call it. She uses it on me occasionally, when I leave my socks on the floor, or when I've had a few too many beers and gotten overly vociferous about the Lakers.

She is calling to me from the garage. I know exactly what has inspired her stern voice. My euphoria vanishes instantly.

The jacket.

I pretend not to hear her. My thoughts race. How could I have been so stupid, leaving it by the washing machine? That was definitely a *bad decision*. I stuffed it into my dry cleaning bag last night, made a mental note to take it to the cleaner's today. But I should have anticipated Rachel getting a jump on laundry. It's the first thing she does when readying the house for visitors, even if it's only Ruth. She throws in tablecloths and guest towels, even though they're already clean; she worries that accumulated cupboard dust has made the linens dull and will inspire sneezing fits. It's one of her slightly bizarre rituals that I choose to ignore. But now . . .

Shadow starts barking from the living room window. Rachel's voice cuts above the din.

"Sam, I need to talk to you *right now*. Would you come here? Please?" Her *please* doesn't sound sincere. It doesn't even sound like an afterthought. Her *please* sounds a little bit like *fuck you*.

"Daddy, Daddy!" Jonah bounds into the kitchen. I can't give him my attention. I'm too wound up. What do I say to Rachel?

The truth. Tell her the truth.

Perhaps subconsciously, I left the jacket there on purpose, knowing Rachel would find it. Maybe a part of me wants her to know so that there will be no secrets between us.

"Daddy?"

I push past my son. My legs feel like lead as I stomp from the kitchen, past the staircase, and head down the hall toward the garage.

Greta's face fills my mind, her repellent lips, wandering hands, cloying perfume—that same perfume that permeates my jacket.

"Daddy, I have to—I have to—Daddy!"

Jonah trails me. I stop in my tracks and whirl around to face him.

"Not now, Jonah!" I bark at my son. Rarely do I use that tone, and I turn away from him before I can see the aftermath of my outburst, his trembling-lipped response.

Rachel waits for me at the threshold to the garage. She stands in front of the washing machine, my jacket in her white-knuckled grip. Her eyes search my face.

Thirty minutes ago, she rode atop me, gazing into my eyes with passion and lust and unswerving love. Now she looks at me as though I'm a felon. And I am.

The truth, Sam. Tell her the truth.

SEVENTY-ONE

Rachel

No way, not possible.

When I bring the linens to the washing machine in the garage, I'm assaulted by a strong and familiar smell. At first I think it's my laundry detergent, but I just started testing a detergent for one of my sponsors that has no dyes or perfumes. This fragrance is more citrusy. No, not citrusy. Peachy. Peaches and vanilla, like cobbler.

The realization hits me.

I drop the linens to the floor and gaze at the black net bag hanging from the wall that holds my husband's dry cleaning. I take a tentative step toward the bag, and the scent of peach cobbler grows more intense. Partially obscured by the netting, but not obscured enough, is Sam's olive jacket, the one he wore to work yesterday.

My mind is blank, at least for the moment, as I grab the bag and plunge my hand into its contents. I pull out the jacket and drop the bag. It falls to the floor and lands next to the Easter linens. I press my nose against the jacket.

Peach and vanilla. Nonnegotiable. *Greta.*

"Sam," I call. "Can you come here? Now?"

My mind reels as I try to make sense of something totally incomprehensible. The saturation level of Greta's perfume on my husband's jacket—aka, his person—is not the result of a quick hug, which Sam has been known to impart upon his employees. The hug that created this had to have been long, drawn out. To get your scent embedded in someone else's clothing would require a certain amount of grinding, pressing, *hugging*.

I shake my head. *No, no, no. Can't be.*

Shadow is barking from somewhere in the house, loud and urgent. I almost don't notice.

"Sam, I need to talk to you *right now*. Would you come here? Please?"

Sam's been a little off lately, and I . . . I'm not sure what it is.

Is he having an affair?

No. It's not that.

Are you sure?

I think of this morning, of making love with Sam. His sudden passion, his intensity, his urgency. *Guilty conscience?* I feel like I'm going to retch.

It can't be.

I defended him to Ruth. I told her, told myself, *Sam would never do that. God, how could I have been so stupid?*

Sam stands in the doorway, and the look on his face tells me everything. I don't even need to ask the question. I throw the jacket at him with as much force as I can. "Greta? What the hell?"

"It's not what you think." He takes a step closer to me, and I mimic it with a step back.

"Don't even, Sam. What a freaking cliché."

"It's nothing, Rach. I swear to you. Nothing happened. On my life."

"Nothing? Then how did Miss Thing's perfume get all over your jacket? Wait, let me guess. She was cold and you were chivalrous and gave her your jacket to keep her warm."

He shakes his head.

"You took her out to the site. Was Carson there?"

312

Again, he shakes his head. My anger erupts. My heart pumps at double speed and my mouth is dry, and I'm afraid if I say anything, I'm going to start screaming. He swears nothing happened. But something was *going* to happen. Which means something *did* happen.

"I don't know why I took her out there, Rach."

"Shut up!"

"No, let me explain."

"Mommy?" Jonah calls from the house. An instant later he appears at the door, face flushed.

I rush to him and grab him by the shoulders and forcefully shove him back into the house.

"Private time," I tell him, then slam the door shut.

SEVENTY-TWO

RUTH

I pull to the curb in front of Rachel's house and check the clock on the dash. I can't believe it's already close to ten. I haven't spent that long in Target in ages. But I was in such a good mood, I allowed myself to roam the aisles and peruse all the bargains, unbothered by the mothers shopping for Easter presents for their brood. I think I could have run into Charlie's wife and I would have been fine, wished her a happy Easter. Of course, I can say that now, since it didn't happen. But I like to think I would have been fine.

I look up to the house and see Shadow at the front window, his paws against the glass, which I know is a no-no. *Damn dog.* I suppose, by canine standards, Shadow is a good dog. He's gentle with the kids and fairly obedient, and very good-natured. I'm just not a dog person. I shudder at the thought of picking up after a dog his size. And forget about the expense of a dog. I'll bet Shadow costs as much to care for as one of Rachel's kids. Try telling my sister that. She *loves* dogs. Always has.

I climb out of my car and walk around to the passenger side. I grab my Target bags. They are numerous. Along with the hair dye, I bought Rachel and the kids some little love presents, and I can't leave the ingredients for the pies in the car, as they are perishable.

Halfway up the path, I lose my balance and drop two of the bags. My meds are in effect, but my joints still protest as I kneel down to retrieve my bounty.

I stand up and see Shadow, still barking furiously. He sees me and thumps his tail, then redirects his focus to something behind me. I glance back and see the Persian cat from across the street sitting on the sidewalk, swinging its tail back and forth violently, like a scythe.

"It's just a cat, Shadow," I call to him, although he probably can't hear me over the ruckus he's making.

I trudge to the porch, the bags growing heavier with each step. Perhaps I went a little overboard at Target, but the children's clothes in the clearance section were hard to pass up. And the model *T. rex* that makes noise for 50 percent off? I know Jonah's into bugs, but I think he'll like it. Then there's the Our Generation doll for Eden. I'm pretty sure she still plays with dolls. At least I hope so.

I climb the porch steps and bypass the doorbell, loop my right hand through the handles of two of the bags, then grasp the doorknob. I turn the knob and push the door open. It swings wide, and I step into the house. I reach out with my foot to close the door, but it doesn't close all the way.

Jonah comes bouncing down the stairs holding something in his hands, the stuffed monkey on his hip.

"Hi, Aunt Ruth!" he says breathlessly, then rushes past me to the front porch. I hear him shriek, "Gigi, no!"

Just then, Shadow bounds from the living room, and I think he's coming to greet me, but instead, he shoots through the open door.

"Damn it!" I shout as I hurry to the kitchen. "Rachel, Sam! Shadow got out!"

My sister and brother-in-law are nowhere to be seen. It's my fault for leaving the door open, so although I know it's going to cost me in the pain department, I don't wait for them to come to my rescue. I set the bags down on the counter and retrace my steps to the front door, cursing Shadow under my breath. I remember his leash, curse again, then rush to the hall closet to retrieve it.

SEVENTY-THREE

Shadow

I hear Little Male say, "Gigi, no!" And I know I'm not supposed to be outside, but I won't stop, can't stop even if I wanted to stop, but I don't want to stop.

Because I'm finally going to get the cat.

SEVENTY-FOUR

The earsplitting shriek of brakes echoes through the morning air, followed by a grotesque thump.

Barking, screaming, moaning, crying. The wail of a teenager, newly behind the wheel, his life forever altered by one error in judgment.

Sirens howl in the distance, swiftly moving closer until their sound is cacophonous.

Neighbors gape from front porches, front windows, sidewalks, driveways, hands over mouths, faces drawn, tearstained.

Swirling red lights atop shiny red trucks. Uniformed men work futilely, jaws tightly clenched. Blood slowly seeps across asphalt.

A cat watches, ambivalent, from a lawn.

A katydid hides in a tree, awaiting nightfall.

A stuffed monkey, unscathed save for a tiny spot of oil on its cheek, lies discarded on the far sidewalk.

PART SIX:
THE VERY BAD DAY
REVISITED

SEVENTY-FIVE

JONAH

I don't know how many days have gone by since the very bad day. Time is different for me than it was. Maybe I'm like Shadow. Not long before I died, I remember Dad telling me that dogs have no sense of time. I didn't know what that meant when he told me, but I do now.

I'm still here, in my house, and my family is still broken. There isn't as much crying as before. Mom still does, Dad and Eden, too, and even Aunt Ruth. But less. There's not a lot of talking. There's no laughter at all. Shadow only seems happy when I'm with him, which I can't do very much anymore. The rest of the time, he mopes.

I feel different from when I was alive. Not just that I'm dead—duh, *that* is different. But I feel like I understand things more than I did. Grown-up things.

This one time at church, the Sunday school teacher said that when we die and go to heaven, we all are the same age as Jesus was when he died, which was like thirty years old. So maybe I'm thirty now.

What I understand, too, that I didn't before, is that everyone in my family thinks it's their fault that I died. I also understand that if I don't, somehow, let them know what really happened, they'll always blame themselves, and they will never get unbroken.

I know they're seeing someone to help them. A doctor. I can tell from their energy, whenever they get back from seeing her, that she's helping. Not much, but a little. I tried to go to her, the doctor, tried to sneak into her dreams, but she's too far away from this house. Kind of like the hospital was when I tried to go to Mom that time she was there. I don't know if I made it to the doctor. I don't think I did.

I'm fading from this place. I sense that, too. I don't want to leave my family how they are now. But I'm starting to feel a pull to *elsewhere*. Maybe heaven. I'm not exactly sure yet, but it feels good and warm and nice, and I know I should let myself go there soon.

But I can't go until I fix my family. I know that's why I'm still here.

I've been trying to figure out how. I don't have much strength left. Last night, I went to Mom. She started to cry and was begging me to forgive her, and I tried to tell her that it wasn't her fault, but all I could do was shake my head, and she thought I was telling her I didn't forgive her, and I know she feels even worse and more guilty than she already did.

It takes a lot of energy to go to her and Shadow. It's easier to go into their dreams. That takes energy, too, but not as much. I was thinking maybe I could go into all of their dreams, Mom's, Dad's, Eden's, Aunt Ruth's, even Shadow's. And instead of trying to tell them it's not their fault, I could show them what happened that day, so they can see for themselves.

I know that going into all of their dreams at the same time will take all of my strength. I wonder if I can possibly do it, and also I wonder if, afterward, I'll have enough energy left to go *elsewhere*. Maybe I won't. I'm not worried or afraid. I remember those emotions, but I don't feel them anymore. The only emotion I feel now is love. And it's still so strong. I love my mom and dad, my sister, my aunt, my dog. Which is why I know it doesn't matter if I use up all my energy and can't go to the next place. I have to try.

I am very small today. I have packed myself so tight, I could be a tarantula or a titan beetle or a praying mantis. I don't go to Shadow.

He is restless, perhaps searching the house for me, but I am trying to conserve my strength.

When my family returns from the doctor, Mom goes upstairs right away. Eden turns on the TV, and Dad goes to the garage to do some work on his laptop. Aunt Ruth goes to the kitchen and starts on dinner.

I wait. And wait.

Pictures go through my mind. Picnics and finger painting and roasting marshmallows; riding my Big Wheel; riding in a stroller; rolling down the grassy hill at the park; Dad making faces; Mom striking a pose with a wooden spoon as her microphone; Eden giggling, dancing, holding my hand; Aunt Ruth rocking me to sleep; Shadow curling up next to me in my playpen, licking my cheek, bringing me his ball. So many pictures. So much life in so few years.

I know when I go, I will lose these pictures. I've already lost so many others. It's okay. I know that's part of going. And I know that even though the pictures won't come with me, the love will. Because love is always. Love lives on.

Later, after the pictures fade, the house is dark. Everyone is asleep.

If I were alive, I would take a deep breath. But I don't breathe anymore, so I gather up all my strength and energy and love and hold it close.

It's time.

SEVENTY-SIX

The Dream

I spotted the monarch first. It was beautiful. I know you don't like bugs, Mommy, but butterflies are bugs and you like them, right? I wanted to catch it and bring it to you, but I never want to hurt my insect friends 'cause that wouldn't be right. And anyways, he was too high up for me to catch and he flew off the flower—you know, Mommy, the big pink flowers on the hedge?—and went over into the Martins' yard.

Anyways, I kept going along the hedge, and that's when I saw it. At first, I thought it was a leaf, but it was sort of shimmering, and when I got closer, I saw that it wasn't a leaf at all, but a katydid. Right there on the hedge!

I yelled to Marco, "Marco, Marco, it's a katydid! It's a katydid!" I couldn't believe it. It was, like, a miracle. Because everyone knows that katydids mostly come out at night. Well, you guys might not know it, but the 'cyclopedia you gave me, Auntie Ruth, says that katydids are nocturnal. The even weirder thing was that when I woke up in the morning, the 'cyclopedia was open to that very page! The katydid page! It was like . . . what do you call it, Daddy? Mental *teleopy* or something!

But there it was, sitting on the end of a leaf, its wings all green, like if you weren't looking for bugs, you'd never ever see it, not in a million trillion gazillion years.

I stepped closer to it, but I didn't want to scare it. But, oh my gosh, it was so cool, like the coolest thing I ever saw. I never saw one that close up before, and I wanted to get closer to it. I wanted to see the wings better, and the brown eyes and everything and see if it was a girl or a boy katydid, 'cause you can tell if you look close enough.

Just then, it jumped from the hedge and sailed over my head and landed right on the grass, right next to the corner of the path at the bottom of the porch. I ran after it, then bent down and looked at it. Away from the hedge, its wings and body looked even brighter green than before, with all these veins running through it like real leaves.

Right then, I knew what I needed. My magnifying glass! I should have gotten it before I came outside, but I forgot.

"Please stay right there," I whispered to the katydid. I'm pretty sure he couldn't understand English, but I hoped he wouldn't go anywhere before I got back.

I ran into the house and up the stairs to my room. But I couldn't find my magnifying glass anywhere it was supposed to be, not in my desk or in my toy chest, or the cubby drawers on my shelf, not anywhere. I thought maybe you borrowed it, Eden, so I ran to your room and called your name.

You were FaceTiming with your friends, and you said something to me, Eden, something I know you feel bad and guilty about, but I didn't hear what you said, Eden, not even a little bit of it, 'cause I suddenly remembered that Daddy borrowed my magnifying glass to get a splinter out of his foot—remember, Daddy? You said your reading glasses weren't strong enough so could you please borrow it?—so I raced back down the stairs to ask you.

I called you, Daddy, and you came out of the kitchen, and I kind of followed you, but then I realized that the splinter happened a really long time ago, and I knew I used the magnifying glass after that. You said, "Not now, Jonah," and that was okay because I already knew you wouldn't know where it was.

I went back outside, just really quick to make sure the katydid was still there, and he was. I thought maybe you might know where my magnifying glass was, Mommy, 'cause you always know where everything is, so I ran to the garage to ask you.

You gave me a squeeze on my shoulder, and I always like your squeezes, Mommy, 'cause I know you love me so much and you squeeze me tight, and you did right then, and then you said something about "private," and when you said that, Mommy, when you said the word *private*, it was like how it is in cartoons when a lightbulb goes on above your head. I knew 'zactly where my magnifying glass was. I left it in my private eye kit! So I ran back upstairs and found it, right where you said it would be, Mommy! In my private eye kit!

I rushed downstairs, just as Auntie Ruth came in. And when I went out to the porch, I saw that Gigi, the cat from across the street, was pawing at the katydid. And I screamed at the cat, which was kind of mean 'cause she's a cat, and eating bugs is sort of what she's supposed to do. And then Shadow rushed outside and went after Gigi, and the cat sort of scooped up the katydid in her mouth and ran away, and Shadow chased her, and then so did I, 'cause I didn't want her to hurt the katydid.

Shadow was barking and running, and I know you thought I was chasing him, Auntie Ruth, and that it was your fault for leaving the door open for him to get out, but I wasn't paying any 'tention to Shadow, Auntie Ruth, 'cause I was chasing Gigi and the katydid.

Gigi raced right across the street. And I know I'm supposed to look both ways before I cross the street, but I wanted to get to the katydid so bad, I just forgot.

When the car came, I felt a big bump, but it didn't hurt at all. I felt floaty almost as soon as it happened.

And that's the truth, the whole truth, and nothing but the truth, so help me. I promise, Mommy.

Shadow, you're a good boy. Auntie Ruth, don't let yourself be lonely. Eden, you will always be the best sister ever. Daddy, keep making funny faces. Mommy, I'll need you forever. I love you all so so so much. And I'm taking that love with me.

Sweet dreams.

PART SEVEN:
ANOTHER DAY

SEVENTY-SEVEN

Sam awakens early, before seven. He rises from the couch and stretches. The rest of the house is still asleep, even Shadow, who is curled up on his bed. The dog chuffs in his sleep and wags his tail as though he is having a good dream. Sam smiles. He had a good dream, too.

He folds up the blankets of his makeshift bed and sets them on the chair, then carries the sheets to the garage, where he drops them into the washing machine. He feels well rested for the first time in ages.

He can't quite grasp the dream. Jonah was in it. Usually, when Sam dreams of Jonah, he awakens feeling drained, anguished, his insides twisted into knots. But not this morning. This morning he feels a sense of peace, of calm.

He gets dressed in the garage, as is his habit of late. It's Saturday, and he throws on jeans and a long-sleeved Nirvana T-shirt that he refused to part with despite Rachel's repeated entreaties.

Sam knows what he has to do. Has known since the moment he opened his eyes. He grabs the spare set of keys for the minivan from the drawer in the kitchen and quietly lets himself out of the house.

Eden lingers in bed for a while. She stares at a spot on the ceiling and thinks about her little brother. She doesn't know why, but she feels her love for him so strongly this morning, and it doesn't hurt like it did before. In her mind, she tells him she's sorry for all the times she was ever mean to him, and suddenly her mind is filled with all the times she helped him, all the ways she was there for him, all the things she did to protect him, like a big sister is supposed to, and she feels like he kept those times with him and that's why he thought she was the best sister ever.

She throws back the covers and gets out of bed. It's Saturday and she doesn't have to get dressed, but she does anyway, pulling on a pair of leggings and a T-shirt with a big purple cicada on it. She goes to the bathroom and brushes her teeth and pees, then walks into Jonah's room through the adjoining bathroom door, something she hasn't done since the very bad day.

Eden stops just inside his room and looks around. The bug encyclopedia is still on the floor. She kneels down and gazes at the open page, at the picture of the katydid. She dreamed of Jonah and a katydid last night, but the details of the dream elude her. She closes the book and sets it on the bottom shelf of his bookshelf.

She gazes at his bed, stands, and walks over to it. Marco the Monkey lies haphazardly across the pillow, where Sam threw him so many nights ago. Eden picks him up and holds him to her chest for a long moment. Then she carries him back through the bathroom and into her room and tucks him into her backpack. Mrs. Hartnett might not want him anymore, but it's time to take Marco back to school.

Ruth sits up and pushes herself to the head of the convertible sofa bed. She gazes at her surroundings, the small guest room in her sister and brother-in-law's house, with its beige walls and sand-colored blinds. This is not her home. Over the course of the past year and a half, she has never felt a longing for her one-bedroom apartment with its outdated appliances and shabby furniture. She longs for it now.

Her joints don't ache this morning. She doesn't question it. She pushes herself out of bed and heads for the guest bathroom. She does her business, and as she washes her hands, Ruth lifts her eyes to her reflection. And what she sees surprises her.

She is not the frumpy hag she thought she'd become these last months. She is an attractive middle-aged woman in desperate need of a dye job, but otherwise somewhat fetching and *alive*.

She takes her time getting dressed. She has few choices here, in her sister's house, but she chooses an ensemble that she has yet to wear since staying here, a cotton floral skirt and a pink blouse, the same color as the flowers on the hedge in front of the house.

Ruth stands for a moment, letting her thoughts wash over her. She grabs her purse from the side table and pulls out her cell phone. She swishes the screen open and finds the number of the man she's been thinking of for a while now, the number she has never used. Before she can stop herself, she dials the number. Waits, holding her breath.

"Hi, it's Ruth—hi. Yes, it's me. Sorry to call so early on a Saturday." She listens to a voice that is both foreign and familiar to her and smiles.

A few minutes later, she sets the phone back into her purse.

She strips the convertible bed. For the first time since the very bad day, she folds it up, replacing the cushions on the couch until the bed is merely a memory.

It's time to go home.

Ruth emerges from the guest room just as the front door opens. Sam stands on the threshold, house keys in one hand and a tall bar stool in the other. He sets the bar stool just inside the entry. His eyes meet Ruth's. She walks to the front door and wordlessly follows him to the minivan. He hands her one of the three remaining stools, grabs the others, and the two of them return to the house.

The stools are simple, cloth-covered cushions, wicker backrests, metal foundations, Target price tags. They fit perfectly at the kitchen counter, two on one side of the L, two on the other.

As Sam goes about removing the plastic packaging, Ruth moves to the pantry and pulls out a box of pancake mix. Normally, she eschews premixed anything, but the mix will be just fine this morning.

By the time she's whisking the batter, Sam has finished with the stools. He heads for the coffeemaker, fills it with grounds and water, and presses the button. He glances at Ruth as she readies a pan with butter and heat. She looks at him and smiles. Their silence is amiable.

The coffee percolates. Shadow shuffles into the kitchen, sniffs the air. Ruth leans down and pats his head. His tongue lolls to the side in appreciation.

First dollops of batter hit the pan, sizzle. Eden wanders into the kitchen, absent her usual morning crankiness. She takes in the new stools without comment, then walks to Sam and slips her arms around his waist, lingers. He kisses the top of her head. She shuffles over to Ruth, dips her finger in the batter and sticks her finger in her mouth. Smiles at her aunt.

Eden goes to the cupboard and pulls out plates, sets them on the counter. One, two, three, four, along the L. Adds napkins and forks. She fetches maple syrup from the fridge as Ruth flips the pancakes.

Twelve golden, steaming disks aligned on a serving tray. Sam sits on one of the stools, on the far end of the L. Ruth sits opposite him on the other side of the L. Eden takes the stool next to Ruth. Sam and Eden fork pancakes onto their plates. Ruth follows suit.

The three of them sit for a long time, not eating, pancakes cooling on their plates.

They glance at one another. A silent agreement is made. Forks rise simultaneously.

Then lower simultaneously as Rachel appears at the archway of the kitchen. Showered. Hair combed. Clean shirt, stretch Levi's, black sneakers. Clear eyes.

She allows Shadow to lick her hand, scratches him under the chin, calls him a good boy. Then glances at her family, first at Eden, then at Ruth, and finally at Sam. She looks at the bar stools, her gaze landing on the empty seat beside her husband. She slowly makes her way toward the empty stool. She stops at Ruth, lays her hand on Ruth's shoulder, squeezes gently. Ruth smiles at her. She moves to Eden and cups her daughter's chin in her hand, kisses her forehead, her nose, her lips, wipes a tear from Eden's face with a fingertip.

She lets go of Eden and stares at the empty stool, looks up at Sam. Sam pulls the stool out and Rachel perches upon it. She reaches out and touches the spot between her husband's eyebrows, perhaps wondering at the smoothness of the skin, the softening of the crevasse.

She holds up her index finger and presses it to the tip of her nose. She knows that Jonah has moved on, that he's no longer here to see their secret gesture. And she isn't fine, not yet. But for the first time since his death, she knows she *will* be.

She lowers her hand to Sam's and interlocks her fingers with his.

"Good morning," Rachel says softly. She clears her throat and takes a deep breath. "Something smells good."

EPILOGUE

MADDIE

I've been seeing the Davenports for six months. After two months, I reduced our sessions to bimonthly, although they are free to come in more often should the need arise. So far, it hasn't.

Ruth Glass has returned to her own therapist, although she checks in with me from time to time. She is doing well. Apparently she is seeing someone, her neighbor. They are taking it slow, according to her, but she smiles when she speaks of him, and her demeanor has transformed from bleak and resigned to confident and hopeful.

Eden is in the sixth grade now and is taking middle school by storm. She has a new group of friends who are supportive and loyal. They know about Jonah, but they see the tragedy only as a part of their friend, not the whole person. She likes a boy named Kevin, although she refuses to admit it to me. But a girl can tell. She still brings Shadow to our sessions, and I have grown very fond of him, so much so that I've given serious consideration to getting Cleopatra a canine sibling if I can work out the logistics.

Sam's business is thriving. He and his partner expanded and have turned over a lot of their work to the junior partners, freeing up more time for Sam. His new assistant is male. His old assistant is working for another firm. He wrote her a glowing recommendation and hasn't had contact with her since.

Rachel is completely off her meds and is facing her life with a renewed sense of clarity and purpose. She grieves. She admits to drinking occasionally. But she monitors herself closely, and I see no warning signs at this point. She has resumed her blog and is active in the parent-teacher association at Eden's school.

Rachel and Sam are working through their marital issues. Much of our counseling focuses on their relationship, both as it pertains to the loss of their son, and independent of that. I offered to refer them to a marriage counselor, but they opted to work with me, as I have gained their trust and am privy to the entire picture. I see them together and individually.

That they love each other is not in question. Whether their marriage will survive? They are beginning to see themselves as more than grieving parents. Their grief will always be a part of them, but like Eden, it is not the whole. As to their personal interaction, they are rediscovering each other as people, as a man and a woman, rather than as husband and wife and mother and father. I give them trust exercises. I give them journaling assignments. Along with family dinners, I prescribed a date night for them once a week. They both enjoy date night. Sam likes the trust exercises while Rachel is less enthusiastic about them. Rachel has taken to journaling, Sam not so much. But they are both working hard, and the rewards are already evident. If they make it, and I honestly believe they will, their relationship will be even stronger than it was before Jonah's death.

I am but a facilitator. You can lead a horse to water, right? But I also know that things began to change drastically for the family after I urged each of them to talk about that day. It was like a switch was flipped. As if by finally talking about it they had opened a floodgate of healing. Suddenly, they were all able to let go of their guilt and allow for the fact that bad things happen to good people, to good *children*, and more often than not, no one is to blame.

I'd like to take credit for their dramatic turn, but I'm not certain it belongs to me. I think the credit belongs to Jonah. I don't know why. I just do.

That night, after Ruth and Eden and Sam and Rachel unburdened themselves, I dreamed of Jonah. I couldn't remember the dream the next morning, although I tried desperately to reconstruct it. All I remember is awaking with a sense of rightness, serenity. And an overwhelming feeling of love.

Jonah has not returned to my dreams since. But whenever I see a katydid, for some reason I think of him and smile.

ACKNOWLEDGMENTS

I am a writer. I write funny. I write mystery. Lately, I write serious. With each book, whether humorous or tragic, I try to write stories that touch people, make them think, make them laugh, cry, feel. Because these emotions are what bind all of us. In these times of division, I feel compelled to use my gifts to bring people together in whatever way I can. *What Remains True*, at its core, centers on the idea that when we are united, we can overcome any challenge life puts in our path. I have experienced several major losses over the last few years, and I know this to be true. We are better together.

The publication of a book is also a communal experience, and *What Remains True* is the perfect example. It would not be the book you are reading without the input of so many incredible people.

Thank you to my amazing agent, Wendy Sherman, who has championed me and my work from my first book deal. For several years thereafter, she patiently waited for me to bring her something of value, never losing faith that I would. Thanks for hanging in there, Wendy!

Thank you to Kelli Martin at Lake Union for falling in love with *What Remains True*, and to the entire Lake Union team for so graciously and enthusiastically welcoming me into your family. Kelli, you are a dream come true. I look forward to many more two-hour phone conversations with you.

Thank you to the tremendously talented Melody Guy. Her insightful notes, thoughtful suggestions, and editorial wisdom have made this a better book. Melody, your loving care of *What Remains True* shines through from beginning to end.

Thanks to the Fab Four, who are not only my primary readers, but the women I love and admire most in the world: Shoney, Hilary, Linda, and Penny. Couldn't navigate this life without you.

Thanks to my partner in crime, Ara Grigorian, who boosts my ego and keeps me honest. It's a privilege and an honor to teach Novel Intensive with you.

Thanks to Michael Steven Gregory for your unfailing support, your sharp wit, and your impromptu lounge act. And thanks Wes, Chrissie, Melanie, Rick, Linda, Cricket, Laura, Matt, Jean, Jennifer, Claudia, Marla, Gayle, and the entire Southern California Writers Conference community.

Thank you to Maddie Margarita (yes, that's her real name!) for your love and encouragement, and to Larry Porricelli and the Southern California Writers Association.

Thanks to my brother, Mark, for reading my books, despite the fact that they are considered women's fiction. Love you, bro.

Thanks to the rest of my crazy, wonderful extended family: siblings, cousins, aunts, nieces, nephews, in-laws, friends—both near and far, off-line and on.

Thank you to Sharon and Lenerd, my mom and dad, the two extraordinary people who made me who I am. I miss you both more than I can express, but I feel your love every single day.

To my husband, Alex, and my children, AJ and Elle: everything starts and ends with you. I love you three with all my heart.

I am grateful to you, my reader, who takes the journey with me every time you read one of my books. I'm blessed to be able to do what I do. And you are the reason I do it. Thank you.

ABOUT THE AUTHOR

Janis Thomas is the author of three critically acclaimed humorous women's fiction novels—*Something New*, *Sweet Nothings*, and *Say Never*—as well as *Murder in A-Minor*, the first book in her Musical Murder Mystery series. She has written two children's books with her father and more than fifty songs. As well as being an author and musical performer, Janis is also a writing advocate, editor, workshop leader, and speaker.

Janis likes to hang out with her two amazing children, play tennis, and sing with her sister. She is also an admitted foodie. Along with her husband (a former chef), she likes to throw wild dinner parties with outrageous menus for friends and loved ones. Janis lives in Southern California with her family and two crazy dogs.

Learn more about Janis at www.JanisThomas.com.